Other Books by Shirleen Davies

Historical Western Romance Series

MacLarens of Fire Mountain

Tougher than the Rest, Book One
Faster than the Rest, Book Two
Harder than the Rest, Book Three
Stronger than the Rest, Book Four
Deadlier than the Rest, Book Five
Wilder than the Rest, Book Six

Redemption Mountain

Redemption's Edge, Book One
Wildfire Creek, Book Two, Releasing Winter
2015

MacLarens of Boundary Mountain

Colin's Quest, Book One
Coming in 2015

Contemporary Romance Series

MacLarens of Fire Mountain

Second Summer, Book One
Hard Landing, Book Two
One More Day, Book Three
All Your Nights, Book Four, Releasing Fall 2014

Sign up to learn about my New Releases:
www.shirleendavies.com/contact-me.html

Redemption's Edge
Redemption Mountain
Historical Western Romance Series

SHIRLEEN DAVIES

Book One in the Redemption Mountain

Historical Western Romance Series

Book design and conversions by Joseph Murray at 3rdplanetpublishing.com

Cover design by The Killion Group

ISBN: 978-1-941786-08-6

Description

Redemption's Edge – Book One
Redemption Mountain Historical Western
Romance Series

"A heartwarming, passionate story of
loss, forgiveness, and redemption set in
the untamed frontier during the
tumultuous years following the Civil
War. Ms. Davies' engaging and complex
characters draw you in from the start,
creating an exciting introduction to this
new historical western romance series."

"Redemption's Edge is a strong and
engaging introduction to her new
historical western romance series."

Dax Pelletier is ready for a new life, far away
from the one he left behind in Savannah
following the South's devastating defeat in the
Civil War. The ex-Confederate general wants
nothing more to do with commanding men and
confronting the tough truths of leadership.

Rachel Davenport possesses skills unlike
those of her Boston socialite peers—skills honed
as a nurse in field hospitals during the Civil War.
Eschewing her northeastern suitors and changed
by the carnage she's seen, Rachel decides to
accept her uncle's invitation to assist him at his

clinic in the dangerous and wild frontier of Montana.

Now a Texas Ranger, a promise to a friend takes Dax and his brother, Luke, to the untamed territory of Montana. He'll fulfill his oath and return to Austin, at least that's what he believes.

The small town of Splendor is what Rachel needs after life in a large city. In a few short months, she's grown to love the people as well as the majestic beauty of the untamed frontier. She's settled into a life unlike any she has ever thought possible.

Thinking his battle days are over, he now faces dangers of a different kind—one by those from his past who seek vengeance, and another from Rachel, the woman who's captured his heart.

Dedication

This book is dedicated to my dearest friends, Joe and Rayma-Lew. I hope you already know how much your friendship and love mean to me.

Acknowledgements

Thanks also to my editor, Kim Young, proofreader, Sue Hutchens, and all of my beta readers. Their insights and suggestions are greatly appreciated.

As always, many thanks to my wonderful resources, including Diane Lebow, who has been a whiz at guiding my social media endeavors, my cover designer, Kim Killion, and Joseph Murray who is a whiz at formatting my books for both print and electronic versions.

Redemption's Edge

Prologue

May, 1865

Persistent, thundering explosions enveloped the area in an unending drumming that caused otherwise courageous men to cover their ears and recoil on the ground. Bullets whizzed past as twelve pound cannonballs exploded all around them, shattering everything and everyone in their path.

The incessant screams of those injured and dying intermingled with the shouts of officers who tried in vain to rally their men for a counterattack. The dark night sky became the backdrop for brilliant flashes of white and orange, which turned red as the smoke wafted upwards, choking the air and reducing visibility to a few short yards.

The general controlled his horse with expert movements, while commanding those around him with stern, calm orders that belied his inner turmoil. His aide, a man two years younger, screamed, then fell from his horse, grasping his chest as blood soaked through his clothes.

He had no time to stop and help the wounded soldier as others looked to him for a miracle he knew didn't exist. Outnumbered and outgunned, his troops, although brave and battle seasoned, were no match for the onslaught before them.

"Retreat!" His command rang out over the gunfire a moment before an explosion rocked the ground in front of him. He worked to control his horse, and almost succeeded—until a second explosion crushed everything in sight. The stallion bucked, panic overshadowing the general's skill at directing the fifteen hundred pound animal. A third volley sent dirt, rock, and shrapnel in all directions.

Blood stained everything in sight. A thunderous war cry left the general's lips. His body thrashed as his weight tilted and his arms flailed in midair. He reached up, hands grasping for purpose, yet found nothing except open air.

"General Pelletier, wake up." The major's hands gentled on the general's body as the convulsions subsided. The thrashing stopped and the general's eyes opened to a sliver of daylight penetrating the slim opening in the tent.

"You've had another dream, sir."

Pelletier remained motionless a moment, focusing on his aide, the man who'd died in his dream, then drew in a shaky breath as he pushed himself up.

"How long this time?" He scrubbed a hand over his face and walked to a small table holding a metal bowl and pitcher.

"A couple of minutes. Not long." The major held out a towel as the general splashed water on his face and neck, letting it drip onto his sweat-soaked shirt.

Brigadier General Dax Pelletier slipped into a clean shirt, tucked it into his pants, then pulled on the well-worn boots he favored. As he accepted the belt and sword his aide offered, a shout came from outside the tent.

The major stepped into the sunlight and up to a young officer who stood at attention, holding the reins to his horse in one hand and a message in the other.

"I'm looking for General Pelletier."

"I'm his aide. I'll be sure the general gets it." He took the message and looked at the man before him, who couldn't be more than eighteen years old. "Go get yourself some food—and some sleep."

He returned to the tent. "A message for you, sir."

Dax opened and scanned the note, disbelief crossing his face. He glanced at his aide, then back at the words on paper. "Did you read this?"

"No, sir."

"Lee surrendered to Grant at Appomattox. The war's over."

Chapter One

"I don't understand why you can't at least meet the young man. He's from an excellent family."

"I'm sure he is, Mother."

Rachel Davenport continued to fold and stack clothes into a large trunk. Two others were already filled and waiting in the corner of her bedroom.

"Perhaps you won't feel compelled to follow your uncle west if you meet the right man." Harriet Davenport clenched a handkerchief while watching her daughter clean out the wardrobe she'd been given as a young woman, before she'd grown up and volunteered to help all those injured men during the war.

Rachel closed the trunk and hung her head, biting her lower lip as she tried to come up with the best way to express herself. No matter how she phrased it, she knew her mother would never understand her need to leave Boston, the life for which she'd been bred, and the comforts her family's wealth offered. Rachel glanced around the room, remembering a wonderful childhood and loving family, and wondered why she couldn't do as her mother asked—marry, have children, and settle into a comfortable existence as a well-kept wife.

4

"I know my decision is a disappointment to you and Father." She stood and walked to the window overlooking the rose garden her mother so carefully tended. "This is no longer the life I want. I have skills most women don't and we both know I'll never be hired in Boston, not with our name and status. Besides, this isn't where I'm needed." She turned to face her mother. "Uncle Charles has offered me a position in his clinic, a place where my skills will prove useful."

"My God, Rachel, it's in the Montana Territory. Think about what it will be like—the hardships and isolation."

"It will be no worse than what I've already seen."

"Damn that war," her mother muttered. "You should never have been involved, working with the injured soldiers, witnessing things..." Her already thin voice trailed off as if she, too, could visualize the carnage her daughter had seen.

Rachel stood and walked toward her mother, grasping her hands, searching the eyes of a woman she loved more than she could express. "Please try to understand. This is something I have to do. Uncle Charles needs someone and I'm the best person to go." She dropped her mother's hands and stepped back. "Besides, I may get out there, stay a few months, and find I *do* miss my life here in Boston."

"Or get yourself kidnapped by those savages your uncle treats. Then we'll never see you again."

"Mother, you know that's not at all true. Where have you heard such things?"

"I've read about them." Her indignant response accompanied the defensive tilt of her head.

"In what? Those dime novels your sister gives you?" A smile drifted across Rachel's face at the thought of her mother curled up in the drawing room, reading about outlaws, cowboys, and Indians.

"Well, they're written by people who've been there, so they should know." The annoyed reply almost made Rachel laugh.

"That could be, although Uncle Charles has yet to mention anything more disturbing than ranch hands getting drunk and shooting up the town on a Saturday night." She grabbed her shawl and took her mother's arm. "I leave in two days. Let's try to have a good time until then. Please. I don't want to waste another minute arguing about a decision that's already been made."

Savannah, Georgia, July 1865

Dax stood at the entrance to what used to be his home. It had once been a large, imposing, two-story house on several acres at the edge of Savannah, over a mile from the waterfront where the family kept their shipping fleet. A fleet Sherman's troops decimated during their siege a few months before.

Atlanta fell, and Savannah followed four months later. The massive devastation of both cities crushed both military and civilian morale. When Dax looked away from his home toward the center of the city, the scenery changed little— burned buildings, blocks leveled by Union artillery, starved citizens scavenging for food, and heartbreaking despair. The two great battles during the last months of 1864 signaled the eventual end to the Confederacy's fight.

He walked around the rubble to the back, stepping over the charred remains of furniture that had been in his family for several generations—a family of fur traders who'd become merchants and prosperous seamen, transporting goods between U.S. cities and European ports. Little remained. Everything of value had been taken, and all else burned.

Dax opened the gate into the family cemetery and knelt beside his mother's grave. She'd died within months of Dax enlisting in the Confederacy at the start of the war. His younger brother, Luke, enlisted a year later, leaving their youngest brother, André, to help their father run the business and the home. André had died of pneumonia the previous summer, followed by their father within months. Only Dax and Luke remained. Dax sat back on his heels, idly picking out grass around the cross-shaped marker and trying to accept the loss of so many.

"I promise, Mother. I'll find Luke. If he's alive, I'll find him," Dax whispered.

"You won't need to go far."

Dax twisted at the sound of the familiar voice behind him and jumped to his feet.

"Luke." His voice sounded husky with emotion as he enveloped his brother in a bear hug, then stepped back to let his eyes wander over the man he hadn't seen in almost three years. The youthful features replaced by those burdened by the sight of too much death. Eyes that once sparkled with mischief were now flat and hard.

"In the flesh."

"And that?" Dax nodded toward the cane Luke held in his left hand.

"A shot to the leg. It's almost healed. I returned home in March to recuperate and found this." His arm swept over the devastation. "The neighbors, those who are left, told me of father and André. I hadn't heard."

Dax clasped Luke on the shoulder, pain for all they'd lost consuming him. He had little stomach for rebuilding a new life at the source of his greatest loss. As the oldest surviving son, he knew his responsibilities now included Luke, no matter that this brother was a seasoned twenty-five-year-old ex-major.

Dax strode to one of the stacks of rubble, picked up a broken piece of china, then threw it back onto the pile. "Where are you staying?"

"With the Yanceys."

Dax cast a knowing look at Luke. "So you'll finally succumb to Violet's charms and marry her?" Perhaps it would be for the best if Luke settled down and began a family.

"Violet? No, Dax. I have no plans to marry. And even if I did, she's not the one I'd choose."

They walked to the front, Luke climbing into the carriage he borrowed from the elder Yancey, while Dax mounted Hannibal, the imposing stallion who'd seen him through the war and saved his life on numerous occasions.

"You will stay with me. The Yanceys will be glad to have you, and it will give us a chance to talk of the future." Luke tapped the horses.

Dax rode alongside, unsure how to explain to Luke he had no plans to stay and rebuild what they'd lost. He'd deed his portion of the land to his brother, then set out to find a new life elsewhere, where the skills he'd acquired during the war would be useful. Luke reveled in the social life of a large city, while Dax had preferred to spend his time at the docks, captaining the family ships and expanding their holdings.

The war had changed more than the landscape. Sometime over the long years of battle, Dax had lost his consuming drive to achieve, build the most prosperous shipping fleet in Savannah and help lead Georgia to the glory he felt it deserved—the showplace of the South.

For now, he'd enjoy Luke's company and the hospitality the Yancey's offered. He wouldn't wait long—a week, maybe two—then he'd tell Luke of his decision to leave Savannah forever.

"You're sure of this, Rachel? It's not too late to change your mind and stay here in Boston. I'm certain Charles will understand." Rachel's father, James Davenport, gripped his daughter's last piece of luggage, a satchel she'd keep by her side during the long trip. It held money, two changes of clothes, sundries, a couple of books, and her diary. His voice shook, indicating the depth of his emotions at losing his daughter a second time— once to the war, and now to the western frontier.

Rachel turned to him with the warm smile he'd become used to seeing over the last two months. Today, however, it didn't exhibit its usual glow. Sadness rimmed her eyes, even as determination defined her features.

"This is something I must do, Father. I know my decision is hard for you and Mother, and there's no adequate reason I can offer. It's just something I must do. Please understand and wish me well."

The pleading look she trained on him broke her father's last thread of defense.

"Oh, Rachel. What are your mother and I to do without you?" He pulled her to him and into the type of hug he'd offered as a child. It didn't last more than a few seconds before he turned her loose and stepped back. "You will write to us every week, even while traveling. Don't miss a week, or your mother will demand I go after you."

"Would that be so bad, Father? To come visit me in Montana?" Rachel hoped he hadn't heard the slight quiver in her voice. As strong and determined as Rachel appeared, she still anxious about making the journey alone. But something drew her. An unfamiliar calling that almost demanded she leave the comforts of Boston for the unknowns of the West.

"No, it's not a bad idea. All I need is time to persuade your mother there is life beyond the Mississippi." He waved to their driver, who jumped down from the carriage and began loading the three trunks packed with almost everything Rachel owned.

"Are we ready, James?" Rachel's mother joined them on the front step.

"It appears so, dear." He checked his pocket watch.

James helped Harriet and Rachel into their carriage, then signaled to the driver. He sat across from the two most important women in his life, sobered at the thought this might be the last time the three of them enjoyed a ride through the city, past the park where they'd taken family picnics, and the theatre, which had been a focal point of their life before the war. A tightness formed in his chest as they approached the train station, while pride in his daughter held him together. In his heart, he knew she'd do well, and prayed she'd come back to them soon.

"I see." Luke sat in the old rocker on the porch of the Yancey home, rocking back and forth, holding a cheroot and listening as Dax attempted to justify his decision to leave. "So you'll leave it all, turn your back on what our family built, and find a new life." His voice held a calm understanding, quite unlike the temper he'd often displayed in his youth. "You'll leave me behind?"

Dax knew his decision would appear harsh, even selfish, given he'd fought five long years to preserve their way of life. They'd owned eight slaves, descendants of a family who'd been with their great-grandfather when he'd built the home that now lay in ruin. All had lived through the war, yet they now made their home in an abandoned warehouse owned by the Pelletier family. No one understood how it had been spared when the buildings around it had been reduced to rubble.

"There's money. More than enough to rebuild both the house and business. Although free, our people have stayed. You know Polly and George will keep everyone together and help you rebuild. I doubt much will change, except they will be free to leave if they choose."

"And the shipping business?"

"It can be rebuilt, if it's what you want."

Luke blew out smoke and tapped ash from the end of his thin cigar. "I was never the captain you were, and don't know anything about rebuilding a shipping empire." He looked away, toward the setting sun. "I had other interests at that time."

They both knew to what Luke referred. Although he had a better head for business than Dax, he'd been considered the golden boy, the one who could charm anyone. Their father had once called him an aspiring rake. Had the war not interrupted him, Dax felt certain his brother would have risen to fame within the female circles of Savannah.

"What are your interests now?" Dax stood and placed his hands on the porch rail, looking out into the western sky as the sun finished its descent.

"Guess I'll need to think on it a bit. If your decision is firm—"

"It is," Dax cut in.

"Then it changes everything." He threw the spent cheroot toward the yard. "When do you leave?"

"Four days from now, at dawn."

Luke used his cane to stand, then joined his brother at the railing. "That gives me four days to figure out what I'll do once you leave. Guess I'd better visit George and Polly tomorrow."

"I'll deed my interest in everything to you. It will all be yours."

"No. I won't take what is rightfully yours, what you worked years to build and then defended during the war." His fierce words surprised Dax.

"I don't want it, Luke."

"What you want means little to me right now. No matter what I decide to do, I will not take your half. Besides, you may change your mind and come back."

Dax shook his head, a feeling deep in his gut telling him he'd never set foot in Savannah again. "All right, if that's what you want."

Luke started to turn, then glanced back at his brother. "Come on. Miss Rue still has her place open. I'll buy the drinks, you decide on the women."

"Hello, ma'am. Mind if I join you?"

The soft southern drawl had Rachel looking up to see an incredibly good-looking man staring down at her, a hat in his hand. "Please." She nodded to the seat beside her and watched as he tried to fit his long legs into the small space. She guessed him to be well over six feet tall. "Not quite built for large men, is it?"

"No, ma'am. Most trains aren't. I'm Cash Coulter."

"Rachel Davenport, Mr. Coulter. It's nice to meet you."

"A city girl?"

"Yes. From Boston. And you, Mr. Coulter? Where are you from?"

"The South, ma'am." Cash set his well-worn hat on his head and tipped it down, hiding his face and shutting Rachel out.

It had been three months since the war ended and animosity between those from the Northern and Southern states remained high. Rachel had worked in Union field hospitals, moving from one battlefield to the next as the war progressed. Within a few short weeks with work days stretching to thirty hours at times, the sight of injured men had become normal. During the two years Rachel had worked in the field, she'd treated soldiers from both sides of the line—gray or blue, it didn't matter. If they were injured, the medical staff treated them.

She watched Cash's features as he settled into a light snore. He had what her mother would call patrician features—a straight nose, blond hair, piercing clear blue eyes, and a regal bearing. Something about his attitude, although cultured and polite, warned her away from the man.

The whistle blew as the train approached the final stop in Missouri, pulling toward the station. Cash's head snapped up, his hand moving with lightning speed to the holstered gun as his eyes shifted to the woman beside him. He scrubbed a hand over his face and sat up.

"I believe this is our stop, Mr. Coulter." Rachel's tired voice underscored how exhausting her trip had been, and she still had many miles to go.

Cash stood, signaling for her to step in front of him into the aisle. He helped her to the railroad platform before tipping his hat.

"Guess I'll be on my way, Miss Davenport. It was a pleasure to meet you."

"Thank you, Mr. Coulter. I wish you a safe journey."

Cash glanced back over his shoulder at her words, nodded, then continued on.

She watched him walk toward the back of the train and wait while a worker drew open the sliding door and set up a ramp. He strode into the open car and, a minute later, led out a beautiful buckskin horse with a dark mane and tail. He tied the horse to a nearby post and stepped into the car once more. This time, he emerged holding a saddle and tack.

"Miss Davenport?"

Rachel swiveled to see a boy several feet away, her trunks stacked next to him.

"Yes, I'm Miss Davenport." She glanced behind her once more to see Cash ride away, back straight, head held high, and hoped life would be good to the battle hardened southerner.

"Where do you want these?"

She gave the boy directions to the hotel where she'd be staying until the stagecoach left for Nebraska. From there, she'd travel to a settlement at the southern edge of the Montana Territory to meet her uncle in the territorial capital of Big Pine. His message indicated they'd obtain supplies, then begin the final part of her journey to Splendor, Montana, her new home. Tonight, she looked forward to a hot bath, a good meal, and sleeping in a regular bed.

"What may I do for you, Miss?" The hotel clerk stood erect behind the counter, spectacles perched low on his nose, focused on the paper in front of him.

"There should be a room for me. Miss Rachel Davenport."

He reached below the counter to check a ledger, found her name, then handed her a key.

"Best place for supper is next door. Same for breakfast. Will you be traveling on?"

"I'm taking the stagecoach to Nebraska." She looked around at the quaint, clean hotel, and wondered how her father had found it.

"The stage leaves at dawn day after tomorrow. I'll have someone get your trunks to the station early that morning. Very early." He squinted over the rims of his glasses as if to emphasize the point.

"I'd like a bath."

"Make that two."

Rachel jumped at the sound of the deep, southern drawl behind her. She turned to see Cash Coulter, saddlebags slung over his shoulder.

"So we meet again, Miss Davenport." Cash took off his hat and nodded at the clerk, who had stopped his work to stare at the newcomer.

"It appears so, Mr. Coulter. You're staying here, I take it?"

"Yes. A night, maybe two, then I'll be off."

"Anything else, Miss Davenport?" the clerk asked.

"No, just the bath. Oh, and I'd like you to store my trunks. I won't need them before I leave." She turned to leave as Cash stepped up to the counter. "I guess it's goodbye again, Mr. Coulter. Enjoy your evening."

"Ma'am," he nodded before turning away.

The bath felt wonderful. She had to fight the temptation to fall into bed without a meal, but her need for a decent meal overpowered her need for sleep. Rachel replaced her dirty traveling clothes with clean ones and walked to the restaurant next door.

"Be right with you." A rotund woman set down plates heaped with steaming food in front of a young couple, then walked toward Rachel. "All right. Just you, dear?"

"Yes." She followed the woman toward a table, surprised at the number of people.

"Miss Davenport?"

Rachel's gaze darted to Cash, who stood next to a table near the window. "Good evening, Mr. Coulter."

"Join me, please. It'd enjoy not eating alone." He gestured to an empty seat.

"Thank you. That's quite nice of you."

Cash looked at the server. "Bring her what I'm having, including the pie and coffee."

Rachel set her reticule on the table while Cash pulled out her chair.

"So, you've come out west from Boston?" His clear blue eyes focused on hers.

"Yes. I'm meeting my uncle in Montana. He's a doctor and needs help. I'm a nurse, so it seemed like the right decision."

"Montana. Harsh country. Bitter cold winters, high winds, Indians. A far cry from the life you left behind." He sipped his coffee while they waited for her meal.

"Yes and no. I was a nurse during the war."

She didn't need to say more. Rachel could see the haunted look in his eyes, telling her he'd seen many of the same things she had—maybe worse.

"And you? Where are you headed?"

"A job in Denver."

"I hope to travel there some day. What kind of work are you in?"

Cash watched her, wondering about her knowledge of the west and how much he should say. "I locate people." He glanced up as the server set Rachel's meal down.

"Thank you. This looks wonderful." She smiled at the woman, while inhaling the scent of cooked meat, then looked up at Cash. "This is perfect." She didn't wait a moment longer. Within minutes, half her steak and most of the potatoes were gone. Rachel picked up the coffee cup and took a sip. That's when she noticed Cash had stopped eating, and sat, staring, with a look of grim amusement in his eyes. "What is it?"

"I've never seen a woman eat with such intensity."

Rachel set down her cup. "During the war, I learned to take food when offered and eat as fast as possible. Same with sleep. There never seemed to be enough of either." A vague smile crossed her face. "Guess I should learn to slow down."

"Nothing wrong with a strong appetite." He picked up his fork and finished the last of his supper.

"I saw you unload a beautiful horse from the train. Will you be riding him to Denver?"

"That's right. I need a horse I can depend on for my work."

"I'm sorry, but tell me again what kind of work you do."

This time Cash didn't hesitate. "I hunt people, Miss Davenport. For money."

Chapter Two

Savannah, Georgia

"Guess I'm ready." Dax took one last look around. "Thank you for allowing me to stay with you. Your hospitality means a lot, sir."

"No need for thanks. You're welcome anytime." Mr. Yancey stood on the street next to Dax, feeling sorrow that the ex-soldier felt it necessary to leave his home. "I thought Luke would be here to see you off."

Dax glanced up, then down the street, hoping to see Luke. "He's not too pleased with my decision. Perhaps he'll come around." He mounted Hannibal, tipped his hat to Yancey, then turned toward the west.

"God watch over you, Dax," Yancey murmured as he watched him ride away.

Dax kept turning in his saddle, checking to see if Luke would appear. He didn't think it would matter, his brother not showing up to see him off, but it did. They often didn't agree, had argued as much as any two brothers, yet they'd remained close. He swallowed a lump of regret at the thought Luke believed Dax had abandoned him. How could one explain an action they couldn't describe to themselves?

As the miles continued, the sky turned an angry black and rain began to fall. Dax pulled his great coat from behind the saddle and slipped it on as the sound of pounding hooves came from behind. He reached for his gun. Although the war had officially ended, many still fought out of ignorance of the surrender, pride, or bitterness. Dax meant to be prepared.

"General! General, wait up!"

Dax reined in Hannibal and turned toward the shouts, then watched as the rider pulled alongside him. Luke.

"What are you doing here?" Dax's voice held an edge, although the sight of his brother warmed him clear through.

"I had a few business dealings that needed to be completed before I could leave. They're done and I'm here." Luke pushed his old hat further down on his head and looked at the storm rolling in. "Best we get moving."

Luke watched as surprise crossed his brother's face, followed by understanding. "What? You thought you could get rid of me? Not a chance. I may not agree with the idea of riding away from our life in Savannah, but I'm sure as hell not letting you find adventure on your own. I'm going with you."

Dax stayed silent. He didn't know where his next stop would be, or if he'd even make it across the Georgia border to Alabama before some stray bullet found him. He only had a vague sense of where he wanted to end up. Now he had a brother to worry about. The thought passed as Dax realized he felt more relief than a sense of burden as Luke rode by his side. He nudged Hannibal on, still not saying a word.

Luke kept pace, finally turning to Dax after several minutes. "Where we headed?"

"Texas."

"What's in Texas?"

"Hell if I know. Guess we're going to find out."

Texas, several months later

"You sure this is the right trail, Pat?" Luke rode behind Dax and their fellow Texas Ranger, Pat Hanes. For days, they'd been hunting a gang of bank robbers. The two Pelletier brothers had been teamed with the older, well-regarded Ranger. Both had as much experience in combat as Hanes, yet he offered superior tracking skills and a history of bringing in outlaws when others had given up.

"Yep, it's the right way." Pat's drawl indicated a mixed history of his long years in Alabama, plus his time in Texas. His slow, easy manner hid a quick wit and incredible instincts. Dax and Luke had learned to appreciate the first and rely on the second. "I know it's hard for you city boys to follow how the ground changes when horses move over it. Pay attention and I might decide to show you someday."

He leaned over his horse and scanned the damp ground again. The rolling hills, woodlands, and drop-off canyons could conceal almost anything or anybody, but the soft soil made it hard to hide horse hooves and human steps.

"I got a feeling it won't be long now." Pat pointed toward a series of hills covered in live oak and other brush.

"Isn't that what you told us two days ago?" Dax sat easy in his saddle, while keeping a watchful eye for any movement around them. He had no intention of being caught unawares.

Pat turned to look at him. "Two days isn't long, at least not by my measure."

They rode another three hours, tracking the group who'd killed a bank clerk and injured a customer in the small town of Red Gulch. The haul hadn't been large, but the war had created a new breed of outlaw—homeless, hungry, destitute, and eager to take advantage of any opportunity.

Luke scanned the countryside once more, fidgeting in his saddle and trying to alleviate the boredom. "Tell us more about your ranch."

"Not much to tell." Pat didn't take his eyes off the trail as he spoke just loud enough for his companions to hear. "It's a decent amount of acreage at the base of Redemption Mountain. That's part of the Territory Range in Montana. Finally paid it off last year. I'll be moving that way when I retire."

"How long are you going to keep up this life?" Luke asked, knowing Pat to be a good ten or fifteen years older than Dax.

"Another year, maybe. I've got a couple watching over the place, keeping it up. The area's growing, lots of people moving in after the war. Some are good, some aren't. It doesn't take much

23

to steal a man's land away and I don't intend to have that happen."

"Look up there." Dax pointed to a hill less than a mile away. "Looks like men climbing up on the right side. One has on a white hat. Might be Whitey."

"I see them." Luke reached behind him and pulled out his military field glasses. "Looks like four, going slow. Probably don't believe anyone is still following them."

"Let's move." Pat had already taken off at a gallop, leaving Dax and Luke to catch up.

Luke kept an eye on the men they tracked. His heart rate picked up, the same as it used to before a battle. A rush of excitement accompanied by fear of the unknown.

They were within a couple hundred yards of the outlaws before one of the robbers turned and saw the dust from their horses

Deke Mayes rode to the front, alongside his older brother, Whitey. "We're being followed." He turned and pointed to a spot down the hill.

"How many?"

Deke checked once again. "Looks like three. Could be more."

Whitey looked up the hill. He'd hoped to make it another ten miles before nightfall, which would put them far enough ahead of the law to rest their horses and eat. Looks like his plans had changed.

"Deke, let the others know to follow us up the hill. On my command, they are to ride left and down into the canyon. You and I will cut right, go around the next hill. They know how to reach the hideout. We'll meet up with them there."

Whitey never took his eyes off of the approaching Rangers while he waited for Deke to convey the orders. Within minutes, they were dashing up the hill, away from the lawmen, and heading toward an area Whitey hoped no one would follow—renegade Comanche country. Of course, that would put him and Deke in danger also, but he didn't consider it to be any worse than what would await them in Austin if they were arrested.

Dax caught up with Pat and paced him as their horses climbed the hill. "They're making a run for it. Looks like they've split up with Whitey and one of the other men riding east while the others head west."

"We follow Whitey. He and his brother, Deke, are the ones we want. My guess is it's the two of them who split off east."

The three rode hard, pushing their horses after an already long journey, determined to end the chase today by catching both Whitey and Deke. They cared little about the others.

Pat stopped at the summit and watched as the two outlaws made their way around the back side of the hill, riding in and out of low shrub and live oaks, then venturing into open terrain. He pulled out his Spencer repeating rifle, took aim, and fired. The bullet ricocheted off a rock a foot from Whitey, causing the man's horse to dance around before the outlaw got him under control and took off at a run again, Deke right behind him.

"Damn," Pat cursed as he slammed his rifle back into its scabbard and kicked his horse into a run.

Dax and Luke had pulled ahead, both riding low, guns drawn. They didn't slow as Whitey and Deke rode into a large copse of live oak and disappeared.

"We'll wait for them here." Whitey dismounted and pulled out his rifle, resting it on a low hanging branch. Deke let his horse go and found a spot a few yards away, then waited.

Within minutes, the sound of hooves pounding on the dry ground was followed by the three Rangers coming into sight. Whitey aimed and squeezed the trigger. The bullet flew true, catching Pat in the chest.

He fell from his horse, clutching his chest as blood seeped through his shirt.

Dax and Luke returned fire as they dismounted, pinning the outlaws down, and took positions behind a group of boulders.

"You slip around to the right and go after Deke." Dax waited for Luke to nod and start moving before he took off in the other direction. He skirted around another group of boulders and up an embankment where he had a good view of Whitey below. As Dax prepared to shoot, his boot slipped on loose gravel, sending him into a slide as a shot flew over his head. The outlaw had seen him. Dax stopped his downward momentum when he slid into another boulder. He scrambled onto his knees and peered over the large rock. Whitey had disappeared.

Another shot rang out, followed by a grunt, and Dax knew that either Luke or Deke were down. He retraced his steps, following the path Luke had taken. He came upon his brother, standing over the fallen outlaw who lay motionless on the ground.

"He's dead." Luke holstered his gun, then turned to his brother. "Whitey took off north. Do you want me to ride after him?"

Dax glanced at the dead outlaw once more and shook his head. "We'd better see to Pat."

Pat lay writhing on the ground, his face ashen, as he tried to stop the awful pain in his chest. He choked as Dax knelt beside him and placed a hand under his head, his eyes scanning the wound. He knew there was no hope of saving their comrade.

"Don't leave me out here," Pat gasped. "Take me home."

"To Austin?"

"Montana." Pat reached up to grip Dax's shirt and pull him toward his face. "Promise me. Bury me on my land in Montana." He let loose of the shirt and fell back. "Promise me," he repeated again as his eyes searched Dax's.

Dax swallowed the lump in his throat and nodded. "We'll get you home. I promise. You'll be buried on your land." He watched as his friend's mouth curved slightly before his eyes rolled back and his body went slack. Pat Hanes exhaled his last breath.

Luke stood over them. He'd grown used to seeing men injured and dying. Most times, he didn't know them and could put the carnage behind him. This time, though, it was different. In a few short months, Pat had become a friend, someone he and Dax could trust. His end came much too soon.

"Did you mean it?"

Dax looked up, his face stoic, eyes grave. "About burying him on his land?"

Luke nodded, already knowing the answer he'd hear.

"Yes."

Splendor, Montana, Spring 1866

Rachel choked on the dust that swirled around her skirts as she made her way to the general store. It surprised her that the road could be so muddy while dust clogged the air. Her uncle's clinic had been quiet the last few days. She suspected the weather and windstorms to be part of the reason, and took advantage of the slower pace to clean the clinic and purchase supplies for the home they lived in at the back of the property.

The old-timers, those who'd lived in Splendor more than a few years, talked of how mild the winter had been this year. In Rachel's mind, the large snow drifts and freezing temperatures seemed harsh. It was hard for her to imagine it being worse. The frozen ground of the winter had begun to soften, creating a never-ending mud pool on the main street. She stomped her feet outside the store's entrance and pushed at the door, losing her balance for a moment as the strong winds propelled her inside.

"Quite a blow we have out there today, Miss Davenport." Timmy, the store's teenage clerk, stood on a small stepladder, arranging items on an upper shelf. "Haven't seen too many people today."

"I'm not surprised. It's not too easy to get around with the mud and wind." Rachel rearranged her bonnet and tried to brush off the dust clinging to her dress.

She glanced around at the full shelves and variety of merchandise Timmy's father stocked and, once again, marveled at how he kept the place so organized and clean. She suspected most of it was due to Timmy's hard work.

He jumped to the ground and walked behind the counter. "What can I get for you?" The boy had a broad, infectious smile that couldn't help but put people at ease.

Rachel pulled a piece of paper from the cotton reticule her mother had given her before leaving Boston. "We'll need flour, sugar, coffee—" Rachel halted as the door to the shop slammed open and a man appeared in the entry—tall, dirty, and trail weary by the look of him.

"Where's the doctor?"

Rachel walked forward, taking tentative steps. The combination of crusted dirt, hard features, and abrupt manner warned her to be cautious.

"I'm Rachel Davenport, a nurse at my uncle's infirmary. He's a doctor."

Dax's gaze focused on the young, beautiful woman before him. Her manner and dress indicated she came from privilege, her voice told him she was from the North.

He hadn't seen anyone this lovely in months, maybe years. *That doesn't matter now*, he told himself, and pushed the thought aside. "It's my brother. He's come down with something. He's running a fever and says his head is pounding."

His voice held the familiar accent of the South and Rachel wondered if he'd fought in the war.

She shot a look at Timmy. "I'll be back for everything later." Rachel pushed past the man and rushed outside to the buckboard to see a man covered with a blanket, hard coughs racking his body, overcome with feverish delirium. Beside him lay a coffin, the smell of embalming chemicals seeping through its seams.

"Follow me." She didn't wait to see if the man would heed her order. She pushed open the door of the clinic, threw her reticule down, removed her hat, and turned toward the entrance. "In there." She pointed to a room off to one side. "I'll get my uncle." Rachel hurried to the back and opened a door connecting the clinic to a short walkway which led to the house in back. "Uncle Charles, we have a patient!" She waited a moment, then called again, "Uncle Charles!"

"I hear you, Rachel. No need to shout." Her uncle emerged, pulling up suspenders while he walked at a brisk pace toward the infirmary. He stopped to scrub his hands before stepping into the room he used to examine patients, directing his comment to the man who stood next to the table. "I'm Charles Worthington, the doctor here in Splendor. Tell me what's been happening with your friend." Charles looked into the young patient's eyes, which were red and swollen, as he pulled back the blanket.

"He's my brother. A fever started yesterday. He also complained of stomach pain. It's gotten worse and he mumbles about his head splitting open. He can't hold down any food or water."

Charles could hear the anxiety in the man's voice as he described his brother's symptoms.

"All right. Why don't you wait in the front while Rachel and I have a look?" He paused when Dax began to object, but shook his head. "It's better if you're not in here, young man. Let us do our work." Charles focused back on the sick man. "What's his name?"

"Luke." Dax drew in a deep breath and closed the door behind him, leaving the doctor and nurse to care for his brother.

"Rachel, get me some laudanum, water, and broth."

"What is it?"

"An infection. Probably dysentery." He looked up at Rachel, knowing she'd had firsthand experience with the various diseases and fevers which killed many during the war. "Let his brother know we'll need to keep him here. It's in the early stages, which makes his chance of survival good."

She helped her uncle before stepping into the front area. Dax stood when she walked into the room, fingering the brim of his hat and trying to curb his apprehension.

"What is it?"

"Appears to be an intestinal infection, Mr..."

"Pelletier. Dax Pelletier."

"All right, Mr. Pelletier. The doctor is treating him, but your brother will need to stay with us for now, at least until the fever breaks. The doctor thinks he has a good chance of recovering if we can get fluids into him and relieve the stomach pain. "

He absorbed her words, wanting to feel relief, yet not wanting to put too much hope in her statement. Dax pushed a hand through his ink black hair and let out a breath.

"Thank you for what you're doing for Luke."

"It's what I've been trained to do. I've done it for close to three years now."

"During the war?"

"That's right. I worked in Union field hospitals. Afterwards, I moved back home to Boston for a couple of months before joining my uncle here in Splendor." She watched his expression, but saw no hint of censure. "Did you fight for the South, Mr. Pelletier?"

"Yes, ma'am, I did. So did Luke." He lowered himself into a chair, exhaustion and concern for his brother overwhelming him. It seemed odd. He'd fought in more battles than he could count, killed men, and watched many die at the hands of others. Somehow, this journey from Texas to Montana, bringing Pat's body home and then Luke's sudden illness, seemed to weigh more heavily on him.

"Do you have a place to stay, Mr. Pelletier?"

"Not yet. We just got into town. Been traveling for over a month. We were almost here when Luke..." His voice trailed off as he thought of losing his brother from a fever now after they'd both made it through the war.

"What brings you to Splendor?"

"The request of a friend."

His answer puzzled her. "Does it have anything to do with the coffin in your wagon?" Her tone softened as she guessed what might bring two men all the way to Montana from Texas.

"That's our friend, Pat Hanes. He owned a ranch around here. His last request was to be buried on his land. Did you know him?"

"No, I'm sorry. I've been in Splendor just a few months. Hold on a minute." She poked her head back into the room where her uncle stood over Luke. "Did you know a Pat Hanes?"

"I've heard the name, but never met the man. Why?"

"The Pelletiers brought his body back here for burial. Mr. Pelletier says he owned a ranch."

"Might be the one Hank and Bernice Wilson manage north of here. Best place to check is with Horace Clausen. He knows everyone who owns property in these parts."

She closed the door, looking back at Dax. "You might want to check with Mr. Clausen at the bank."

Dax stood and looked past her toward the examination room.

33

"It's all right, Mr. Pelletier. Your brother will be fine with us. The bank is down the street. If you hurry, you may catch him before they close for lunch."

"Is Mr. Clausen available?"

"He is. May I tell him your name?" The bank clerk set down her pen and took in the stranger's appearance, her face impassive.

"Dax Pelletier."

A moment later, a tall, slender man with graying hair and short beard walked toward him, extending a hand. "I'm Mr. Clausen. How may I help you, Mr. Pelletier?"

Dax looked around at the clerk and two other customers in the bank. "May we speak in private?"

"Of course."

Dax followed Clausen into his office and took a seat as the man closed the door.

"My brother and I are Texas Rangers. Our friend, Pat Hanes, died while we were hunting some bank robbers—shot by their leader. He asked us to bring him here for burial on his ranch. Did you know him?" From the look on Clausen's face, Dax assumed the man did, indeed, know his friend.

"I'm sorry to hear this. Mr. Hanes was a good man. I know he looked forward to the day he could return to Splendor and work his ranch full-time."

"That's what he told my brother and me. If you could give me directions to his ranch, I'll take him out there, make sure he has a decent burial." Dax handed the banker a document signed by a doctor and their captain, attesting to Pat's death.

"Hank Wilson and his wife, Bernice, have been tending the place, along with the hired hands. They'll know what to do." Clausen walked to a file cabinet against a wall.

"Thanks, Mr. Clausen. I guess I'd better get going."

He glanced over his shoulder. "Wait a minute, Mr. Pelletier. It would be best to sign the necessary documents now, before you leave. That way, it will all be legal."

Confused, Dax looked at the man. "Legal?"

"Why, yes. Didn't Pat tell you the provisions of his will?" Clausen pulled out the file and sat back down at his desk, looking over the document.

"What will?"

"Ah, I see he didn't tell you. Pat was a thorough man. He knew his chances of dying on the job were decent so, the last time he visited Splendor, he made arrangements for the passage of ownership. It states that if he died as a Ranger, whomever brought his body back to the ranch would become the legal owner." Clausen looked up at Dax. "Plus, there is a sizable account here at the bank that is also yours." He slid a bank record across the desk for Dax to read. "Congratulations, Mr. Pelletier. You and your brother are the new owners of some prime ranchland at the base of Redemption Mountain."

Chapter Three

Ah, hell, Dax thought as he slumped back into the chair across the desk from the banker.

"By the look on your face, I can see Pat never mentioned any of this."

"Not a word."

"Nothing can be changed now. The property and money belong to you and your brother. I'd like to add, however, that Pat's ranch is one of the best properties around Splendor. Good water, large expanses of grazing land, access to timber, and a house located in a protected valley."

"Pat didn't talk much about it, except to say he owned a decent amount of land."

Clausen chuckled at the statement. "Depends on what you call decent. What would *you* call five thousand acres?"

Dax's head spun from the information. He and Luke now owned a massive amount of land in Montana. He signed for his portion before leaving the bank to take Pat's body to his ranch—well, his and Luke's ranch now.

Clausen provided directions, telling Dax it would take about an hour by wagon to get to the main house, even though the edge of the ranch began a mile outside of Splendor. He tied

Hannibal to the back, intending to leave the wagon at the ranch and ride his horse back to town. He stopped by the clinic to let the doctor and Miss Davenport know he'd be back that evening. They'd been encouraging about Luke's progress. He rested peacefully for the first time in a few days and his fever had lessened, which gave everyone hope he'd pull through.

Dax's thoughts turned to the pretty nurse and wondered why a privileged woman of the North would risk her life traveling to the wilderness and an unknown future. He hadn't been with a woman in months, and never a decent one like her. Before the war, he focused his attention on building the shipping business. He'd courted little, never experiencing the urge to marry or settle down. His female adventures before the war centered on women he'd never consider introducing to his parents. They were a way to kill time and relieve tension, nothing more. Something about Miss Davenport called to him in a way that sent warning signals through his body.

Dax shook his head and concentrated on the rut-filled trail ahead. There were few fences in this wide expanse of rangeland. The only sign he'd entered the ranch appeared on a large boulder with one word, HANES, painted near the top. No matter what Dax and Luke decided to do, keep the place or sell it, the name would remain on that rock as a reminder of the man who'd died before having the chance to enjoy his land.

The wind picked up as he continued, sending a chill clear through him, which didn't ease the remainder of the journey. Dax supposed he should be grateful the rain Clausen warned him to expect didn't appear.

He'd been traveling about an hour when a large barn and house came into view. A woman stood at the back of the home, taking clothes from the line, her hand shielding her eyes from the sun's glare as she turned in his direction. Dax lifted a hand and waved. She didn't respond as she dropped the clothes in a basket and walked toward the front of the house, always keeping him in sight. Dax could hear her yelling before a short and stocky older man appeared from the barn, holding a rifle in his hand.

Dax nodded to both as he pulled the wagon to a stop and jumped down.

"Hold it there, mister. What business do you have out here?" The man didn't raise the gun, although his words held a warning.

"My name's Dax Pelletier. My brother, Luke, and I worked with Pat Hanes down in Texas."

He saw the woman glance toward the back of the wagon, then cast a worried gaze to the man who Dax assumed to be her husband, Hank Wilson, the man Clausen mentioned during their meeting.

"We were chasing a gang of bank robbers when Pat got shot. He didn't make it." Dax nodded at the coffin. "We brought him home to be buried."

The woman gasped and hurried toward the wagon. The man took longer to absorb the news, taking slow steps to join the woman.

"I've got a letter from our captain at the Ranger office in Austin." He reached into a jacket pocket and pulled it out. "Would you like to read it?"

The man took the letter from Dax's hand and read through it. "I'm Hank Wilson. This is my wife, Bernice. We've been running the place with the help of the ranch hands while Pat finished up his duties in Texas." He took a deep breath. "Guess our work here is over."

"I wouldn't count on it. Did Pat ever mention his will? His plans for the place if he died?"

"He did. I suppose you and your brother are the new owners."

Dax didn't explain how he wanted no part of the place and had known nothing of the terms in Pat's will. "We are."

"Then you'll probably be wanting to run things how you see fit, hire your own people. It'll take us a few days to pack up."

Dax understood the uncertainty the man felt. "Let's talk about all that after we bury Pat. Do you know if he had a place in mind?"

"There's a patch out back of the house he mentioned would make a fine place to rest. Guess that's where he'd want to be. I'll get a shovel."

"Two, if you have them." Dax climbed up on the seat, turned the wagon, and followed Bernice toward the site Hank mentioned.

The two men worked for an hour digging the grave, while Bernice notified the hands not out tending the herd of Pat's death. She sent one into town for the minister. By the time Dax and Hank were finished and had lowered the coffin into the grave, the others were assembled and the preacher stood staring down onto the pine box, holding his bible.

"I met Mr. Hanes just once, but I'll do my best to say the right words for the man." Reverend Paige opened his bible.

Bernice walked up and whispered in the preacher's ear, then stepped back.

"It's good to know, Mrs. Wilson, that Mr. Hanes was a God-fearing man."

The service didn't take long. Everyone took a handful of dirt and dropped it on the coffin. Two of the ranch hands took over the job of filling the grave, while the others walked toward the house in a solemn procession. Reverend Paige took coffee, then excused himself for the ride back to Splendor. The others stayed inside, recounting a few stories and speculating about the ranch's future.

Dax counted six people in total—Hank and Bernice, plus four other men. The rest were out with the herd. From what he'd learned as he listened to their conversations, Pat provided room and board, plus a few dollars a month for them to keep watch over the place, make repairs, and tend the herd. From what Dax knew, the arrangement seemed standard for most ranches. At least no one seemed anxious to leave.

"What are your plans, Mr. Pelletier?" One of the men, Dax believed he'd introduced himself as Ellis, stood next to him, looking out the front window toward the barn.

"I don't know for certain." He wanted to say what he felt, that he'd get the hell out of here and head back to Texas, but kept it to himself. "My brother and I need to talk about all this." He turned toward the others, who he suspected would have the same question.

"Guess you're all wondering what will happen next." He saw a couple of heads nod. "The best I can say is I'm not certain. I'd like all of you to stay, at least through the spring and summer, until my brother and I figure this out. Same jobs, same pay as with Pat. If you decide to leave, let Hank know." He set down his glass and looked toward the foreman. "I'm heading back to town for the night, Hank. I'll be back tomorrow and will plan to stay here for a while." He glanced at Bernice. "Is that going to be problem?"

"Not at all. The house has several bedrooms. I'll get two ready for you."

Dax glanced back at Hank. "We'll talk again tomorrow."

"What do you think?" Rachel asked Charles as she stood over Luke, pressing a cold cloth to his forehead, watching the occasional flutter of his eyelids. The sun had set hours before, yet both remained in the room, keeping watch on Luke. They'd tried to get some broth down him without success.

"The fever is lower and he isn't as agitated. His breathing is no longer erratic. I believe this boy may make it. We'll need to keep him another couple of days. Sometimes a relapse occurs. I don't want him back on the trail before we know he's beaten the fever." Charles dropped into a chair. "At least there's been no other emergencies to distract us."

"Let me get you something to eat." Rachel turned toward the door.

"I'm not hungry, Rachel."

"You ate little of the stew and I can see you're tired. What about letting me stay here for a while so you can lay down? I'll call if there's a change."

Charles stood. "Perhaps you're right."

Rachel watched him walk the short distance to their house and disappear inside. She let her eyes drift down to focus on her patient. He had dark hair, but not jet black like his brother. It was more of a deep auburn. The few times he'd opened his eyes, she'd seen they were a deep caramel color, while Dax's were steel gray. She imagined the older Pelletier could stop a conversation with just a look.

"General...," Luke muttered and tossed his head, then fell silent.

"You're all right, Mr. Pelletier. You're safe." Rachel kept her voice low and calm.

"General..."

"He's asking for me."

Rachel turned to see Dax Pelletier standing in the doorway. For some reason, she hadn't realized how tall he stood, well over six feet. He'd taken a bath. His damp, black hair had been slicked back and a clean shirt clung to his still moist skin.

"Luke calls me that sometimes when he wants to get under my skin." He placed his hat on a nearby chair and walked over to stand next to Rachel. "How's he doing?"

His deep voice washed over her, sending a slight shiver through her body. She took a step backward, creating distance, before answering. "The fever is down a little more since you left. He's stopped grabbing his head and his color is better, but he still won't take much broth. Overall, it's encouraging." She walked to a basin and soaked the cloth once more, before placing it on Luke's forehead.

"Were you a general in the war?"

He didn't like to talk of his rank or war experience, yet believed it discourteous to ignore her question. "The last several months, yes."

"And Luke? Did he serve also?"

"He was a major."

Dax watched her work, her concise movements full of compassion, yet he could sense a rod of steel at her core. He bet she'd be a formidable force if someone challenged her.

Rachel didn't know if exhaustion or the elevated warmth in the room had her on edge. She ran her fingers under the collar of her dress to loosen it, hoping no one else would detect the slight shake in her hands. She hadn't noticed it herself until Dax appeared. It was an unwelcome realization.

"Do you have a room yet?" Her words came out sharper than intended, yet they had the desired result. Dax stepped away from her.

"Yes. I'm staying at the boardinghouse."

"Good, then we know how to contact you. It would be best if you got a good night's sleep. My

43

uncle or I will come for you, if needed." She walked to the other side of the table and raised her eyes to the door. "Goodnight, Mr. Pelletier." Rachel then let her gaze lower to her patient.

"Are you dismissing me, Miss Davenport?"

His stern question, devoid of warmth or humor, grabbed Rachel's attention. She looked up to see hard, gray eyes, which had turned the color of gun metal, trained on her, challenging. She imagined this to be the same look he used when commanding troops.

Rachel sighed. "My apologies. I must be tired."

Dax let his gaze wander over her face, noting the lines around her eyes for the first time. Even though her stance and expression indicated exhaustion, Rachel Davenport's beauty couldn't be hidden. She possessed an almost regal quality that captivated him.

"What do you do when you must tend to more than one patient?"

She understood his point as her lips curved upward. "Become a complete witch, I believe."

He nodded and grabbed his hat as his hand grasped the door knob. "Goodnight, Miss Davenport. I will see you in the morning." He shot a glance at Luke, then let his gaze settle on Rachel for a moment before closing the door behind him.

"How is our patient this morning?"

Rachel stirred at the sound of her uncle's voice. She sat up in the chair where she'd slept all night, and rubbed her eyes while looking toward Luke, seeing his color had returned. "He hasn't made a sound in several hours."

Charles bent over Luke, checking his temperature, eyes, and color, concurring with Rachel's comment. "Good," he murmured. "Very good. It seems his fever has broken. We may be able to send Mr. Pelletier on his way a little earlier than I first thought."

Luke stirred at the sound of voices, opened his eyes, blinked a few times, and groaned. "I feel awful." He tried to sit up, then slid back onto the bed.

"That will pass, young man." The doctor held up a glass of water, while supporting Luke's head. "Give it a few more days and you'll feel like your old self."

"Let's hope I'm better than that." Luke tried to swing his legs off the bed.

"Hold on a minute. I don't believe you're ready to leave us yet."

"No offense, Doc, but I'm more than ready. I'll not take up any more of your time than I already have." He glanced around the room. "Where's my brother?"

The doctor stepped back and shifted his gaze to his niece. "Do you know where he's staying?"

"At the boardinghouse down the street."

"Good. I believe you should head down there. Let's see if he can talk some sense into his brother."

They turned at the sound of a brisk knock on the outside door. Rachel pulled the door open to lock eyes on the tall, broad-shouldered figure of Dax Pelletier, looking every bit the ex-military officer. He'd shaved the stubble from his face and stood erect, holding his hat, but the look of concern remained.

"Come in, Mr. Pelletier." He stepped past her. "Or do you prefer General?" Rachel knew she taunted the man, which she never did in her capacity as a nurse. She placed a hand over her mouth in an attempt to stop from embarrassing herself further.

He stopped at her words. "For most, I prefer Dax or Mr. Pelletier. For you, however, I'll make an exception. General will be fine." He turned toward the exam room door, a vague smile playing across his face.

"Ah, Mr. Pelletier. My niece and I were just speaking of you." The doctor motioned toward Luke, who'd made his way to a nearby chair and was attempting to pull up his pants, nearly toppling over in the process. "As you can see, he's doing much better today. The fever's broken and his color has returned, but he insists on leaving."

"Now." Luke didn't look up from the task of pulling on his boots.

"Well, I..." the doctor began, then stopped as Dax reached past him to help Luke.

"You sure about this?" he asked his brother.

"Yes."

"If that's what you want, we'll go. What do I owe you?" Dax reached into his pocket as the doctor named a figure, then handed him the amount, plus extra. "Thank you." He shifted his gaze to Rachel. "Both of you."

He helped Luke stand and, noticing he didn't seem too steady, helped him outside. Luke raised a hand to shield his eyes from the bright sunshine. After being inside and flat on his back for he wasn't sure how long, the fresh air felt good, even if he did have some trouble keeping his balance.

"Where are we going?"

"I'll settle up at the boardinghouse, then we can ride out to our new ranch."

Luke stopped, slack-jawed, and stared at Dax. "What the hell are you talking about?"

"We own Pat's ranch. He had a will stating if he died, whoever brought him back to Splendor inherited the ranch."

"Ah, hell."

Dax didn't respond. He didn't need to. Luke could see the look of disgust pass over his face.

They still owned extensive property in Savannah and hadn't yet made the decision when they'd return to claim it. In the meantime, Luke had made provisions for their former slaves to work the land and keep up the house as paid help. The Pelletier money would keep everything going for a long time, perhaps indefinitely if Polly and George, the married couple who ran the place, did what they promised. For the ex-slaves, profits meant ownership, the right to claim land once they'd built it to a certain level, then continued to expand. Dax and Luke had no doubt the couple would work hard to become true property owners.

47

And now this.

"What do you want to do?" Luke asked.

"Right now? Nothing. We'll stay at the ranch for a few weeks to make sure it's going well and to give ourselves time to make a decision about selling."

"Pat said it's a small place. Probably be easy to sell." Luke stepped up onto the wooden walkway outside the boardinghouse, holding the rail for support, then turned to Dax when he heard him snort. "What?"

"It's somewhat bigger than we both thought."

"How much bigger?"

"Five thousand acres."

After stopping at the bank so Luke could sign the necessary papers, they saddled Hannibal and Prince for the ride to the ranch, Luke insisting he could handle his horse. They arrived at the ranch in the afternoon. Luke had been able to keep up the modest pace most of the time, although a thirty minute ride had doubled when Dax made a couple of excuses to stop. No matter. They had nowhere else to go. Each had taken a leave from their jobs as Texas Rangers. Their captain had insisted on it, requesting they keep him posted about when they'd return.

Bernice stepped off the porch, stuffed a towel into her apron, and waited for the men to dismount. She nodded to Dax, then turned to Luke. "I'm Bernice Wilson. You must be Luke, Dax's brother."

He slid off Prince, steadied himself, and doffed his hat. "Yes, ma'am. I'm pleased to meet you."

"You still look a little peaked. Why don't you come inside and rest. I'll get you something to drink." She turned toward the house, then called over her shoulder at Dax. "You, too."

Dax tipped his hat to Bernice, but stayed in place. "You go on in. Sounds like Hank may be in the barn. I'll take care of the horses and let him know we're here." He grabbed Prince's reins and walked toward the barn, stopping when he heard voices coming from inside.

"I don't know, Hank. Seems to me the man's got no business running a ranch. Besides, I think he's a Johnny Reb, and you know that won't go over well with the men."

"As Pelletier said, you can stay or leave. Makes no difference to me what side he fought on. It's over and time to forget about it, Ellis. But if you can't, then it'd be best for you to pack your gear and go."

"How do we know they have the money to run a place like this? They were working as Texas Rangers. Those men don't have two nickels to rub together."

"Seems to me you're making a lot of assumptions. Pat wouldn't have asked them to bring him home if he thought poorly of them and you know it."

"Don't know why he didn't leave the place to you. Seems fitting after all you and Bernice have done."

"You know the reason. We don't want it. Working here is good enough for us and we hope to stay on. You'd better do some hard thinking pretty quick as I need to find someone else if you leave."

Dax stood his ground, taking it all in and not interrupting. He heard footsteps and guessed Ellis had decided to leave, and perhaps consider Hank's words. Dax pulled on the reins and stepped inside the barn, passing Ellis on his way out.

"Boss." Ellis didn't make eye contact as he continued on toward the bunkhouse.

Dax nodded at Hank as he unsaddled the horses, brushed them down, and pushed open the gate to the pasture behind the barn.

"Did your brother come out with you?" Hank pulled off his gloves and stuffed them in his back pocket.

"He's inside." Dax watched as Hannibal and Prince ran around the large fenced pasture. It had been a long time since they'd been this free to run.

"Suppose you heard Ellis."

"I did. He's free to leave." Dax closed the rear barn doors and turned to Hank. "Are you ready for our talk now?"

"Sure am." Hank followed him into the house and pointed toward an office. "I'll get Bernice to bring us some coffee while you find your brother."

A short time later, the three men watched each other from large leather chairs and sipped their coffee. Dax's eyes roamed over an accounting of the property Hank had scratched out on a piece of paper. He'd been meticulous at keeping records of purchases, payroll, and income from the cattle sold each year.

"Pat kept things simple. He planned to come back and expand the herd, hire more men, maybe get into horse breeding for the army. He expected horse sales to grow with the expansion of forts out west. The cattle operation is profitable with enough coming in to pay the men, buy supplies, and enlarge the herd every year. He was a frugal man, but knew enough to pay the men well." Hank scratched his stubbled jaw. "Took him over ten years to accumulate the land, and he had to fight off King Tolbert, the neighboring rancher, for every acre. He must've put every cent he had into this place. Damn shame he never got to finish his dream."

"What would need to be done to expand the herd, grow the way he intended?" Dax set the paper on the desk and leaned back. Yes, Pat had been frugal, which accounted for the large sum of cash in the bank.

"More cattle and men, but that's about it. There's plenty of good grazing land and water, so those aren't worries. Why? What are you thinking?" Hank needed answers.

Dax looked toward Luke, then back at Hank. "Neither Luke nor I have ranching experience. Farming, shipping, and trade, but not cattle."

"You know business? How to keep what's yours?"

Dax's eyebrows drew together as his eyes narrowed. "Explain yourself."

"This is rough country. We spend as much time fighting off bands of renegade Indians and land thieves as we do tending the cattle. Winters are merciless. Some years, we lose a third of the herd to weather and theft. You have to be prepared to kill and die if you run a place like this. It's no business for the weak." Hank leveled his gaze at Dax.

This time, Luke's eyes narrowed on Hank's. He straightened in his chair, then leaned forward. "I don't believe any man who's served under his leadership would call Dax weak."

"That's enough, Luke." Dax's calm voice held a slight censure. He didn't need his past to defend him.

"You two fight in the war?"

"For the South." Luke responded in a tight voice, ready to defend their decision to support the vote for secession.

"Makes no difference to me on which side you fought. There were good men on both. What does matter is that living out here is another war. You have to decide if that's what you want—to continue to fight for what you want every day of your life, or settle back into something more peaceful."

"Like being a Ranger?" There was no humor in Dax's tone.

Hank chuckled, then sobered. "Mind me asking where you two are from?"

"Savannah, Georgia." Luke set his empty cup on the desk.

"Been there. I heard Sherman tore it apart. That true?" Hank could see the shadows pass over each brother's face, looks of disgust and pain, which told him the talk was accurate. "Well, this is as good a place as any to build a new life." He pushed up from his seat and stood when he heard commotion from out front, then loud pounding on the front door before it flew open and Bull Mason, one of the hands, entered the study.

"We've got trouble. Tolbert's foreman is riding in with some of his men. They don't look like they want to talk."

All three men followed Bull outside to see a group of riders approaching.

"You recognize them?" Dax asked Hank.

"The one in the lead has been with Tolbert several months. His name is Drake. Mean hombre who travels with a gang, mostly ex-soldiers. I heard he also served in the Confederate army. Guess we'd better meet them." Hank stepped off the porch, not aware of the way Dax stiffened at the mention of the man's name. Dax's reflexes kicked in and he moved a hand to the butt of his gun.

"We're looking for the new owner." The one Dax guessed to be the leader nudged his horse a little closer and looked at Dax, cocking his head, but not showing any recognition of the general under whose command he served. "Are you him?"

"My brother and I own the place."

"My name's Drake. My boss, King Tolbert, wants to meet with you. Follow us." He started to rein his horse around, but stopped at Dax's words.

"Another time. Of course, he's welcome to come by, pay us a friendly visit and talk." Dax and Luke each moved further into the yard, putting about six feet between each other, and watching for any movement from the riders.

"I don't believe you heard me right. Mr. Tolbert wants you to follow us—now."

"Well, Sergeant Drake, I guess we're at an impasse."

Drake glared down at the man, narrowing his gaze, a sense of unease washing over him when he realized who stood before him. "General Pelletier. I'm surprised you recognized me."

"I recognize most faces and all names of the men who deserted during a battle. In your case, I remember both. If we were back home, I'd shoot you where you sit, as I can't abide cowards. As it is, I'll let you ride out. Tell Tolbert if he wants to see me, he'll send a proper invitation or ride out here himself. No lackey as a go-between."

Drake bristled at the insult and started to reach for his gun.

"I wouldn't, Sergeant." Dax and Luke both drew in unison, pointing their guns at Drake's chest. Bull Mason followed their lead and aimed his gun at the other riders.

"You ain't no general anymore, Pelletier." Drake moved his hand away from his gun and rested it on his thigh. "I'd keep a close watch on your place and your men. Accidents happen all the time out here." He smirked and kicked his spurs into the side of his horse, riding away with his men, a cloud of thick dust rising in their wake.

Chapter Four

"Good morning, Mr. Brandt." Rachel slid off her horse, an older dun, and walked him into the livery.

Noah Brandt, the town's blacksmith, looked up, then stepped away from the horse he'd been tending. "Ma'am. What can I do for you?"

"Old Pete lost a shoe." She indicated the right front hoof. "May I leave him here with you?"

"Yes, ma'am. That'd be fine." Noah took the reins and led the horse to a back stall. "Can't get to him until later today, though."

"That's fine. I'll stop back later." Rachel stepped into the sunlit morning as a group of riders approached from north of town. It appeared to be King Tolbert with a few of the men from his ranch. She'd met Tolbert several times, and he'd extended invitations for supper on a couple of occasions. Her uncle had always refused. Rachel figured he had a good reason, although she found King to be quite appealing with exceptional manners and a charming wit. Regardless, her uncle had warned her to be careful around the man.

"Good morning, Miss Davenport." King stopped and tipped his hat.

"Mr. Tolbert." Rachel gave a slight nod, not letting the smile she felt appear. She wanted to heed her uncle's advice, yet saw no real danger in the man.

"I've been remiss in not pursuing a supper engagement with you. Would you be available tonight?"

Rachel hesitated a moment before answering. "I do appreciate the invitation, Mr. Tolbert. However, I take care of my uncle and never know when a new patient will arrive."

"I'm certain your uncle will understand you taking one night away, Miss Davenport. Why don't I speak with him?"

"Oh, no. That won't be necessary." She pursed her lips, coming to a decision. "Perhaps one evening away will be all right."

"Splendid. I'll pick you up at six tonight." He tipped his hat once more, then rode down the main street, tying his horse outside the bank, while the others dismounted and milled about.

Rachel noticed none made a move to head toward the general store or saloon. It seemed as if they were standing guard, watching out for their boss and any perceived danger. She shook her head at the thought of a threat against such a prominent rancher and continued on to the clinic. A wagon had arrived since she'd left so she hurried inside.

"Uncle Charles?"

"Back here, Rachel."

She stepped into the back room to see a small girl on the table, two adults and two other children standing around watching the doctor's efforts to help.

"What is it?"

"This is Mr. and Mrs. Weston. Their daughter has a fever and can't hold her food down." Without saying another word, he motioned for Rachel to guide the family to the waiting room so they could work.

"I'm Rachel Davenport, the nurse. It would be best if you and your children wait in the front." She saw the reluctance on the mother's face and understood her concern. "This is a small room and the doctor needs all the space to treat your daughter." She led the parents and children to the other room. "I'll be back to let you know how she's doing. What's her name?"

"Janie," Mrs. Weston replied in an unsteady voice.

Rachel closed the door and joined her uncle beside the little girl.

"We need to get her fever down."

Rachel went right to work, gathering what they needed. She'd begun applying a cold cloth to the girl's face and chest when the door slammed opened.

"Doc, you got to come quick. There's been an accident and we need your help." The dirt-covered cowboy pulled his old hat off when he spotted Rachel.

"Son, I've got me a sick girl. I can't go now."

"But our foreman, Hank Wilson, has been shot. Pelletier, the new owner, said to get you right away."

Rachel glanced up at the mention of Dax. "Perhaps you should go. I can take care of this."

Charles looked at his niece, then at the cowboy. "Where's the bullet?"

"In his shoulder, near his chest."

"Rachel, I can't be in two places at once. You have good experience with bullet wounds. You take my bag and head out to the Pelletier ranch. See what you can do while I tend to the child. She has a high fever and may convulse. You don't have as much experience with the reactions of young children to illness. I'd better stay with her. Take what you need from the cupboard."

"But—"

"Rachel, you're a solid nurse and, frankly, better than most doctors I've seen. You go. Do what you can for Mr. Wilson."

She bit her lower lip, deciding it would be futile to argue further. She grabbed her uncle's medical bag, inserted a few items from the shelves, and turned toward the waiting man.

"I need to get the buggy ready."

"You ride behind me, ma'am. It'll be quicker." The cowboy jammed the hat back on his head, grabbed the bag from her, and dashed out.

"You're sure...?"

Her uncle glanced up. "Go. You'll do fine."

She followed the man outside, offering a brief explanation to Mr. and Mrs. Weston before closing the door. Rachel grabbed the hand he offered and, in one move, he swung her behind him.

"I'm Bull Mason, ma'am," he called back to her as his horse galloped out of town.

"Rachel Davenport," she answered, but doubted he'd heard.

It didn't take long before she saw the ranch house in the distance. Bull stopped and helped her down, handing Rachel the bag before escorting her inside toward a downstairs bedroom. She walked into the room and halted at the sight of Dax leaning over the injured man, trying to stop the bleeding, while an older woman wiped the man's forehead with a cloth.

"General." She nodded at Dax as she set the bag down and opened it. "Let me see."

Even under the circumstances, Dax couldn't keep a wry smile from forming. It vanished when Rachel pulled back the bandage to examine the wound.

"Rifle shot?"

"Appears so." Dax stood and pulled the chair away to give Rachel more space. "What can I do to help?"

"Hot water, alcohol, bandages—and wash your hands if you're planning to help." She didn't look up, focusing all her attention on the injured man.

"All right. Everyone out." Luke herded the others out of the room. "I'll get the water and alcohol. Bernice, will you grab some bandages?"

She nodded and scurried away, returning a moment later with a handful of makeshift bandages and a couple of towels, handing one to Dax, who'd finished washing his hands in a basin on the nightstand. Luke walked in with a pan of hot water and a bottle of whiskey, then left, closing the door behind him.

Most of the men didn't leave. Instead, they congregated outside on the porch, talking of the shooting and possible man, or men, behind the action. The only other person with Hank on the western edge of the property was Bull and from his description, the person who pulled the trigger rode a large roan, like the one Drake had ridden onto the ranch several days before.

"Was there anyone else with him?" Luke asked as he leaned against the porch railing, arms crossed.

"Not that I could see. Odd, as I figured him for someone who'd give the order, not pull the trigger." Bull rubbed a hand over his unshaven jaw.

"But you're sure it was him?"

Bull paused a moment. "He sat on a big roan, dark hat—same as Drake. Wish I could've seen his face."

"May not be good enough for the sheriff." The others looked up at Luke's comment, then glanced at each other.

"We don't have a sheriff. Haven't since ours showed up dead a few months ago. Shot in the back." Ellis threw the piece of leather he'd been working on to the ground.

"The town can't find a replacement?" Luke asked.

"No one wants the job." Bull walked down the steps. "I'll be in the barn." Even though the ranch often used Noah Brandt as a blacksmith, Bull could do a good job when they couldn't get to town. It was often the way he chose to think and blow off steam.

Luke watched Bull disappear into the barn. He thought over the man's words and wondered how hard it would be to attract a lawman to this isolated town at the foot of the Territory Range. The land mass stretched north and south between the border of Montana and Idaho. It seemed a good place for anyone who wanted to start over or get lost. Luke wondered which category he and Dax fell into.

"There it is." Rachel mumbled more to herself than to the other two who hovered over the bed. She made a slight sound of satisfaction as the bullet clinked into a metal bowl. "Alcohol." She reached over to accept the bottle Dax offered and poured a generous amount on the hole, then looked up at Mrs. Wilson. "He's fortunate. The bullet went more into the shoulder area and didn't clip a lung. Overall, if there's no infection, he should be ready to ride in a few weeks."

"I'll let the men know." Dax walked to the door, then turned back. "Nice work, Miss Davenport. Thank you."

The door closed behind him, allowing Rachel to take her first deep breath since she'd arrived. She didn't know what about the man triggered such intense reactions in her. She'd never experienced anything like the surges of heat, racing heart, and halting breath that seemed to occur around Dax Pelletier. Rachel had seen many men in her job as a nurse. He was, quite simply, the most compelling man she'd ever met.

It had been all she could do to keep her focus on the injured man and not the feelings an innocent touch of his hand would arouse. The reaction unnerved her. She'd wanted to reach over and stroke his arm, touch his face, but held her curiosity in check.

"Miss Davenport?"

The sound of her name pulled Rachel out of her rambling thoughts. "Yes?"

"I can sit with my husband now. You're probably exhausted. Why don't I fix you some coffee or tea so you can relax a bit?"

Rachel let out a sigh. "Tea would be wonderful."

Minutes later, Bernice returned and handed her a cup.

"He'll be in pain for a while. I can leave some laudanum, if you'd like." She sipped at her tea and felt the tension flow out of her.

"Hank has no use for that kind of stuff, but you can leave it." Bernice sat down and took hold of her husband's hand.

"I believe I'll get some fresh air." Rachel walked out the front door to see that everyone had dispersed. She chose a seat in a large rocker and leaned her head against the back, closing her eyes. She must have lost track of time because when she opened them again, the sun had begun to set and Dax stood over her, a slight grin on his face.

He'd been watching Rachel for a long time, her face now eased of the tension he'd seen while she worked on Hank. She seemed to be in a deep sleep, her eyelids fluttering as the cooling breeze washed over her face. At one point, she started, then settled back when whatever menace haunted her had passed. He'd wanted to stroke his knuckles down her cheek, feel the softness and the warmth. More than anything, he wanted to kiss her, feel her lips against his.

"I'm sorry. I must've dozed off." She started to rise, then stopped as Dax placed a hand on her arm.

"No hurry. Supper's almost ready. You need to eat before we head back to town."

"Town? Oh, I'd forgotten. I rode out with Mr. Mason."

"I'll be taking you back." Dax took a seat next to her, stretching out his long legs and crossing them at the ankles, folding his arms over his chest.

She stared over at him, swallowing a lump in her throat, already dreading such close proximity to Dax on the ride back. She couldn't recall ever being physically drawn to a man, at least not to more than a handsome face. Dax Pelletier elicited feelings that were so much more than she ever thought possible, as if a magnet drew her toward him. At the same time, she found it difficult to form a cohesive thought. The entire situation seemed ridiculous.

"I could borrow a horse and get it back to you later." Rachel shifted to her side in an attempt to create more space.

"No. I'll take you back." Dax didn't say how much he looked forward to riding back with her sitting in front of him on Hannibal. He'd been thinking about it the entire time he'd watched her sleep, thinking about slipping his arm around her waist and holding her tight against his chest as they rode back to Splendor.

Not that anything would ever come of it. He and Luke planned to stay a few weeks, get an understanding of the value, then put the ranch up for sale. Neither had a desire to be tied to a place in the northern reaches of the country, no matter how beautiful or tempting the majestic scenery or the woman who sat next to him. Someday, he might regret the decision. For now, it wasn't a part of his future.

"Tell me about Splendor." Dax did have an interest in learning more about the town. However, what he needed now was to hear her voice.

Rachel relaxed and leaned back in her chair. "Well, let's see. It's a wonderful town. Everyone is friendly and obliging, always offering what they can to help out a neighbor. About anything you need is available. Not extravagances, you understand, but the basics. I sometimes miss the type of merchandise available in Boston, but not often." She paused a moment and closed her eyes. "Reverend Paige and his wife are perhaps the nicest people I've ever met. They have this...I don't know...welcoming way about them. Everyone is accepted at their church."

Dax followed her lead and closed his eyes. "So tell me what you *don't* like about it."

"Dust storms, although there's been just one since I've been here. Apparently, they rise up in minutes and, before you know it, you can't see three feet in front of you. A slight one blew through town the day you and your brother arrived, but they get much worse. When the storm blows through, it leaves grit and dirt everywhere."

They sat a moment in relaxed silence. Dax could hear her soft breathing and wondered if she'd fallen asleep.

"The sunrises and sunsets."

"What?" Dax asked, his brows drawing together in a confused frown.

"I love the way the sun peeks up over the eastern mountains and cloaks the town in a soft, yet brilliant light. At sunset, the sky can turn the most amazing shades of pink, orange, yellow, and violet. I've never seen anything like it. It truly takes your breath away."

He glanced over to see her smiling as if she were picturing the scene she'd described.

"You'll stay then?"

"For a while, at least. I've been here since early fall, so not quite a year. According to the people who've been here the longest, the winters are the worst and I've lived through one already."

"Was it bad?" Dax had fought through harsh winters during the war and never imagined ever living through them again.

She chuckled. "If you consider snow storms that last a week, leaving mountains of snow behind then, yes, it was a challenge. At the same time, it was exhilarating in a way I can't describe."

Dax let her voice wash over him. Something about the tone and intensity worked on his senses, causing his body to respond. He shifted in his chair, attempting to hide his body's reaction.

"When the snow melts, the grasslands turn an almost translucent green. The countryside is thick and lush. I'd run my hands over it, marveling at the silky feel." She ran a hand along the arm of her chair in a slow movement, almost stroking it.

Dax watched her hand travel along the wood of the chair, caressing it, and let out a groan.

"Are you all right?" Rachel gazed over at him.

He cleared his throat and stood. "Yes. I guess I'd better see how Luke's doing in the kitchen."

"He's fixing supper?"

"Let's say he's heating up some stew from last night and attempting to make biscuits. I'd suggest you do your best to ignore the results." He held out a hand to help her up, taking a moment before letting it go.

Supper didn't take long. Leftover stew, biscuits, and coffee, but Dax couldn't take his eyes off of her. Strands of her lush, auburn-colored hair had escaped the bun, framing her face. Her hazel green eyes flashed with warmth, irritation, or amusement, and he wanted to learn what triggered all of those responses. He found he wanted to learn everything about her.

"Luke, you did a mighty fine job with those biscuits." Bernice picked up the plates and started for the kitchen.

"Uh...thank you, ma'am." He knew they were passable, but not much more.

"Let me help you, Mrs. Wilson." Rachel reached for the empty stew bowl.

"Nope. You've done enough, and I appreciate it."

"She's right. It would be best to get started back." Dax grabbed his gun belt and strapped it around his waist, adjusting it low on his hips. He pulled on a worn great coat. "I'll get my horse."

The ride back to town took longer with Dax keeping a steady pace, and not the full-out run as when she rode behind Bull. She sat in front, nestled between his thighs, one of his arms wrapped around her waist. The sensations she felt as his body moved against hers had Rachel playing word games, trying to think of anything except the hard-bodied, rugged man who held her close.

"Relax, Rachel. If you don't, you'll be sore tomorrow." His whispered words did nothing to stem the growing agitation at being this close to him.

She took a deep breath and tried to relax her muscles, letting her back rest against his chest.

"That's it." His breath washed against her neck, sending shivers up and down her spine.

Within minutes of getting on the horse, Dax regretted the decision to ride back with her. He should've taken her back in the wagon, let her sit a foot away. Or, even better, asked one of the ranch hands to take her home. He had no business being this close to someone like Rachel, especially with his growing attraction to her. When the war ended, he'd made up his mind not to get attached to any one place or woman for a long time, perhaps ever. Rachel posed a threat to his resolve.

She remained a mystery. Her sophisticated ways and upbringing hid a strength he found fascinating. Everything he discovered about Rachel made her more desirable. No matter her beauty, the grit she'd developed during the war, what he'd seen her do today, or his strong attraction to her, he had to hold himself in check.

Although she hadn't spoken much while working on Hank, Dax had learned they'd both grown up attending fancy balls, eating fine food, and enjoying undisputed social standing, where who they married meant more than emotions or love. None of those meant anything to him now. He had yet to figure out what *did* matter. Even as those thoughts rolled around in his head, he could feel his arm tighten around Rachel, pulling her closer, inhaling the rose scent of her hair.

"Will you keep the ranch?" Rachel felt his arm contract and fought for breath. Not because he held her too snug. The sensations came from the incessant pounding of her heart, the tightening in her chest, and the feel of his body aligned with hers.

He didn't want to answer questions about the ranch. Each answer would lead to another question, then one more.

"We'll stay a while, then decide."

"Do you have family in Texas?"

"No, we're from Savannah. Luke and I moved to Austin after the war. That's when we took jobs as Rangers." He willed himself to focus on the road ahead and not the feel of her nestled close. "We wouldn't have come up here if it hadn't been for Pat's request."

She settled a hand on top of his and squeezed lightly, thinking how lucky Mr. Hanes had been to have selected the Pelletiers as friends.

Dax stifled a groan at the feel of her hand on his.

He rounded the last bend to see lights from a few kerosene lamps still burning inside various buildings. The clinic stood near the center of town, the livery and school at the north end, and the church at the south end. In between stood the Wild Rose Saloon—or the Rose, as locals called it—the general store, boardinghouse and restaurant, barber shop, bank, land office, gunsmith, jail, Western Union, and stage office.

Dax stopped Hannibal in front of the clinic. He didn't release Rachel right away. Instead, he pulled her close once more, then reluctantly let go and slid to the ground.

"I'll help you. Swing one leg over the horn." He lifted his arms and grabbed Rachel around the waist, slowly lowering her and letting his eyes lock on hers, the steel color having turned a stormy, dark gray.

She gazed up at him, her hands resting on his arms, and made no move to back away. The invitation he saw both warned and encouraged him.

"I'm not certain how long we'll be in Splendor, but I'd like to call on you, if you'd allow me to, Rachel." He closed his eyes, surprised that he'd voiced what he wanted, knowing he had no business showing an interest in her.

She'd wanted him to ask, yet hadn't allowed herself to hope. "I'd like that, Dax."

He continued to stare into her luminous eyes, wanting nothing more than to capture her lips with his. She didn't move or turn away, continuing to hold his gaze. He bent lower before a gruff cough from behind drew his attention.

Dax let his hands drop from her waist and stepped away before turning to see Doc Worthington in the doorway. He cleared his throat. "Good evening, Doc."

"Mr. Pelletier." He looked around him at Rachel. "I wondered what happened to you. How's Hank Wilson?"

Rachel tried to control her breathing as well as her pounding heart. "Mr. Wilson is doing fine. The bullet didn't do as much damage as I'd first thought. I took it out and he should make it, if the wound doesn't become infected."

The calm tone of her voice surprised Rachel. Her insides were anything but still, her heart continuing to race from the brief contact with Dax. If her uncle hadn't interrupted, she felt certain he might have kissed her. The disappointment surprised her. Her rational mind told her she hardly knew him, the attraction toward him too new. So much about what she felt stunned and confused her.

"King Tolbert stopped by to see you."

"He did? I wonder..." Her voice trailed off when she remembered the invitation.

"I guess you were supposed have supper with him tonight." Her uncle's eyes narrowed at her, disappointment clear on his face.

Dax stepped away, saying nothing. He hadn't thought about Rachel being courted by anyone else. The knowledge affected him more than he'd have thought, especially the name of the suitor—King Tolbert, the man most on the ranch suspected of ordering Drake to shoot Hank.

"Well, I should be leaving."

Rachel watched Dax swing up on his horse in a movement so smooth, it seemed as if he'd done it a thousand times before which, of course, he had.

"Mr. Pelletier...wait." Rachel hurried to the horse's side and looked up to see the same stormy gray eyes trained on her. "Thank you for bringing me home. I appreciate it."

"No problem, ma'am. You did a real good job on Hank. I'm the one who's grateful to you." He looked at Worthington and touched the brim of his hat. "Doc."

Dax rode off, knowing he'd been saved from doing something stupid. If Worthington hadn't appeared, he would've had Rachel in his arms within seconds, keeping her there as long as she would have let him. It didn't matter. She had an interest in Tolbert, and Dax had no place in his life for a small town Montana nurse, no matter how much he felt otherwise. The solitary ride back took much longer than the ride with Rachel. He pulled the great coat around him, settled his hat further down on his head, and ignored the tight feeling in his chest.

Chapter Five

"Who else could it be cxccpt Tolbert?" Bull Mason grumbled as he sat whittling a piece of wood. "That man's been after Pat's land for years. Hell, we've spent more time fighting his men than growing the herd. Someone needs to set him straight."

"How many acres you think he's got now?" Joe, the newest ranch hand, asked as he sipped his evening coffee.

"Maybe a couple thousand more than here." Ellis threw out the last of the grounds and rinsed the coffee pot with water. "No one seems to know for sure."

"He runs more head and has double the number of men." Rudolph, or Rude as he preferred to be called, had been on the ranch as long as Hank and Bernice. He'd met Pat when he'd first arrived in Splendor and liked the man right away.

Dax and Luke leaned against the wall of the porch and listened to the conversation. They'd learned quite a bit about four of the ranch hands in the last few days. There'd been little time to get to know the others who sat with them, relaxing.

Bull and Ellis had fought for the North during the war, both mustering out in 1863. Neither Rude, the oldest, nor Joe, the youngest, had fought, both already settled in Montana when the war broke out. If they *had* fought, their sentiments were clear. Neither agreed with the South's determination to secede, splitting the country in two, yet no one voiced a word against Dax or Luke. They'd seen how the general, as they'd started to call him, had insulted Drake and stood his ground, Luke right alongside him. Their respect for the two had grown, even as their sentiments against the war stayed intact.

"What are we going to do, General?" Bull asked, not looking up from his whittling. "We can't let Tolbert get away with this."

"I don't have a good answer for you. I will say, whoever shot Hank won't go unpunished."

"What do you want us to do in the meantime?" Ellis crossed his arms and leaned against the porch. Of all the men, he found it hardest to shift his allegiance from Pat to the Pelletier brothers, but Dax sensed that once they'd won his trust, he'd be a strong ally.

"Luke and I will be going to town tomorrow for more men. Joe, you'll stay here to watch the place while the others join the rest of the men, round up the herd, and bring them closer to the house."

"We won't be able to graze them all close in for long." Bull stood and shoved his hands in his pockets.

"More men would allow us to split the heard into smaller groups and keep them close." Luke spoke more to Dax than the others. The plan wasn't much different from guarding prisoners during the war.

"Bring them in tomorrow. We'll split the herd into small numbers as we hire more men. Ellis, you'll ramrod tomorrow." Dax straightened his tall frame. "Goodnight, gentlemen."

Luke followed him inside. "You think Ellis is the right choice? Seems Bull might be a better pick."

"You're right, but Ellis is the one doing the grumbling. Besides Rude and Hank, he's been here the longest. I want to see how he handles the others. By tomorrow afternoon, we'll know how he does and perhaps more about how far we can trust him."

"Do you have any idea who may have shot Wilson?" King Tolbert asked as Drake relayed the news one of the men had heard about the Pelletier foreman.

"Nope. Could've been anyone."

King Tolbert sat behind his desk, deciding how to handle the new owners of the Hanes ranch. He thought he had plenty of time. The sudden death of Pat Hanes changed things, as did the unexpected passing of the land into someone else's hands. He'd thought the property would go up for auction, which would mean a cheap price compared to what Hanes had paid for each parcel.

It still burned how the absentee landowner had been able to steal property out from under him. King lived in the valley, knew everyone, yet each time a rancher had trouble, they reached out to Pat through Hank Wilson. Never had anyone contacted him. Those sales had allowed the Texas Ranger to build a ranch into something to rival his own holdings.

From what Drake had told him, the Pelletiers came from old southern money. Drake didn't appear to fear the two brothers, but King could sense the caution in his man when he spoke of them. One, an ex-general. The other, an ex-major. Drake said he knew Dax better, having served under him. He knew less of the younger one, but he heard stories from others. Both had superior fighting skills, although Dax made more calculated moves, while Luke tended to be somewhat brash in his actions. Drake warned King that both had reputations for never giving ground. Well, Tolbert would see about that.

"The new owners won't take kindly to their man being shot, And no matter who pulled the trigger, they'll look to me. What else have you heard?"

"The Pelletiers plan to ride into town this morning to hire more men. They've got the others bringing in the herd, circling them close." It had been a good move to insert one of their men into the Pelletier ranch. They'd learned much over the last few months.

"That's good. Means they're scared."

"I wouldn't count on it, boss. Those two just don't give up. I'm thinking their plan is to grow the herd, maybe get the place ready to sell. A few hundred more head of cattle and more men would challenge what you have. Some Englishman with money could swoop in and snap up that property real quick if they plan it right. They've still got property in Savannah, and jobs in Texas. Why would those two want to stay here? No, I think they'll get the best price they can for the place and move on."

King listened to Drake's comments, not sure he bought into them. He felt certain once they learned the true potential of the land, they might make the decision to stay and build up the ranch. It would be, in King's mind, an unwise decision if that's what they did. He wouldn't tolerate anyone else taking more land from him or keeping what he felt should rightfully be his. They weren't ranchers—hell, from what he'd learned, they didn't know the first thing about the cattle business.

"How many men are they after?"

"Don't know for certain. My guess is at least a half-dozen."

King thought about the number, which would bring them up to about the same number of men as him. It made a statement. They were willing to fight for the ranch, and that was unwelcome news. Tolbert stood and walked to the window, pulling back the curtain to look out at the distant mountains.

"When are they bringing in the cattle?"

"Today."

King narrowed his eyes at Drake. "Get the men out there, scatter the herd, and don't let them get close to the inner pastures. No gunfire. And don't let them see your faces. I don't want them tying it back to us." His goal wasn't to kill, only to show the Pelletier brothers the true nature of ranching and discourage them from staying. When they give up, he'd be ready to buy them out.

"And if they get in our way?"

"No killing, Drake. Scare them. If you have to fire, aim into the air. I don't want anyone shot. Do you understand?"

"Sure, boss." Drake's heavy footsteps echoed in the hall as he left. King could hear the front door close and knew the man wasn't happy about the last instruction.

He looked up at the soft knock on his office door and guessed it to be his daughter, Abigail.

"Come in."

"Good morning, Father." Her soft voice and quiet ways always tugged at her father's heart. "I thought I heard you in here."

King watched Abby close the door. She'd always been the exact image of her mother. Beautiful, deep red hair, creamy complexion with a sprinkling of freckles across her nose, and a smile like the morning sun. She reached up and placed a kiss on her father's cheek.

"Drake had some things to talk over with me. What are your plans?" He noticed her eyebrows arch at his question.

"You didn't forget about taking me to town today, did you?"

He had, and felt a pang of guilt, but that was easy to correct. "Of course not. When will you be ready?"

King watched her eyes light up. "Now, if it suits you."

"Get what you need and I'll have someone ready the buggy."

As she rushed out of the room, he wished life could be different for the young woman. Her mother had passed away a few years after Abby's birth. He'd just started building the ranch and the time he could spend with his daughter had been slight. She'd attended boarding school and finishing school in Philadelphia, surrounded by other girls from well-to-do families. Abby returned to Montana before Christmas, asking him to allow her to stay. He'd agreed. The time had come for her to be courted, yet the possibilities were few in this remote area.

King couldn't worry about the quality of her suitors now. He had more pressing matters, such as the land he coveted, which rested in the hands of two ex-Confederate soldiers. He walked outside and called for one of the hands to prepare the buggy.

"I'm ready, Father."

The cowhand who'd harnessed the rig helped Abby onto the seat. King watched as the man's eyes roamed over his daughter, making him reconsider his previous thought. Perhaps he'd need to *make* time to identify someone suitable for his daughter sooner rather than later. He had many ties in the territorial capital of Big Pine. Perhaps he'd look there.

King slapped the reins, deciding to give both his daughter and his troubles with the Pelletiers more thought.

"That's five men." Luke and Dax sat at the restaurant connected to the boardinghouse and finished their noon meal. They'd been lucky. A rancher across the line in Idaho territory had sold out. The new owner brought in his own men, letting many of the others go. A group had ridden into Montana, some rode south to Utah, and others rode toward Washington and Oregon. Dax had spotted them at the livery, and after a few minutes, the five had found work. They were now on their way to the ranch, while the brothers stayed to pass the word around town.

"We're fortunate we saw them before they spoke with Tolbert. He might have hired them to keep the men out of our reach." Luke placed the last bite of food in his mouth and clasped his hands behind his head.

Dax finished his meal and leaned back in the chair, looking outside toward the livery and the Rose Saloon across the dirt street. He thought about Rachel, had been thinking about her since the day he'd taken her back to town. It irritated him that he couldn't get the woman out of his mind. Dax had considered staying in town that night, going to the Rose, and finding one of the women to take the edge off. A couple of them were pretty enough. The trouble seemed to be that none were worth the effort and he'd still leave with an ache for the beautiful nurse. The best course was to follow their plan to get the ranch ready to sell, find a buyer, and ride back to Texas and the jobs they'd left behind.

Luke rapped him on the arm. "Isn't that Miss Davenport walking toward the livery?"

Dax sat up and debated only a moment. "It is." He stood and looked down at his brother, his jaw working.

Luke suppressed a grin. "Might be a good idea to go say hello. You can never thank a pretty woman too much." He ignored the contemptuous look Dax shot him as he turned toward the door. Luke had thought his brother might have something on his mind. He just hadn't connected it to Miss Davenport. In Luke's opinion, the time had come for Dax to show a little interest in a woman. Someone who might bring sense back into his brother's life. Rachel Davenport might be the perfect woman to do it.

Dax followed her toward the livery and stood back, leaning against the wall of the Western Union office next door while she spoke to the blacksmith. Dax had met the tall, bruiser of a man with broad shoulders and muscled arms. He towered over Rachel and had to lean over as they spoke. She reached into her reticule, pulled out some money, and placed it in the smithy's hand, smiling up at him.

"Thanks again, Mr. Brandt, for doing the work and keeping Old Pete a couple of extra days. I hope that covers it." She nodded to the coins in his hand.

"That will cover it fine, ma'am." He grabbed the horse's reins and handed them to Rachel before turning back to his work.

Dax watched as Rachel whispered a few quiet words to her horse, then led him outside. Her eyes registered surprise when she spotted him.

She raised her hand to shield her eyes from the sun and smiled up at him. "Hello, General. What brings you to town?" She fought the hope he'd come to visit her or even ask her to supper.

Her smile speared clear through him, almost painful in its intensity. He'd never been affected by a woman to this degree before and didn't quite know how to take it.

Dax touched a finger to the brim of his hat. "Good afternoon, Miss Davenport. Luke and I rode in to see if we could hire some additional men."

"And did you find any?" She pushed aside the disappointment at not being the reason for his visit.

"We were fortunate. Five were at the livery having Brandt check their horses. They'd just ridden in from Idaho and were looking for work. We hired all of them." He ran a hand down the horse's withers. "He yours?"

She threw an affectionate glance at the horse. "This is Old Pete. He belongs to my uncle, but I'm the one who usually rides him. Poor boy threw a shoe. Mr. Brandt took care of him for me." She looked back over her shoulder. "Uncle Charles told me he and another ex-soldier came to town almost two years ago. Mr. Brandt stayed, but his friend rode on. Restless, I guess."

"They fight for the North?"

"I believe so. I've never asked him. All I know is he's a nice man and does good work. He's a good choice if your ranch ever needs a blacksmith."

Dax looked down, letting his eyes lock on hers as he crossed his arms over his chest. "That so?"

Rachel cleared her throat at his close scrutiny. "Why, yes. I believe he'd provide excellent work for you." She glanced away and looked past him toward the main street, spotting King Tolbert and his daughter coming their way. "Have you met King Tolbert yet?"

Dax's brows lifted at the sudden change of subject and his body went on alert. "No, I haven't had the pleasure."

She noticed his voice held an edge. "Well, now's your chance." She nodded behind him.

Dax turned to see a man, perhaps ten or fifteen years older than him, driving a buggy, a young woman sitting next to him. He stopped at the livery and jumped out.

"Good afternoon, Miss Davenport." He doffed his hat and walked around to help his daughter down.

"Hello, Mr. Tolbert. I don't believe you've had a chance to meet our newest resident, Dax Pelletier. He and his brother are the new owners of the Hanes ranch."

King's grin fell enough to let Dax know the man hadn't expected to meet him so soon, and definitely not in the company of Rachel.

"Pleased to meet you, Tolbert." Dax extended his hand, which the man accepted.

"Mr. Pelletier, this is my daughter, Abigail. Abby, this is Mr. Pelletier. He's part owner of the ranch to the west of us."

Abby gave a slight curtsey before looking up into haunting gray eyes and an incredibly handsome face. "Good afternoon, Mr. Pelletier." Abby inched to one side, glancing behind Dax and into the livery. Her eyes landed on Noah Brandt at the same time her heart rate picked up a beat. She'd met him a few times while in town with her father. Abby knew her father would never approve of her attraction to the town blacksmith, yet she couldn't help her reaction to the taciturn ex-soldier.

"It's a pleasure, Miss Tolbert." Dax shifted his attention back to Rachel. "You'll have to excuse me. It's time I met up with Luke and headed back. Good to see you again, Miss Davenport." He glanced over at the others. "Good to meet both of you."

Abby couldn't speak past the lump in her throat. To her father's disgust, her wide eyes told it all, except he'd mistaken the object of her fascination. He thought she'd become enamored with the rugged Texas Ranger, never suspecting her true interest lie with the smithy hidden in the shadows.

"Mr. Pelletier," King nodded.

Feeling bereft, Rachel's gaze stayed focused on Dax as he crossed the street to the boardinghouse and restaurant. She wanted to run after him and talk further. He was a complicated man. One she wanted to get to know better.

"Sorry to have missed you at supper the other night, Miss Davenport."

His comment brought her attention back to the man in front of her. "I do apologize. Mr. Wilson, at the Pelletier ranch, was shot and needed immediate attention. I didn't get back to town until late."

King noticed she offered no further explanation. But she didn't need to. Tolbert already knew about the shooting.

"Your uncle told me there had been an emergency. Perhaps another time?"

"Yes, perhaps. I never know when someone will come into the clinic seeking our help. I'm glad you understand. Speaking of the clinic, I'd better get Old Pete back into his stable. Uncle Charles won't eat unless I'm there to remind him. Good day, Mr. Tolbert, Abby."

"See you soon, Miss Davenport."

Abby listened to the discussion. Being in Philadelphia much of the last several years, she'd paid little attention to her father's social life, and never wondered if he courted other women. It appeared he did. She glanced once more over her shoulder and into the livery as King escorted her toward the Western Union office a few steps away.

"Father, do you mind if I wait outside while you send your telegrams? It's such a nice day."

"Of course, Abby. Just stay close. I won't be long." The minute the door closed, Abby retraced her steps to the livery. She felt her resolve falter as she got closer and noticed Noah look up, locking his gaze on hers.

84

Noah straightened, wiping his blackened hands on his pants, then shoving them in his pockets. "Good afternoon, Miss Abigail."

She made a slight nod. "Hello, Mr. Brandt." Abby looked around the large structure. It sat back a few feet from the main street, the forge placed near the middle and stables in the rear. "Appears you have quite a bit of work."

Noah knew his interest in the young woman was foolish. King Tolbert would never allow his daughter to be courted by someone like him—a broken down ex-solider. Still, he couldn't tear his eyes away from Abby whenever she visited. It was enough to be near her, talk to her once in a while. At least, that's what he told himself.

"Yes, ma'am. I seem to keep busy."

She stood a moment, unsure of what else to say. Thankfully, Noah broke the silence. "When do you return to Philadelphia?"

"Oh, I haven't had a chance to tell you. My father has agreed I won't be going back. I'm staying here to help him with the house." She cleared her throat and glanced at Noah in a conspiratorial way. "He doesn't know I learned how to keep the books while back east. My hope is he'll allow me to help with ranch business." Her slight blush at confiding something quite important to her touched Noah.

"I'm sure you'll do fine at whatever you do, Miss Abigail."

"Abby? What are you doing?" Her father's rough voice startled her and she turned abruptly to see his face harden at seeing her with the blacksmith.

"I had a question for Mr. Brandt. Daisy has developed a slight limp and I thought he might know of something I could use to wrap her leg." She cast a worried glance at Noah.

"Like I said, Miss Abigail, sometimes warm compresses do the trick. If you find comfrey, mash it and include it in the wrap." His eyes wrinkled at the corners in amusement and his mouth quirked into a small smile.

"Thank you so much, Mr. Brandt." She bit her lower lip, then turned back to her father. "Are you ready?"

King eyed her, looking for signs of any untruth, but found none. He held out his arm to his daughter. "Yes. I still need to stop by the bank." He looked toward Noah. "Mr. Brandt."

"Good day, Mr. Tolbert."

"That's all of them, Ellis." Bull reined in his horse next to the other cowhand. "I'll take drag if you and Rude want to ride toward the front. The others can spread out in between."

"Wish we had a few more men. At least we don't have to drive them too far." Ellis secured his hat and rode to the front of the herd.

Bull looked around. He'd felt a prickling sensation along his neck a couple of times. He always heeded the warnings his body sent out, knowing from his past that to ignore them was a mistake. Ellis had settled into a spot on the left side of the herd, while Rude rode on the right. Bull's head snapped up at what seemed to be a flash of light coming from a nearby ridge. He rubbed the dust out of his eyes, blinked a few times, and tried to focus. Seeing nothing, he let his gaze roam across the moving cattle, keeping track of the other men.

A series of loud cracks sounded from overhead, sending the cattle into a full run. Rude, Ellis, and the other men tried to turn them into each other to slow their progress. Bull kicked his horse, riding full speed to catch Rude and help him reverse the herd's course. Ellis had reined up and circled around toward the others, firing into the air and yelling at the bawling animals, trying to get them to follow his commands.

Bull and Rude also fired into the air, getting the reaction they wanted. The lead animals began to turn, the others following, circling around to join the back of the herd. It took time before the cowhands got the cattle settled down. Their success wasn't a matter of luck as much as an expectation they knew they could control the herd.

"What the hell happened?" Ellis glared at Bull after he'd pulled down the kerchief covering his face.

"Gunfire. It came from the ridge a couple miles back."

Ellis let out a string of curses. "It's time we go after that son-of-a-bitch."

Like the others, he was certain who ordered the stampeding of their herd. The same person who shot Hank and who'd tried to run Pat off the land for years—King Tolbert. He'd tried this same tactic several times over the years, yet they'd never been able to prove his men had been the ones to do it. Most of the time, they'd stopped the running cattle and recovered any who'd become separated. A couple of times, they'd lost more than a few head, and on one occasion, a wrangler had been injured, breaking a leg and cracking a few ribs.

Bull nodded, as angry as Ellis at the continued attacks, wanting to hunt down and punish those responsible, but accepting they'd do nothing until the Pelletiers gave the word. He glanced at Rude, who sat astride his horse on the front edge of the herd, drinking from a canteen, and looking in the direction of the gunshots. Bull knew someone had been tipping off Tolbert to their daily routine. He couldn't believe any of the ranch hands, his friends, would put the others in danger. Still, he planned to be more vigilant.

"Let's get the cattle moving and talk to the Pelletiers. With luck, they were able to find more men." Bull made a slight clucking sound and his horse pulled out, following the cowboy's subtle commands.

It took three hours to get the cattle to a large pasture not far from the ranch house. Joe and the new men joined them and helped to split the herd into groups. By dusk, the tired ranch hands slid off their horses and headed for the supper Bernice had set out in the bunkhouse.

"How'd it go?" Dax asked as he sat alongside Luke on a long bench and grabbed a plate.

Ellis spoke up. "We've got more trouble. Someone tried to scatter the herd, but we got them under control. It had to be Tolbert's men."

"What do you think, Bull?" Luke asked.

"I agree with Ellis. I saw a flash of light from a ridge not long before the shots rang out. They didn't aim at us. Their goal seemed to be to spook the cattle, get them out of control, and make us lose a few." He glanced at Rude. Something about the man's silence didn't sit right. "We're good, though. Still have the same count."

Ellis scrubbed a hand over his whiskered jaw. "When we going to go after them, General?"

The new men glanced up at the mention of the military title. Rude knew his bosses were from the south. Now he also understood at least one had fought in the war.

"I met Tolbert in town today. Seems it's time Luke and I paid him a visit."

Luke agreed. "We'll ride over tomorrow morning."

Chapter Six

Rachel sat up and rubbed her eyes, having been roused awake by the loud knocking. "Coming!" She grabbed her wrap, slipping it on before yanking the door open to see Al, the bartender at the Wild Rose.

"We need the doctor, Miss Rachel. There's been a fight at the saloon. One of the men has been shot pretty bad. We've got him out front of the clinic."

"I'll get the doctor."

Charles hurried through the back door. He'd thrown on pants and a shirt, but still looked disheveled from Rachel shaking him awake. He looked down at an unconscious man, covered in blood and laying on the table.

Al and another man stood to the side, the eyes of the younger one showing a combination of fear and anger as he watched the doctor strip open the man's shirt to expose the wound.

"Who is he?"

"Jeff Decker. He's my brother."

"What happened?"

"A man at the card table didn't like losing and accused Jeff of cheating. Jeff stayed calm, told him maybe he shouldn't be playing if he couldn't afford to lose, then started dealing the cards. The man pulled a gun and fired, then took off. Can you help him?"

"I'll do what I can." Charles glanced at his niece, who took the cue.

Rachel settled the young man out front while Al went back to the Rose.

"What's your name?" she asked him.

"Stephen." He rested his elbows on his knees and covered his face with both hands. "Hell, it was just a friendly game. This shouldn't have happened."

"The doctor will do everything he can. Would you like some coffee?"

Stephen looked up, his eyes red. "No, thank you, ma'am."

Rachel left him alone and joined her uncle.

"It's not good. He's lost a lot of blood. I need to get the bullet out, but his chances are slim."

By dawn, the bullet had been removed, the area bandaged, and Jeff continued to cling to life. Still in grave danger, the young cowboy fought for each breath, giving Charles and Rachel hope he might make it. The biggest concern was infection. His brother had fallen asleep in a chair out front, knowing Jeff had made it through surgery.

"This has to stop." Charles scrubbed a hand over his face.

Rachel turned to him. "What?"

"This is the fourth shooting since the sheriff was murdered, and that doesn't include the foreman out at the Pelletier place. Men think they can ride in, do whatever they want, then ride out. We have no one to protect us." His eyes met Rachel's. Her safety weighed heavily on him, knowing his sister would never forgive him if anything happened to her daughter. Charles knew he'd never forgive himself, either. "You should leave. Go back to Boston where you'll be safe."

"We've talked about this before. I'm not leaving."

"Rachel, listen to me. It's been months since the sheriff was killed. No one in Splendor is interested in taking the job, and we've had no responses from the inquiries we've made around the territory. The country has a lot of angry men roaming around who've lost their homes, families, and their way to make a living after the war. They're desperate and preying on smaller settlements where raiding is easy. I'm afraid it will get worse. You'll be safe in Boston."

She sat down on a nearby chair and tucked stray strands of hair behind her ears, too tired to have this discussion tonight. "I won't leave unless you do."

"You know I can't do that. Who'd care for these people?"

"Then neither of us goes. We'll have to find another solution to the problem. There must be someone who'll take the job. Even if it's just temporary." She thought a moment, then blew out a breath. "I have an idea."

Charles looked at her.

"The Pelletier brothers are Texas Rangers. They plan to stay for a while, until they decide what to do with the ranch. Maybe one or both would help out."

Charles considered the idea. "Seems to me they have their hands full with the ranch. However, it would solve the problem, at least until we can find someone to permanently take the job."

"Fine. I'll ride out to their place tomorrow." She leaned her head against the wall and closed her eyes.

"Maybe one of the men should ride out. Mr. Clausen at the bank, or Griggs at the telegraph office. A man might have better luck."

Rachel's eyes shot open. "You don't believe I can do something as simple as riding out and talking to the Pelletiers?" Her sharp retort told Charles he'd stepped over some imagined boundary.

"Fine. You go. Right now, I need some sleep. Will you be okay here alone?"

"Yes. I'll be fine." She relaxed again and slumped into the chair. "I'll let you know if there's any change."

"Good morning, Miss Tolbert. We've come to see your father, if he's home."

"Mr. Pelletier, correct?" Abby asked.

"That's right. This is my brother, Luke."

She glanced between the men, noting the similarities and differences between the two.

"Please, come in. I'll let Father know you're here." She showed them to Tolbert's study. "May I get you anything?"

"No, ma'am. Thank you."

They didn't wait long. King Tolbert walked in, his lack of warmth an indication of how much their visit displeased him. "What can I do for you, gentlemen?" He took a seat behind his desk and sat back.

Dax leaned forward in his chair. "You wouldn't know anything about an attempt to stampede our herd, would you?"

King eyed his visitors, surprised at the speed with which they'd confronted him.

"Certainly not. I sincerely hope no one was injured."

"No one was injured and we lost no cattle. So, the time was misspent for whoever ordered the action." Dax stood and walked to a nearby window and glanced out, then turned back to Tolbert. "You, of course, know of Drake's past, the accusations against him?" Dax noticed the look of surprise on the man's face.

"Past accusations mean nothing to me."

"And what is it that he does for you...besides intimidate other ranchers?"

"It sounds as if you're accusing me of more than the unfortunate incident with your herd. I'd be careful of false accusations if I were you." Tolbert's voiced hardened with each word. He stood, walked around his desk to the office door and pulled it open. "I believe it's time for the two of you to leave."

They walked to the open door, Dax stopping within inches of Tolbert, glaring down at the man. "Listen well, Tolbert. We won't tolerate the actions made against our men or property, and we will not bend to intimidation. If we discover you or any of your men are involved, there will be hell to pay, and you'll be our main target."

They pushed past Tolbert to walk outside and mount their horses as Drake and a few men rode in from the direction of town.

"General. Major." Drake touched the brim of his hat with a finger, his sarcastic tone not lost on Dax or Luke. Neither acknowledged the man, other than to keep their eyes trained on him until they'd ridden past.

"The man's dirty," Luke commented.

"As much as any man I've ever met." Dax nudged Hannibal into a gallop, knowing events would get worse, much worse, before Tolbert and the actions of his men were stopped.

"Hello, Mrs. Wilson. I apologize for dropping by like this." Rachel had ridden to the ranch late that morning, hoping to catch Dax and Luke during their midday meal. She'd had to fight butterflies in her stomach the entire way, knowing the source of her unease. He'd never followed up on his request to call on her and Rachel suspected she knew the reason.

"Nonsense, Miss Davenport. It's good to see you again. Please, come in." Bernice stepped aside to let Rachel in.

"How is Mr. Wilson? Would you like me to check on him while I'm here?"

"He's doing fine. Cranky, of course, and ready to get back to work. I figure I can keep him down about another two days. How about something to drink?"

"No, thank you. Actually, I've come to speak with the Pelletiers. Are they around?"

"I expect them and the others any minute. They don't waste much time when there's food waiting." Bernice began to untie her apron when the sound of approaching horses caught her attention. "That must be them."

Rachel stood at the pounding of boots on the front steps. The sound kept rhythm with a similar hammering in her chest. The door burst open as Dax and Luke strolled in first, followed by Bull, Ellis, and Rude. They stopped when Rachel came forward.

"Miss Davenport," Dax greeted her as he pulled off his hat and placed it on the hook of the hall stand. "I thought I recognized your horse outside. To what do we owe this visit?" His gaze wandered over her, settling on the cautious smile she offered.

"I came to see you and your brother." She looked at Luke, who stood a foot away. "If you have the time, of course."

"We'll make time. Join us for dinner first, then we'll take as long as you need." He motioned to a chair and sat across from her, deciding sitting next to her would be too much of a temptation and would test his already slim control when it came to Rachel.

Dax's intense gaze rarely left her during the meal. The men told stories, eliciting smiles and full-fledged laughter from her. He liked the sound—deep and genuine.

"Guess we'd better get going." Ellis stood. "Thanks, Bernice."

The others followed his lead and within a minute, Rachel had been left alone with Bernice and the brothers.

"I'll clean this up while you three talk."

"I'm happy to help," Rachel offered.

"No, dear. You go ahead and meet with the boys before they have to head out. I need to check on Hank anyway."

The corners of Rachel's mouth lifted at her use of the term "the boys." She had a hard time seeing either as anything other than full-grown, and quite attractive, men.

Dax ushered her into the study and to a divan against one wall. "What can we do for you?"

He'd spent much of their meal focusing on her mouth, remembering how much he'd wanted to taste her lips, wondering what her response would have been if he'd taken her in his arms for a proper kiss. He imagined her proper, sophisticated exterior might crumble once she met the right man, someone who could kindle the passion he believed hid within her.

"Did either of you hear about the shooting in town last night?"

Dax blinked, her question yanking him out of his daydream and back to the present.

The men glanced at each other and shook their heads. "No, can't say we have," Luke answered as he took a seat in one of the chairs across from her, Dax sitting in the other.

"Several men were playing cards when one of them accused a young cowhand of cheating. Everyone ignored the man, which must have angered him more. He pulled out a gun and shot the cowboy. My uncle removed the bullet and is still keeping watch over him. We hope he'll pull through."

"Can anyone identify the man who shot him?" Dax leaned forward in his seat, his eyes fixed on Rachel.

"Perhaps the bartender or others who were there last night can. He wasn't alone. Apparently, they all rode out of town after the shooting. That's the fourth shooting in six weeks, not counting Mr. Wilson."

"And why are you telling us this?" Dax asked, knowing there must be a reason why she'd taken time out of her day to ride all the way to their ranch to deliver this information.

She straightened, moving up to the edge of the divan and folding her hands in her lap. "No one in Splendor is interested in taking the position as sheriff. My uncle and several others have sent queries out, without success."

"And you came here to see if one of us would be interested in the position, correct?" Dax stood and walked over to the desk, crossing his arms and leaning a hip against the edge.

"You must understand. The town wasn't like this before the sheriff was murdered. He kept the town clean."

"Appears someone didn't appreciate the fine job he did." Luke stretched his legs out, trying to relieve the ache in the one with the old bullet wound.

She looked from one to the other, hoping to see some spark of interest. Both faces remained impassive.

"I know you have a ranch to run and you plan to return to Texas. All I'm asking is that you consider helping us while you're here."

Her tongue flicked out to moisten her lips, a nervous reaction which created an immediate impact on Dax. He shifted his stance and dropped his arms to his sides before taking a seat behind the desk.

"I appreciate the confidence you have in us, Miss Davenport, but I've got more than I can handle with the threats to our men. Luke?" Dax's dismissive tone sliced through Rachel.

"I'm sorry, but I agree with Dax. Right now, we need to focus on this place, then get back to our regular jobs."

"As Texas Rangers." She'd hoped at least one of them would offer to help. She believed they'd see and acknowledge the need. Her hopes fell at the realization neither felt the town merited their help.

"Yes." Dax felt a pang of guilt at declining her plea. "We could send a telegraph to our captain. Perhaps he'll know of someone who'd be interested." He watched as her face fell and wished it could be otherwise.

Rachel grasped her reticule and stood, moving toward the door. "Well, thank you both for your time. I'm certain you have work to get back to." Her voice held no censure, only disappointment.

"Miss Davenport, wait." Dax took a few steps forward, stopping a foot away. Neither said a word.

"Guess I'd better get back to the men." Luke glanced at his brother as he walked past them. "It was good to see you again, Miss Davenport." He closed the door behind him, leaving the two alone in the study.

Rachel kept her gaze fixed on Dax, making no attempt to leave. She felt her chest rise and fall, incapable of drawing a full breath. Resentment rose within her at his refusal to assist her friends and neighbors. At the same time, desire flared, and with it, an almost desperate need for him to reach out and pull her close.

He couldn't look away. He'd meant to ride into town, take her to supper, and spend a quiet evening getting to know her, asking all the questions that had been swirling through his mind. Yet the knowledge of her agreement to share a meal with King Tolbert held him back. Dax wondered about her relationship with the rancher and why it even bothered him. There was no place in his life for a woman from Montana, regardless of the attraction he felt.

He lifted a hand toward her face, intending to stroke his knuckles down her cheek, then pulled back and dropped his arm.

"About the night outside the clinic... I should never have asked to call on you." He spoke in a gentle voice. "I'm sorry I haven't said anything sooner or told you my plans had changed."

Rachel tore her eyes away from him, confused by his comment and angry he'd apologized over something she'd hoped would happen. She'd been looking forward to a visit, perhaps supper with the captivating southerner. Now she knew why he'd never come by. He regretted asking her.

She drew herself up, lifting her chin and feeling a wave of humiliation at his regret over asking to call on her. She could feel the heat of embarrassment rise up her neck and face, but refused to turn away.

"It's quite all right, Mr. Pelletier. I'd forgotten all about it." She turned toward the door, then stopped. "Again, thank you for hearing me out. If you do learn of someone with an interest in helping us, please let my uncle know."

Rachel walked the few steps to the front door and dashed down the porch steps. She grabbed Old Pete's reins, mounted, and turned him toward town, not looking back to see Dax standing on the porch, hands shoved into his pockets, a look of disappointment and confusion playing across his face. She wanted to get as far away from him as fast as possible and, with luck, not lay eyes on Dax Pelletier for a good long time.

"Perhaps we should consider it." Luke rode alongside his brother a few days later, watching the ranch hands circle up the cattle in a nearby pasture.

"What?"

"Taking the sheriff job until they can find someone else."

Dax cocked an eyebrow and cast him a disbelieving look. "Is there a reason you think we should take on more work?"

"I'm not looking to take on more work, but this is something we're trained to do and the town needs help. We could split it up." Luke tipped his hat lower on his forehead, shading his eyes from the intense sun. "It may be something we should think about a little more."

They rode in silence, combining the small herds into a large pasture until the sun began to set over the Territory Range. There were mountains in the eastern states, long ranges of unending forests and clear lakes. Yet neither Dax nor Luke had ever seen anything to rival the size and majestic beauty of the mountains in the western region.

"Have you selected men for tonight's watch?" Luke slid off Prince and picked up a foreleg to inspect a hoof.

"Bull and Ellis are staying, along with several others. I think it would be a good idea if you and I circled the outer perimeter to keep watch for a while."

"Out of sight?"

"That's right."

"I'd sure like to catch those doing the shooting. You think anyone else besides Tolbert is behind the attacks?"

"Hank doesn't know of anyone else who'd attempt something like this. There's a large ranch on the other side of Tolbert—too far away from this property to make any sense to pursue. Another good-sized ranch lies to the west of us. It's owned by two brothers Hank's known for years. He swears there's no chance either would be involved in what's going on. The other ranchers have small spreads and not enough men. His money's on Tolbert, the same as ours."

"What about Drake? Could he be working on his own?"

"Perhaps. He sure as hell would like to see us back in Texas. The man's got a real temper. It got him into trouble several times under my command. He's fearsome in a fight, but doesn't know how to let it go afterwards. Tends to bring his mean streak back into camp. He has a history of gathering followers, those who don't possess the brightest minds. He's also the type others hire to carry out actions too dangerous or too beneath them." Dax scanned the area once again and wondered if Drake could be working on his own without direct instruction from Tolbert.

"Did you recognize any of the men riding with him?"

"A couple were in my unit. Disappeared the same time he did. I would've ordered the lot of them shot if I'd had the extra men to track them down." Dax signaled to Bull, letting the man know he and Luke were leaving to take positions on the outer perimeter. He looked at this brother. "You call it."

"I'll head up there, take up a position near that ridge." Luke pointed toward a rocky outcropping a couple hundred yards away.

"I'll be opposite you." Dax turned Hannibal, continuing to watch the men and cattle, as something nagged at him about the whole situation.

He didn't know what bothered him the most. Tolbert and his henchman, Rachel's request and his subsequent refusal to help the town, or the woman herself.

She'd weighed on his mind each day and night since she'd ridden off after his poor attempt at explaining his decision not to call on her. He'd wanted to assure Rachel his change of heart had nothing to do with her, at least not in the way she may have thought. She'd responded quite different from the way he'd expected, leaving before he had a chance to explain.

He kept thinking of the gleam in her eyes when he'd asked to call on her. She'd been eager to see him again. He remembered all of it. The feel of her against him as they rode to town, the disappointed look she'd cast him when her uncle stepped outside. Every detail replayed over in his mind.

Then the mention of King Tolbert. It had been as if someone had thrown cold water over him, and with it, a dose of reality. Dax wanted her, no doubt about it. At the same time, he believed his stay in Splendor would be short and he understood, without hesitation, that Rachel Davenport would not be a short-term woman. No. She'd be someone a man could get hooked on, marry, and build a life around. None of those were part of his future.

Dax dismounted, settled under a stand of pine, drew out his rifle, and leaned against a boulder. The position gave an excellent view of the pasture below, as well as the majestic skyline of the Territory Range. He could just make out Luke's form opposite him. He glanced up at the darkening sky and thought more of Rachel, wishing he could find a way to purge her from his mind.

Chapter Seven

For hours, Rachel had failed to fall asleep. The combination of too many thoughts rambling through her head and worry over the town made it difficult for her to relax. Her tired body drifted off more than once yet, each time, something woke her.

She felt herself sinking into sleep again, then gave up, tossed her thin blanket aside, and walked to the window, opening it enough to let a cool breeze wash over her. She stood, her nightdress billowing as soft waves of air entered her room.

A quiet knock sounded. She turned, watching as the door to her room cracked open just a few inches, enough to make out the figure of a man. She stifled a gasp, wondering, hoping she knew the identity of the intruder. He strode toward her and stared down, letting his hands rest on her waist.

"You've been waiting for me." He let his gaze wander over her, his body tightening at the sight.

Rachel locked on the face she dreamed of each night and nodded. "Yes." The word came out as a soft whisper. "How did you get in here?"

"Does it matter?" He let his hands move up her arms in an intimate caress. "Do you think of me often?" His gentle, southern voice washed over her, drawing her eyes to his full lips, hovering inches from hers.

She didn't answer, her heart hammering in her chest as he closed the distance between them and began to caress her lips with his. She let the sensations build, wanting him to do more, yet he held back.

"I've wanted this since I first met you." He lowered his head once more for what she'd been waiting...

"Rachel? You going to sleep the morning away?"

She jolted and sat up, rubbing her eyes as she noticed the bright sunlight filtering through her drawn curtains. Morning. She'd had another dream. The same one about Dax she'd had almost every night. Still somewhat disoriented, Rachel threw off the covers and trudged to her nightstand, splashing water on her face and scrubbing hard in an attempt to rid her thoughts and mind of the man. Although it had been several days, it still stung the way he'd told her in that calm, yet still commanding manner of his, he regretted his request to call on her.

In her world, men did not ask to call on a lady, then tell her they no longer had an interest. Behavior such as that was unthinkable.

What galled her the most was the realization that his lack of interest bothered her so much. He'd changed his mind, and rescinded his request—nothing more. It wasn't as if he'd broken off an engagement or anything of note. All he did was imply she no longer appealed to him.

Rachel groaned, dropped the brush on the dressing table, and covered her face with her hands.

She hurried to the kitchen, smelling fried bacon and seeing a stack of flapjacks waiting on a plate. Her uncle stood at the wood stove, concentrating on his task. It was the same stance she saw each time a new patient came into the clinic—thoughtful and questioning.

"You all right?" Rachel asked as she stood on tiptoes to place a quick kiss on his cheek.

"Tired. Couldn't sleep. I kept thinking about the situation in town and our lack of a sheriff." He turned toward her, looking down into her eyes, pleading. "It would relieve me a great deal if you'd leave Splendor and go home. Your idea of approaching the Pelletiers made sense. If they won't do it, we need to face the fact it may be too dangerous for you to stay."

She took a seat and spread butter across the flapjacks before covering them in syrup. She cut a bite-sized stack, speared it with her fork, and took the mouthful. "Oh, these are great. Just perfect." She cooed again before cutting another bite.

"You're changing the subject, young woman. Don't think I don't know it." He quirked an eyebrow at her.

"I'm not ignoring the danger, just trying to find a solution." She savored another mouthful, then set down her fork. "What about Mr. Brandt? Perhaps he'd consider being the sheriff."

"The blacksmith?"

"I've heard he earned a reputation during the war as a hard fighter, quiet, determined, and quick. Some say he was a hero."

"You're speaking of the man who runs the livery, correct?"

"Yes, why?"

"No reason. He's so withdrawn, quiet. I guess I figured he'd gotten out because he didn't have the stomach for it. Where'd you hear about him?"

"From Timmy at the general store. He said his father would take great exception to him passing along confidences, but he thought I should know in case we had trouble."

"Timmy is a smart lad. Even *he* recognizes danger."

"Uncle Charles, I know there are instances where lives are threatened and people die. You're here and haven't made the decision to leave. I have no plans to leave, either. You'll need to accept it." She stood and rinsed her dirty plate. "Besides, the number of patients you see increases each week as word spreads there's a doctor in town. You need me." She poured a cup of coffee and scrunched her face as she sipped at the tepid brew. "Ugh, I don't know how you can drink this awful stuff."

"I'll have you know I learned how to make authentic western coffee from the sheriff before he was killed. Even the cook at the boardinghouse said the sheriff made the best coffee around."

She handed her cup to her uncle. "In that case, I won't throw it out. I'll give it to you." She walked toward the door. "I guess it's time to check the supplies in the clinic. You know how busy it seems to get as soon as we've had a few hours of quiet."

"Do not think our discussion about you leaving is over, Rachel, because it isn't."

Her mouth twitched at his words. She had no plans to leave. He could do all the complaining, rationalizing, and arguing he wanted. It wouldn't have any effect. She pushed open the back door to the clinic, then methodically opened and closed drawers and cupboards, jotting down supplies they needed. Most of the time, they were able to purchase them at Big Pine, the territorial capital southeast of Splendor. It took a full day by wagon to get there and one more to get back. They'd start at first light and wouldn't reach their destination until after dark. Charles never lingered to enjoy the entertainment available in the larger town, always concerned about the need to return home and not leave their neighbors without a doctor. At close to four hundred residents, Splendor seemed small, but Rachel always had to remind herself that many outposts had less than one hundred inhabitants, making Splendor one of the larger towns in the Montana Territory.

A sharp rap at the front door drew Rachel's attention, alerting her she hadn't unlocked the entrance.

"Good morning, Mr. Henderson. What can I do for you?"

"Is the doc in, Miss Rachel?"

"He's in the house, but I can go get him." She started to turn when his voice stopped her.

"Actually, it's one of my girls. She's got some kind of fever. Maybe you could come over, check her first to see if she needs to see the doc."

Rachel liked Amos Henderson, the owner of the Wild Rose Saloon, even if she disagreed with the role of his female workers. From what she'd heard, he treated the girls well, kept his place clean, and didn't abuse them like some establishment owners did.

"I'd be happy to look at her but, the truth is, she'll most likely need to see my uncle."

"That's fine. I just think she'd be more comfortable speaking to you first."

She grabbed a shawl and followed Amos to the saloon and up the side stairs to the rooms above. He stopped at one of the doors and knocked.

"Tilly, you awake?" Amos pushed the door open enough to see the bed. Tilly lay covered, soft moans escaping, followed by racking coughs.

Rachel rushed to her side. "She has a fever." She pulled back the covers, not expecting the sight before her. "Mr. Henderson, perhaps it would be best if you left Tilly and me alone."

He blushed and backed out of the room as Rachel pulled a chair next to the bed.

"When is the baby due, Tilly?" Rachel asked in a soft, kind voice.

Tilly's eyes were red and swollen, her voice scratchy. "Less than four months." She choked once more and curled into a tighter ball. That's about what Rachel would've guessed by the look of her.

111

"How long have you been coughing and running a fever?"

"Just since yesterday. I thought it would pass, but it got worse."

"Does Mr. Henderson know about the baby?"

"He's known for a while now. I had to tell him when I couldn't, uh...do my work." Tilly turned her head into the pillow, away from Rachel.

"All right. Let's get you over this fever, then we'll talk about the baby."

Rachel sent word to her uncle, who joined her in Tilly's room, working alongside her to help bring down the fever.

"There isn't much else we can do, except wait. The fever isn't getting worse and she's resting. I'm going to head back over to the clinic. Why don't you stay here until she wakes up?"

Charles stepped toward the door when it slammed open, a cowboy standing in the entrance, a look of rage mixed with fear on his face. He didn't say a word before walking past the doctor and straight to the bed, staring down at the sleeping woman. "Is she all right, Doc?"

The doctor joined him by the bed. "Why don't we go out in the hall to talk?"

"No. I'm staying right here."

Charles glanced at Rachel, who gave a slight shrug. "This is my nurse, Rachel Davenport. Rachel, this is Ty Murton." He looked back to the young man. "You must know Tilly."

The cowboy's eyes never wavered from Tilly's sleeping form. "It's my baby." His emphatic words permitted no argument.

Charles set down his bag, abandoning his plan to leave for the clinic. "All right. If she wakes up and wants you to stay, that's fine. If she doesn't, you'll have to leave." He pulled another chair over for Ty. The cowboy nodded, ignoring the offered chair.

Ty watched her, overcome with concern for the woman he'd come to love.

He'd met Tilly the first day she'd accepted a job at the Rose. She'd never worked in a saloon before, but lack of money, hunger, and desperation had left her no choice. He'd been her first, had tried to talk her out of it, not understanding why someone as pretty and sweet as her would choose such a path. They'd talked for a long time before he accepted her decision and made up his own mind to do whatever he could to get her out of this life.

She woke coughing, but not the spasms of earlier, which had racked her body. Rachel applied another damp cloth as Tilly opened her eyes.

"There's a young man here to see you." She indicated across the bed.

Tilly's head swiveled, then her eyes grew wide. She offered a weak smile.

"Hello, Tilly."

"Tyson. What are you doing here?"

He grabbed her hand in his and squeezed. "Where else would I be?" He stared at her, challenging her to argue. "I'm here to bring you home. Our home. That's where you'll have our baby."

113

"Tyson, I..." Her voice trailed off, eyes filling with tears as she absorbed his words.

"I know you're not sure, but I am. I'll send for the preacher. I'm thinking the doc and Miss Davenport here will stand as witness." He squeezed her hand again, then stood and looked at Charles. "I'm getting Reverend Paige. You'll stay with her?"

"Of course." He watched Ty disappear into the hall.

"Is that what you want, Tilly? To marry Tyson?" Rachel asked, believing it to be a possible answer to the girl's situation.

"I love him, but I'm not certain he's the father. Someone like me, well...I can't be sure." She wiped the dampness from her cheeks and rested a hand on her stomach. She looked up as Amos Henderson walked back into the room.

"Ty Murton says he's the father. He's off to get Reverend Paige. You willing to marry the boy, Tilly?"

"Yes, Mr. Henderson. I am."

"And you know he's the father?"

She looked at the others. "No."

Amos shook his head. "Well, I guess it doesn't matter. Don't know what we'd do with a baby around here anyway."

Tyson came through the door minutes later with Reverend Paige and glared at Henderson. "You here to cause trouble, Amos?"

"No. Making certain Tilly's doing what she wants." He stepped back, allowing Tyson to take his place.

An hour later, Tilly lie in the back of Tyson's wagon, wrapped in blankets, her fever gone, and wearing a plain gold band. Ty shook everyone's hand, including Rachel's, climbed onto the seat, and slapped the reins.

"Will they be okay, Mr. Henderson?" Rachel asked as the wagon pulled away.

"They just might be. He, his mother, and two brothers own a small ranch south of town. Good people, hard workers. I don't believe they'll have a problem accepting Tilly. She didn't have much experience before coming here." He scratched his head. "Fact is, I don't think she had any. I saw the way Tyson looked at Tilly her first night at the Rose. He came back darn near every night and paid for her time. Don't know where he got the money or how he made it in so often as their ranch is quite a distance away, but he did. I doubt that girl was with more than one or two others the entire time she was here, and those were early on." Amos walked up the steps and through the saloon doors, letting them swing behind him.

"You all right, Rachel?" Charles asked.

She looked up as a tired smile broke across her face and nodded toward the wagon as it pulled out of sight. "It's the people, Uncle Charles. That's why I want to stay in Splendor."

"Where are you headed?" Luke sat in one of the big leather chairs in the study, feet propped on a table, sipping whiskey and eyeing Dax.

"Into town. Thought I'd see how the doc is doing."

"The doc, huh?"

"That's what I said." Dax ignored the skeptical look on his brother's face as he buckled his gun belt in place.

"Are you going to talk to the doc any more about the need for a sheriff?"

"I hadn't thought about it. Are you still thinking you may want the job?"

"Not unless you have an interest to splitting it between us. Neither of us has time to handle it alone."

"Like you, I have no interest. They'll need to find someone else."

Luke knew when Dax made a final decision, it stayed that way—final. He watched Dax head for the front door.

"Say hello to the, uh...doctor for me," Luke called after him, chuckling at the thought Dax had been hooked by a nurse in the frontiers of Montana. A nurse from the North, no less.

Dax rode at a brisk pace, wanting to reach Splendor before Rachel had time to eat. He hoped she'd accept his apology and agree to spend some time with him, perhaps even let him take her to supper. He'd thought over and over about what he'd said and her reaction. He'd never have done the same to a lady in Savannah. Even if she no longer held any attraction, he would've honored his request and taken her to tea, or supper, or some activity to fulfill his obligation. Doing otherwise would've been humiliating for the woman and cast him as a cad.

116

Why did he think he could skirt convention because they lived in the wilderness? He shook his head at the sheer stupidity of his actions.

Even though he still felt a strong pull back to Texas, and building a relationship with Rachel would be a huge mistake, Dax felt drawn to her and wanted to learn more about her. He knew his actions were selfish. Perhaps the more he learned, the less appealing she'd become and he could leave without a backward glance. He almost laughed at the thought.

"I'll get it." Rachel pulled the door open to stare at the man who'd embarrassed her and haunted her dreams. As had become her habit when facing Dax, she straightened her spine as if doing so would fortify her against the way her body responded to the man.

"General Pelletier. To what do we owe the honor of your company?" As much as Rachel told herself she never wanted to see him again, a part of her hoped he'd reconsidered his previous comments. She wanted to be the focus of his visit. And wanted to decline any offer he made to make amends.

The sarcastic sweetness in her voice had Dax on alert. He fingered the brim of his hat, never taking his eyes from hers. "Miss Davenport." He made a slight bow. "Business brought me into town and I thought I'd pay my respects." It surprised him how the lie fell from his lips with little effort. "Is the doctor available?"

Disappointment washed over her at the realization he hadn't come to see her. She dropped her gaze. "Why, yes. I'll get him for you."

Rachel left Dax standing outside and knocked on her uncle's bedroom door.

"What is it?"

She inhaled a deep breath and did her best to calm her features. "Dax Pelletier is here. He'd like to see you."

"I see." At least he thought he understood the source of his niece's agitation.

She hadn't quite been herself since the night Pelletier brought her home from tending to Hank Wilson. And, after his refusal to help the town, she'd been downright disdainful any time his name came up.

"Well, I guess I should see what he wants." He started for the door, then turned back. "Would you care to join us?"

"No." She barked out, feeling instant regret at her caustic tone. "I have supper to prepare. Please, go on ahead."

Dax stood ramrod straight, chastising himself for what he'd said to Rachel. He should've come right out and apologized for his callous behavior. He seemed destined to be the worst kind of fool where she was concerned.

"Good evening, Mr. Pelletier."

"Doctor. I hope I'm not interrupting." He looked behind the doctor, disappointed he didn't see Rachel.

"Not at all. Rachel just started supper. You wished to see me?"

Dax looked down at his boots, then back up at the doctor before clearing his throat. "The truth is, I came to see Rachel, hoping she'd allow me to escort her to supper."

Charles nodded, understanding the dilemma. Rachel had always been stubborn. He knew something had changed between her and Pelletier after the night she'd ridden out to request their help. She'd told him they'd refused, but nothing more.

"You know, Rachel is an excellent cook. I don't know what she's preparing tonight, but I do know there will be plenty. She makes enough for an army." He chuckled, visualizing the portions of food she always served. "I believe the girl is trying to fatten me up. Anyway, why don't you join us? It would be nice to share a meal with another man." He gave Dax a conspiratorial wink.

Dax hesitated a brief moment. "If you're sure I wouldn't be intruding."

"Not at all. Follow me."

Rachel heard voices before she saw anyone come through the door. She turned her back to the entry and, standing straight, focused on the pot of stew she'd prepared the night before.

"Just put your hat on one of the hooks and I'll let Rachel know you're joining us for supper."

Rachel heard her uncle's words and fumed. She would *not* share a table with Dax Pelletier.

"Rachel—"

"I heard." She turned on her uncle. "How could you invite him here without asking me? I may not have enough food," she hissed. "In fact, I'm sure I don't. He'll have to come another time." She glared at him, trying to swipe errant strands of hair out of her face with one hand, while gripping a large wooden spoon in the other.

As if she couldn't feel worse, Dax Pelletier appeared behind her uncle.

"It certainly smells wonderful in here. I hope the invitation from the doctor still stands." He grinned at her, fueling her irritation.

She plastered on her most ingratiating smile. "Of course it stands. Why wouldn't it?"

Her voice wreaked of insincerity, something her uncle had never witnessed.

"Rachel, if—"

"Uncle, why don't you offer the general a drink while I finish supper?" She grabbed another plate from the cupboard, along with utensils, and marched past the men and into the dining room.

"What may I get you to drink?" Charles asked as they walked away from the kitchen.

"Whiskey would be perfect, if you have it."

"Well, I guess you're safe," the doctor whispered to Dax as he handed him his glass.

The men relaxed in the living room, chatting, giving Rachel time to ladle stew into a large bowl, place biscuits in a warming basket, and set them both on the table. She clasped her hands in front of her.

"Supper is ready, gentlemen."

Dax walked to the table, holding a chair for Rachel. She took her seat, then glanced at him for a mere moment, her eyes frosty. "Thank you."

He'd expected a smart retort and almost missed her quiet words.

Charles said a brief blessing before the three filled their plates.

Dax waited a moment, then dug in. "This is excellent, Miss Davenport." Bernice, at the ranch, prepared good meals—hot, flavorsome, and filling. But the stew Rachel made could have been served at a fine restaurant. And the biscuits with blackberry jam were the best he'd had in years. "Did you make the jam also?"

Rachel looked at Dax and thought how odd it felt to be sitting at the supper table with a man she'd sworn to stay as far away from as possible, but her uncle had given her no choice.

"No. Mrs. Petermann, at the general store, made it last summer. She's going to show me where to find the berries this year so that I can put them up myself." Her agitation lessened somewhat the more she spoke, although her irritation at their guest remained high.

"Do you enjoy cooking?"

She didn't want to like talking with him, sharing parts of herself, allowing him to learn more details of her life, no matter how trivial. And she did not want to learn any more about him. Rachel had no doubt the more she knew about Dax and his life, the more her attraction would grow.

"It depends on who's at the table."

He didn't take the bait, just continued to enjoy the meal and the company. No matter how hard she tried to put him off, Dax found himself fascinated by Rachel and her many talents. If he had to identify one quality that drew him to her the most, it would be her total lack of self-absorption. She was a woman unaffected by either her looks or talent. They were a part of her life, not what defined her.

"Any more trouble in town?" Dax directed the question at Charles, eager to move beyond the issues between him and Rachel. He felt certain that, given enough time, they would sort them out and perhaps become friends.

"Nothing more. Jeff Decker, the young cowhand who was shot, seems to be doing well. It's a miracle the boy made it."

"His healing had everything to do with your treatment, Uncle Charles. And prayer."

"I'll concede to the prayer part, Rachel." He looked back at Dax. "It's a real dilemma. One the town needs to solve soon, before it gets worse. I understand Rachel spoke to you and your brother, and I have no issue with your decision. Might you know of anyone else who would have an interest in Splendor?" He set down his fork and sat back. "At this point, the town will do what is needed to find someone, Mr. Pelletier."

"Do you have an idea of who is causing the trouble?"

"Al, the bartender at the Rose where Decker got shot, didn't mention a name. The description could have fit about any cowboy around here."

"What about the other trouble, before and after the sheriff died?"

"No one has ever gotten a good look at anyone. Shootings, murder, fires, cattle get run off..." His voice trailed off, thinking about the violence which had occurred over the last year. "Before he was killed, the sheriff mentioned he thought Mr. Drake might be involved somehow.

Unfortunately, he never said anything about proof." Charles picked up his cup of coffee and took a sip.

Dax's gaze narrowed at the mention of the deserter. "King Tolbert's man?"

"That's the only Drake I know of around here. Have you met him?"

"He rode out to the ranch a few weeks ago to deliver a message from Tolbert." He glanced at Rachel. "The message wasn't cordial." He allowed himself small satisfaction when he saw a look of surprise cross her face. "Drake served under my command when we were in the Army of the South. The man and I have a history."

"Why would Mr. Tolbert hire someone like him?" Rachel knew her uncle had grave reservations about King.

Dax gave her a pointed stare. "I don't know. However, I do plan to find out."

Rachel scooted back from the table and began to gather the empty plates.

"I'll help with that." Dax followed her into the kitchen, glad to have a few minutes alone with her.

"Here." Rachel tossed him a towel. "You don't mind drying the dishes, do you?" Sarcasm filled her voice. She chastised herself, hating the feeling of sounding rude, even toward someone who thought so little of the town...and her. She told herself he deserved whatever she threw at him.

"Whatever you need." His quiet response made her feel even worse about her behavior.

"Why are you here?" She glanced over her shoulder at him, but didn't stop scrubbing the dirty pan. If anything, her movements became more forceful.

Dax swiveled to face her, his eyes riveted on hers. "At your home?"

"Yes. Why did you come tonight? I know it wasn't to see my uncle, and you've already told me you have no interest in helping out the town or calling on me. Why not stay cocooned at your ranch, instead of riding all this way for a meal of stew and biscuits?" She stopped scrubbing long enough to dry her hands on the towel draped over her shoulder and turn toward him.

He set a plate aside and moved to stand a foot away. "I believe it had something to do with you."

"Me?" She thought he'd make up some pointless excuse about picking up supplies or having the blacksmith check out his horse. Instead, he'd surprised her with his simple answer.

"That surprises you?"

"Well, yes." She stepped back, trying to create space, but halted as she hit the edge of the sink. "You made it clear you'd made a mistake asking to call on me."

"I was a fool."

Her brows furrowed, creating a crease with tiny lines between her eyes. Dax could see his answer made no sense to her.

"I want to be clear, Rachel. First, I'm sorry for my callous behavior. I didn't mean to imply I regretted asking to call on you, I meant I should

124

never have asked in the first place, not without thinking it through."

"There's no difference." She turned back to the sink and picked up the pan, beginning another onslaught against the iron skillet.

"The truth is, I want to spend time with you, more than you know." He edged closer, resting one hand on the sink, but not hemming her in with the other. Not yet. "I'm not sure how wise it is, knowing I may leave for Texas."

She turned toward him and glanced down at his hand before moving a couple of inches away.

"I came tonight to apologize for my previous behavior and ask you to supper. However, you'd already started cooking, which worked out well for me, even if not so well for you." He gripped the edge of the sink with his other hand, trapping her between his arms.

She swallowed, feeling heat creep up her face. "Why not so well for me?" She tried to steady her voice. Instead, her words were thick and shaky.

"You ended up cooking for me. Which, by the way, was quite good." He leaned closer, wanting to capture her mouth with his, yet knowing it wouldn't be wise.

She took a shallow breath and looked behind him, her eyes darting toward the outside. "Does it feel hot in here to you?" Rachel felt a desperate need to open the door and let in a cool breeze.

Dax lifted a hand and let his knuckles trace a path from her ear, down her cheek, across her jaw. "Feels fine to me." His deep voice clouded her brain even more. "I still want to take you to supper." His darkened eyes held a magnetism, drawing her in.

"I don't think it's a good idea." Her words came out in a broken whisper. She rested a hand on his chest. She could feel the insistent beating of his heart as he moved his fingertips to the base of her throat, then raised them in a slow, almost intimate pace to her cheek, setting her body aflame.

Dax inhaled a deep breath and stepped away. He gazed down at her, glad to see she mirrored his own feelings of desire.

"I think it's an excellent idea." His husky, uneven voice surprised him. It was a few, soft caresses, nothing more, yet it felt as if his body had been set on fire. "I'll call on you next week."

Rachel straightened and stepped toward the back door, pushing it open to allow the cool air inside. She didn't respond as he left the room.

Chapter Eight

The night had grown late when Dax rode back toward the ranch, feeling good about stopping to see Rachel, even as his mind wrestled with his intentions toward both her and the ranch. He knew Luke had begun to form a bond, not just with the men, but with the land itself. Dax could see it in his brother's eyes as he gazed to the mountain range at sunset, or made suggestions about expanding. He guessed Luke may have found something he could truly love, as well as a way to release the pent-up aggression and sorrow his brother believed he'd been able to hide so well.

Once more, his thoughts turned to Rachel and the guilt he felt at refusing her plea to help the town. He'd offered to do what he could to spread the word, see if they could come up with someone with experience to take the sheriff's job. The pay seemed reasonable, the house provided by the town sounded better than in most towns, and the monthly stipend at the general store was generous.

He hadn't mentioned to Rachel or Charles the decision he and Luke had made to jump in if the town did come under attack from either external or internal threats. As Texas Rangers, they could do no less. They would hold the information close, hoping they'd never need to step up to the task.

From what he'd heard, the town had been quiet for a long time under the keen eye of the previous sheriff, at least up until a few months before his death. Afterwards, instances of shootings, unexplained fires, and missing property had increased. The town leaders wanted the lawless actions stopped.

Dax rounded the last turn before something in the air caught his attention. Smoke. He kicked Hannibal into a gallop, racing forward until he saw what he'd feared. One of the ranch buildings blazed, long streams of red flames spearing into the sky while smoke filled the air. Men were lined up, passing buckets to each other and tossing water on the fire. He drew to a stop and jumped down, racing to Luke's side.

"What can I do?"

"Replace Bull at the pump." Luke's voice carried over the wind whipping through the flames and the neighing of scared horses. "Have him check on the horses."

Dax pumped water as the men increased the speed of passing the buckets toward the fire. He could see the damage as the flames died down and the sparks gave way to ash floating through the air.

They continued their pace until Dax and Luke were certain all the flames had been extinguished. The men scattered the burning ash, dumping dirt and kicking it around on lingering embers.

"What the hell happened?" Dax asked as Luke stopped beside him.

"Don't know. Ellis saw it while he took his evening smoke. At least we contained it to the storage building behind the bunkhouse."

"The furthest building west." Dax continued to stare at the damage, relieved no one had been injured.

"Easy to sneak in, start a fire, then take off. No one would hear or see you." Luke responded as if he'd read his brother's mind.

"Ellis!" Dax looked to the man who stood several yards away and motioned him over. "You see anything at all when you noticed the fire?"

"Nothing, boss. Just flames. I didn't do much except alert everyone to the fire. Wanted to get it out before it jumped to the bunkhouse."

Dax turned to Luke. "We'd better go check it out."

They searched behind the shed, finding nothing except horse prints, until Dax saw boot impressions a few yards from what had been the back wall of the wooden structure. "I can't tell how long they've been here, but my guess is not long."

"Well, Horace, I don't know the reason neither of the Pelletiers are interested in the job. They said no and I accepted it." Charles spoke to the town banker, Horace Clausen, as well as Stan Petermann, owner of the general store, Amos Henderson from the Wild Rose, and Bernie

129

Griggs, proprietor of the Western Union office and the town postman. Clausen had called them to the bank to discuss how to find a new sheriff. "Dax Pelletier did say they'd send out messages, see if they could come up with someone."

"He came in yesterday with his brother. Sent two messages, one to Austin and another to Independence. He got a short reply from Austin, saying they'd spread the word."

"These things take time, Horace." Bernie Griggs glanced at his pocket watch as he spoke. "You know, we could talk to Noah Brandt again. Maybe he'll change his mind."

"It's doubtful. The man seemed pretty firm when he rejected the idea the first time. I doubt if anything's changed." Horace paced his office, frustrated at their lack of progress. "We have women and children we need to protect. If we allow it, those threatening and killing people will keep at it. It will spill into our private homes. It's only a question of when." He pulled out a kerchief to wipe his brow.

"What about the man who rode into town with Noah?" Griggs asked.

Stan stroked his short beard. "The one who served in the war with him?"

"That's the one."

"He stayed a couple of weeks. Had no interest in a town this small. According to Noah, he took off for San Francisco." Stan knew Noah Brandt better than anyone, yet still saw the man as a mystery. "Of course, it's been over a year. Perhaps he's changed his mind. Couldn't hurt to ask Noah."

"You'll talk with him?" Clausen asked.

"Be glad to. Someone should ride to Big Pine, talk to the sheriff again. Maybe one of his deputies would have an interest. I'd go, but can't be away from the store that long."

"Rachel and I are due for a trip. Give me the sheriff's name and I'll speak with him."

The men were ready to adjourn when Clausen's secretary interrupted. "Mr. Tolbert is outside to see you. He asked about the meeting." The woman glanced at the others in the room. "I told him I didn't know anything about it."

"Thank you, Mrs. Phelps. I'll be right out."

Charles stood to leave and looked over at Clausen. "Why didn't you get word to Tolbert about this meeting?"

Horace cast a worried gaze at the others. "Frankly, I'm not sure King doesn't hold some responsibility for what's going on. Understand, I have no proof, but it's hard to forget the way he threatened our previous sheriff when he stood up to King about something the man wanted to do. Tolbert showed no regret when we lost him to a bullet. Why do you ask?"

"No reason. Well, guess I'd better head out, let Rachel know we'll be riding to Big Pine sooner than expected."

The men filed past Tolbert on their way out, acknowledging the man, but doing little else.

"What was your meeting about?" Tolbert asked as Clausen held his office door open.

"Usual stuff, King. Fourth of July's in a few months and they want to start planning some type of shindig." Clausen knew Tolbert expected

131

to be invited to all meetings of those considered town leaders, or at least apprised of the topics discussed. It irritated most how he acted as if he owned the town, yet contributed little to it, even buying the majority of his supplies in Big Pine. "What can I do for you?"

"I want to know the terms of Pat Hanes' will. Make sure him passing the land to the Pelletiers was legal. You understand, don't you?"

Tolbert's obvious accusation angered Clausen. "Are you accusing me of something illegal?"

"No, of course not. I want to be certain, that's all."

"I hate to disappoint you, but the details, as well as the documentation, are private documents and not available for public inspection. You'll have to believe what transpired happened according to Pat's wishes. I'll be glad to submit them to the territory judge when he comes through."

"He may not be here for months."

"It's the best I can offer." Clausen held his ground. The accounts he held for Tolbert were five times larger than any other customer. It would be disastrous to lose them.

"You know what an impact my ranch and I have on Splendor, right?" Tolbert's eyes bore into the banker's. "Sure would be a shame to change banks, or find it necessary to start my own."

Although Clausen believed both were idle threats, he had to consider King's words.

"Mr. Tolbert, you'll do what you feel is best for the town, I'm quite certain of that. If you don't believe my bank is serving your needs, you'll have to seek alternatives. A Big Pine bank is one, as is starting a new bank. I would mention, however, there aren't enough people in Splendor to support two banks." And both men knew who the locals would choose.

King eyed the banker, knowing he had no other options, at least right now. "We'll wait for the judge." He stormed from the office, unhappy with the outcome, and knowing there was little he could do, short of finding a way to get to Clausen's files without the man knowing.

"Dax, you hear what happened near Big Pine?" Luke had spent the day in Splendor, picking up supplies and going by the Rose before riding back. He stopped the buckboard and jumped down, heading toward Dax and Bull standing outside the barn.

"No. What happened?"

"Renegades attacked a group of settlers on their way to Oregon. Killed several before they were run off."

"How'd you hear about it?"

"The settlers are in Splendor. They decided to stop for a couple of days to replenish what was lost in the raid. By the sounds of it, a few might stay." Luke started unloading what he'd purchased at the general store, then stopped and turned to his brother. "You think we should do anything about the renegades?"

"Why would we? Sounds as if no one knows for sure who attacked the wagons. Most travelers understand the dangers before they set out."

"Doc Worthington and Miss Davenport are leaving for Big Pine tomorrow." Luke's casual response hit Dax like a fist to his stomach.

He didn't wait to hear more. Within minutes, he'd saddled Hannibal and tore off toward town, determined to stop the doctor and Rachel from doing something so risky.

Splendor's main street hadn't seen so many people in months. Five covered wagons stood at the north end, near the livery. Men gathered in groups, talking, and pointing in various directions. He rode up to the livery and slid off his horse.

"Gentlemen." Dax tipped his hat at the closest group of men. "I heard you had some trouble."

"A group of Indians, Sioux is what our guide tells us, attacked us between Big Pine and here. Took off with one of the wagons after killing the driver and his wife." He stuck out his hand to Dax. "I'm Percy Slater."

"Dax Pelletier. My brother and I own a ranch north of town. Where are you headed?"

"Planned to go to Oregon. But, now, my wife and I have been talking and we might stay here."

"Are you farmers, Mr. Slater?"

"Grew up farming, but the war pretty much destroyed what little we had. I owned a restaurant in Missouri. Might try that here. My wife's a seamstress. Mr. Petermann at the general store said there might be a need for that as the town grows."

Dax looked up the street to see Rachel emerge from the clinic and hand a small child to a couple, then walk back inside.

"Excuse me, Mr. Slater. There's someone I need to see." Dax grabbed Hannibal's reins and started up the street, determined to talk some sense into Rachel and her uncle.

He knocked, then walked inside, not waiting for Rachel to open the door. "Rachel, are you back there?" He pushed through the door that divided the front area from the examination room and saw her putting away supplies. She turned at his approach.

"Hello, General. I thought I saw you at the livery." Truth was, her chest had tightened and her heart picked up several beats when she glanced up to see a group of men talking with Noah. Dax stood with them. She'd hoped he might come by so she could tell him of her decision not to allow him to call on her.

"I've been speaking with the settlers." He stood not a foot away, wanting nothing more than to reach out and draw her to him, but he had to be careful around her. The woman had a way of getting to him and crumbling his willpower. "I heard you and your uncle are thinking about going to Big Pine. Is that true?" He had to find a way to ignore the rising apprehension he felt. Perhaps Luke had been wrong.

"Yes. Tomorrow, if Uncle Charles has his way."

"It doesn't appear to be a wise idea, given what's happened." He felt a contained fury build.

"Perhaps not, but I fail to see how it's your concern."

He stepped to within inches of her, crowding her space. "Not my concern?" His voice took on an ominous tone, coming out thin and hard. "It *is* my concern if you plan to ride into an Indian attack. You did hear about the settlers who were killed, right?"

Rachel took a shaky breath and bit her lower lip. She had no intention of letting him know how his closeness disturbed her. She put her hands on her hips and glared at him. "Of course. I treated one of the children from the group. The man told me it sounded much worse than what actually happened."

"So a man and his wife getting killed and their wagon stolen isn't enough for you? What would be worse?" He stared down at her with narrowed eyes, daring Rachel to argue with the facts.

Their eyes locked and, for a moment, neither said a word.

"Of course that's bad," she stammered. "I just mean..." Her voice trailed off as Charles walked through the back door.

"Well, Dax. What a nice surprise."

Dax ignored the greeting. "I've come to talk you out of leaving for Big Pine tomorrow."

"I see. Unfortunately, it's a trip we must make. We're low on supplies and someone needs to speak with the sheriff there to see if he knows of someone who'd like to enforce the law in Splendor. Maybe one of his deputies."

Dax crossed his arms and planted his feet shoulder width apart. "Who's going with you?"

"What do you mean?"

"Is anyone riding along for protection?" Dax's patience began to wear thin at the lack of precautions Charles had made to protect Rachel from attack.

"No one. Rachel and I are going alone."

"Excuse me, but that's not acceptable."

Rachel's eye flared. "Not acceptable to whom?"

Charles held up a hand to warn her off. "You may be right. Nonetheless, we're leaving tomorrow, with or without protection. If our trip is fruitful, we may have a new sheriff riding along on the way home."

"Or you may not make it back at all." His already intense voice displayed the exasperation he felt. These were educated people. How could they not understand the risks?

Dax clenched his jaw, wondering how far he could push the doctor to reconsider his decision. He guessed not far by the determined set of the man's face.

Rachel stood to the side, trying to respect her uncle's wishes and stay out of the exchange. After what had transpired in her kitchen, she knew Dax had at least some interest in her, even if he'd refused the job as interim sheriff and would be leaving Splendor as soon as a buyer could be found for the ranch.

She'd reminded herself over and over after he left to keep her feelings in check and not succumb to the strong attraction she felt for Dax. Rachel had always considered herself a strong woman, yet he triggered emotions she'd never experienced before. It would be all too easy to fall under his spell and do something she'd regret. She'd woken the following morning with a firm conviction to decline his supper invitation and keep her distance. She knew it would be painful, yet accepted it as the price she'd have to pay to protect herself from a broken heart.

"Well, it appears we're at an impasse." Charles' voice sounded tired, resolute.

Dax's eyes shifted from Charles to Rachel, and held. "Fine. I'll take one of my men and we'll ride with you."

"No." Rachel's firm response surprised her uncle as much as Dax. "We don't require your help. We'll be fine."

"Now, Rachel, what Mr. Pelletier says makes sense. If he's willing to ride along and provide protection, I'm not going to refuse."

"I'll find someone else. Perhaps one of Mr. Tolbert's men would join us."

"No," Charles and Dax said in unison.

Her uncle narrowed his eyes at her. "We will not rely on one of Tolbert's men to help us. I'd go alone before I'd approach that man."

"You won't be going alone. I'll be back in the morning with one of my men." He nodded at the two, then left, frustration and anger still coursing through him, yet not entirely unhappy with the outcome. Although he didn't have the time to spare, at least he'd be able to spend time with Rachel. If they were determined to go, he wanted to be the man riding along.

Rachel turned to her uncle. "What are you thinking, having him ride along with us?"

"I'm not certain what your issue is with Mr. Pelletier, but I'll not refuse his offer. He's right. The attack makes the trip more dangerous and we should have protection."

"But you said—"

"I know what I said. The smart course is entirely something else."

The truth dawned on Rachel. "You purposely baited him so he'd offer to help." Her uncle didn't respond. "Fine, don't admit it. But know this. It will be a long and miserable trip."

She stormed from the clinic, anger rolling off her. After making her decision to distance herself from the source of her unease, the last man she wanted to spend time with would be accompanying them on their trip. Dax and another cowboy from his ranch would be a part of their lives for at least four days. She groaned at the prospect of being in his company for so long.

Rachel grabbed a small bag and started to throw her necessities inside, along with a gun and bullets. It had been a long time since she'd had to fire the weapon and sincerely hoped she didn't have to use it on this trip. However, a body would be foolish not to go prepared after what happened to the settlers. She set the bag near the door and undressed, pulling on her nightgown, then brushing out her hair before braiding it into a long strand.

She glanced into the mirror and winced at the slight wrinkles in the corners of both eyes. Most women were married by her age, or that seemed to be the custom before the war anyway. It sobered her to think she might never meet the right man, marry, and have children. Her mother had made it her mission to sort through the eligible beaus in Boston and present Rachel to them. She'd been unimpressed with each one. Only one man held her interest, triggered her heart to race and her body to experience wonderful, yet frightening emotions—Dax Pelletier. Admitting it galled her.

"Bull is the best man to take with you. We'll be fine for a few days without him." Luke worked on a frayed spot in Prince's halter, then set the rope aside. "Unless you want me to go."

"No, you're needed here. I want to talk to one of the bankers in Big Pine, let him know the ranch may be for sale and discuss prices. I'll speak to Horace Clausen when I return."

"Sounds like the decision is final."

Dax took off his hat and speared a hand through his hair, letting his arm drop to his side. "I'm not certain of my decision. All I do know is I'm not ready to assume leadership of a ranch, not even if the responsibilities are shared with you."

Luke strolled to the back of the barn and threw open the doors, framing a spectacular view of the Territory Range. "It's a sight, isn't it?"

Dax joined his brother and stared out. "It surely is."

"You're ready to walk away from this?"

Dax glanced at his brother, unaware he'd begun to develop the same fondness for the land and the growing town as Luke. "I'm not ready to be tied to it, the same as I wasn't ready to reclaim our place in Savannah. There's more out there I need to see before settling down. And even when I am ready to stay in one place, I doubt it will be in a small town in Montana."

"And Rachel?"

This time Dax's head swiveled, his eyes locking on Luke's. "What's that supposed to mean?"

"Are you going to deny you have feelings for her? Hell, Dax, I've seen the way the two of you are with each other. I don't know anything about her, but you? I can't recall the last time a woman affected you the way she does. Are you certain you can ride out and leave her behind?"

Dax's jaw worked, but he held his silence. He would not let a few lustful urges dictate what he did with his life. He'd make a choice to stay in Splendor or head back to Austin based on what he wanted, as he always did. No one dictated how he lived his life, certainly not one pretty nurse who lived in the far northwest frontier—and served on the wrong side of the line.

"You hear me good. She means nothing to me. I'll make up my mind, regardless of how I feel about any woman." He turned without another word, his face set in stone, and left the barn.

141

Dax's indignation rose with each purposeful stride. Luke knew him better than anyone. How could he believe, even for a moment, his mind would be swayed by a saucy, smart female who irritated him more than anyone he'd ever met? He stormed up the front steps, almost slamming the front door on his way to the study. There wasn't a chance he'd let a woman get under his skin enough to alter whatever he decided to do. Not...One...Chance.

Luke watched as Dax disappeared into the house, amusement sparking in his deep caramel-colored eyes. His brother was well and truly caught. He just hadn't figured it out yet.

"Everyone ready?" Dax watched as Rachel settled onto the wagon seat next to her uncle and arranged her skirt. The sun had begun its climb over the eastern skyline. The day promised to be long. Dax expected they'd reach Big Pine at dusk, in time to take care of the horses, find rooms, and eat.

"We're ready." Charles signaled the horses with a gentle slap of the reins.

Bull rode behind the wagon. He waved to his boss and they were off.

The group stopped near a riverbank at noon, watered their horses, and ate the cold chicken and biscuits Rachel had packed. Bull leaned against a tree trunk, talking with the doctor, while Rachel walked along the edge of the water, listening to the ripples and watching the occasional trout resting in a nearby eddy. So far, the trip had been easy and, in Rachel's mind, a relaxing change from the hectic pace at the clinic.

"We appreciate the food. Bull and I were prepared to eat jerky and hardtack." Dax sipped from a canteen and then offered it to Rachel, who took a long drink.

She shrugged off his gratitude. "I'd made extra last night, knowing we'd need it today."

"How long will you stay?" Dax heard the words tumble from his mouth, surprised he'd voiced the question he'd had on his mind since they'd met.

Rachel understood what he was asking. "I'm not sure. Perhaps two years, maybe forever. I know a life in Boston isn't what I'm after. It's so..." Her voice trailed off when she realized she'd started to reveal more about herself than intended.

"So?" Dax prompted.

She took a slow breath, considering her words. "Normal, I guess. When the war ended, I traveled home for a couple of months before starting the journey out here. Nothing much had changed since before the war. Friends still spoke about the same topics—fashion, social affairs, appropriate marriages—as if the relevance of those issues had remained unchanged. I no longer held similar interests. Perhaps I'd seen too much." She glanced up at him. "Does that make sense?"

It made tremendous sense to Dax, although his neighbors and friends in Savannah had experienced a different type of war than those

143

who lived in Boston. The south had been devastated, while the northeastern seaboard emerged relatively unscathed.

"It's hard to imagine anyone not touched by the war. You and I experienced the carnage firsthand. Many didn't." His voice took on an introspective tone. "I haven't decided if the experience will make me a better or worse person."

Rachel absorbed his words, knowing his words could have come from her. She had yet to regain the light, frivolous attitude so much a part of her before the war, and doubted it would ever be within her grasp again. She turned to face him, staring into the depths of his deep gray eyes, and thought she understood what those eyes had beheld.

"From what I've seen, General, you are an honorable man and, I'm guessing, a better person for your experiences." She flashed him a brief smile.

The impact of her words and smile shouldn't have surprised Dax, yet they did. She had a way about her. The cloying banter, so much a fixture in conversations with women of the South, were lacking in Rachel's life. Syrupy praise and false platitudes weren't a part of her character.

"Rachel, I—" Dax's words were cut off when both turned at the sound of Bull's voice.

"Boss! You and Miss Davenport ready to head out?"

Dax waved to him. "We're on our way." He looked at Rachel. "It's time we left." A part of him was glad for the interruption. He wasn't even certain what he'd been about to say. Rachel's closeness had Dax wishing for things he'd pushed to the back of his mind, not to be visited until well into his future. She made him want to reexamine what he believed important, including his desire to return to Texas.

Within minutes, they were continuing their journey. All were surprised by the relative ease of the trip. It took over ten hours to reach Big Pine, yet they'd experienced not a single threat, nor had they seen another human being the entire day. They'd taken care of the horses, found rooms, and finished a quiet supper before turning in.

Rachel lay in bed, exhausted and glad half their journey was over. She'd spent most of the time trying not to focus on Dax and his unnerving presence. She'd hoped by walking away from the wagon during their noon meal, she'd be signaling her desire to be alone. A stroll along the river seemed perfect. But, within minutes, he'd come up beside her. It seemed strange how she'd felt, more than heard, his approach. She'd briefly considered telling him she needed space, then thought better of it. After all, he had taken several days of his time to escort them to Big Pine and deserved her appreciation, no matter how unwanted his company.

Their discussion by the river had done nothing except increase her interest in the man. Now, like at home, he haunted her thoughts, making her incapable of sleep. All she asked tonight was to be free of the persistent dream of him entering her room. One night of complete rest, without his presence during her sleep. Was that too much to ask?

Chapter Nine

Big Pine, Montana, the Territorial Capital

"You're certain I can't talk you into staying, planting roots in Big Pine?" Sheriff Parker Sterling made his last plea, hoping to lure the young man into signing on as a deputy. The town's population had exploded over the past few years, making it the choice as the territorial capital. Along with the growth came an increase in incidents of theft and murder.

"I appreciate the offer, but my answer stands." Gabriel Evans lifted his well over six foot frame from the chair and headed toward the door.

"Gabe?"

He looked over his shoulder at the sheriff.

"What rank were you anyway?"

He didn't know why people still cared. For whatever reason, they did. "Colonel."

Gabe walked into the cool night air, looking up and down the street, searching for a quiet place to have a couple of drinks and maybe play cards before turning in. He'd be up early the next morning, ride to Denver, then south again to Texas. He thought he might try his hand at riding as a Texas Ranger. He'd already been through California, staying in San Francisco a few months and working as a deputy before realizing the lifestyle in the bawdy town wasn't what he sought.

He'd ridden through Utah, stopping briefly in the small settlement of Salt Lake before traveling north. He might not have headed toward Big Pine, except some liquored up fool and his partner jumped him not far from the capital. He'd overpowered them, trussed the men up, and hauled them to Big Pine and Sheriff Sterling. Gabe had been in town a week. Time to move on.

"Good evening, Gabe. What are you looking for tonight?" Dolly, a cute, petite redhead, sashayed his way, offering more than a drink and cards.

He tipped his hat and offered a warm smile. "Hello, Miss Dolly. Thought I'd come by for a whiskey, maybe some poker before I call it a night."

"Sure there isn't anything else you want?" She ran a slim finger up his arm.

"Not tonight, sweetheart." He headed toward a table with an empty chair, nodded to the others, and took a seat as Dolly placed a whiskey before him.

"Let me know if you change your mind." She shot him a seductive wink before walking away.

He followed her progress, somewhat regretting his decision to decline her offer.

"Looking for a more peaceful evening?" The cowboy dealing had been in the night before when a fight broke out at another table. One man had been shot before Gabe interceded, wrenching the shooter's arm behind his back and slamming him into a wall. The man collapsed at Gabe's feet and now sat inside a cell, awaiting trial.

Gabe nodded as he fanned out his cards and threw down a couple. Within the first few hands, he could often tell if luck entered a card game with him, or stayed on the outside. Tonight, she'd stayed by his side. A couple of quiet hours passed with friendly banter, a few drinks, and one winning hand after another for Gabe. He settled up near midnight and walked outside, letting the night breeze wash over him.

Something ate at him. He couldn't figure out what, although he'd had a nagging feeling in his gut for several days. Maybe he'd ride north, check up on a friend, stay a few days, then leave for Denver.

Gabe strode up the stairs to his hotel room, withdrew his Remington .44 from its holster, and placed it by the bed. He undressed, then fell back onto the bed, finalizing his decision. His obligation in the Colorado town could wait. It had waited for four long years, a few weeks would make no difference. His next stop would be Splendor, Montana.

"What the hell?" Gabe grumbled as he shot straight up in bed. The sound of gunfire split the night air, along with shouts and the rumble of horses thundering down the street. He grabbed his gun and dashed to the window, looking out onto the spectacle below. A group of riders, perhaps six or eight, fired guns into the air and circled in front of the sheriff's office, demanding the release of the man Gabe had marched to jail the previous night. So far, it appeared all their actions were meant to gain attention and frighten the locals.

Gabe didn't wait to see if it would escalate. He threw on clothes and stormed out of his room, running smack into another guest, also with gun in hand and a fierce look on his face. They ran down the stairs, stopped at the door, and peered outside.

"We'll ask them to leave. If they don't..." The stranger's voice trailed off as Gabe nodded and indicated with this fingers—one, two, three—and the two burst outside, guns in hand.

"Enough! Put your guns down." Gabe's commanding voice cut through the noise as he and the stranger stood next to each other.

The attackers turned and fired.

The two men aimed their guns, firing bullets around the horse's legs, causing them to buck.

The two rolled to the ground and reloaded as the attackers aimed in their direction. Gabe finished first, aimed and fired, hitting one of the men in the shoulder. He toppled off his horse. The other man hit his mark in the thigh. The wounded man screamed before sliding to the ground. Gabe and the stranger shot off another round toward the rest who had scattered, leaving their fallen comrades behind.

Gabe rose at a cautious pace, keeping his gun trained on the injured men. He spoke to the man next to him, never taking his eyes off those on the ground.

"Gabe Evans."

"Dax Pelletier." He glanced at the men thrashing around on the ground and started to step off the wooden walkway to the dirt street. "Do you have any idea what got them so riled?"

"My guess is they took exception to an arrest made last night. A friend of theirs killed a man."

Dax kicked one of the men in his injured leg. "Get up." The man grabbed his leg and screamed. He ignored the man's agony and looked at the one holding his shoulder. "You, too." Dax indicated with his gun for the man to stand. He nodded toward the jail. "Let's go."

Dax marched the two inside, helping the one who dragged his injured leg and moaned, receiving no compassion for his efforts.

"They need a doctor." Gabe kept watch outside for the others, hoping they'd be smart enough not to return.

"He stopped by a few hours ago on his way out of town to let me know one of his patients went into labor. It could be hours until he's back." The sheriff looked at the injuries. "They don't look too bad. Probably could let them sit for a while."

"Hell no, Sheriff. You got to get us some help." The man with the injured shoulder gritted his teeth, holding his arm to his side.

"Just shut your mouth, Pauley. It's your own fault you're in here. What the hell were you thinking anyway?" Sheriff Sterling glared at the young man as he locked the cell door. "Your ma ain't gonna be too happy with you."

Pauley dropped onto the wooden bed's thin mattress and fell back against the wall, careful to land on his good side. "You know you don't have to tell her, Sheriff."

"Boy, you know she's gonna know all about this by morning. There's nothing I can do to save you from her." The sheriff walked over to the other man and, along with Gabe, carried him into another cell. "Irving, you're old enough to know better than to do what those others tell you."

"I know, Sheriff. I don't know what got into me." Irving lay flat on the mattress, pressing a hand to his injured leg and whimpering with each movement.

"Do either of you even know that man?" Sheriff Sterling pointed to the prisoner in the third cell. Irving and Pauley each mumbled something unintelligible, indicating they didn't know the man they'd gotten shot over. "That's what I thought." The sheriff's disgusted tone told them how he felt about their stupidity. "Who else was out there tonight?"

"Don't know their names and I've never seen them before. They rode into town tonight. We met them at the saloon and they mentioned how one of their pals got thrown in jail." Irving tried to sit up, then fell back. "Things got a little blurry with all the whiskey being passed around."

"Did you get a name?" Sterling asked.

Irving rubbed his throbbing temple. "One of them mentioned someone." He squeezed his eyes tight in an attempt to think. "I don't think he was with them, though. It's all fuzzy."

"You must remember something." Hands on hips, the sheriff glared at Irving, still mystified as to why they'd let themselves get talked into such a misadventure.

"Blake, or something like that," Pauley shouted from his cell.

"No," Irving called back. "It began with a 'D'. I'm sure of that."

"Yeah, that's it. They called him Drake," Pauley said, then fell silent.

Dax's head snapped around toward the cells. "Are you sure the name you heard was Drake?" He spit out the words, staring into the prisoner's eyes.

"Uh...yes, sir." Pauley flinched away from the hard, cold stare of the man outside the cell. "That's what I heard."

"Shit." Dax cursed under his breath. "Gentleman." He looked at the sheriff and Gabe. "I'd better get back to the hotel. I'll send over a friend of mine to check on the prisoners. He's a doctor."

"Wait a minute." Sheriff Sterling walked up beside him. "Do you know the one they call Drake?"

"Maybe. If he's the man I know, he works for a rancher named Tolbert back in Splendor."

Gabe shifted his eyes to Dax's at the name of the biggest rancher in the area, and the town where his friend lived. "Are you talking about King Tolbert?"

"You know him?"

"Everyone in Montana has heard of King Tolbert." Sterling leaned a hip against his desk and crossed his arms. "The man even owns property around Big Pine. Doesn't run cattle here, at least not yet. I heard someone say he might be looking to buy a couple of the businesses in town. How do you know him?"

"My brother and I own a ranch north of Splendor. His hired gun is named Drake and we suspect he's behind some of the shootings we've been having in town." Dax looked back toward the cells, then turned his gaze on Gabe. "Are you familiar with Splendor?"

"A friend lives there. Noah Brandt."

"The blacksmith?"

Gabe nodded.

"Don't know him well. From what I can tell, those who do think real highly of him."

"I'm on my way to Splendor. A stopover, nothing more."

"Why don't you ride back with us after we finish our business?"

"Us? Who's with you?" Gabe asked.

"Doctor Worthington and his niece, Miss Davenport."

"That wouldn't be the nurse, would it?" A vague smile flicked across Gabe's face. A smile Dax didn't like.

"It would. How do you know her?"

"Never met her, but Noah sent me a letter a few months back, saying a real attractive nurse arrived in town. It was his way of trying to draw me back. You know, I might take you up on the offer to ride along. It's sometimes better to move in a small group rather than alone."

Less than forty-eight hours later, the group rode out of Big Pine, leaving the sheriff to wait for the territorial judge to arrive and oversee the murder trial of the man Gabe had brought in a few nights before. Sterling had already sent the two younger miscreants home to face the wrath of their mothers.

Once more, Dax took the lead with Bull at the back. This time, however, Gabe rode alongside the wagon, maintaining a watchful eye on their surroundings while keeping up a running conversation with Rachel and Charles. Every once in a while, Dax would turn in his saddle so he could judge the wagon's progress. Each time, half of Gabe's attention focused on locating any dangers, the other half focused on Rachel.

At noon, they broke for lunch. This time, Rachel stayed close to the wagon. Bull, Gabe, and Dax posted themselves around the perimeter, no one believing they'd make it to Splendor without a visit from either Drake's men or the renegades who had attacked the settlers a week before.

Dax glanced at Rachel, wishing she'd stayed in Splendor. He'd mentioned it to her before they'd left home, saying they could pick up the supplies, talk to the sheriff, and she could stay in town to treat anyone who came to the clinic. She refused, telling him he could stay if he wanted, but she had no intention of staying behind. He'd let it go. Now he had a bad feeling in the pit of his stomach. During the war, he paid close attention to his body's reaction to anything which seemed out of the ordinary and he found himself doing the same today. Trouble taunted them, he'd bet his last dollar on it.

"We need to pick up the pace the remainder of the trip, Charles. Do you think you can keep up?" Dax took off his hat and set it on the wagon seat, continuing his scan of the surrounding hills.

"Don't worry about us. We'll keep up." Charles capped his canteen. "You expecting trouble?"

Dax cast a look at the doctor. "Just being cautious. The closer we get to Splendor, the faster someone can ride for help if needed." He grabbed his hat and settled it on his head.

Charles understood the gravity of their situation. He'd treated the two cowboys Gabe and Dax had shot, listening as they spoke of the men who'd caused the disturbance and threatened to break their friend out of jail. Their words gave a chilling image of men without conscience, believing they had a right to challenge and intimidate others while being entitled to impunity for their own actions.

"We'll be ready." Charles climbed onto the wagon and turned to Rachel. "Get your gun out of your bag. We may need it." He pulled his rifle out from under the seat and set it next to him.

Bull and Gabe mounted their horses, this time both riding toward the back, one on either side of the wagon. They had at least four hours left on their journey—it would seem like much longer by the time they arrived in Splendor.

They'd traveled two more hours, when Bull spotted dust rising from a hill to their right.

"Riders!" He pointed toward several horses cresting the hill and riding toward them at a full gallop.

The instructions from Dax had been clear—don't run, hold their positions and, if shot upon, kill as many attackers as possible. Charles pulled the wagon to a stop and secured the reins as Rachel jumped off. She slid onto her stomach under the wagon and took aim at the approaching riders, who'd leveled their guns and began to shoot.

"Let your horses go." Dax's stern command could be heard over the gunfire. Bull and Gabe dismounted and took positions next to Charles on the opposite side of the wagon as shots pelleted the ground. He looked around and spotted Rachel under the wagon, hoping she'd be safe.

Bullets ripped into the side of the wagon, splitting wood, but nothing more.

"Hold...hold," Dax ordered in a low voice. "Now!"

The four men fired almost in unison, toppling two intruders and sending the rest in various directions.

"Don't let them get behind us." Dax aimed and fired once more, missing his target at the same time Gabe hit his mark.

Aim and squeeze, Rachel reminded herself before firing. She missed and aimed again. This time, she hit one, but he didn't fall.

"Let's get out of here!" One of the attackers pulled up, motioning for the others to join him. Within a few minutes, the violence had ended.

"Rachel?" Dax dropped to one knee and looked under the wagon. Relief flooded over him as he saw she'd come through without injury. He watched as she slid toward him, then offered a hand to help her stand. "Are you all right?" He ran his hands up her arms as his gaze wandered over her. He noted dirt, but no blood. For the first time since shots had been fired, Dax took a slow, deep breath. He rested his hands on her shoulders a moment before letting them drop to his sides.

"I'm fine." She shivered at the feel of his hands moving up her arms. She wanted to lean into him, wrap her arms around his waist and hold on. Instead, she turned in a quick circle, noting the others were also unhurt.

Bull and Gabe were checking the men they'd hit. Both were dead.

"What do you want to do with the bodies, Dax?" Gabe stared down at one of the men who'd tried to kill them.

"Load them in the wagon. We'll see if anyone in town recognizes them."

The trip took on a more sinister feel as they placed the bodies on top of each other in the wagon already full of supplies. Gabe took one more look around.

"Did you recognize any of the riders?" Gabe asked Dax as they gathered their horses.

"No, but I've only seen a small number of the men who work for Tolbert. Whoever they are, it's certain they have a grudge against us for disrupting their fun at the jail, and they're not above killing."

"How's Miss Davenport?" Gabe mounted and turned back toward the wagon.

"She's doing fine. Tough lady."

"I figured that."

Dax looked at Charles. "Are you ready?"

"We are."

"Let's get them to Splendor." Dax moved out in front, watching as Gabe and Bull took positions on opposite sides of the wagon once again. The danger had escalated with the deaths of two men, making them the target of ruthless thugs out for vengeance.

The typical orange, yellow, and pink evening sky turned a menacing black as they approached Splendor. Clouds, heavy with moisture, opened up as Charles pulled to a stop at the clinic.

"Rachel, go inside and pull out what we'll need to prepare the bodies."

She nodded and turned to jump down as Dax approached, holding out his arms. She hesitated a mere instant before accepting his help.

"We'll bring in the bodies." Dax let his hands fall from her waist, wishing he had more time to prolong the contact. "Is there anyone we should notify?"

"Without a sheriff, there's nobody. Uncle Charles will let Mr. Clausen and Mr. Petermann know. Perhaps someone will recognize them."

Dax, Gabe, and Bull unloaded the supplies, pulled the wagon around back, and unhitched the horse. Everything in town, except the saloon, had closed for the night.

"Do you have a place to stay?" Dax asked Gabe. "If not, you're welcome at the ranch."

159

"Thanks, but I'll bunk down at Noah's. I'd like him to look at the two bodies, see if he recognizes them." He swung up on his horse.

"I'll check on the doctor and Miss Davenport once more before riding out. You'll send word if there's trouble?" Dax hoped someone would claim the bodies once word got out. If not, they'd be buried in the common cemetery on a knoll behind town.

"I will." Gabe touched a finger to the brim of his hat and rode off.

"I'll stay out here while you check on the doc, boss." Bull shifted in his saddle, still watching for threats. Like the rest of them, he knew the danger hadn't passed just because they'd reached Splendor.

"Anything else you need before we leave, Doc?"

Charles looked up from where he and Rachel worked on one of the dead men.

"Not tonight. If it's not too much trouble, I'd like you to meet with some of the other men. We need to talk about what's happening."

"I'll be back tomorrow." Dax shifted his attention to Rachel. "Do you have a minute?" They'd had little time to talk since the first day of their trip to Big Pine. There were things he needed to say.

"All right." Rachel followed him to the front of the clinic, lit a kerosene lamp, and turned toward Dax.

"Have supper with me after the meeting tomorrow."

160

She knew he'd ask. He'd said as much in her kitchen the week before. "As much as I enjoy your company, I don't think that's such a good idea."

"Having supper?"

"Spending time together." She tucked a loose strand of hair behind an ear and licked her lips in an unconscious gesture, making Dax's body tighten. "You'll be leaving for Texas soon and my life is here, at least for now. There's no sense in spending more time together. It will just make it worse when you leave. Do you understand?"

He reached up and ran a finger down her cheek, noticing she didn't flinch at his touch. "No, Rachel, I don't." He lifted her chin, locking eyes with hers. "What's the harm of spending time together?" He dropped his hand and stepped away. "Unless you have plans with King Tolbert."

A bucket of ice water thrown over her couldn't have killed the moment more. Her face turned to stone at his words.

"I have no plans to see Tolbert, and I have no plans to see you. It's late and I need to help my uncle. Thank you for accompanying us to Big Pine. We're both grateful." She turned to walk away, but stopped as a firm hand seized her arm and spun her back.

Dax pulled her to within inches, his hard gaze softening at the anger that flashed from her eyes. He leaned toward her, tilting his head, waiting for her to jerk away, but she kept her eyes fixed on his.

"Are you certain you don't want to see me, Rachel? Because I certainly want to see you again." His voice washed over her as his lips hovered so close she could feel his breath.

Her heart pounded so hard he'd have to be deaf not to hear it. She sucked in a breath, wanting him to close the small space between them and kiss her. She tilted her face up, encouraging him to act, knowing she'd pay for it later. He brushed his lips across hers in a soft caress that shot sensations streaking through her limbs. She gripped his arms, holding tight as he settled his mouth on hers, deepening the kiss.

Dax knew he shouldn't do this, not with her uncle a room away. He wanted to pull her tight, kiss her senseless, let her know that no matter what his decision, she meant something to him. She was a woman he would never forget, and if he had her, would never be able to let go. He lifted his head at the thought, drew a breath, and took a step backwards.

"I'll come by after my meeting to take you to supper." He opened the door and strolled outside, berating himself for his brash action while already looking forward to tomorrow.

Chapter Ten

"I don't recognize either one of them." Horace Clausen stared down at the bodies, wincing at the chemical smell. He looked up at Stan Petermann. "Have you ever seen them?"

"Not me. You say there were more than these two?"

"Maybe three or four others rode off. I was so busy shooting and ducking that I didn't get a chance to count." Charles threw the cover back in place.

"Do you think Noah would recognize them?" Horace asked.

"Noah took a look earlier. Said he's never seen them." Charles looked into the front room at the sound of boots pounding on the wood floor. "Ah, Dax. I hoped you'd make it while Horace and Stan were still here."

"Doc." Dax pulled his hat off and joined the others. "Any luck?"

"No one recognizes them, and that includes Noah Brandt. Come on back to the house. I'll get us coffee while we talk."

Dax glanced around the house, then took a seat.

"She's at the general store." Charles handed Dax a cup filled with hot, black coffee, then did the same for the others and took a seat. "What are your thoughts?" He addressed the question to

Dax, understanding the man had a history with Drake.

"Do you know if anyone's sent word to Tolbert about the shootings?"

"Not yet. I wanted to see if anyone in town recognized them first." Doc sipped at the hot brew before setting his cup aside.

"I'll take a couple of men with me and ride out to his place. It might be best if I take the bodies so I can gauge the look on their faces when they see them."

"Any luck finding someone interested in being the sheriff?" Clausen looked at Charles, already seeing the answer in the man's face.

"Sheriff Sterling is looking for a deputy himself. He offered the job to Gabe Evans, who turned him down flat." A look of disappointment crossed the doctor's face.

"He said he had no interest in being a lawman in Big Pine. That doesn't mean he might not have an interest in Splendor." Dax had thought about Gabe on his ride back to the ranch the night before. The man had a quick gun, seemed slow to anger, and held strong convictions. For a Northerner, he seemed all right.

"We asked him when he and Noah rode into town last year," Horace said. "Turned us down, too."

"Men change their minds. Maybe I'll have a talk with him."

Dax and the others turned at a knock on the door. Charles opened it to see Horace's secretary,

Mrs. Phelps, standing outside, wringing her hands.

"Is Mr. Clausen here?"

"He is. Please, come inside."

"Maybe for a moment. I need to let him know Mr. Tolbert is at the bank and ready to bust a gut." She clamped a hand over her mouth when Charles smiled.

"I heard you, Mrs. Phelps. I'm on my way. Guess I'll speak with you gentlemen later."

"I'll go with you, Horace." Dax grabbed his hat and followed the banker out the door, then turned to Charles. "Let Rachel know I'm still counting on taking her to supper."

The two men entered the bank to find Tolbert in the office, pacing, his anger escalating with each passing second.

Horace held out his hand. "It's good to see you, King."

Tolbert waved off the extended hand. "What's this I hear about two of my men being killed?"

Horace and Dax glanced at each other before the banker spoke. "News does travel fast. I didn't know you were aware of the shootings. I just found out myself this morning."

Tolbert's face reddened, realizing he'd said more than he'd intended. He shrugged it off. "Doesn't matter how I heard. Is it true?"

"Might be, if the two bodies at the doc's are your men." Horace slid back into the coat he'd just hung up. "Come with us."

Horace didn't knock before throwing open the clinic door and walking in with King and Dax, and heading to the back room. "Do you recognize them?"

Tolbert took one look at the bodies and stepped back. "Yes. Those are two of the men I hired to keep watch on my land near Big Pine." He glared at Dax. "Did you do this?"

"They attacked the doctor, Miss Davenport, Bull, Gabe Evans, and myself while we rode back to Splendor. Came out of the hills west of Big Pine and started shooting. I believe they got more than they expected." Dax stood his ground. The fault rested on Tolbert for the death of the two who lay before them. "I want the others brought in for trial, Tolbert. Were they acting on your orders?"

"Hell no. I don't know what they were thinking shooting at the doctor and Miss Davenport, but I aim to find out." He slammed through the door, heading for his horse.

"I'm going with you." Dax grabbed Hannibal and mounted before King could object, all thoughts of supper with Rachel forgotten.

"I can deal with my own men, Pelletier."

"I'm sure you can, but I'm still going."

They rode in silence, not speaking until they dismounted in front of Tolbert's ranch house.

"Drake!" Tolbert stomped toward the barn, anger pulsing through him at the thought his men could've been so reckless as to shoot at Rachel and her uncle. He spotted one of the hands working on a horse near the back. "Where's Drake?"

The ranch hand jumped at the hard tone of Tolbert's question. "He and some men rode over to the Pelletier property, like you asked." The man shut his mouth when he spotted someone standing behind his boss.

"What the hell did you send them to my place for?" Dax moved up to within a foot of Tolbert, planting his feet, a hand resting on the butt of his gun.

Tolbert glared back at Pelletier. "We're looking for a stray bull. Drake thought perhaps he'd gotten lost on your place."

"If he did, my men would've sent him back. You sure there wasn't another reason? No orders to shoot at my men or stampede the cattle?"

"I never gave an order to shoot at any of your men. Wilson getting shot had nothing to do with me."

The ranch hand looked behind the men who faced off, seeing Abigail Tolbert walk into the barn. "Good afternoon, Miss Abigail."

King and Dax turned at the man's words.

"Father, is everything all right?"

He shot a look at Pelletier, warning him not to say anything further in front of Abby. "All's fine, Abby. I need to speak with Drake. You remember Dax Pelletier, our neighbor?"

"Of course. Hello, Mr. Pelletier." To King's disgust, she made a slight curtsey.

He pulled off his hat. "Miss Tolbert." He turned from the young woman, his focus on her father again. "I'm heading to my place to make sure your men aren't doing anything more than looking for a stray bull. You will hear from me if I find otherwise." He stormed from the barn, swung onto Hannibal, and made good time to the ranch.

He slid to the ground and tore up the front steps. "Bernice, do you know where Luke and the others are?"

"Well, let's see. I believe Luke and some of the men rode to the western property line, checking for strays, while Ellis took a group north. Luke spoke with Hank before he left. He came inside to lie down if you want to talk to him."

Dax followed Bernice. He knew Hank had been giving his wife a hard time for days, pushing himself too hard and not resting enough.

"How are you feeling?" Dax asked as he took a seat next to the bed.

"I feel great, but the woman keeps telling me I'm pushing myself too hard. How about talking to her for me, Dax?" Hank glanced at his wife who stood by the door, not at all vexed by her husband's words.

"Sorry, Hank, but from the looks of you, it seems Bernice may be right. You need to take it easy before you can handle the normal load. Until then, did Luke tell you exactly where he and the others would be working today?"

"Sure did. He and some of the boys are working on the west side, near Wildfire Creek. I swear your brother picks the spot because he likes it. Says it's one of the nicest places on the ranch. Anyway, he told me they'd be looking for strays."

Surprise registered on Dax's face. Luke had never even mentioned the creek as far as he could recall. He'd have to ask him about it. "And the others?"

"North end, near Survivor Pass. Ellis and the boys are checking for strays. They all plan to be back for supper."

Supper! Dax had forgotten about Rachel and his invitation to take her to supper. He looked at Bernice. "What time is it?"

She walked over to the dresser to pick up Hank's pocket watch. "'Bout six o'clock. Why?"

"I've got to head back to town. When the boys get back, tell them that Drake and his men have orders to find a stray bull. Tolbert thinks it's on our place. No trouble. I want them to keep a look out for him and his men."

Dax's quick strides had him out the door and riding out of the ranch within a few seconds, not taking time to change into a clean shirt or shine his boots. He didn't want to take a chance on being late and giving her an excuse to refuse supper with him.

"All I know is he rode out to the Tolbert ranch with King." Charles watched Rachel pace back and forth, her irritation increasing with each turn.

"Well, I'm not waiting any longer." She started for the kitchen to ladle up her own bowl of soup when a knock sounded.

"Shall I answer that for you?" His condescending tone wasn't lost on Rachel.

She set down the spoon, cast her uncle a contemptuous look as she walked past, and opened the front door. One hand on the doorknob, the other on her hip, she shot Dax a disinterested look, trying to hide her irritation.

He held his hat in both hands, fingering the edges and looking a bit mussed. "My apologies. I had to take care of a situation at the ranch and didn't have a chance to change. I hope you'll still agree to have supper with me."

The sheepish look on his face softened her mood, making her think perhaps she'd misjudged him—at least in some ways. She understood the danger he posed to her heart. The wild emotions his kiss elicited the night before confirmed it.

"Truthfully, I had given up on you. You caught me just before I'd decided to prepare a bowl of soup. You wouldn't care for some, would you?" Her slight smile told Dax she already knew the answer.

"Not tonight. However, I'd like to accept the invitation at another time." He held out his arm. "Shall we?"

She reached for her wrap. "We're leaving now, Uncle Charles. I won't be late."

"Don't worry about me. Have a good time. You, too, Dax."

"I plan on it, sir."

The night air held a slight chill. Rachel secured her shawl and looked up at an almost full moon knowing, in a few nights, it would illuminate the entire town as it became a brilliant ball of light. Dax followed her gaze, then came to a stop, keeping his eyes aloft.

"I used to watch the moon at night, often after a hard-fought battle, and wonder about Luke, as well as the rest of my family. I'd hear other men—fathers, brothers, husbands, uncles—moaning in pain and prayed my family would be spared." Dax's solemn voice mirrored his feelings on those nights he lay awake, wrestling with concerns for his family and his men.

"It appears Luke came through unscathed. What about the rest of your family?"

He dropped his eyes to Rachel's. "No one remained when Luke and I returned to Savannah." He reached for her hand and proceeded down the wooden walkway toward the boardinghouse restaurant.

"You left it all behind when you traveled to Texas?"

"Yes and no. Luke set up the men and women, who had been our slaves before the war, as Pelletier employees. They work the land, keep everything running well, and they receive wages. If the profits grow, they obtain a percentage of the land over a period of time. One of our bankers handles the details. Luke corresponds with him a few times a year. I would have left it all to Luke, but..." His voice trailed off when he remembered the day he'd left Savannah. "Luke didn't show up to see me off when I left. A couple hours later, he rode up to my side during a pouring rain. He refused to let me ride out alone and I don't believe he's ever looked back." Dax opened the restaurant door to the rich aromas of beef, onions, and spices drifting through the air.

"I'm guessing it's pot roast night." Rachel inhaled deeply, filling her lungs as her mouth began to water. "She cooks it just right."

"Take a seat anywhere, Rachel." Suzanne Briar busied herself pouring coffee for a table of cowboys.

Dax led her to a table near a window. They could see the saloon lights across the street and the livery a couple of doors down. He could make out the outline of two men inside and guessed them to be Noah and Gabe.

"Good evening, Rachel, Dax." Suzanne placed two cups down and filled each with coffee. "What can I get you?"

Rachel hid a smile. Suzanne served one choice each night plus a couple of desserts. "I believe I'll have the pot roast." She looked at Dax.

"I'll have the same."

Suzanne nodded. "Won't take long."

"I wonder why she always asks. Everyone knows she serves one choice each night," Dax said and sipped his coffee.

"Maybe she thinks it's hospitable." Rachel looked around the simple restaurant and recalled all the opulent places to dine in Boston. It would be hard to find two more different worlds. She'd grown up in one, and come to love the other.

"When we spoke before, it sounded like you plan to make your home in Splendor." Dax picked up his knife and fork and cut into the meal Suzanne had set before him.

"For now, yes. My parents don't understand how I could shun a society wedding, grand home, and family. Most days, I don't quite understand it myself. All I know is, this town feels right."

"So no marriage, no children?" It surprised Dax that Rachel wouldn't want both.

Her eyes darted to his. "I *would* like to marry and have a family, but not with any of the men I know in Boston. The life is so rigid and women's choices are few." Her gaze wandered back to her plate, her eyebrows knitting together as if she were formulating a complex thought. "My world back east consisted of a string of nannies, visits to approved parks, private schools, and every assortment of social event imaginable. Friendships and activities were decided within certain social boundaries." She focused again on Dax. "Did you live that way in Savannah?"

He let out a soft chuckle. "Not at all. Don't misunderstand. We had social functions we were required to attend, and no excuse on earth would allow us to miss school. We were also expected, from an early age, to work in the family business. I chose the sea trade, while Luke worked in the warehouse and distribution office. Both of us understood and worked in the farming and horse breeding part of the business. Our choices suited us both."

"You've ridden your entire life?"

"I can't remember a time when I didn't own a horse. My mother joked about us learning to ride before we could walk." A vague smile appeared at the mention of his mother and he realized how much he still missed his family.

"How about some pie tonight?" Suzanne walked up with two large slices.

"I wouldn't turn it down." The plate she set in front of Dax had to be a quarter of the pie.

"Neither would I." Rachel's eyes widened at the huge portion, but her mouth still watered. "This looks wonderful."

"Just baked them a few hours ago. I'll get more coffee."

Rachel didn't wait for the coffee to dig in, not noticing Dax's expression as he watched her uninhibited enjoyment of the dessert. She looked up after a few bites to see his eyes on her and his pie still untouched.

"What?" She grabbed her napkin, thinking a stray piece of pie must be the reason for his stare.

"Nothing. Just enjoying watching you eat."

Her face reddened as a grin broke out. "That's another reason I belong out here. At home, we get small portions, not enough to feed a bird. Here, I can eat as much as I want."

"Most women in Savannah fretted about their weight. I don't suppose that worries you." He picked up his fork and took a bite.

"I guess not because I never give it a thought."

They finished their pie and walked out into the cool night. Rachel stifled a yawn. It would be considered early by east coast standards. Most people were in bed early and up before dawn in the small town.

"I'd better get you home before you fall over."

"Sorry. I always get sleepy after I eat." She glanced up at Dax's strong profile set off by the bright moonlight, remembering how his lips felt on hers. Her stomach tightened at the memory. "I'm glad you invited me. I had a wonderful time."

They walked behind the clinic to her front door. One light burned from inside, indicating Charles had already turned in for the night.

Dax turned her to him, his words gentle. "I don't know what I'm going to do, Rachel. Whether I'm staying or leaving. This," he let his arm make a wide arc, "is something neither Luke nor I anticipated. We did a favor for a friend and are now the owners of a big spread hundreds of miles from where we planned to settle." He took a deep breath, inhaling the fresh scent of the evening air. "Knowing how uncertain my future is, would you still allow me to call on you?"

She clasped her hands in front of her, knowing her heart would be in danger whether she continued to see him or not. She'd accepted the fact her heart had already been captured by the rugged Southerner. Whether he stayed or left wouldn't change it. She could enjoy what time they had or walk away, perhaps regretting the opportunity to know about him.

"I'm sure it's no surprise how much I like you, Dax. Much more than I should, knowing you'll most likely leave..." Her voice trailed off as she contemplated life in Splendor without Dax and how he'd become so important to her. "Once you decide how to handle your half of the ranch, there will be nothing to keep you here."

Except you, Dax thought.

"A part of me wants to keep seeing you. Another part warns me away, believing the pain will be so much worse the more time we spend together." Her soft green eyes captured his.

He lifted her chin with a finger. "What are you saying, Rachel?"

"I'm not sure, except I already care for you too much knowing you don't plan to stay." Resignation and a sadness she'd never felt before tinged her voice.

Her words pierced his heart. Most women he knew would never voice their feelings unless they already believed they knew how the other person felt. Rachel's honesty meant a great deal to Dax and he had no idea the best way to respond. He couldn't make promises, yet he had no desire to walk away.

He hesitated a heartbeat before bending down to place a kiss on the corner of her mouth, then one on the other corner before capturing her lips in a heated kiss. He moved his hands to her back and pulled her toward him, intensifying the contact as a sigh escaped her lips. Rachel's hands rested on his arms, steadying her from the fiery contact that felt both right and terrifying.

His hands moved up her back, one supporting her neck, holding her in place as he shifted his mouth one way, then another. She moaned as he traced the edge of her lips with his tongue, encouraging her to open for him.

Rachel felt like fire in his arms. Her response surprised him, while warning him she wasn't like any other woman he'd known. He'd never felt his heart trip over itself, yet it did with Rachel. He drew back, placing one more kiss on her mouth.

"We'll take it a day at a time." The huskiness in his voice betrayed how far he'd already fallen. "Save every Saturday night for me, and any other time I can make it into town." He placed one more kiss to her temple, offered a smile, then turned to leave. He stopped at the corner of the clinic and looked back to see Rachel glancing over her shoulder at him as she stepped inside.

She closed the door, leaned her back against it, and took a deep breath. A hand rested on her chest, feeling the staccato rhythm of her racing heart. Common sense warned her she should let him go. Without ever experiencing it before, she knew what she felt for the wandering Texas Ranger was love. Until now, she'd had no idea how frightening falling in love could be.

Chapter Eleven

Austin, Texas

Duff Mayes sat on his horse, drenched and cold from a late spring storm that had him arriving late to his destination. He'd waited months to let things cool down before making this trip. The bank robbery his two brothers and cousins pulled off hadn't been forgotten. Rangers never forget when one of their own dies at the hands of an outlaw, and Duff Mayes hadn't forgotten his youngest brother, Deke, had been shot dead by a Ranger named Pelletier.

Whitey Mayes knew who followed them after the robbery—Pat Hanes and the two Pelletier brothers. He'd met them in Austin on one of his trips to check out the bank. Hanes had been well known and liked within the Texas Ranger community. The other two were a mystery. No one knew much about them, except they were ex-rebel soldiers and had been successful in tracking down all the outlaws they hunted. Just one had been brought in alive.

Duff and Whitey meant to hunt them down.

Duff slid off his horse in the front of the Rangers' office, shook off the rain, and pushed open the door to see three men sitting around a desk. The oldest one looked up.

"Something I can do for you?"

"I'm looking for the Pelletiers."

"That so. And who would you be?"

"Henry Johnson. I fought in the war with them." Duff looked nothing like his wanted poster. The injury from another bank job months before had almost killed him, wasting away his muscles as well as leaving him with a permanent limp. He'd grown a scraggly brick red beard, in sharp contrast to his wavy light brown hair.

"Well, Mr. Johnson, they've taken some time off. I don't know when they'll be back. You can leave a message if you want, but I can't guarantee they'll get it." The captain's eyes narrowed on the man. Something seemed familiar—the stance, the eyes that darted around the room, never making direct contact with any of the men.

"I don't have any plans. Maybe I'll head their direction, see if I can catch up with 'em."

A short, lean Ranger dropped his boots from where they rested on the desk onto the floor. "Aren't they up in Montana, Captain?"

"Yeah, that's where Pat had his ranch," another said, then stopped when his captain shot him a warning glare.

"That's all we know, Mr. Johnson. Like I said, you're welcome to leave them a note." The captain stood and started around the desk, his eyes never leaving the man's gun hand.

"I think I'll ride up to Montana. Maybe someone's heard of them. Don't matter. There's nothing keeping me in Texas." The lie rolled off his lips with little effort. He and Whitey still owned a ranch north of Red Gulch, deeded under false names, where they raised horses and enough beef to feed them and their men.

"Up to you."

"I appreciate the information." Duff tipped his hat and walked back out into the storm, which had slowed to a soft rain. He'd get a room and be off early the next morning for the ranch. Within three days, he, his brother, and their cousins would be on their way to Montana and the vengeance they were due.

Splendor, Montana

"What are we going to do, Drake? We can't let those deaths go unpunished."

Drake assessed the man next to him, still fuming from the idiocy he and his companions had shown by attacking the group riding home from Big Pine. They'd brought it on themselves and Drake was sorely tempted to cut all of them loose. He didn't need hotheads around to jeopardize his plans to run the Pelletiers out of the territory—or kill them.

"Well?"

The cold stare Drake shot him shut the man up. No one wanted to cross their boss, a man with little patience and no conscience.

"Drake." They turned as King Tolbert walked toward the corral where one of the men attempted to break a green horse.

"Yes, sir?"

"I'd like a word with you." Tolbert shifted his gaze around the group of men, some who'd been with him a long time, others Drake had hired. Those men warranted closer scrutiny.

Drake followed him into the house and closed the door as Tolbert took a seat behind his desk, not offering the man a drink. "I want to know what happened between Big Pine and Splendor. And don't tell me you know nothing of it. I'll not abide a lie."

"All I know is what the men told me. Two of the men started off from your property in Big Pine earlier than the others. The rest took off some time later. They heard shooting several hours out, but by the time they reached a place where they could see what was happening, a couple of bodies were being loaded into a wagon. Must've been the wagon the doctor and Miss Davenport took to Big Pine for supplies. Three other men on horses were with them. That's all I know."

"The men didn't consider those bodies might be the two who rode out ahead of them? Did they even think about riding up to the wagon and questioning anyone?" King's words had hardened more with each question.

"They didn't want to get shot at. At least that's what they said."

"Pelletier said more than two attacked them. Are you certain the others weren't involved?"

"They insist they weren't."

"And you believe them?"

"No reason not to."

181

King sat forward, leaning his arms on the desk and not missing the slight unease he saw in Drake's eyes. "You'd stake your life on that?"

"I don't stake my life on any man's word, Mr. Tolbert."

King sat back as a wary tension sliced through him. "I want you and a few men to ride the western property line. From there, you can see the comings and goings at the Pelletier place. Don't cross onto their land. Just keep watch. I heard they're buying more head from one of the ranchers south of town. I want to know if it's true."

"That all?" Drake asked as he stood to leave.

"For now." Tolbert waited a beat. "No violence, Drake."

Tolbert heard the click of the door close, then a tapping before Abby poked her head into his study.

"Hello, Father. Do you have time to take me to town today?"

Guilt tugged at King. He had no time to take his daughter to town, yet knew he'd not refuse her. He pulled out his pocket watch. "Be ready in an hour. You can do your shopping before we have dinner at the boardinghouse."

A huge smile split her face, reminding him it wouldn't be long before she would find someone and begin a life of her own. He'd have to make certain she decided on the right man.

"Good day, Mr. Tolbert, Miss Abigail. Take a seat anywhere you'd like and I'll be right with you." Suzanne had never taken to King Tolbert and the way he'd shipped his daughter off at an early age to be raised in the east, moving from one private boarding school to another as she got older.

"I'll be right back, Abby. I need to speak with Horace." He crossed the few feet to where the banker sat alone, finishing his meal.

Abby took the opportunity to follow Suzanne to the kitchen. She'd been on the woman's heels from a young age, always curious as to the happenings in the restaurant. Suzanne felt certain the girl's education hadn't included cooking classes.

"Are you sure it's all right with your father to be in the kitchen with me?"

"Oh, yes. He's speaking with Mr. Clausen. I won't bother you long."

"Abby, it's never a bother to have you join me. You're welcome anytime." Suzanne had lost her own daughter and husband during a severe snowstorm years before. The attractive widow had never remarried, telling people she'd already had her one great love. Abby hadn't known Suzanne's daughter, even though they were of similar age. In Suzanne's mind, Abby had turned into the type of young woman she thought her daughter would have become—smart, quiet, pretty, with a ferocious curiosity.

"What are you making?" Abby peered over Suzanne's shoulder into a large pot.

"Lamb stew. Noah Brandt got the meat on trade for some of his work, then traded it to me for a couple dozen suppers. A good deal, don't you think?" Suzanne noticed Abby's eyes light up at the mention of the blacksmith. She suspected the young woman had a crush on the man and felt a pang of sorrow, knowing Tolbert would never approve of his daughter's interest in him. An impish thought crossed her mind. "In fact, it's time I took a bowl of this stew over to him at the livery. I'm swamped right now. Would you mind taking it over?"

Abby couldn't conceal her enthusiasm even as she tried to hide it. "I'd be happy to help."

Suzanne ladled up a large bowl, wrapped cornbread in a cloth, and handed both to Abby. "There you go. By the time you're back, I'll have your meal ready."

Abby didn't even glance at her father, just walked straight to the livery, being careful not to spill the stew.

Noah's eyes grew wide at the sight of Abby carrying a bowl and knew Mrs. Briar had sent her with his meal.

"Miss Abigail, let me take that." He set the food aside, wiping his blackened hands on his pants and pulling a handkerchief from his pocket to clean what he could from his face. "Does your father know you're here?"

She glanced behind her. "No. He's speaking with Mr. Clausen and, well...Mrs. Briar needed the help." She looked around Noah to see a beautiful stallion in a back stall. "Oh my."

"He belongs to a friend of mine. Gabe Evans. Gabe raised him from a colt. Handsome, isn't he?"

"More than that. He's one of the most stunning animals I've ever seen." She walked toward the horse, admiring the lines and strength of the stallion's muscles. "He's quite tall and, well...sort of devilish-looking, don't you think?"

"That he is."

Abby turned at the sound of the unfamiliar voice behind her.

"Miss Tolbert, this is Gabe Evans. He owns Blackheart. Gabe, this is Abigail Tolbert."

"Oh, what a perfect name for him. Blackheart." She turned back to the magnificent horse who'd given a loud snort at the sight of Gabe walking into the livery.

"He thinks I'm here to take him out. He's never been a patient beast." Gabe stood beside her, admiring the pretty young woman who showed no fear at being close to the impressive creature.

"And will you? Take him out, I mean?"

"In a while. I want to ride to the Pelletier ranch. Do you know them?"

"Yes. I've met Dax Pelletier, but not his brother."

"You're welcome to ride along."

Noah's eyes shot to Gabe, who didn't notice the scowl warning him he may have made a mistake.

"Thank you, but I'm in town with my father. In fact, he's waiting for me at the restaurant."

185

She looked up at Noah standing on her other side. "It's good to see you again, Mr. Brandt."

"It's my pleasure, Miss Tolbert. Stop by whenever you'd like." Noah's gaze trailed Abby as she made her way across the street to join her father. If he had any dreams left, she'd be it.

Gabe knew the look a man showed when he wanted a woman, and Noah wanted Miss Abigail Tolbert. He knew his friend wouldn't act on it, though. He'd convinced himself no woman would want him if she learned what he'd done during the war. Gabe knew his friend was wrong, but acknowledged everyone had to make their own choices. Noah had made his.

"Why don't you court her? She's a beautiful young woman who doesn't hide her interest in you."

"No. She deserves someone far better. You know as well as me I'm not fit for any woman." Noah swallowed hard, wishing he had something to offer a woman like Abby.

Gabe clasped his friend on the shoulder. "You may think that, but I don't. Someday, you'll realize what you did during the war has nothing to do with the man you are." He grabbed Blackheart's blanket and saddle. "I'm off to see the Pelletiers. You want to ride out with me?"

"Too busy today."

"I'll be back for supper."

Noah focused on his work, then set his hammer down and glanced up as Gabe rode from the livery. The thought his friend, the ex-colonel, would be a much better match for Abigail crossed his mind. Hell, anyone would be better than him.

186

He wrapped his large hand around the hammer and started back to work, the lamb stew and cornbread Abby had brought to him forgotten.

Gabe headed north, following the directions Noah gave him to the Pelletier property. Billows of dust followed a herd of cattle a couple miles out of town. He recognized Dax as one of the men working the herd and rode to join him.

"Moving them to another pasture?" Gabe brought Blackheart alongside Dax.

"Bought these from the Murton family. Tyson's got a family on the way and needs cash. Luke and I need the cattle." Dax looked over his shoulder, and satisfied nothing seemed amiss, turned back to Gabe. "What brings you out here?"

"Curious if you've had any other trouble."

"Not yet. I'm expecting it, though."

"Tell me about Drake." Gabe had figured out a history existed between Dax and Drake, and he guessed it went back further than their time in Splendor.

Dax gripped the saddle horn with both hands and leaned back, eyeing the man next to him and deciding how much to say. It had become a personal matter between him and the deserter. No officer respected or trusted a man who left others to die in his place.

Gabe stayed silent, waiting for Dax.

"He was a sergeant in my division. Hell of a fighter, but an unstable leader. He couldn't leave the hostility on the battlefield. He'd bring it back to camp and take it out on his men. One almost died. The decision had been made to bust him to corporal. He disappeared the same night."

"Deserted?"

"That's right. Happened the night before an important battle and I needed every man. I sent in a replacement, a friend of mine, to lead his unit. He died fighting in the sergeant's place."

"Anything could've happened. The man's death wasn't your fault."

Dax cast him a quick look. "True, except the man I sent in was already too injured to fight. I'd originally ordered him to stay at the rear due to wounds in an arm and leg. He shouldn't have been in the battle at all." He rested his steady gaze on Gabe. "A few weeks ago, Drake showed up at the ranch. It's the first I'd seen him since he deserted."

Dax went on to tell him about the shooting of Hank Wilson and the scattering of his cattle.

"Have you spoken with Tolbert?"

"I've confronted him. He's adamant no orders to shoot anyone came from him."

"Bull wants to split off part of the group and take another trail back. You okay with that?" Luke slowed Prince down to keep up with this brother, Bull pulling up next to Dax on the opposite side and nodding a greeting to Gabe.

"I'm good with it. Luke, this is Gabe Evans."

"Gabe." Luke reached across Dax to shake the outstretched hand. "Dax told me about how you helped out during the attack. We're all

188

obliged to you." He turned in his saddle at the sound of gunfire. "Get down!"

Another shot rang out, grazing Dax's arm and hitting Bull. The big man muttered a curse as he fell from his horse.

Luke and Dax took off toward the shots, Gabe sliding off his horse to kneel next to Bull, using his hands to stem the flow of blood. He looked up when more rounds echoed through the valley, but saw only Dax and Luke riding back to join him.

Luke slid from his horse and dropped to Bull's side, checking his pulse, while Dax tore a piece off his shirt and wrapped it around his injured arm.

Gabe glanced up. "He has a pulse. We need to get him to the doc—now."

Luke pulled an old shirt from his saddlebag and used it to protect Bull's wound.

"It will take too long to get a wagon from the ranch. He'll have to ride." Dax spotted Bull's horse, rode after it, and grabbed the reins.

It took all three of them to get Bull into the saddle and tied down, throwing a blanket over him. Luke swung up behind him.

"I'll go with them." Gabe paced Luke, while Dax stayed behind to check on the other men.

Just like before, cattle were scattered. Besides the nick to Dax's arm, Bull appeared to be the only casualty.

"I've got this if you want to head to town, boss." Ellis had the look of a man ready to explode. "If those bastards come back, we'll be ready for them."

"Circle up the cattle and post the men around. Send some of them to the other herd. No telling where those riders will go next." Dax turned Hannibal around and took off to catch up to Luke and Gabe.

Luke almost lost Bull twice, the big man's weight shifting even though ropes secured him to the saddle. Gabe stood by his side a moment after reaching the clinic, untying the ropes and helping Luke slide Bull off.

"Doc!" Luke threw one of Bull's arms over his shoulder, while Gabe did the same on the other side. "Doc!"

"I'm coming." The clinic door opened as the two men struggled to get Bull inside.

"Gunshot," Luke said.

"Oh, my God," Rachel murmured when she saw who'd been shot. She grabbed clean cloths, bandages, hot water, and a bottle of whiskey from the cupboard.

They lifted Bull onto the table as blood continued to flow from the wound.

"We've got him now. You boys wait outside." Charles spared them no other thought as he put all his concentration into saving the man on the table.

Luke and Gabe had just closed the door behind them when Dax burst in and started for the back room. Both men blocked his path.

"Doc says to wait out here." Luke didn't move until his brother nodded. "You need to get that tended to." He nodded toward Dax's bandaged arm.

"It's nothing." He'd forgotten about his injury, his concern focused on Bull, his anger on those who'd shot at them.

An hour passed, then another without word. They didn't speak or leave, each dreading the door opening to be told Bull hadn't made it. Almost three hours later, an exhausted Rachel appeared to tell them their friend had survived—for now.

"Honestly, I don't know what kept him alive. I thought we'd lost him more than once."

Dax walked up and placed an arm around her shoulders. She leaned into him, absorbing his strength, finding comfort in his touch. Before she realized it, he'd pulled her around in front of him with both arms circling her, his chin on the top of her head, her head resting on his chest.

"That's good news, Rachel." His soft whisper sent chills through her body, and she wished they were in a place where she could look up and accept the kiss she knew he'd offer. She pulled back and, for the first time, noticed his blood-soaked shirt.

"You're hurt." Without another word, she ushered him into the room where Bull lay unconscious so she could treat his wound.

A moment later, Charles came out and turned his attention to Luke and Gabe. "He's resting. I don't believe he even knows how hard he fought to stay alive. By all medical definitions, the man should be dead."

"Can we see him?" Luke asked.

"For a minute, then you'll need to leave."

The three stood next to the bed while Rachel finished securing a clean bandage to Dax's arm.

"Any idea who did this?" Charles asked.

"I'll wager the same men who attacked us coming back from Big Pine." Gabe ran a hand through is hair, frustrated and tired.

"Whoever it is, the sons of bitches will pay." Luke glanced toward Rachel. "My apologies, ma'am."

She turned toward Luke. "I understand and feel the same."

"What now?" Dax asked Charles.

"We need to keep Bull here. Rachel and I will take turns watching him. You three might as well head out. No sense all of you sitting around."

"I'm staying. I'll keep watch on him while you and Rachel rest." Dax's stern features told more than his words. It didn't matter what they said. He wasn't going to leave.

"I'll find out if the others saw anything and make sure the herd gets settled. We'll need to rebrand right away. I don't want any mix-ups." Luke grabbed his hat and looked at Charles. "Thanks, Doc."

"He's not healed yet." The doctor turned his weary body back toward the room where Bull lay unconscious.

"Like you said, he shouldn't have made it this far," Luke called over his shoulder.

Gabe looked between the brothers. "You understand the bullet that hit Bull may have been meant for one of you."

Rachel shot a look at Dax.

"I've thought of that. We won't know until we've caught the men who shot at us." Dax's hard voice rang with command.

Gabe nodded. "Let me know when you plan to ride out to Tolbert's. I want to go along."

"Tomorrow, if Bull has a good night. I don't want to put it off."

"I'll wait for the two of you at the ranch and we'll head out from there." Luke started outside, then stopped at Dax's words.

"Watch your back."

Chapter Twelve

Denver, Colorado

"You boys stay here. I'll go inside and see if anyone has heard of them." Duff Mayes left his brother, Whitey, and three cousins to sit in the fading evening sun as he walked into the sheriff's office in Denver.

Clark, Bill, and Jed Olin had grown up on a farm next to the Mayes' place. Their mothers were sisters. Both sets of parents had died during the war and the boys had joined forces to build a new life as bank robbers in Texas.

A few minutes later, Duff emerged from the sheriff's office and walked toward his horse. "Appears we're headed in the right direction, boys. They came through here, riding north to Montana."

"What town?" Whitey Mayes had been patient with his brother's insistence they be careful about going after the Pelletiers. Both were still Texas Rangers while taking time off for personal business. Even with that knowledge, Whitey wanted revenge against the men who'd killed his brother.

"Someplace called Splendor."

"Let's go."

"No. It's late. We'll stay here tonight, then take off early tomorrow. Besides, I need a drink."

"Can't it wait?"

"No, it cannot." Duff drawled before riding up to the nearest saloon. The others followed, knowing that arguing would be a waste of time. Besides, the Olin brothers felt the same as Duff. A night of whiskey, cards, and female company sounded damn good.

Splendor, Montana

Rachel woke from another dream, grabbed her wrapper, and walked the few steps to the clinic. She stared at the man who sat sprawled in a chair before her. Her nights were plagued with visions of Dax and now he seemed to be invading her days, as well. It wouldn't be so difficult if her body didn't respond to his presence, all senses on alert.

Dax shifted in the chair, a hand moving to the butt of his pistol as his eyes flew open.

"How's he doing?" Rachel asked while checking Bull's color and heart rate.

Dax sat up and looked at his ranch hand still sleeping on the table a few feet away. "He hasn't made a sound or moved since you left." Dax stepped up beside her. "What do you think?"

"I think this man is indestructible." Her face tilted up and Dax caught a glimpse of a tired smile. "Uncle Charles gave him a small dose of laudanum, enough to deaden most of the pain. However, I'd expect him to still be restless, groaning."

Dax's gaze moved in a slow perusal from her slippered feet to her face, traveling over the dress she'd worn the day before. She'd braided her hair and let the long strand drop down her back, a few wisps of hair falling free. He stepped behind her and used a forefinger to brush them from her neck, then bent to place a kiss on the soft column.

She tried to concentrate on Bull, ignoring the intense sensations washing over her as Dax's lips traced a line up her neck to below her ear. He wrapped his arms around her waist. She leaned back into him and took a slow, measured breath, trying to keep herself from giving in and turning into his arms.

Dax felt his body harden as his hands splayed across her stomach. He turned her around to face him. His mouth covered hers as he tightened his hold, one hand on the small of her back, crushing her to him. He felt her immediate response as her arms wrapped around his neck and she buried her hands in his hair.

Rachel reveled in the way his mouth claimed hers. She arched against him, seeking something more, but not knowing what. The hunger in his kiss intensified, shattering any remaining control. His tongue traced the fullness of her lips until she opened and he plunged inside.

She'd never felt so on fire, and squirmed against him in an attempt to get closer. She was shocked at her own response as her hands drifted down his back and pulled him tight, feeling the full length of his body against hers.

Dax marveled at the way she matched him kiss for kiss. Her eager response drove his body to a heated pitch he found hard to keep under control. He couldn't get enough of her.

The yearning he felt for this woman never eased and, in fact, had become his constant companion. As much as his mind told him to push her away, he couldn't bring himself to heed the warnings.

Since he'd first set foot in Texas, he believed that it held his future. It had become a place for new beginnings where growing towns and men with enormous vision ruled the land. Dax wanted to be a part of its progress. He foresaw an exciting and endless future for those willing to brave the lawlessness that still claimed the state.

Splendor had beauty and majestic landscapes found nowhere else. Yet it occupied a space at the far north of the country, in a land of little civilization and slow growth. It did have something Texas didn't—Rachel.

He'd fallen in love with her—doubt no longer existed in his mind. If they sold the ranch, could he leave her behind? He thought not.

She had become anchored in Splendor, and he didn't believe his life could ever be content in this small town. Dax saw no prospect of changing their separate journeys. His heart squeezed at the realization they faced an insurmountable impasse.

His raised his mouth from hers and gazed into her eyes, knowing Rachel had been right in her reluctance to continue seeing him. To continue would only result in more pain—for each of them. Dax hated the decision he believed with all his being he must make. His arms dropped to his side and he stepped back, resting his forehead against hers before placing a kiss on the tip of her nose.

"Would you mind making us coffee?" He needed space, distance from her before he did something they both would regret. From her body's response to his, he had little doubt she'd let him take her, and that would be the worst situation for them both. No, he had to keep his distance, remove the temptation, and find a way to break the hold she had over him. He needed to fall out of love with Rachel.

On a slow sigh, Rachel pulled herself free from the intense emotions of Dax's touch. "You're right. We could both use coffee, and I'm certain Uncle Charles will wake soon." She could still feel herself vibrating from the feel of her body aligned with his. He'd taken his time, exploring her mouth, creating a heat like nothing she'd ever felt. She wanted more, much more from Dax Pelletier.

He watched Rachel with hooded eyes, wondering what she was thinking and knowing he had to tell her his thoughts. He felt as if he was being torn in two. One part wanted to own her, keep her with him always. Another sought a life far away from the woman who'd found comfort in the small town of Splendor. His customary self-control eluded him when she was near. He feared their fierce attraction would eventually break his restraint, creating a situation resulting in him having no choice. And Dax needed the ability to choose.

He stared down at Bull, wondering if he'd make it. Although he'd had a good night, there were still no guarantees. Dax had been warned more than once about getting to close to his men. Forming attachments in time of war could affect an officer's ability to lead. He felt the same now. He'd already grown close to those at the ranch. It had to stop.

Today, he, Luke, and Gabe would ride out to see Tolbert and confront the man. In Dax's mind, only one rancher would dare send men to harm those around him, and Dax meant to put a stop to it.

"Is your father at home?" Dax asked Abigail as he stood with Luke, Gabe, and Noah outside Tolbert's front door. Noah had stayed out of the town's problems since he'd arrived, yet the growing belief Abigail's father might be involved in ordering other men killed had gotten his attention. He needed to hear what Tolbert had to say for himself.

"Yes, he is, Mr. Pelletier. Please come in and I'll get him for you." Abigail stood aside as each of the men filed past, noticing Noah made fleeting eye contact as he entered, offering none of his usual warmth or smile. As she stared at his back, it hit her how much his lack of attention hurt.

She tapped on the study door and entered, not waiting for him to respond. "Father, there are some men here to see you."

"Who are they, Abby?"

"The Pelletiers, Mr. Evans, and Mr. Brandt."

"Four of them. Well, I won't keep them waiting."

He entered the parlor and offered his hand to Dax, who ignored it. "We need to speak with you, Tolbert. In private."

"Of course." He ushered them into his study. "How about something to drink, gentlemen?"

Dax disregarded the offer. "Did you order your men onto our land?"

King studied the four men, knowing this visit had bigger implications than checking cattle movements. "Yes. I asked Drake to see if the rumors of you purchasing more cattle were true. I understand they are."

"You could have asked Luke or me. We would've told you."

"I'll note that for the future. Is there anything else?"

"Did you also order them to kill?"

King's eyes blazed at the question. "Of course not. I'd never order the shooting or killing of a man."

"Then someone on your ranch went beyond your order to check on cattle and shot at us, critically injuring Bull." Dax walked up to within inches of Tolbert, glaring into the older man's eyes, sending a not-so-veiled threat. "We want those responsible. No more games, and don't take this as idle conversation. There will be a

200

major battle between us if you don't give us whoever shot Bull."

"So you can lynch him without a trial?"

"No, so we can take him to Big Pine to wait for the territorial judge. They'll be no lynching in Splendor, but we *will* have justice." Dax spat the words out, his hostile features leaving no doubt of the fury he felt about the attacks on the ranch and Bull.

Tolbert didn't let Dax's rage sway him. "I won't turn anyone over to you until there is proof one of my men pulled the trigger. Do you have proof?"

"You told us you ordered your men onto our land the day of the shooting. Are you telling me there are others who'd go to the lengths you would to secure more land?"

"I have no idea to what you're referring. Yes, I'm interested in more land, and I'd pay a fair price for yours. As a businessman, I also keep track of what my fellow ranchers are doing. You purchasing more cattle interests me, as I'm sure it would you if the situation were reversed. However, I don't condone violence to get what I want. Now, if you have no proof, I'll ask you to leave. If you find something that implicates my men, which is doubtful, show it to me. As I've told you, I've never ordered anyone shot, on your land or anywhere else." He walked to the door and pulled it open. "I'm certain you can find your way out."

"Make no mistake, Tolbert. We *will* find the proof we need, and when we do, we'll expect those guilty to be handed over." Dax's even tone and measured steps belied the rage he felt toward the rancher and his band of thugs. They'd find the proof and God have mercy on those responsible.

They'd ridden from Tolbert's ranch to Splendor, where Dax took a few minutes to check on Bull while the others went straight to Horace Clausen's office at the bank.

"We need to talk," Gabe told Clausen once Dax joined them.

"Is this about bank business?"

"No. Town business."

"Then I'd like to send Mrs. Phelps for Stan Petermann, Amos Henderson, the doc, and Bernie Griggs. Unless you have an objection."

"Not at all."

It didn't take long for the office to fill with the town leaders, everyone except Charles Worthington, who begged off to keep watch on Bull while Rachel got some much needed rest. All wondered at the summons from Clausen.

"Dax, why don't you tell them what happened?" Gabe asked.

Twenty minutes later, the calm atmosphere had turned solemn as the men assimilated the new threats.

"What do you suggest we do?" Stan Petermann asked.

"First, keep watch on everyone and everything going on in and around Splendor," Dax said. "The four of us will talk with ranchers closest to town, let them know of the shooting and potential threats. You need to escalate the search for a sheriff. There's only so much we can do as citizens. There needs to be an official lawman. Someone who won't cower under men such as Tolbert."

"I'm not sure what else we can do," Clausen said. "We've sent telegrams, asked anyone with experience to come forward, and approved a generous wage. You went with Doc Worthington when he traveled to Big Pine, Dax, and know he came back with little encouragement. There've been no takers." He removed his spectacles and pinched the bridge of his nose between a thumb and index finger.

"I can't blame anyone for not wanting the job, especially since the last sheriff was murdered," Amos Henderson said and leaned forward, placing his arms on his knees.

The businessmen began to murmur amongst themselves, their conversations escalating as their fear intensified. They knew the threats were not just against the Pelletiers. Anyone going against Dax, Luke, and their armed men wouldn't hesitate to go after citizens with little ability to defend themselves.

"But I don't know anyone west of here, Horace," Stan said in a heated tone. "Just because I passed through some towns doesn't mean I met anyone who'd be interested in the job."

"We could send word to Denver and a few other towns, see if someone's interested."

"We've already done that, Amos, without any success." Stan pulled a handkerchief from his pocket to wipe his damp forehead. "What a fix. Who'd have ever thought we couldn't find anyone to protect Splendor."

"There must be someone," Bernie Griggs said, frustration obvious by the exasperation in his voice.

A tense silence enveloped the room as each man pondered the consequences of not locating a lawman to protect the citizens.

"Ah, hell. I'll do it."

Noah turned to Gabe. "What?"

"I said I'll do it." Gabe's voice rose so there'd be no doubt of what he meant. "But on a temporary basis, until this mess is cleaned up or you find a permanent sheriff. Then I'm gone."

Luke and Dax exchanged looks, neither believing Gabe would make the offer. He'd been firm on his refusal, even when they asked him again on the ride from Tolbert's ranch to town.

Horace didn't waste another moment. He yanked open a desk drawer, pulled out a piece of paper, administered the oath, and handed Gabe the badge. "Sheriff Evans, welcome to Splendor."

"Do not get it into your head I'm staying. This job is temporary, until the town finds someone else or the problems with Tolbert are resolved." Gabe shoveled supper into his mouth, still wondering why he'd volunteered. He had no intention of taking the job or staying in the tiny hovel Noah called home.

Gabe had grown up in New York. His mother, father, and brothers still lived there in big homes with servants, barely touched by the war and its destruction. When the fighting ended, he hadn't been prepared to return. He needed time to clear his head and reconcile his confusion over the last few years. Gabe liked the big city, flourished in it and, unlike Dax and Luke, he knew he'd return.

"Whatever you want. It's your choice."

Gabe grunted in reply.

Noah took a sip of strong coffee, then cradled his cup in both hands. He'd been as stunned as everyone else at Gabe's announcement, hopeful his friend would offer, yet not anticipating it.

"You interested in being a deputy?"

"Hell no. The livery keeps me plenty busy. Anyway, you already know you can count on me. I don't need a badge for that."

"More coffee, gentlemen?" Suzanne topped off their cups when each nodded. "So I hear you're our new sheriff. Congratulations."

"It's temporary, Mrs. Briar. Don't count on me being around for supper the rest of my life."

"Oh, certainly not. I expect you'll meet some pretty young woman, marry her, and settle for good in Splendor. Raise a passel of children." She winked at Noah, who returned a thin smile.

"Only when the earth freezes over, Mrs. Briar, and not before."

"Well, you know that's likely to happen here in Montana. You'd better watch what you say." She turned her attention to other customers.

"She does have a point, Gabe."

"And what point is that?"

"You never know what will happen. You might meet the perfect woman and settle right here in cow-town Montana."

Gabe shook his head, stood, and reached into his pocket for some bills, throwing them down on the table before turning toward the door. "I'm headed to the Rose for a drink. You want one?"

"Why not?"

The two walked toward the saloon, hearing the piano music and muted laughter before they'd reached the swinging doors. No one spared them a glance as they took a seat at a table against the wall.

"What can I get you two gentlemen?"

Gabe looked up into the softest green eyes he'd ever seen and a pretty face framed with golden brown curls. He cleared his throat. "A whiskey, ma'am."

"The same for me, Ginny."

"Sure, Noah. Two whiskeys."

Gabe kept his eyes riveted on her as she walked toward the bar and ordered their drinks.

"She's new," Noah said when Gabe kept staring.

"What?"

"Ginny. She got into town a couple of weeks ago. Came in with the settlers, along with her young sister. Don't get any ideas, though. She's strictly a server and nothing else."

206

Gabe dragged his eyes away as she turned back toward their table. He had no intention of getting ideas about any woman, least not one in Splendor. He intended to spend no more time than needed to help out the town, then he'd move on to Denver.

"Here you are. Let me know if you want anything else."

Noah saluted Gabe before taking a sip of the amber liquid, letting the warmth trickle down his throat and pool in his belly. Gabe did the same and signaled Ginny to bring them a bottle.

"Why do you stay?"

Noah knew what his friend asked. They'd been close since they were kids, even though Noah's family had lived from one paycheck to another, working for Gabe's father. They'd enlisted in the Union army together and, over time, Gabe had risen to the rank of colonel, while Noah had been promoted to major. Their skills were different—Gabe a natural leader, Noah an extraordinary sharpshooter. They'd planned to return to New York after the war, perhaps go into business together. It hadn't worked out, at least not yet.

"I've got my reasons." Noah reached for the bottle and poured another glass.

Although Gabe understood the tragic event that plagued his friend, the one that had changed him and almost destroyed his soul, he also knew the person behind the self-condemnation. Noah had the biggest heart of anyone Gabe had ever known. He'd always planned to marry, have a family, and build a business. Now he found contentment in solitude and working with his hands. Over time, Noah's unreserved nature had deteriorated into a cloak of loathing at what he'd done. Gabe tightened his resolve, determined to find a way to pull his friend out of it.

"Come with me when I leave. We'll start a business in Denver or someplace in California. Maybe we'll even go back home and do what we planned before the war. Give ourselves a fresh start."

Noah remained silent, his eyes neutral, rolling the shot glass between his fingers.

Gabe slammed back one more drink, then placed his empty glass on the table and stood. "Think about it."

"You need rest, Dax. There's no need for you to keep watch over him." Rachel rested a hand on Dax's shoulder, finding her own comfort in the brief contact. He'd been there since after his meeting at the bank and Gabe's announcement he'd take the sheriff job. She looked down at Bull, whose breathing was slow and measured. He hadn't stirred in hours. "We'll send word when there's a change."

Dax looked up from where he sat, knowing Rachel's words made sense, yet unable to leave the injured man. He understood the dangers and bloodshed faced as a Texas Ranger and had witnessed the unimaginable during the war. It hadn't occurred to him a war of a different kind waited for Luke and him when they brought Pat's body home. He stood and picked up his hat.

"You're right. I'm not doing Bull any good by sitting and waiting." He started for the door, then turned back and grabbed Rachel's hand. "Walk outside with me."

She glanced at Bull to make sure he hadn't stirred. "All right. For just a moment."

The late night air chilled against her skin as she allowed Dax to take her hand and guide her toward his horse. She loved the feel of his warm, calloused hand, and wondered how it would feel against her body. The thought prompted a slight shudder as heat rose up her neck and face. He stopped in the shadows and pulled her to him, grasped her shoulders, and lowered his head.

She'd anticipated this, yearned for it. His lips felt warm and firm as they brushed across hers, then claimed her mouth in a demanding kiss. She felt his hand move from her shoulders to splay across her back and pull her close. The feel of his strong, hard chest and continued kisses elicited intense sensations beyond anything she ever expected. A throbbing urgency shot through her body and she longed to get closer. She wanted more and wrapped her arms around his neck, one hand holding his head, the other caressing a shoulder.

Rachel felt the wood siding of the building as Dax inched her further back into the shadows, never breaking contact of his lips with hers.

He trailed hot kisses down her neck, then up to nibble at the sensitive area below her ear, causing a moan of pleasure. He pulled back an inch, waiting for her eyes to open and meet his. What he saw in them stopped his heart and terrorized him all at once. Her feelings for him were clearly visible in her glazed eyes—eyes that searched his, looking for understanding and perhaps something he'd be unable to give.

He stepped back and took a deep breath before saying what he knew would change everything between them. "I've made the decision to leave Splendor, Rachel. As soon as the ranch sells or Luke buys me out, I'm riding back to Texas." The pain in her eyes ripped at his heart, causing his stomach to clench and his throat to tighten.

She moved away and straightened her dress, smoothing it down her hips. Her eyes fixated on her hands, now clasped tightly in front of her. After what had been happening between them, the intimate kisses and shared feelings, his announcement caught her by surprise.

"And this?"

Dax understood her confusion and felt horrible for making the break more difficult. He'd meant for it to be a quick kiss, something they'd both remember. Instead, it had exploded into an unanticipated, passionate embrace, leaving him reeling. He glanced away before locking his gaze back on her.

"I'm sorry, Rachel. When I'm with you, it seems all good sense leaves me."

She continued to stare at him, disbelief and anger replacing the passion of moments before.

"You were right. Being with you makes the inevitable worse. You're a part of Splendor, and

I'm an outsider. No matter how I try to make myself think otherwise, I know it won't happen."

"I see." She moistened her lips, struggling to find a way to hide the extreme ache and disappointment she felt at his words. The reality he'd made his decision slammed into Rachel, stripping away her breath and paralyzing any attempt at further speech. If she tried to speak, she knew tears would flow and she absolutely refused to cry over this man. She slipped closer to the clinic door and reached for the handle, grasping it tight as if it could provide her the strength she needed, and turned the knob.

"Rachel, wait." Dax reached for her, but she stepped further away and into the open doorway. She stopped and turned toward him, waiting.

He pulled off his hat and ran a hand through is hair, searching for the right words, words that would make her understand his need to build a life outside of Splendor.

"This, a ranch in Montana, isn't what I'd planned or wanted. We came as a promise to a friend, with no intention of staying." His strained voice vibrated with tension and regret. "Meeting you..." His voice trailed off as he moved toward her. "You weren't supposed to happen."

Rachel's chest tightened, making it hard for her to breathe. She had no idea where her words came from as her chin jutted out and her eyes, firm and intent, held his. "I understand. This town is a mere stop on your journey, as am I." She backed up, obscuring her damp, pain-filled eyes in the darkness of the clinic. "I'll keep you no longer."

The door closed and Dax heard the lock click. It sounded as final as the ache in his heart he feared would haunt him well beyond his return to Texas.

Chapter Thirteen

Luke paused in his work of cleaning his horse's hooves as a lone rider approached. Gabe Evans had visited twice in the last four days. He hadn't expected to return today, and Luke's stomach tightened at the prospect he may be relaying news about Bull. He dropped Prince's hoof and straightened.

"Gabe. Didn't expect to see you here today."

"It's Bull." The sheriff slid off Blackheart and walked the few feet to stand in front of Luke. "He's awake, yelling for someone to get him back to the ranch." A smile split Gabe's face. "That boy is a handful when he gets agitated."

Luke couldn't contain the breath he'd been holding and let it escape in a whoosh. "I guess we'd better help the doc and Rachel out. Get our cowboy off their hands." He returned Gabe's grin and motioned for him to follow. "Let's tell Dax."

Luke opened the door to the study where Dax stood, staring down at some papers on the desk.

"Great news. Bull's doing well and he's ready to come home." Luke walked around the desk and looked over his shoulder. "What do you have there?"

Dax glanced up and nodded at Gabe, but didn't reply to Luke. He folded the papers and shoved them in a pocket. "That is good news. Why don't you take a couple of the boys and a

213

wagon to pick him up? I'm sure the doc is more than ready to get him out of there."

Luke's narrowed gaze focused on his brother. "I thought you'd want to go. You know, see Rachel. You haven't been to town in several days."

"No. You'll have to go without me. I've some things I need to finish up here."

Luke didn't budge. Dax's mood had deteriorated every day since the last time he'd visited Bull. The brusque behavior and almost dismissive attitude weren't unusual, except Luke suspected it had more to do with Rachel than anything else this time. He turned to Gabe.

"I'll be right out. I need to speak with Dax about something."

Gabe turned and walked back outside.

"Do you want to tell me what's going on? And don't say nothing because I'll know it's a lie." Luke crossed his arms over his chest and planted his feet shoulder width apart.

Dax slumped into a chair and leaned back, glancing out the window toward the barn where Gabe stood talking to Ellis and Rude. He shifted his gaze to Luke.

"I plan to head back to Texas as soon as the ranch business is handled. The plans I made are there, not here."

Luke had been prepared for something, but not the announcement his brother would be leaving. "And when were you going to tell me?"

Dax saw the anger begin to form on his brother's face, and he regretted his procrastination in letting Luke know his plans.

"Today." He pulled the papers out of his pocket and threw them on the desk. "These sell my rights in the ranch to you for one dollar. You pay a dollar, we both sign, the ranch is yours. Simple and clean."

Luke didn't speak. He walked to the cupboard and pulled out a bottle of whiskey. He downed one glass, then poured another before facing Dax.

"That's crap and you know it. First, you want to turn everything in Savannah over to me and ride out alone. That didn't happen. Now you want to do the same with the ranch." He finished his whiskey, stomped to the desk, and slammed the glass down, creating a scar in the wood from the impact. "The same applies here. It's not going to happen. I'm not buying you out, not even for a measly dollar. Whatever is under your skin, you damn well better work it out because I'm not giving you what you want."

Luke cursed under his breath, pushed his hat on his head, and stormed from the house.

Dax watched him leave. He couldn't remember the last time he'd seen Luke this angry. He scooped up Luke's glass, filled it to the brim, and downed the whiskey in one gulp, taking a measured breath as the liquid burned its way down his throat. He began to pour another, then stopped and slumped into a chair, resting his head on the back and staring at the ceiling.

Hell, why didn't anyone understand his life lay in Texas? Not Montana, not Savannah, and not anywhere he'd be responsible for people's lives—and deaths. Watching Bull hover between life and death convinced Dax his desire to walk away from being responsible for others was the right decision. He wanted a simple life, where his decisions and orders to others were few. For now, his work as a Ranger suited him fine.

Maybe he'd buy a home outside of Austin. A small place with one ranch hand and nothing more. Someone who knew the job, asked few questions, and required little guidance. A man he didn't have to lead.

"Hell," he murmured under his breath. He stood to look outside as Luke and a couple of men left with Gabe and the wagon. His natural instincts urged him to lead the charge, set the direction, and march toward his goal without hesitating. But now, at this point, he felt bone tired with the weight of too many commands and tough decisions, over too many years, pressing down on him. He needed time, a respite from being at the front, from being the man everyone looked to for direction and guidance.

"Dax?"

He jerked at Bernice's voice and turned to see her holding out a cup of coffee to him.

"Hank would like to speak with you, if you have time."

Dax took the cup and walked toward the kitchen, sitting next to the ranch manager. Hank had started working full days the week before and already seemed like a different man. Being cooped up too long could work on a man in a bad way.

"I hear Bull's doing better, ready to come home." Hank glanced at Bernice and caught her slight nod.

"That's right. No doubt you saw Luke, Ellis, and Rude ride out with the wagon. Now we'll be the ones to put up with his nasty temper until he heals." Dax sipped his coffee and waited for Hank to say what was on his mind.

Bernice pulled out a chair and sat next to her husband, putting a hand over his. Warning bells rang in Dax's head, yet he continued to stay silent.

"You know, we've been here a long time. First with Pat, now you and Luke. It's been good, Dax, real good, but Bernice and I, well...we think it's time we moved on."

Dax set his cup down and leaned his arms on the table, staring into Hank's eyes and seeing the man's struggle. He knew they'd lost their only child to cholera years before. They had no other family, no grandchildren to visit, and he wondered at the real motivation to leave.

"Is it the pay?"

"No, the pay is good. The house you provide is fine. You and Luke are more than fair. No complaints about anything. We're not getting any younger, and this last bout with a bullet wound took a lot out of me."

Bernice squeezed Hank's hand. "You and Luke are fine people and that makes the decision hard. Truth is, we're ready for some peace. Find a place where Hank can fish, and I can catch up on my sewing."

"I can't fault you for wanting to slow down, enjoy yourselves. How old are you, Hank? Forty, forty-five?"

Hank snorted. "I've got a couple years before I reach fifty."

"Fifty, huh? That means you'll most likely be around another twenty years or so, right?"

"Maybe…" Hank's voice held a cautious tone.

"And you're going to fish every day for the next twenty years? Sitting on the bank alone, praying for a bite and reminiscing about all the things you did before?"

"Well, I'm sure there'll be other chores. You know, stuff Bernice needs done."

The hesitancy Dax heard in Hank's voice and the way Bernice squirmed in her seat made him wonder if this might be more about Bernice than Hank. She sat up nights, sent unending prayers, and worked tirelessly to keep Hank comfortable after the shooting. Her concern and care had touched everyone.

"You know, there might be other choices." Dax let the sentence hang. He could see Hank's throat working, as if he wanted to say something, but held back. "You could do work around here which wouldn't require riding out with the herd, managing the men."

Hank shot a quick look to Bernice and leaned forward. "Like what?"

"It's no secret Luke and I have talked about expanding the ranch. We've already added to the herd from what we bought off the Murtons. We can see the place doubling in a year, then doubling each year afterwards. Luke's good with business, planning our next steps, but hates keeping the books. I'm better with hiring the men, getting them to do the right work when needed."

He stopped to listen to himself. Isn't that exactly why he'd made the decision to leave? He shook his head and continued, "We need someone to handle the supplies, do the books, and keep us on track with the money. That should still leave you plenty of time to fish." He looked at Bernice. "The boys can take care of their noon meal, but they need breakfast and supper. That will free you up to do your sewing."

"I can't do that." Bernice threw him a disbelieving look, challenging him to argue. "Those boys need three hot meals a day, unless they're out on the trail. I can't just give 'em two."

Dax fought a smile at her offended tone. "I'm saying we can make some changes around here that I believe might work for you. Besides, we all know you aren't going to find any better fishing than what's right here on the ranch."

"I can't take the same pay for doing the books and keeping the supplies current." Hank's disgruntled voice came through real clear.

"What would you say is fair?"

"We stay in the back house. I get half the pay and Bernice gets two-thirds pay. She gets weekends off and does those boy's laundry once a week. That's a good offer."

Dax reached a hand across the table. "Done."

Hank clasped his hand and sealed their bargain.

"I guess I'd better get back to my work. You've made a good decision." Dax walked out, glad to have the matter settled. Now he needed to finalize a few more issues with Luke, then he'd be off to Texas.

Doc Worthington helped Bull into a clean shirt Rachel had found in a drawer. It barely fit the bulky cowboy, but it looked a whole lot better than the shirt he'd been wearing when he arrived.

"You need some help, Bull?" Luke offered and started to reach for the front buttons.

Bull slapped his hands away. "I got it. I'm not helpless."

Ellis and Rude masked their amusement, each glad to see him grumbling and carrying on as before.

Rachel stood back, watching Luke and wondering if she should ask after Dax. She hadn't seen him since the night he'd told her she held no place in his future. Each time she remembered his words, the pain in her chest flared, then settled near her heart. She knew it would lessen over time—all wounds did. What hurt most was her belief she'd meant something to him, yet he'd shown no signs of it when he'd told her of his plans to leave. She believed if Dax held any feelings for her, he would've asked her to join him. He didn't and, of course, she probably would have refused. Her uncle needed her here, in the clinic that had become his life. Regardless, it would've been nice to hear the words. At least she'd know he felt something for her and hadn't just been passing the time during his stay in Splendor. She slumped against a nearby wall, feeling the pain tighten across her chest once again.

"It seems I'm always thanking you. For me, for Hank, and now for Bull. I don't know what the town would do without you." Luke stood close by, his eyes studying her face. He knew it wasn't his place, but the pain he saw in her eyes wiped away the caution. "He told you he's leaving, didn't he?"

"Yes," she breathed out. "As soon as he settles the details with you."

"Ah, the details. I wouldn't count on us working out anything soon. We have many details to discuss."

Luke could see the pain pass over her face and anger surged through him. He loved his brother, would risk his life for him, but he knew Dax was making a huge mistake. Luke had choices, too, and he'd decided the world would freeze over before he bought Dax out and allowed him to dump everything, including Rachel Davenport.

"You ready, boss?" Ellis asked. They had begun to help Bull up, Rude under one arm and Ellis under another.

"I'm not helpless." Bull swore under his breath as his legs almost gave out under him.

"Now you just concentrate on moving one foot in front of the other, boy. Rude and I will do our part so you don't topple over." Ellis's breath already came in labored gasps as he took on more of Bull's substantial weight. "You get the door, boss."

It took a little while before Bull lay in the wagon, a blanket pulled up to his chest. Luke climbed up and glanced behind him. "You okay back there?"

"I'm fine. Let's get out of here."

"Thanks, Doc. You and Rachel worked a miracle." Luke slapped the reins.

Rachel stood on the wood walkway and watched the wagon disappear around the bend. She thought of Luke's words and wondered if there might be more to Dax's leaving than either man had said.

Luke didn't sound pleased with his brother's decision, which didn't surprise her. From what she'd seen, they were close. Too close for Dax to leave Luke behind. Perhaps the man she'd fallen in love with might be stuck in Splendor a little while longer.

"Where are you headed?" Dax took in Luke's shiny boots and slicked back hair. The look reminded him of the nights before the war when his brother used to attend one social event after another.

"To supper and the Rose." Luke spared Dax a cursory look. "You're welcome to join me."

"You eating alone?"

"No."

Dax's gaze leveled on Luke. "That so? And who's joining you?"

222

"Miss Davenport." Luke didn't turn his head or give any indication he believed the announcement of his supper partner would cause a stir. Out of the corner of his eye, he saw Dax stand and walk toward him in slow, measured steps. He turned a fraction to see Dax's fierce stare bore into him.

"You asked Rachel and she agreed?" His voice vibrated with anger directed at Luke, at Rachel, and himself.

"She did."

Dax strode away, arms slack at his sides, trying to understand why it affected him so. He'd made his decision, been upfront about his intentions, and walked away from Rachel. Although they'd never made any kind of commitment, never spoken of love, Dax felt the pain as much as he'd feel a bullet to his chest.

"Join us. You don't need to stay here alone." Luke walked up beside him. "It isn't as if I'm courting her. It's supper, nothing more. Afterwards, we'll walk her home, then go to the Rose, have a few drinks, and play cards."

The offer tempted Dax. He'd thought of little else except Rachel for the last few days. He tried to convince himself he'd made the right decision and his interest in her would pass once he left Splendor. It wouldn't take long for Rachel to realize his decision was for the best and move on. With her intelligence, beauty, and kind heart, some good-looking cowboy would scoop her up in no time. His body bristled at the thought. He swallowed a lump in his throat and tried to convince himself what he felt for her couldn't have been love. He wanted and desired her more than any women he'd ever met. Love took time, grew over the years—didn't it? It had been a few short months. If it wasn't love, why couldn't he rid her from his thoughts and purge her image from his mind?

"You go ahead. Enjoy yourself and try to make it home sober." Dax clasped Luke on the shoulder and turned away.

"You look stunning." He shouldn't have been surprised. Rachel darn near took his breath away. She wore a blue evening dress and styled her hair to rival any east coast beauty.

"Why, thank you, Luke. Come in for a minute. I'm serving up my uncle's supper." She turned toward the kitchen, while Luke made himself comfortable in the front room.

"Hello, Luke. How's Bull doing?" Charles walked from the back and shook his guest's hand.

"He's a beast."

Charles laughed and took a seat.

"I mean it. He's a real bear. Gripes all the time, won't let anyone help him, and insists he can do everything himself. Hank caught him in the barn yesterday and you should've heard the yelling."

"Who won?"

"Hank." Luke smiled as the vision of Bull sulking back to the bunkhouse and slamming the door flashed across his mind.

"Are you ready?" Rachel asked as she set her uncle's supper on the table.

"I sure am." Luke's eyes roamed over Rachel and he silently cursed his brother for being such a fool. It would serve Dax right if someone came along and snatched her up before he came to his senses.

They made their way down the street, the sun still glowing over the tips of the nearby mountains. Rachel waved at a few people finishing up their day. She saw light coming from the livery and knew Noah Brandt hadn't stopped working.

"That man never rests."

"Who?"

"Noah Brandt. He starts his day before anyone else is up and works late, way beyond most of us. There's something about him..." Her voice trailed off as she thought of the man everyone saw as a mystery.

"Are you interested in him?"

"Me? No, not in the way you mean. He's so private, yet one of the nicest men you'll ever meet—if he'll open up and talk with you."

Luke let the information settle in. He knew Gabe and Noah were close, yet he'd met Noah just a couple times. Once when they'd visited King Tolbert. He'd been silent as he took in every word during the meeting, his sharp eyes missing nothing. Luke agreed with Rachel. There was a lot more to Noah than he wanted people to see.

"Here we are." He opened the door to Suzanne's restaurant and followed Rachel inside.

"Good evening. Follow me." Suzanne led them to a table by the window. "Where's your brother?"

"Sulking at home. I invited him to come along."

"What a shame, a good-looking man like him alone." She shot a quick glance at Rachel, who averted her eyes.

They got settled, ordered the night's special, and looked out the window toward the glow of the fire in the livery.

"You said you invited Dax to come. He refused?" Rachel had tried not to ask, but her good sense surrendered to the pull of her curiosity.

"He didn't refuse as much as decline." Luke told himself he didn't want to get in the middle of whatever had happened between the two of them, yet the sadness in her voice wrestled with his restraint. "I'm not sure what's going on with him. There's something weighing on him, dragging him down, but he won't talk about it."

"He told me his life is in Texas, not here. Sounds pretty simple to me."

Luke thought about it a moment, believing the cause to be more complex. He chose not to share his concerns with Rachel right now. "You may be right. It could be a simple desire to live somewhere else."

Two hours later, he walked her home, recognizing how much he'd missed going out with a lady. It had been quite a while since he'd cleaned himself up and spent an evening discussing whatever came to mind with a beautiful woman, not worrying about the next battle or what outlaw may be coming up behind him.

"Thanks so much for this evening, Luke. I had a wonderful time."

"The pleasure's mine, Rachel." He made a slight bow, then cast her a vague smile before turning to leave. "Don't give up on him. He hasn't left yet."

Rachel stayed by the door and watched him leave, his last words playing over and over in her mind. No, Dax *hadn't* left. He still had to work out the details with Luke or find another buyer for his half of the ranch. That didn't mean he wouldn't leave. Rachel had thought about Dax day and night, lying awake in bed while trying to find a way to rid him from her mind. She'd come to accept that no amount of hope would get him to stay. He'd fixed his sights on Texas, a vast state with unlimited opportunities. This small town in Montana couldn't be more different than the big southern state on the border of Mexico.

No, Dax Pelletier would never be a true part of Splendor, never claim the town as his own, never be happy with someone like her. He'd arrive and leave as most did—seeking a dream hundreds of miles away where she held no place.

Chapter Fourteen

Big Pine, Montana

"We'll stay here tonight." Duff Mayes slid off his horse, casting a look at his brother and cousins before walking up the steps toward the hotel in Big Pine. "I need a bath and food. Then a drink." He nodded toward the saloon next door.

"How long are we staying?" Whitey Mayes had grown increasingly frustrated over the two weeks it had taken them to reach Montana. He wanted to reach Splendor, kill the Pelletier brothers, and get back to their Texas ranch. The trip had already taken up too much time.

"We'll leave in a couple days. Splendor should be a day's ride from here."

"Why wait? We need to get this over with."

The glare Whitey shot his older brother had no impact on Duff. Over the years, he'd learned to ignore most of Whitey's ramblings. They used to come to blows over them. Now he let him fume.

"I want to talk with the sheriff, maybe a few others, and find out if anyone has heard of the Pelletiers. We need to know what we're riding into." He continued through the entrance toward the front desk and ordered rooms.

228

Duff signed his name in the register, threw a couple of bills on the desk, then glanced at the clerk. "Big Pine have a sheriff?"

"We're the territorial capital. Of course we have a sheriff. Parker Sterling." He pointed down the street in the direction of the jail.

"Thanks." Duff grabbed his saddlebag and started up the stairs, tired and as ready as Whitey to get this over with and head home. What worried him, caused him to be more cautious than normal, had everything to do with what he'd learned about the two Texas Rangers they hunted. It didn't seem to matter to his brother that both were ex-Confederate officers and had excellent reputations as Rangers, even though they'd been with the agency a short time.

The three Mayes and three Olin brothers had been robbing banks for close to two years, and up until Duff had been shot in the leg months before, no one had been injured. In fact, no one had gotten close to tracking them toward their ranch. The robbery in Red Gulch changed everything, leaving the youngest Mayes brother dead. The one difference between that robbery and the others was Hanes and the Pelletiers.

Whitey told Duff the Rangers didn't give up like the others, even though the outlaws had set up numerous false trails to throw them off. Each time the gang believed they'd lost them, the lawmen would show up on their trail within hours. It had been the first time they'd been tracked by the three Rangers. Whitey believed the lawmen had gotten lucky. Duff thought not. He figured the brothers were more accomplished, with more skills than the lawmen they'd encountered in the past.

Whitey grabbed Duff's arm, stopping him before he could enter his room. "We should get out of here tomorrow. Talk with the sheriff, then leave." Whitey looked behind him, making certain they were alone. "Something's not right. We're being tracked. I can feel it."

Duff pulled him inside and closed the door. "You're imagining it. We've seen no one, no signs we're being followed."

"And there may not be any until it's too late. I'm telling you, someone is hunting us the same way we're hunting those Rangers."

Duff threw his saddlebags on the bed and turned back to Whitey. "Don't you think I know there are posters out on us? Anyone could pick one up and come after us. But we've seen no one. Besides, who's going to follow us all the way north to Montana?"

"There are some men who would."

"Few who'd give up other opportunities to track us all the way up here." Duff sat on the bed and rubbed the leg, which had never healed, grimacing at the pain a day in the saddle caused. He knew his brother had good instincts, a skill he'd used to save them more than once. If his leg didn't hurt so bad, Duff might have been more inclined to focus on Whitey's comments. But he needed time for the pain to subside before climbing back on his horse.

"We'll get out of here after I speak with the sheriff tomorrow, and not before. We're a day's ride from finding who we're after, and nothing will change before then. I'm going to grab some food and a few drinks. You can come along or stay here. It makes no difference to me."

Whitey looked out the window to the road below. Seeing nothing, he dropped the curtain and looked at his brother. "We're making a mistake not getting this over with quick."

"It'll be done soon, but it will be done *my* way."

Whitey watched Duff leave, knowing nothing good would come from continuing to put off the inevitable.

Splendor, Montana

"What are you drinking?" Al, the Wild Rose bartender, asked.

"Whiskey." Luke leaned against the bar, eyes locked on the saloon girl who passed among the tables. He'd noticed her clothes and hair right off. She wore a simple calico dress and had pulled her golden brown hair into a bun with soft ringlets escaping to frame her face. He'd had drinks at the Rose several times since arriving in Splendor and had never seen her.

"Who's the new girl?" Luke asked as Al set down his drink.

"Ginny. She arrived in town a few weeks ago with her little sister. They came in with the settlers and decided to stay." Al chuckled when he noticed the look of appreciation on Luke's face. "She's a server a few nights a week. No upstairs business with her."

Luke glanced at Al, then back at Ginny. "Guess I might want to introduce myself to your new server." He grabbed his glass and found a seat, ignoring an empty chair at one of the card tables. She came by as he'd finished off the last of his drink.

"May I get you another?"

He tilted the chair, balancing on the back two legs, and let his gaze drift up to her. "I don't believe we've met. I'm Luke Pelletier."

Her easy smile stalled at the wide grin he gave her. "Hello, Mr. Pelletier. I'm Ginny."

"Ginny, it's nice to meet you. Al says you're new to Splendor."

She worried her lower lip and looked at Al. His nod told her it would be all right to speak with him. "Yes. My sister and I have been here a few weeks. Can I get you a drink?"

Luke let his other questions wait, knowing there'd be plenty of time to get to know more about the pretty young woman. "A whiskey, please."

He watched her avoid a couple of cowboys on her way to the bar. He thought she couldn't be older than seventeen, and wondered about her sister, where they lived, and what happened to their parents.

"Here you are." Ginny set down the glass. "Let me know if you need anything else."

"I will, Ginny. Thanks." He wrapped fingers around the glass and studied the golden liquid before bringing it to his lips. His eyes wandered back to the pretty server standing at the bar, talking with Al. He wondered about her. Why did she have to support her younger sister? Where were their parents? What was she doing working in a saloon? Luke made the decision to find out more about the intriguing newcomer.

"You wanted to see me, boss?" Drake strolled into King Tolbert's study, shut the door, then folded his arms and leaned against it. The ranch had been quiet since the shooting of the Pelletier ranch hand. He'd lived, but the wrath from Tolbert had been significant. Drake knew his boss believed there might be some truth to the Pelletiers' accusation. Drake had ordered his men to stay out of King's way and not create any trouble. Those who didn't would answer to him.

King looked up, then set his pen down and stood. "I need to make changes. We're going to cut some of the men loose. Most are from the group you brought in or hired." He crossed his arms and leaned against his desk. "I'm keeping all the men I hired. I've prepared a list of the men I don't need." He turned to pick up a paper behind him, but didn't offer it to Drake.

Drake had wondered when King would trim the number of ranch hands. He knew that when it happened, his men would be the first to go. There were a few he'd like to cut loose himself, but others needed to stay. They'd been with him since his departure from the Confederate Army. He owed them.

"I'd like to see it."

"As long as you understand I'll make all decisions on who leaves." He held out the paper.

Drake scanned the list. All the men who'd ridden in from Big Pine were on it, as well as a few others, two of them he couldn't lose. "Pruett and Swaggert need to stay."

"Why's that?"

"They're more experienced than the others and hard working. They've been with me for years."

King listened. He didn't know the two well. They did whatever Drake ordered—no questions asked. That worried him. He understood loyalty, as well as the fact it could be taken too far.

"I'll think about it. In the meantime, I'm letting the others go." He walked back around to his chair and sat.

"When will you tell them?"

"Tonight. They'll be paid through the month. I expect them to be off the ranch tomorrow morning."

Drake kept his temper as he left the house and headed toward the barn. With each step, his unease grew. He'd learned about Tolbert from another soldier. The man had traveled west years before and worked for Tolbert, then moved back east to help his parents after the war broke out. He'd told Drake of Tolbert's plans to expand, take over the neighboring ranches and control the cattle business in the growing territory of Montana. He'd said the man would need people like Drake to achieve his goals. The two of them,

234

plus Pruett and Swaggert, had planned to leave together.

The solider died a few weeks later. The others had taken off in the middle of the night after a brutal battle, deciding their future didn't exist in the South. They headed west, as far away as possible from those who knew them. He'd recruited others who'd fought for the South and lost everything, forming his own roving gang. It had taken them a year to cross the country, stealing what they needed and killing those who tried to stop them. All the while, Drake never let his focus stray from Tolbert, his Montana ranch, and a start at a new life away from anyone who knew of his desertion from the army. He never expected to see General Pelletier again, especially not in an isolated town like Splendor. He had to protect the secrets of his past, and that meant ridding the area of the Pelletier brothers.

Denver, Colorado

"You're certain these are the men who rode through here asking about the Pelletiers?"

"That's the one who spoke to us." The sheriff pointed to the wanted poster in Cash Coulter's right hand, then pointed to the one in his left. "This one stayed outside with three others. Duff Mayes came inside, except he called himself Henry Johnson. He also said he and the Pelletiers are friends, known each other for years. He just wanted to catch up with them."

Cash folded both posters and stuck them in his shirt pocket, knowing their journey had nothing to do with finding old friends. It had to do with locating and killing two Texas Rangers.

He'd started in Louisiana months before, searching for another band of outlaws who'd killed a family on their farm—Cash's uncle, aunt, and two cousins. From what he'd learned, the gang had stopped for food, then taken the horses and killed his kin. A lone worker had survived, identifying the leader as Parnell Drake, ex-sergeant in the Confederacy, deserter, and murderer.

After following their trail for several weeks, Cash lost them near Austin, Texas. He'd learned of a man named Henry Johnson, who'd been looking for the brothers. Cash had spent time with their captain, finally matching a wanted poster of Duff Mayes to the man who called himself Henry Johnson. The real reason for their search became obvious—locate the two Texas Rangers who'd killed his brother and murder them. Now Cash tracked the gang who hunted men he'd known since childhood. He'd still go after Parnell Drake, hunt him down, and kill him. First, he had to warn his friends.

Big Pine, Montana

"What did the sheriff say?" Whitey stood at the bar, waiting for his brother to speak with Sheriff Sterling, who'd ridden out of town early and returned in the afternoon. He'd hoped they'd be on their way to Splendor by now. Their journey would have to wait until tomorrow.

Duff signaled for a drink. "He knows Dax Pelletier—doesn't know the brother. He was in Big Pine a few weeks ago to pick up supplies with a couple of other people. They have a ranch in Splendor. He says it used to be belong to Pat Hanes."

"The man I killed," Whitey said under his breath.

Duff nodded. "Looks like they may have decided to stay a while, which means they'll be easy to find."

Whitey sipped his whiskey, a smile spreading across his face. He could feel the rush of getting close to the men they sought. Within days, the Pelletiers would be dead, Deke's life avenged, and they'd be on their way back home. "When do we leave?"

"First light tomorrow." Duff looked behind him at the table where their cousins—Clark, Bill, and Jed Olin—sat playing cards. "We'll send one of them to find out where the ranch is. I have yet to see a wanted poster on them, but our faces are all over. Big Pine and a couple other small towns are the only places where ours weren't up."

"Who's the sheriff in Splendor?"

A grin split Duff's face. "They don't have one. He got himself killed several months ago. That's another reason Pelletier rode here. To get the word out the town needs a sheriff."

"No sheriff and the Pelletiers don't know we're coming. Should be pretty simple. While we're there, we might as well relieve their bank of any excess funds, don't you think?"

Duff held his glass up in a salute. "I think it's an idea worth considering."

An hour after the sun appeared the following morning, the five outlaws rode out of Big Pine and straight toward Splendor. Their stops were quick. They took enough time to water the horses, eat hardtack and jerky, wash both down with water, then moved on. Well before sunset, they camped a few miles outside of town.

"Try the saloon first. Someone there is bound to know where their ranch is located." Duff stood next to Clark, as his oldest cousin prepared to leave. "Remember, you're an old buddy from the war and heard the Pelletiers were up this way. Nothing more."

"I got it, Duff. Hell, you've been telling me what to say for twenty minutes. How about I bring back some whiskey?"

"No. We stay sober until this job is done."

"And the bank?" Whitey asked.

"I'll take a look while I'm in town. See if it looks worth it," Clark called over his shoulder as he turned his horse toward town and started off.

"Truth is, I don't know how we'll be able to take care of the two Rangers and the bank. It's going to be one or the other." Duff stood, hands on hips, and watched Clark ride off.

"Unless we split up," Whitey said.

"That'd be plum foolish. We came here for one purpose. To avenge Deke. Robbing a bank will need to wait until after those boys are in the ground."

Whitey knew better than to argue with Duff, especially when he'd settled his mind on something. A small town, no sheriff and, more than likely, little resistance. It seemed a waste to leave money in the bank.

Dax wrapped the gun belt around his waist, buckled it, and slid his Remington into the holster. He adjusted the black vest he'd slipped on over his white shirt, and glanced at the black coat he hadn't worn in months. It lay on the bed, waiting for him to slide it on. Dax wasn't sure why he'd even brought it with him from Austin. The decision had been made at the last moment, before they'd left town with Pat's body.

He'd been out with the herd for the last two weeks, learning the ranch boundaries and locating missing cattle. All the while, his mind worked through the dilemma he'd created. Luke still hadn't budged. If anything, he'd become more adamant about his refusal to buy Dax out. They both knew he wouldn't sell to a stranger and, the truth was, he didn't know if he could walk out on Luke.

His brother's plan was simple. Resign from the Rangers and work the ranch for a year, figuring a year would give them time to see if they wanted to stay or sell. They both knew their captain would take them back anytime. He'd told them as much when they left.

As he left the herd and rode back to the ranch, he realized the thought of one more meal at the house, no matter how good the cooking, didn't appeal. Supper at Suzanne's, followed by cards and a few drinks at the Rose sounded real good. Luke had decided to head into town earlier with the rest of the boys. Dax had declined, saying he might join them later.

The sun hadn't set as Dax rode out on Hannibal. He took his time, watching the sun drop behind the western peaks of the Territory Range. The clouds began to turn light pink, then yellow, before transforming into a vibrant orange as he rounded the last turn toward Splendor. The beauty of the evening sky turned his thoughts to Rachel, and the familiar tightening of his chest began. It occurred each time her image formed in his head, and no matter how hard he tried, he couldn't stop his reaction to her memory.

Every day, he woke up wondering if he'd made a mistake by walking away and leaving the one woman he'd ever known who could stir his blood with a quick glance. And for what? To pursue an unknown future in Texas. He'd believed time away from Rachel would be all he needed to wipe her from his life. He'd been wrong. If anything, his feelings for her had grown stronger, more intense, and he found it rare when his thoughts didn't turn to her. He'd never forget the look on her face when she'd learned he'd decided to leave. That's when he knew.

Rachel had fallen in love with him, as he had her. What a mess.

Dax heard the music from the saloon as he passed the schoolhouse. To his left, he could see Noah still working in the livery. As the sun settled behind the mountains, he rode up to the boardinghouse, threw Hannibal's reins over the hitching post, and glanced down the street. A couple doors down, a lantern still burned in the clinic and he thought of Rachel. Would she be there, or in the house fixing supper? Had she thought of him at all the last few weeks?

He continued to stare as the clinic door opened and the woman who'd captured his heart walked outside to shake a blanket. She didn't notice him as she shook the material several times before throwing it over her arm and turning to go back inside. That's when she saw him and stopped.

Dax found himself taking a couple of steps toward her. He raised a hand in acknowledgement. She responded with a grim smile and slight nod before looking at the ground and walking inside. He started to go after her, then halted. Nothing had changed. He still believed he'd leave Splendor at some point in the near future. He needed to work things out with Luke which, given his brother's less than friendly attitude toward Dax's determination to leave, could take a while.

Rachel's life remained here, or perhaps in Boston. Seeing her again would only start the process over and that's not what he wanted, did he? Doubts continued to plague him. What was so important about Texas? Could there be a chance to find contentment on the ranch? He shook his head and walked toward the restaurant door, taking one more glance down the street before disappearing inside.

"Good evening, Dax. Table for two?" Suzanne asked.

"It's just me tonight."

"One special coming right out for you." She started to turn, then changed her mind. "You want anything else? You know, I keep a stash of whiskey in the back—for emergencies, of course."

With a slight smile, Dax answered, "Do I have the look of a man needing a drink?"

"Let's just say I've seen you look better." She patted his shoulder and left for the kitchen, returning within minutes with a large helping of roast beef and potatoes. "I'll bring you some coffee."

Dax busied himself thinking of Drake until Suzanne set down his plate. He stared at the food. He'd been ravenous by the time he'd reached town, his mouth watering for Suzanne's cooking, including a large slice of pie. When had he lost his appetite? He cut a piece of the meat, placed it in his mouth, and chewed, not expecting the bland taste and dry texture. He used a generous amount of coffee to swallow it down, and cut another slice. It tasted the same. Knowing her menu consisted of one main dish each night, he glanced around, surprised at the pleased faces of others.

His head turned at the slight squeak of the entry door and his eyes lit upon Rachel, followed a moment later by Gabe Evans. His already dry mouth tried to swallow the lump he felt at the sight of her with their new sheriff. She wore a different dress from the one he'd seen her in not thirty minutes before. A smile lit her face when she glanced up at something Gabe said.

"Two? Or will Noah be coming along?" Suzanne asked.

"Just the two of us tonight." Gabe placed a hand on the small of Rachel's back as they followed Suzanne to a table not far from Dax.

"Good evening, Dax." Gabe stuck out his hand as Dax stood. "Why don't you pull up a chair and join us?"

Dax shot a quick glance at Rachel before shaking Gabe's hand and returning to his seat. "Thanks, but I'm almost through."

"Here's your pie. I'll take that if you're finished." Suzanne picked up the half-eaten roast and refilled his cup. "It wasn't to your liking tonight?" She nodded toward the plate.

"Guess I wasn't as hungry as I thought. I'll settle up now." He reached into his pocket and pulled out some coins. "Thanks, Suzanne."

He stayed to eat a few bites of pie, glanced once more toward Gabe and Rachel, then left. He hesitated a moment by the front door before stepping outside. He almost turned back, wanting to at least speak with Rachel a moment, hear her voice and, well...be in her company, if only for a few minutes. He stopped himself when he realized she'd moved on. Gabe came from the North, had served in the Union Army and, from what he'd heard, had a similar background to

Rachel's. It made sense the two would be attracted to each other. He hadn't expected her to move on so soon. The thought warred with his common sense. Had he meant so little to her?

Dax settled his hat on his head and started across the street. A shiver ran up his spine, almost like a warning, causing him to stop and look up one end of the street, then the other. He saw no one. The loud music and lights of the Rose drew him inside and he forgot the odd sense of foreboding which had passed through him moments before.

"Over here, Dax."

He turned his head toward Luke, who sat a couple of tables away and pointed to an empty chair.

"You in?" Ellis asked as Dax took a seat.

"I'm in." Once again, a strange warning flashed through him. His narrowed eyes searched the saloon for any odd behavior or suspicious action. A man leaning against the bar glanced at Dax, then shifted his gaze elsewhere. As before, he saw nothing that would trigger the hairs on his neck to bristle.

Within minutes, he held cards in one hand and a whiskey in the other. His eyes continued to scan the saloon. He noticed the man at the bar continue to study the room, his eyes landing on Dax a few times before glancing away. The tense feeling began to subside as the alcohol warmed his blood and his body relaxed. One game after another passed, with him holding the winning cards on a rare occasion. Luck wasn't his partner tonight. He looked up as the man who'd been standing at the bar shoved through the swinging doors and left.

"Gabe stopped by earlier. Asked if you were in town." Luke watched the faces of the others at the table and pushed some chips forward. "I told him you were at the boardinghouse."

"I saw him." Dax threw his cards down and leaned his chair back on two legs.

Luke shot him a look, but kept quiet, already knowing the sheriff planned to take Rachel to the boardinghouse restaurant. He didn't believe there was more to Gabe's invitation to supper than friendship. Anyone who saw the way she looked at Dax could see he held all of her interest, if only he'd claim the prize right in front of him.

Dax had this notion that Texas held his future. Luke felt otherwise. He'd grown to like Splendor, the ranch, and the people. He couldn't imagine a more beautiful place in the entire country, and they held a treasured piece of it. Luke wasn't about to give his share up, and he sure as hell wasn't going to take Dax's. It left Dax in an odd position. Of course, he could ride out, like he'd tried to do in Savannah. If he'd planned on abandoning the ranch, Luke believed he'd already be gone. No, his brother still struggled with something and, whatever it was, it kept him in Splendor—at least for now.

Chapter Fifteen

"Thank you, Gabe. I had a wonderful time." Rachel offered a sincere smile. Gabe had been a perfect host, attentive and interesting, and getting out of the house had been a welcome break to her daily routine.

They'd finished their pie and the last of the coffee. Rachel rotated the cup in her hands and glanced out the window to the main street. The saloon stood straight across from them. She wondered if Dax had gone there for drinks, cards...or something more. The thought he'd seek companionship with another woman hurt.

"No need for thanks. I appreciated eating a meal without staring at Noah's ugly face. And it's far better than my own poor excuse for cooking." In truth, Gabe had enjoyed a chance to sit down with a pretty lady, something he hadn't done in a long time.

"Does Mr. Brandt know you speak of him so?"

He chuckled. "Believe me, he says worse about me."

"Everyone is so glad you took the sheriff's job. It's hard to describe the sense of unknown that's plagued the town since the previous sheriff's murder, plus the violence around Splendor and attacks against the Pelletiers. It means a lot to everyone to have you here."

Gabe shifted in his seat, uncomfortable with the confidence Rachel and the rest of the town placed in him. He'd yet to prove himself. "I'll stay for a while, until the trouble is gone or a new sheriff is found. I'm not quite ready to settle in one place. I guess I'm still searching."

"Like Dax."

"Excuse me?"

"Dax says the same, except he knows where he wants to settle."

"Texas."

Her eyes lifted to his and, for a brief moment, Gabe saw pain pass over them before she masked it.

"You, better than most women, know about war, the responsibilities someone like Dax carried, and the kinds of decisions he had to make. I don't know him well, but it could be he needs time away from command, away from being responsible for anyone except himself."

"Is that what you need?"

"Perhaps. I was an officer, but didn't carry the same load Dax did. As an officer, you feel the weight of your decisions and how they affect the men in your command."

"You may be right, except some men are born to lead. It's in their blood. I suspect you and Dax are much alike."

One corner of his mouth crooked upward. "All I know is I'm not ready to settle down."

"And would it matter if you met the right woman?"

His brows drew together. "I don't know. The problem is a man's got to be comfortable with himself, believe his life is in order, before he can commit to someone else. There's a tremendous responsibility associated with settling down with a woman and taking on the role of husband and provider."

"And are you comfortable with yourself?"

"Most days. Others..." His voice trailed off as if he'd pondered the same question himself.

"All right, you two. I'm bushed and ready to close up." Suzanne stood over them.

Neither had noticed they were the last ones in the restaurant. "Apologies, Mrs. Briar," Gabe said as he stood and pulled back Rachel's chair. "I lost track of time."

"No problem, Sheriff. It's good to see you in here."

Rachel tried to hide the fact she glanced at the saloon as they walked back to her house.

"Do you want me to go over to the Rose, see what he's up to?"

She shot Gabe a murderous look, uncomfortable her feelings were so easily read. "No! It makes no difference to me what he does. It's his decision." Her words did nothing to still the regret she felt at Dax's choice to leave her behind when he left Splendor.

Rachel turned when they'd reached her door. "Well, thank you for the meal and conversation."

"We'll have supper again before I leave. You can count on it." Gabe tipped his hat as he turned away.

She slipped inside, closing the door behind her.

"Did you and the sheriff have a good time?"

248

Her uncle's voice startled her. "I didn't realize you were still up. You do know I'm a grown woman and you don't have to wait up for me."

Charles set down the book he'd been reading. "Who said I waited up for you? I couldn't sleep, that's all." He stood and walked down the hall to his room. "Goodnight, Rachel."

She shook her head at his poor attempt to hide his concern. Rachel prepared tea, then took a seat in the parlor, balancing the cup on her lap. She closed her eyes, remembering the sound of Dax's voice, the touch of his lips to hers, and the feelings which invaded her whenever he stood near. The air vibrated around them, as if they shared a private language no one else understood.

If she tried hard enough, she could feel his arms tighten around her, a hand drifting to her head, holding her in place for his intoxicating kisses. Her face burned as she remembered the thrill of being held so close and the urge she felt to surrender to his powerful touch. She'd never wanted the sensations to end, but the decision had always been out of her control. Her eyes drifted open as she inhaled a deep breath, attempting to calm the hammering in her chest.

She leaned back in the chair, willing herself to make sense of his decision and allow herself to move on. Her eyes closed as she remembered how he'd looked tonight.

He'd taken scant notice of her when she'd walked into Suzanne's with Gabe. The look on his face showed no trace of regret, as if any feelings they held for each other had evaporated, leaving them little more than mere acquaintances. She took a sip of tea and tried to put it all into perspective.

She'd known Dax less than three months, although her fascination had begun from the first time they'd met. Something inside told her he'd felt the same tug toward her. The attraction grew whenever they were together, and before she knew what had happened, she'd fallen in love with the man. She'd even allowed her imagination to take over, believing she'd become important to him and fantasizing he'd be a permanent part of her life. How wrong she'd been.

Her path seemed clear. Forget Dax Pelletier and focus on the reason she'd come to Montana in the first place—the clinic and her uncle's medical practice.

They'd talked of traveling to visit folks at remote ranches, the ones who made the trip to Splendor only when forced to by a lack of supplies. Most handled illness and injury alone, and many died without proper care. The fact the Westons brought their daughter, Janie, to the clinic had been a positive sign. Now she and her uncle needed to reach out to the other families.

He'd also treated the occasional Blackfoot Indian who'd visit the white man's doctor when all else failed. The visits were rare and not encouraged by the tribe. However, each time, Charles had been able to expand their trust in his cures and his sincere desire to help them. On more than one occasion, he'd expressed an interest in visiting their village, and had extended an invitation for Rachel to join him. She had to admit the thought interested and scared her.

Most people in town discouraged the doctor from reaching out to the Blackfoot, believing it would lead to nothing good. Living in Boston, she'd grown up on stories of the savage tribes who inhabited the frontier, reading of attacks and torture against white settlers. She now understood much of what had been written may not have been accurate. As she'd come to accept, there were two sides to the actions behind the Civil War. She believed there must be two sides to the stories told of Indians, as well.

She thought more of the plans she and her uncle had spoken about, and her mood lifted. She recognized she had a full life in Splendor, without the need for a romantic entanglement. Supper out once in a while, a ride in the country on occasion, but a relationship? Not now.

Rachel changed into her nightdress, snuffed out the light, and climbed under the covers. Tomorrow, she'd start fresh—with Dax forgotten.

"I got the location of their ranch and something more," Clark said as he swung off his horse, poured some coffee, and lowered himself in front of the fire where everyone sat. "I saw both the Pelletiers in the saloon. They were playing cards with some of their men." He took a sip of some of the awful coffee his brother Jed had made and grimaced. "Damn, Jed. You've got to learn how to make this stuff." He shifted his gaze to Duff. "Those two don't look so tough to me."

Duff ignored the comment. From their actions, the Rangers had already proven Clark wrong. "How far is their ranch from town?"

"A few miles northwest," Clark answered.

"How many men?"

"I didn't ask. Figured it wouldn't matter since we've already decided to go after them."

Duff swore, pinning his cousin with a disgusted glare. "Your momma ever say you ended up with half a brain?"

Clark threw the last of his coffee on the fire, trying to ignore the anger at Duff's comment. "There's five of us and they don't know we're anywhere around here. Unaware we're even after them. We gonna leave if there's ten or fifteen of them, forget about Deke, and ride back to Texas?"

"He's right, Duff. We came here for one reason. To kill the Pelletiers. No matter how many men they have, there will come a time when they'll be alone. That's when we strike." Whitey lit a hand-rolled cigarette and inhaled with a deep draw, releasing the smoke in a slow stream.

"Oh, we'll get rid of them, but we need to handle it in a different way than I'd planned. They'll definitely recognize you and me, Whitey, and possibly Clark. I doubt they've ever seen a wanted poster on Bill or Jed. Here's what we'll do..."

"Rachel, come quick." Charles pounded on her bedroom door, trying to wake her at the early hour. "There's been an accident at the Pelletier ranch and I'll need your help." The sun hadn't yet begun to rise as Charles grabbed supplies from the cabinets and picked up his satchel. "I'll harness Old Pete and get the wagon ready. You dress and go out front. Tell Ellis we're on our way." He ran to the back to get the wagon.

Rachel tried to clear her sleep-fogged brain as she dressed, reached for her bonnet and shawl, then raced out front.

"What happened?"

"Most of the boys were out with the herd last night, bedded down, when something spooked the cattle. They plowed straight through camp. Two of the new men are pretty broken up. Rude's got a knot on his head but, other than that, he's okay." Ellis looked up to see Charles drive the wagon onto the main street and stop to let Rachel climb up.

The doctor drove as fast as he dared, pushing Old Pete to his limit and hitting every rut in the dirt road.

Dax and Luke had ordered the three injured men to be taken to the bunkhouse, where Bernice and Hank had done what they could. Two of them were in bad shape with broken bones, bruises, and who knew what else, while Rude nursed a bump on his head. It could've been worse.

"What's taking Ellis so long?" Dax opened the bunkhouse door to peer out for the third time in ten minutes. He and Luke had been bunked down under some trees not far from the herd, yet far enough they'd missed being trampled.

"They'll be here. It takes time. My guess is the doc will bring the wagon and all they have is Old Pete." Luke bent over Johnny, one of the injured men, doing his best to clean the dirt and rocks from the numerous cuts that covered his arms and face. Bernice had muttered it was a mercy Johnny and the other cowboy, Tat, remained unconscious.

Dax tore outside when one of the men yelled that the doctor's wagon had drawn into sight. He reached up to help Rachel down. She avoided him and jumped to the ground on her own.

"Where are they?" Charles asked as he grabbed the supplies.

"In the bunkhouse." Dax watched Rachel follow her uncle inside, a sharp pang of regret slicing through him at the way she ignored him. It was no more than he deserved.

Charles made a quick examination of Johnny, then did the same with Tat, noting how young each appeared. "We'll need help to set limbs and keep them still. Both may have injuries I can't see. I'll do what I can."

"Luke and I will stay," Dax said.

"So will Bernice and me." Hank walked up to stand by his wife.

"All right. Everyone else outside," Dax ordered.

Charles and Rachel worked as fast as possible, checking the injuries, applying splints and setting broken limbs. The others helped as needed. Dax marveled at the way Rachel focused on her work, calming Johnny and Tat as they moved in and out of consciousness, assisting Charles in a quiet, efficient manner. He'd seen her work on Hank using the same expert care.

"We've done all we can do for now. Rachel and I will need to stay here tonight." He looked around the bunkhouse, realizing all the ranch hands needed to be in this one large room tonight. At least the injured men were on bunks close to the door.

"We'll set up a bunk for you next to them, Doc. Rachel should stay in the house. There's no use in her staying all night in here with the rest of the men." Dax had no intention of letting Rachel stay in a room surrounded by a bunch of ranch hands.

"I'm staying here. This is where I'm needed."

"Rachel—"

"No, Dax. I'm staying." She'd placed her hands on her hips and glared at him. "Where do you think I slept during the war? I'll tell you. In a tent with injured men like these, except there were many more to watch over. You and the others stay in the house. Uncle Charles and I will be fine out here." She turned her back to him, ending any further argument.

"Come one, Dax. They know what they're doing. We'll only be in the way." Luke touched his brother's arm, encouraging him to let the decision stand.

255

Dax didn't like it. "If that's your decision, then I'll stay also."

Checking Tat's bandages, Rachel glanced over her shoulder at him. "No."

He moved around to look down on her. "Let me remind you, Miss Davenport. This is the Pelletier ranch. It doesn't belong to you or anyone else, and no one tells me what to do on my own property. I'll bunk down wherever I please."

She kept her head angled away, hoping Dax wouldn't notice the heat which crept up her face, certain she'd turned scarlet.

He watched her, waiting for a response. It didn't come. "Do we understand each other?"

Rachel pinned him with a heated glare, the sarcasm in her response hard to miss. "Yes, General. We understand each other just fine."

His mouth quirked up the slightest bit, glad he'd hit a nerve. She could be tough, he'd give her that.

Luke listened to the exchange, surprised and pleased at Dax's response. Perhaps his brother *had* started to come around to the idea the ranch might be worth keeping.

"I'll take care of getting everyone fed. Let me know what else you need." Bernice took off for the house, Hank not far behind.

"I'm going to check on the men watching the herd, make sure nothing else has happened since we've been gone. Bull's already here, still not healed enough to ride, and with his head injury, Rude needs to stay behind. Do you need me to send anyone else back?" Luke asked.

"No. You'll want every man left to keep watch on the cattle. Take Ellis with you."

"Someone started the stampede, Dax. A couple of the men heard gunshots before the cattle spooked."

"I know."

"Tolbert's men?"

"That's my guess." Dax shot a look at Johnny and Tat, both in such bad shape they might not make it until morning. He clenched his jaw as anger rose at the human destruction King Tolbert and his men had caused. He shoved the bunkhouse door open and headed toward the house in long, determined strides, taking the front steps two at a time and slamming the door open as he entered.

"What are you thinking?" Luke kept pace, knowing Dax had come to a decision.

"I'm riding to the Tolbert ranch. It's time to end this."

"You're not going alone." Luke grabbed his arm and spun him around. "It's suicide riding in there without the rest of us."

"The hell I'm not." Dax shook off Luke's hand and opened the gun cabinet, pulling out his rifle, a revolver, and ammunition.

"At least wait until I get back with some of the men. I'll send Ellis to town for Gabe. We can all ride to Tolbert's together."

Dax narrowed his eyes at Luke. "I'll wait an hour. If you're not back, I'm going alone."

Ellis rode into town, bringing Gabe and Noah back with him.

Luke ordered most of the men to guard the herd, selecting a few to ride with him, believing they needed a show of force to accomplish anything. He knew Dax wouldn't do anything stupid, yet he'd never witnessed the type of rage he'd seen on his brother's face when they brought the injured men back to the ranch. He had reached his limit with Tolbert, and Luke was capable of holding Dax off for just so long before he rode out to confront the man.

Dax mounted Hannibal in one fluid motion. He'd waited long enough for Luke. The time had come to confront King, with or without additional men.

"Where are you headed, Dax?" Hank rushed out of the house to stand next to his boss, afraid he'd decided to ride out alone.

"I'm leaving for Tolbert's. Don't try to stop me." Dax turned his horse toward the neighboring ranch.

"Don't believe I'll have to." Hank pointed toward Luke heading toward them from one direction while Ellis, Gabe, and Noah approached from the other.

"You weren't planning to leave without us, right, big brother?" Luke reined Prince to a stop next to Dax.

"Another minute and I'd have been gone."

They waited as the others joined them, Gabe pulling up alongside Dax. "I'm in charge here, Dax. No shooting. We're going to get Tolbert's side of what happened, then I'll decide from there. You understand?"

"You know as well as I do that King is responsible for what's been happening. He won't talk his way out of it this time."

Gabe leaned toward Dax. "And I'll arrest you if you do something stupid. Now, let's get going."

"Father, there's a group of riders approaching." Abigail had bounded from her seat on the front porch and dashed to her father's office at the sight of a large group of men heading toward their house.

"Guess I'd better see what they want."

He waited as Gabe, Noah, Dax, and Luke dismounted. Noah glanced at Abigail, who stood next to her father on the porch, and wondered how much she might know about her father's actions. He couldn't believe she could have any knowledge of such violent events.

"Sheriff, what can I do for you?"

"Someone stampeded the Pelletier cattle. Two men are critical, may not make it, and a third has a head wound. You know anything about it?"

"I'm sorry to hear about it. My guess is you're here because you suspect me of ordering the stampede. Whatever happened didn't come from me." King said the words as doubt spread through him. Too many instances of violence had been directed against the neighboring ranch, none of it ordered by him. However, all of it seemed to be traced back to his ranch.

"Where's Drake?" Gabe asked.

"He and some men have been away from the ranch, checking for stray cattle the last three days. They're not due back for a couple more days."

"Where?"

"Started at the southwest line and were to move north."

"The line bordering the Pelletier ranch?"

Irritation began to burn within King. His gut told him Drake had to be involved, yet he'd allowed the man to convince him otherwise.

"That's right."

Everyone turned at the sound of an approaching rider.

King walked down the steps, passing Dax and Luke without a glance, and watched as Drake stopped in front of him. He hadn't expected to see the man so soon.

"What's going on, boss?"

"There's been another incident on the Pelletier ranch. You know anything about it?"

"No." He glanced around, recognizing most of the men who'd ridden in with the sheriff.

"You telling us you know nothing of a stampede that injured three men? It happened close to the same area where you've been riding. A couple of the Pelletier cowhands heard gunshots before the cattle spooked." Gabe rested a hand on the butt of his gun, uncertain how the volatile ex-soldier would react. Noah noticed the movement and edged closer, ready to act if needed.

Drake stepped up within inches of Gabe's face and planted his feet. "You accusing me of something, Sheriff?"

"Not yet." Gabe stood his ground, narrowing his eyes on the man he knew was lying. To his disappointment, Drake's jaw worked, but he stayed silent.

Drake turned toward King. "I had nothing to do with a stampede and neither did any of the men. I'll be in the barn if you need me."

"I want to see you when you're finished." King turned to the others. "If there's nothing else, I'll return to my work. Good day, gentlemen."

"We're not done, King," Gabe said. "I still have a lot of questions. I'd like to meet with the men who were with Drake the last few days."

"Of course. I'll send word to you once they return."

"Be sure you do." He turned to Dax and Luke, who'd stayed remarkably silent. "Let's go."

King shoved his hands in his pockets, coming to the realization he'd made a mistake hiring Drake. He should have cut him loose with the others. It would've left him shorthanded, but that seemed insignificant when faced with what he believed the man had done. In his gut, he knew Drake had something to do with the acts against the Pelletiers, even though he'd been warned not to harm them. The man, and the rest of those loyal to him, had to go.

Chapter Sixteen

"He's not going to make it, is he?" Rachel's heart sank at the way Johnny struggled for every breath. They'd done all they could, and he'd fought hard. Yet, with each heartbeat, his body sank further into decline.

"There's always hope." Charles suspected the cowhand suffered internal injuries. Nothing more could be done, but the doctor refused to believe the worst. He'd seen more miracles in his life than he could count, patients without a chance would rally and prove him wrong. "I won't give up on him."

Tat began to improve within the first few hours after Charles and Rachel arrived. Although severe, his injuries hadn't been as extensive as Johnny's. Charles felt certain Tat would recover.

"Is there anything more we can do?"

"Keep watch and make him comfortable. It's up to his body, and God."

The bunkhouse door scraped open as Bull stepped inside, carrying food and coffee from the main house. He set everything down on a nearby table before looking at both men.

"Dax, Luke, and the others are back. I expect they'll be over here any time."

No sooner had he finished than the door opened to reveal the group who'd ridden to

Tolbert's ranch. Their expressions signaled the displeasure and frustration each felt.

Gabe walked up next to Rachel, staring down at Tat, then Johnny. "Are they improving?"

"Tat is, Johnny is hanging on," Rachel said as she applied a damp cloth to the face of the young man who'd yet to rally. "We'll know more by morning. Tat should recover real well, although Charles is certain he'll end up with a limp." She looked toward the second bed.

"You and the doctor have done a good job. From what I've been told, it's surprising either of them still has a chance."

Dax watched the easy exchange between the two and felt what could only be described as jealousy swell within him. He'd always been cocky, even arrogant in his attitude toward the emotion. He kept a tight hold on his feelings, never before allowing a woman to get under his skin, mess with his mind. The control had vanished when Rachel entered his life.

He replayed the warning he'd given Rachel earlier. *Let me remind you, Miss Davenport. This is the Pelletier ranch. It doesn't belong to you or anyone else, and no one tells me what to do on my own property.* He'd been surprised at the intensity of his words, as if he believed them. Had he been lying to himself, to Luke, and to Rachel? Did the ranch mean more to him than he'd been willing to admit?

"I'll be in the house. Thanks for riding out, Gabe." He shook the other man's hand, nodded at the doctor and Rachel, then disappeared outside.

She set down the damp cloth and fought the urge to go after him. The need to be near Dax, touch him, had swelled to the point of suffocation. Weren't her feelings for him supposed to recede, give way to an acceptance that whatever had begun between them had ended? Why did it seem her desire for the man continued to build? It wasn't supposed to be this way.

"Go to him, Rachel. He won't talk to me. Perhaps he'll open up to you."

She hadn't noticed Luke walk up beside her. "It would be a wasted effort. He wants nothing to do with me."

"You might be surprised at what he wants. Fact is, he may not realize what's important to him. The man hides his feelings well."

Rachel considered Luke's words. "What makes you think he'll speak with me?"

"Perhaps he won't. You'll never know if you don't try."

Rachel let her hands run down the front of her dress, more in nervous agitation than as a way to smooth the creases. Before she had time to talk herself out of it, she pulled the door open and, with determined steps, followed Dax to the house.

He'd reached the front door when he heard footfalls on the steps behind him. He glanced over his shoulder, surprised at who stepped up next to him.

"Is there something you want?" His sharp eyes narrowed as he studied her.

Her courage began to slip as she focused on the set of his face and clamped jaw, wondering why she'd taken Luke's advice. Then she caught herself, determined to forge ahead.

"Do you have a minute to talk?" The calm, even tone surprised her.

"About?" Dax's breath hitched as her tongue skimmed across her lips. The small action sent heat rushing through his body and he crossed his arms in an attempt to hide his reaction.

What could she talk about? The attacks on the ranch, his plans, her love for him?

"The clinic." The words popped out before she even realized it. Her look of surprise wasn't lost on Dax.

Amusement crossed his face as it dawned on him her request might not have anything whatsoever to do with the clinic.

"All right. Come inside and we'll talk about *the clinic*." He let the two words stretch out. "Would you like some coffee, or a glass of sherry?"

Rachel took a seat in one of the large leather chairs, a mischievous look flashing across her face. "Whiskey would be nice."

Dax's brows shot up, offering no comment on her choice. He poured their drinks, then selected the chair across from her, moving it forward so their knees touched. He noticed her face color at the implied intimacy.

"Here's to our first whiskey together." He lifted his glass in a slight salute, then took a swallow. "Now, what is it about the clinic you want to discuss, Rachel?" He spoke in a quiet tone, the smooth, rich sound creating a warmth that flowed through her.

She held the glass of whiskey in both hands as if it were a shield between her and Dax. She studied the tawny color a moment before raising the glass to her lips and taking a slow sip. Rachel hadn't indulged in whiskey since leaving Boston. Unlike many women, she enjoyed it, had cultivated a taste for the drink during her time in the field hospitals where it had been plentiful. She took one more sip, then trained her eyes on Dax, noticing for the first time how his had turned a deep steel gray and were filled with an emotion she couldn't quite define.

Rachel continued to roll the glass between her hands and cleared her throat. "Uncle Charles would like to expand his practice to include those families who live miles away. Establish a pattern of visiting them every few months to make sure everyone is fine."

"Like a circuit judge?" Dax asked.

"Why, yes." She took a breath, glad he'd followed her meaning. "To do this, we need to stock more supplies and, at some point, buy another horse. I don't know if Old Pete is up for what he plans."

Dax sat forward, resting his arms on his knees. "Would you accompany him?" He didn't like the idea of Rachel traveling into open, and often wild, territory without more protection than what her uncle could provide.

"On occasion. He'd be gone several days, perhaps a week, which is a dilemma as the town would be without a doctor."

"They'd have you."

"I'm not a doctor."

"You're better than most I've seen." He inched forward, letting his knees rest on either side of hers, trapping Rachel in her seat. "Because of your field experience, you possess skills some doctors don't. You're efficient and steady, and patients feel safe with you. That's a skill not easy to learn, yet you come by it naturally."

His unexpected praise surprised her. She had no idea he had so much confidence in her abilities. The knowledge warmed her, as did the nearness of his body, which also sent a warning. She needed space. Rachel tried to move her chair back a few inches, only to find the rug underneath held it in place. Having no other choice, she stood, forcing him to inch backward, allowing her to step around the chair.

"Why, thank you, although I believe you may be exaggerating my skills."

"Not at all. Remember, I saw many doctors during my time with the Confederacy, and few had your capacity to not just heal the wound, but calm the patient. It's a gift not many possess." His eyes caught and held hers. He stood and reached up to move loose tendrils of hair from her face and tuck them behind her ear. The movement was slow as he let his fingers trace a path along her cheek. "What do you need from me?"

She held her breath at the feel of his fingers on her skin, burning a trail that caused her heart to race to such an extent, she knew he must have heard it. The sensations were so right, so perfect, she'd felt an immediate loss when his arm dropped away.

"Rachel?" His voice sounded raspy and thick, even to him.

"I'm sorry. What did you say?" She lifted her face, displaying the same confusion he felt.

"I asked what you needed from me. I assume there must be a reason you're telling me about these plans." He stepped back and poured himself another drink, admonishing himself for his impulsive action.

"Yes, of course there's a reason." The reason...What was the reason? "I wondered, if it might be possible, for you and Luke to help fund the additional supplies. It could be a loan, or perhaps a donation, or..." She'd only come up with this idea seconds before, surprised she'd thought of anything at all.

"And what would we get out of it?" He stepped a few feet closer, stopping in front of her chair.

"Get out of it?" His question confused her.

"If we provide the funds, what can we expect from you?" Dax didn't understand why he kept baiting her. He still believed his time in Splendor would be short, yet he couldn't seem to rid his thoughts of this woman. She now stood before him, asking for his help, and he couldn't get the vision of them kissing and embracing out his mind.

Her mind raced. "Well, we could perhaps name the clinic for you. Yes, that's exactly what we could do. The Pelletier Medical Clinic." She stood and smiled up at him. "What do you think?"

The excitement in her voice and the radiant smile she shot him were more than he could handle. He stepped closer, wrapped an arm around her waist, and tugged her to him, lowering his mouth to hers.

At first, Rachel offered no resistance. This is what she'd dreamed of and wanted ever since he walked away. She let her hands glide up his arms to his shoulders, then wrapped them around his neck as he deepened the kiss.

"Ah, Rachel," he breathed against her mouth as his tongue outlined her lips until she opened for him and he eased inside, tasting the whiskey, as a moan escaped her lips. He let his hands roam her back as he aligned her body with his. "I want you, Rachel," he whispered.

His quiet words brought Rachel back to her senses. She dropped her hands from his neck to his shoulders, and pushed without success. She pushed harder and he let her go, allowing her to gain the distance she sought.

"We can't do this, Dax. *I* can't do this." Her voice shook with emotion.

He took a ragged breath and stepped away. "I'm sorry. It shouldn't have happened—"

"Don't say that. There isn't much I understand about my reaction to you except it feels right, and good, and perfect. I don't understand any of it." She placed one hand on her forehead and turned away from him, unable to meet his gaze.

"I wish I could explain." His resigned, broken voice stirred Rachel, and she wanted nothing more than to wrap her arms around him and pull him close.

She turned, her gaze questioning. "Why, Dax? Why leave a prosperous ranch, your brother, and people who believe in you to pursue a future hundreds of miles away, when the dream is already right in front of you?" I'm right in front of you, she thought.

He'd been asking the same questions of himself for weeks, believing he knew the reason, yet not finding a solution.

"I don't know if I can do this anymore, Rachel." The despair in his voice cut through her.

"Do what?"

"Be the person they need." His gaze focused on her. "The person *you* need."

She didn't break eye contact as she stepped closer. "You don't have to be anyone except yourself. You're already the person I need."

He reached out and ran his knuckles in a soft caress from the corner of an eye to the contour of her jaw, letting it drift down the soft column of her neck, and feeling a sense of desperation at his inability to explain his doubts. How could anyone understand his absolute certainty he could perform his duties as a Texas Ranger, track and bring in dangerous outlaws, yet he couldn't face the thought of leading men again? How could he have them look to him for answers when he felt so uncertain himself?

He'd led men to victory in battle after battle, watching good men die, yet continuing to believe in the Confederacy's right to secede. Then the momentum shifted. Battles were lost, more men died. Still, he pushed on in the war against the Union. He'd been prepared to continue as long as needed to achieve their goal. Until the day all chance of victory had been erased with the signing of the surrender.

All those battles, all the men who'd sacrificed so much. Had it been for nothing?

A year ago, he couldn't imagine feeling this way. His craving to lead had been as much a part of him as his arms and legs, pushing him to accomplish—first as the captain of merchant ships, then as an officer, culminating in the rank of general. Yet here it was, staring him the face. He'd lost his desire to be the man others looked to for solutions, and he had no idea how to reclaim it.

Dax dropped his hand and stepped away.

"Talk to me. Help me understand."

He started to speak, then pulled back at the sound of voices a moment before Luke opened the door and stepped inside with Ellis.

"I thought you might be in here." If Luke suspected he'd interrupted anything, he didn't let on. "Ellis and I are riding out to stay with the other men guarding the herd. Bull's insisting he's healed enough to go with us. What do you think?"

"Take him. I'm going with you." Dax moved around Rachel and toward the door.

"I thought you'd say that. Ellis already saddled Hannibal." Luke glanced at Rachel. "Doc says he has to go back to town tomorrow morning. He'd prefer to take both men with him, but doesn't think it's wise in their condition. He'll come back tomorrow night to check on them."

"I can stay while my uncle's in town." She directed her comment to Dax.

"I'd appreciate that." He let his eyes drift over her once more before following the others outside.

Rachel watched them leave, more confused than ever about Dax, his reasons for leaving, and their own reactions to each other. Regardless, she had learned something. Luke was right. Dax struggled with demons he couldn't define and perhaps didn't understand himself.

"Sit down, Drake." King indicated a chair across from the desk where he sat. He leaned forward, his eyes fixed. "When will the men be back?"

"I expect them by supper tomorrow. Why?"

"The sheriff wants to speak with them about the stampede. He's certain my men are responsible. If either of the Pelletier men die, it will be murder."

"I already told you none of the men were involved. They were with me."

"How far were you camped from their herd?" King knew Drake must have known the Pelletier herd was close by. You don't move a large number of cattle without hearing them.

"Not close, but we were aware of their location. We camped in the hill area and they were in the valley below."

"And no one spoke of how interesting it could get if some of those cattle were spooked? No mention of the Pelletier herd at all?"

"No."

"The sheriff said gunshots were fired. Are you telling me no one heard anything?"

"That's what I'm saying."

King had no proof the man lied, although he suspected it. Most cowhands were honest men, working hard to earn a living. A few always wanted to stir up trouble. You didn't need to look for them. They were the vocal ones, men who might joke about it, then go ahead and do it. Men like that had no place on his ranch.

"Send the men to me as soon as they return."

"Sure. Anything else?"

"No."

Tolbert waited until Drake left, then stood and walked to the window facing the barn. He didn't know if Drake ordered the stampede or not, but gunshots and moving cattle could be heard for miles in the quiet of the night. The bigger question remained—Drake's motivation for going against his orders and threatening the Pelletiers, shooting at their men, and stampeding their cattle. What did the man have against them? Tolbert considered himself a good businessman, willing to go to extremes others weren't to achieve his goals. However, he had never ordered men hurt.

"Father?"

He turned as Abigail opened the door and stepped inside. "I'll be retiring now. Tomorrow is a big day." She walked up and placed a kiss on his cheek.

"Tomorrow?"

She tilted her head. "The ladies at the church are having a luncheon and I've been invited. You didn't forget, did you?"

"Uh...no, of course not."

"I'll be leaving late morning. Do you need me to check for telegrams or mail?"

"Who's riding with you?"

She smiled up at him. "No one, Father. I'm riding Willie." She saw the concern on his face. Her father seldom allowed her to go anywhere alone. In fact, he hadn't allowed her to travel anywhere by herself for quite some time. "There's nothing to worry about."

"I'd prefer to have someone ride with you. Let me check with Drake."

She kept her voice calm, even though irritation swelled within her. "There's no need to send anyone. I'm perfectly capable of riding to town and back by myself. You used to let me do it all the time before..." Her voice faded at the realization she'd started to mention a subject her father preferred to ignore.

King shot a quick look at his daughter, clearing his throat before turning away at the reminder of what had happened a few years before. He knew he'd been keeping a tight watch over Abigail, demanding someone accompany her any time she left the house. He understood her need for a measure of freedom. All young men and women wanted to feel they could make their own decisions, set their own course, and his daughter was no different. Most women were already married or had plans for marriage by her age. Keeping her close, allowing her contact with others only when he or another man he trusted accompanied her to town could not last. He wanted to keep her safe, yet needed to let her go. She remained all he had left.

"When will you return?" A lump formed in his throat as he accepted the time had come to allow her more freedom.

"No later than midafternoon."

He clasped his hands behind his back. "All right."

"Thank you!" She kissed him once more and rushed from the study before he could change his mind.

Chapter Seventeen

"We're looking for the boss." Bill and Jed Olin looked down from where they sat atop their horses at the older man who'd come out to meet them.

"Neither of them are here. What do you want?" Hank shielded his eyes from the early morning sun. He didn't care for the look of either one. Their appearance gave the impression of gunfighters, rather than ranch hands.

"We heard you might be looking for cowhands. That true?"

"Might be. Like I said, the Pelletiers run this place and neither of them are around."

"When are they due back?" Bill persisted.

"Not sure. They're out with the herd, so it could be days." Hank looked behind the two men to see a welcome sight as the doctor's wagon rolled up the road. He hadn't expected the man for a few more hours. "You'll need to come back."

Bill shifted in his saddle, not pleased with the idea of riding back again tomorrow. "You mind if we wait a spell."

"Suit yourself." He wanted to discourage them, send them on their way. However, with the four men laid up, they were shorthanded. Ellis and Bull should be ready for work pretty quick, but Johnny and Tat had a lot more recuperating to do. Hank had to consider Dax and Luke might

276

feel different about them and hire both on. "You can put your horses in the corral."

Jed and Bill rode the short distance toward the barn, released the saddles and threw them over the fence, then opened the corral gate. They needed everything to appear normal, like any two cowhands looking for work, even though not having their horses ready to ride didn't seem right. Bill rested a hand on the butt of his gun and leaned against the fence, watching the doctor pull his wagon to a stop and climb down.

"You got here earlier than I expected." Hank watched as the doctor grabbed something from the back of the wagon.

"How are they doing?"

"Rachel's done a great job. Doesn't leave their side for more than a few minutes. She could use a break, if you can get her to go along with it." Hank kept pace with Charles as he walked toward the bunkhouse.

"I'll see if I can get her to rest, at least for a while. It would be best if she rode back into town tonight. I can stay here, if needed." Charles pushed the door open. His eyes landed on Rachel, who leaned over Johnny as he spoke to her in a raspy voice. She nodded at something he said before turning to see her uncle in the doorway.

"Uncle Charles. Come over here. Johnny's awake." Both doubted the young man would make it through another night, yet he'd rallied and appeared to be on his way to recovering.

Charles gazed down at the boy, which is how he thought of him, and smiled. "Glad to see you're better, young man."

"Johnny," he whispered, wincing as the word came out.

"Johnny it is." He glanced at Rachel. "Why don't you take a rest? I can handle these two for a bit." Charles turned back to Johnny and pulled back the covers.

Rachel watched for a moment before removing her well-used smock and hanging it on a hook by the door. She ran the back of a hand across her forehead, then let her arm drop, feeling the fatigue which had progressed over several hours.

She stepped into the bright sunlight, her eyes landing on two men leaning against the corral. Too tired to introduce herself, Rachel ignored them and made her way toward the house, ready for some of Bernice's tea and a slice of the cider cake she'd baked the night before.

"Hello, ma'am."

She turned at the greeting, not wishing to start a conversation, yet unable to be rude. "May I help you with something?"

"We're waiting to speak with the boss about a job. We heard he might need some help." Jed stood a few feet away, hands on hips, and let his eyes wander up, then down. He hadn't seen a woman as pretty as this one in a long time.

"I'm sorry I can't help you. The men who own the ranch aren't here right now. It may be best to come back another time."

"The older man said we could wait. I think that's what we'll do."

"It's up to you." Rachel walked up the front steps and through the door. Something about the man didn't seem right. It wasn't so much the way his gaze moved over her, which was irritating, though not threatening. The eyes—flat and cold—were what triggered a sense of unease, prodding her to take a small step back when he spoke. She hoped he didn't notice the apprehension his presence caused.

"I thought I heard someone come inside. How about something to drink and a piece of cake?" Bernice dried her hands on a towel slung over her shoulder and took down a cup. "Tea?"

"Thanks. I'd appreciate it." She took a seat at the kitchen table and let her mind drift back to the conversation she'd had with Dax. Until last night, she hadn't realized the extent of the burdens weighing upon him. The calm strength he always displayed belied an inner turmoil, one she knew other military men faced when the battles ended. Unless he confided in her, there was nothing she could do. She wanted to help, get him to talk and release his burdens. Perhaps someday he would.

"Here you are." Bernice set down a cup of tea and a plate with a large slice of cider cake. "Now you relax while I go outside to check the laundry."

Rachel didn't respond as Bernice disappeared outside. She slipped a piece of cake in her mouth and let her thoughts drift once more to Dax. He could stay or leave. His future hung in the air, and hers along with it. Whatever troubled him would be the deciding factor. Even if he stayed, there were no assurances he'd still want to see her. She might be a temporary respite in his search for a new life or a path back to the man he used to be. Would he still turn to her when he figured it all out? Right now, there was no way to tell.

The back door swung open, allowing Bernice to walk through. Her arms full of clothes and linens.

"Let me help." Rachel stood and took some of the load, then set everything down on the table before grabbing a clean shirt. "Luke mentioned you and Hank talked of leaving. I'm glad you worked something out. It's certain the Pelletiers would've been lost without you."

She grabbed a towel and made quick work of folding it. "Oh, I don't know about those two being lost. They're pretty capable." Bernice chuckled. "Truth be told, it was more me than Hank who wanted to leave."

Rachel's brows drew together and she set down the trousers in her hand. "Why?"

"The shooting. We've been together a lot of years and I couldn't bear the thought of losing him to the violence taking over this area. It's getting worse all the time."

"Are you talking about the threats to Dax and Luke, or is it something more?"

"It all started months before the sheriff was murdered, before you came to Splendor. Ranchers on the other side of town were the first targets. Missing cattle, fires, random shootings.

The sheriff arrested some of King Tolbert's men, but had to let them go. He didn't have the evidence needed to hold them. A few months later, someone gunned the sheriff down on his way to check on another shooting." Bernice lowered herself into a chair and rested her arms on the table.

"He died not long after I arrived. I spoke to him a few times. Seemed like a decent man." Rachel remembered him as tough, hardened, with kind eyes and a ready smile. His leathered skin and slight streaks of gray in his hair caused him to look much older than his true age of thirty-nine.

"We're hoping Sheriff Evans can make some sense of everything." Bernice stood as Hank came through the back door.

"Dax rode in with a couple of the men. I let him know Johnny's improving." He poured a cup of coffee and looked at Bernice. "He's going to put Hannibal away, then talk to those two gents who rode in a while ago. Thought I'd take him some coffee."

"I'll take it." Rachel reached for the cup and started toward the front.

Bernice watched her leave before turning to Hank. "Those two would be good for each other."

"Dax and Rachel?"

"Of course. Haven't you seen the way they look at each other? Dax doesn't take his eyes off her when she's here. Same goes for her."

Hank leaned down to place a kiss on his wife's cheek before heading back outside. Bernice usually had things right. He wondered how he'd never noticed the attraction between the two.

Dax walked out of the barn and heard the sound of the front door open and close before looking up to see Rachel walk down the steps toward him. He worked hard to ignore the way his body responded to her presence.

"Hank thought you'd like this." She handed him the coffee.

"Need it is more accurate." He took the cup and turned toward the two men standing nearby. "I'm Dax Pelletier. You wanted to see me?"

"I'm Bob Jones and this is my brother, Ted. We're looking for work." Bill glanced between Dax and the woman next to him, his eyes not settling long in one place.

"Where did you two last work?"

"We've been at several ranches the last few years," Bill said, although they sure didn't *work* the ranches. "Texas and Colorado, mostly."

"The work available here might not last long. I've four men laid up, but two will start back within a few days. I'm not sure about the other two. Once they're recovered, I may not have room for additional men." He eyed them, annoyed at the younger one whose gaze kept wandering to Rachel. Dax stepped closer to her in an attempt to warn the man off. "If you can accept those terms, you're welcome to start. The bunkhouse is over there." He indicated with the hand holding the coffee cup. "My brother, Luke, will let you know where you'll be riding." He rested his other hand on Rachel's shoulder.

Jed looked between the two of them, the message coming through clear. "Thanks, boss."

Rachel watched them leave, then looked up at Dax and felt his arm fall from her shoulder. "What was that about?"

"Nothing." He drank the coffee in a couple of swallows and handed the empty cup back to her. "I'm going to check on Johnny and Tat."

She lifted a brow, choosing to ignore his response. "Tell Uncle Charles I'll join him in a few minutes."

Dax pushed open the bunkhouse door as the doctor looked up.

"Ah, Dax. Just the person I want to see," Charles said.

Dax stood between the two bunks, looking toward Tat first. "How are you feeling?"

"I've been better, boss. Could've been worse, I suppose." Tat attempted to shift in his bunk, even though the splints kept him in place. "I hope to be back with the herd soon."

"Take it easy. You'll be back out there soon enough." He turned toward Johnny, surprised at how much the young cowhand had improved. "You look much better than last night."

"The doc says I almost didn't make it. Glad I proved him wrong." His voice still sounded raspy and dry.

Dax could see the pain flash through his face, understanding the lad still had a long recovery ahead. "Take your time healing, Johnny. I've hired a couple of men to ride herd until you and Tat are back."

"That'll be soon, boss," Johnny said, although everyone knew it wasn't true.

"You won't ride until the doctor says it's okay." He glanced at Charles. "Do you have a minute?"

Charles followed him outside and closed the door.

"Tell me your thoughts."

"Tat is coming along well, considering it has been just a couple of days. Still, I doubt he'll be able to ride for several weeks. Johnny's got a longer healing spell. Problem is, they'll both want to get back to work sooner than they should. I'll come by at least once a week to check on them, and can send Rachel out if I'm not available."

"Rachel coming out would be fine, Doc."

Charles's mouth quirked upwards at the corners. "I suspected it might be." He turned to go inside, then stopped. "You know, it's none of my business, Rachel being a grown woman and all, but I'll say my piece anyway. She's taken a liking to you, Dax. I understand you may not feel the same. If you don't, I'd have to ask you to think about staying away from her. She's a great nurse and a big help to me, but she's also my niece and I don't want to see her getting her heart broken."

Dax shoved his hands in his pockets, feeling like he did years ago when his father would lecture him. Except this wasn't a lecture and Charles wasn't his father. He was a concerned uncle trying to do his best for his niece.

"I care a great deal about Rachel and my intention isn't to cause her pain. She knows I may leave, return to Texas. You'll have to accept whatever she decides to do while I'm here. She's free to walk away any time."

Although the response didn't satisfy Charles, he felt a sense of relief knowing Dax understood his concern. He began to say something else before his eyes lit on the subject of their conversation. Rachel flashed a tentative smile at the two men, having no idea she'd been the focus of their discussion.

"Bernice asked me to let you know there's roast beef and biscuits ready. Why don't I keep watch on Johnny and Tat while you two go inside and eat?"

Dax's eyes searched hers and he quelled the urge to reach out and pull her to him. "Have you eaten?" he asked instead.

"Well, someone had to test it and make sure it was fit to eat." Her serious expression turned to a soft laugh as she disappeared into the bunkhouse.

"Hard to walk away from someone like that, isn't it, son?"

"Harder than you know." Dax lowered his head as his long, slow strides carried him into the house.

"Thank you so much for inviting me. I had a wonderful time." Abigail stood next to Ruth Paige, the reverend's wife, who had hosted the church lunch.

"I'm so pleased you could join us, Abby." Ruth looked behind the young woman. "Did you come alone to town or did your father accompany you?"

"It took a bit of persuading before he gave his permission for me to ride without a chaperone. I'm hopeful each trip will be a little easier for him." Abby still felt remorse at alluding to the tragedy a few years before, but perhaps the comment had been what swayed her father to let her make the trip alone.

"We'll certainly hope that's the case. Perhaps you'd like to join a group of young women for tea at our home sometime? You've been gone so much and a number of women about your age have moved to Splendor. I doubt you've met most of them."

"That would be wonderful." Abby had hoped to meet more people, especially those her age, once she returned home. This would be her opportunity.

"Tilly, come over here a minute." Ruth waited while the young, pregnant woman made her way across the room. "Tilly, I don't believe you've met Abigail Tolbert. Abby, this is Tilly Murton, Tyson's wife."

Abby cast a surprised look at Tilly. "I'm so glad to meet you. I didn't know Tyson had married."

Tilly glanced away, a hand resting on her protruding stomach.

"They were married last month. Edward performed the ceremony." Ruth took Tilly's hand. "They'll have a new member of the family before long." She smiled at the young woman, indicating she had become a welcome friend.

"That is exciting news. I hope you'll let me come and visit sometime. I haven't seen Tyson in a long time." Abby understood the awkward situation Tilly found herself in. Not everyone accepted conditions such as this the way Reverend and Mrs. Paige did.

"I would love to have you come to visit." Tilly's grateful look warmed Abby.

"Well, you two may talk about it more at our next young ladies tea. You *will* be able to make it, right, Tilly?"

"Oh, yes. Tyson already said he'll bring me to town. He's been wonderful."

Abby caught a glimpse of the way Ruth's nose scrunched as another woman approached.

"Good afternoon, Abigail. I've been meaning to come over and see how you're doing."

"It's good to see you, Mrs. Poe. How are you?" Abby did her best to hide her amusement at the way Ruth stood guard near Tilly, as if daring the woman to say anything disparaging.

"I'm doing fine." She glanced at Tilly. "Looks like you're coming along." The woman's voice took on an inflammatory tone.

"Yes, ma'am," Tilly glanced down and placed her other hand on her stomach.

"It certainly was good of the reverend to go ahead with a church marriage. Some wondered about how appropriate it was given your advanced state."

"Now, Gladys, you know it pleased my husband to marry Tyson and Tilly. He enjoys nothing more than seeing two young people unite in marriage."

"That may be, Ruth. I'm just saying not everyone felt the same. Of course, I'm not one of them. Well, I suppose I should find my husband for the ride home. Looks like the wind is kicking up. Could be facing a dust storm before too long." Gladys nodded at Ruth and Abby, ignoring Tilly in her effort to get away.

Abby felt the chill as silence washed over the three.

"Don't pay any attention to her, Tilly. Gladys Poe has a different view, that's all, and few people share it." Ruth rested a hand on the young woman's arm and squeezed.

Tilly didn't answer. She knew some accepted the fact Tyson had married his pregnant saloon girl and treated her well. Others didn't.

"Is Tyson waiting outside?" Abby's attempt to change the conversation worked.

"Yes. He's probably out there now."

"Wonderful. I'd love to say hello, plus I need to start riding back. My father will have a fit if I'm late. I'll see you Sunday, Mrs. Paige."

Ruth hoped the introduction might encourage the two young women to be friends, believing both had needs the other could fill. One wealthy, yet lonely, who'd been separated from everyone for years—the other poor, somewhat scorned, yet full of life and dreams.

Abby preceded Tilly down the steps to see Tyson's wagon several feet away, with him standing alongside it. She waved, hoping he'd still recognize her, then turned to Tilly, whose

288

broad smile signaled her pleasure at seeing her husband. Abby placed a hand on her bonnet to hold it in place. Gladys Poe had been right. The wind had picked up since she'd arrived at the church.

"Why, Abigail Tolbert. It's been a while." Tyson wrapped an arm around Tilly's shoulders and pulled her close, as she also tried to keep her bonnet on her head.

"Hello, Tyson. Tilly and I met inside. Congratulations on your marriage."

He cast a warm gaze at Tilly. "We made the decision pretty quick. Sorry we couldn't invite everyone."

"Well, you'll have to make up for it by letting me visit. It's been such a long time since I've seen your family."

"I told her it would be all right for her to come out once the baby's born, Tyson."

"Of course it is. You're welcome before then if you get a notion to take a ride. You know Gil would be real pleased to see you again."

Abby laughed. "I'm sure he's forgotten all about me by now." She watched as the wind began to whip furiously around the tree branches, sending leaves and twigs into the air. "I should start for home."

"You riding alone?" Tyson's voice held concern as he felt the gusts of wind, fused with dirt, increase. He didn't much care for women riding alone in this part of the country, especially in a dust storm.

"Yes, but you know it's not far. I'm so glad we met, Tilly. I'll see you again soon."

Their eyes followed Abby as she walked toward her horse. She grabbed the reins and hoisted herself up before straightening her dress and waving.

"What did you mean about Gil and Abby?" Tilly asked.

He helped his wife up on the wagon seat, then climbed beside her. "He's had a spark for her since they were kids. Never amounted to anything. They were too young and Abby was always being sent away to school." He slapped the reins, wanting to start for the ranch before the winds picked up anymore. The dust already swirled around them, making it hard to see.

"Well, now may be his chance." Tilly wrapped a hand around Tyson's arm and leaned into him.

"You never know." He chuckled at the thought, knowing it would never come to pass. There would be no chance King Tolbert would ever let his daughter get near a poor rancher like Gil. Tilly didn't know it, but she'd learn. The Tolberts were worlds away from the Murtons.

Abby rode straight down the main street through town, fighting the dust swirling around her. She'd thought of stopping to say hello to Suzanne at the restaurant, then decided against it as the wind increased. The distance between the church and boardinghouse amounted to a couple hundred yards, yet the gusts had increased to a point where it had become hard to see. She brought a hand up to rub the dust from her eyes, realizing in the course of a few minutes, visibility had been lost. She tried to see in front of her, reining Willy one way, then another before she felt a tug on the reins. Someone had grabbed the horse and was leading them.

A moment later, they entered the safety of the livery, Noah's hands lifting to help her down. "What do you think you were doing trying to ride out in this storm?" Noah's voice held a concerned edge and none of the usual warmth.

She dusted dirt from her dress and tried to spit sand from her mouth before answering.

"Here. Drink some of this." He handed her a canteen.

"Thank you." The mumbled words were lost as the sounds of the intense wind continued. She drank a few swallows before handing the water back to Noah and accepting the cloth he held out so she could wipe the dirt from her face. She felt the grit and realized how horrible she must appear.

"Do you want to tell me why you were out in this wind storm?" He sat on a bench and leaned forward, waiting for her answer.

Abby tossed the dirty cloth back to him and crossed her arms in front of her chest, embarrassed at being treated like a child. "I thank you for your kindness, Mr. Brandt, but I don't owe you an explanation." She straightened her spine as her chin jutted out, trying her best to look insulted.

His mouth crooked upward at her show of defiance. He'd never seen this side of Abby and found he liked it. Noah stood, picked up his hammer, and walked to the forge.

"You're right, Miss Tolbert." He turned from her to focus on his work.

Noah's reaction, turning his back on her as if she held no significance, irritated Abby even more. Deciding the time had come for her to leave, she glanced outside to see the winds had become even stronger, obliterating the view of the boardinghouse across the street. Her arms fell to her sides as she lowered herself onto the bench Noah had vacated moments before.

She watched him work, his strong arms raising and lowering the heavy hammer, and wondered what pushed him to work so hard. He never seemed to close the livery. Even when she and her father would ride past on their way to Sunday services, he'd be inside, the forge burning hot, concentrating on the task before him. Abby stood, debating if she should keep her distance or move closer. Her curiosity won out.

"What are you working on?"

Noah didn't turn or answer right away. After a few more heavy strikes of the hammer, he set it aside and looked over at her.

"New bars for the jail. The sheriff doesn't like the current ones."

Abby wandered toward the wall where Noah hung his tools and ran her finger over several of them, trying to figure out how he used each one.

"Is this for Suzanne?" She picked up a half-completed pot and held it out to him.

"It is."

"And this?" She pointed toward a flat piece of metal.

"A frying pan." He studied Abby as she walked around the livery, fingering one item, then another, trying to pass the time until the windstorm subsided.

"What do you do when you aren't working, Mr. Brandt?"

"Noah."

She turned to him. "What?"

"My name is Noah."

A smile broke across her face. "All right. Noah. But you must call me Abby. So what do you do when you aren't here?"

"Eat, sleep, play cards sometimes." He picked up the hammer once more.

She pursed her lips. It sounded like a solitary life.

"Will you be going to the church picnic in a few weeks?" The question popped out before she'd thought through it.

"No."

"Why not? It's such fun, with lots of food, games, and even music. The whole town will be there." As she spoke, Abby realized how much she wanted him to attend.

"I don't go to picnics, Miss Tolbert."

"Abby, remember?"

"Abby."

"You wouldn't have to bring anything. I could pack enough food for you." Her gaze lifted to his when she realized what she'd said.

A grin split Noah's face. "Are you asking me to accompany you, Abby?"

She could feel heat creep up her face and wished she'd learn when to stay quiet. "I, well... I thought—"

"Abigail, are you in here?" The sound of her father's voice cut her off and she shifted to see him looming in the entry. "What are you doing in here? I expected you home long before now."

She noticed the wind had stopped, no longer blowing and forcing her to remain in the livery. Even so, she didn't want to leave.

"The windstorm began as I left church. It blinded me and Mr. Brandt was kind enough to lead Willy inside. I was waiting for the wind to pass."

King glanced from his daughter to Noah, giving the blacksmith a hard stare.

"Well, it has stopped. Get Willy and we'll leave."

"I'll get him." Noah walked over to the stall and brought the horse out, helping Abby onto the saddle.

"Thank you again, Mr. Brandt. I appreciate your kindness."

"You're welcome, Miss Tolbert." He shot a look to her father. "Mr. Tolbert."

Noah waited until they'd ridden out of sight, then turned back to his work. A small weight lifted each time he saw Abby. Everything about Abigail Tolbert caused him to feel better. He knew nothing would ever come of it, yet he couldn't keep himself from wondering if things were different, if he'd come out of the war a different man, perhaps he might stand a chance. He shook his head at the foolish thought, poured water over his head, then walked back to the forge.

Chapter Eighteen

"Whiskey." Cash took off his gloves and laid them on the bar before turning to survey the other occupants of the Wild Rose. He'd gotten an early start. By midafternoon, he'd spotted a camp south of Splendor and gotten close enough to identify Duff and Whitey Mayes. He didn't recognize the third man. He'd accounted for three of the five men Sheriff Sterling had seen leaving town early one morning a couple of days before Cash arrived in Big Pine. Now he had to find the other two. He'd ridden around to the north end of Splendor, hoping to avoid running into the two outlaws who weren't in camp with the others.

"Here you are." Al set the whiskey down and picked up the coins Cash handed him. "You're new in Splendor."

"That's right." He took a sip of whiskey, looking over the rim of the glass at the bartender. "I'm trying to locate Dax and Luke Pelletier. Do you know them?"

Al eyed the stranger. This was the second gunman to ask for the Pelletiers in as many days. "What do you want with them?"

"That's my business."

Al glanced up as another man joined them at the bar. "Sheriff. What can I get you?"

"Whiskey."

Gabe turned toward the stranger and extended his hand. "Gabe Evans."

"Cash Coulter."

"You just get into town?" Gabe picked up the whiskey Al placed in front of him and tossed it back.

"Yep."

"Staying or passing through?"

"Don't know yet. Depends if I find the men I'm looking for."

"And who would that be?" Based on the man's distinct southern accent, Gabe thought he already knew.

"Dax and Luke Pelletier. Do you know them?"

"I do."

The two men fell silent, each waiting out the other.

"He's looking for the Pelletiers," Al said as he topped off each whiskey glass.

"I heard." Gabe turned his attention back to Cash. "Have you known them long?"

"We grew up together in Savannah, but I lost track of them after the war. It's important I find them."

Gabe finished his whiskey and clasped Cash on the shoulder. "Finish up. I'll take you to them."

"I thought it best to get this to you right away." Bernie Griggs, the Western Union and mail proprietor, had ridden to Tolbert's ranch to deliver the telegram. He'd known the rancher had sent urgent messages to several contacts in the east. Tolbert had received his first response.

King opened the message and read it, his brows furrowed, exposing deep creases between his eyes. "Of course, you know what it says."

"Yes, I do."

"Have you heard any of this before?"

"No. Most of us have had a bad feeling about the man ever since he arrived."

"I see." King set the message on his desk and walked to the window.

"Do you need to send a response?"

"No. Thank you for bringing it to me," King said over his shoulder, never turning his gaze away from the circle of men standing by the barn, his foreman one of them. He'd sent the messages a few days before, hoping for a quick response. He now understood the motivation Drake had for creating a war with the Pelletiers. The problem would be deciding what to do with the information.

He picked up his gun belt, strapping it around his waist before grabbing his hat and walking outside. Abigail sat on the porch in one of the rocking chairs, engrossed in a book. She looked up at his approach and set the book down.

"Are you going somewhere?"

"I need to go to the Pelletier ranch. Would you like to ride along?"

She saw as well as heard the concern in his voice. "That would be lovely. I'll be right back." Abby hurried into the house while King continued toward the barn, motioning for one of the men.

"Boss?"

"Saddle my horse and Abigail's."

"Yes, sir."

"Are you going somewhere?" Drake asked as he walked up beside Tolbert.

"Abigail and I are taking a ride. I doubt we'll be gone long."

Drake had seen Bernie Griggs go into the house, then leave about ten minutes later. He wondered if Tolbert leaving had to do with Griggs' visit, or if it was a coincidence. He didn't put much stock in coincidences.

"I'm ready, Father." Abby strolled past Drake and straight into the barn. Within minutes, she and Tolbert were riding out.

"I'll watch the place while you're gone."

"You do that, Drake," Tolbert said, glad to get Abby away from the ranch and the menace he unwittingly welcomed into their lives.

Cash followed Gabe out of town, heading northwest on an old rutted road.

"You're now on Pelletier land." Gabe pointed to a whitewashed post to the side of the road. "It won't be much longer to the ranch."

"How long have you been in town, Sheriff?"

"Not long. I stopped by to visit a friend."

"And they persuaded you to take the sheriff position?"

Gabe eyed Cash. "Something like that."

"Sheriff Sterling in Big Pine said they'd been looking for a sheriff for some time."

"You interested?"

"Why? The job doesn't suit you?"

"Suits me fine, but I told them I'd take it on only until they found a replacement who wanted to settle in Splendor permanently."

"Sounds like you don't."

"No."

They rode in silence a while longer before coming in sight of the ranch house. A group of men were pulling saddles off their horses when Gabe and Cash stopped and dismounted.

"Hey, Gabe. What brings you out this way?" Bull walked up to the sheriff, eyeing the other man.

"Brought a friend of Dax's and Luke's. Are they around?"

"Both are in the bunkhouse, checking on Tat and Johnny. I'll take care of your horses while you go inside." Bull reached for the reins, not taking his gaze from the tall, blond man who accompanied Gabe.

Dax stood over Rachel, watching her change Johnny's bandages. She'd ridden Old Pete to the ranch earlier to keep watch on the two injured cowboys while everyone except Bull, Hank, and Bernice were out with the herd.

"The swelling is almost gone and your cuts and bruises are healing. You'll need to relax and let the broken bones heal." Her words were gentle and encouraging.

"I'm already tired of laying around." He fumbled with the blanket and tried to sit up, then fell back on the bunk.

"I understand." She smiled at Johnny. "Be glad you were hurt and not killed. You're a lucky man." Rachel had yet to look at Dax, although she could feel his presence and knew he stood close behind her. "I'm going to check on Tat. Let me know if you need anything."

She stood and turned, facing the man she'd most wanted to avoid today. Her hope had been to check on the two ranch hands, then ride back to town without coming into contact with the older Pelletier. After their conversation the other night, she realized he needed space, time to figure out what troubled him. And she needed space, as well.

"Hello, Rachel."

She raised her eyes to meet his. "Hello, Dax." She tried to move around him, but he didn't budge. "Excuse me," she said and tried again.

"How about some coffee after you've seen to the men?" His gaze locked on hers in almost a silent plea.

"Perhaps."

Both turned at the sound of the door opening, and Dax's jaw dropped at the sight of the man accompanying Gabe inside.

"I'll be damned. Cash Coulter. How are you?" He walked up to his old friend and took his hand, drawing him into a hug and slapping him on the back, causing Luke to look up from where he sat next to Tat.

"I'm doing fine, Dax." Cash looked around the bunkhouse and spotting Luke, held his hand out to him. Seemed his friends had a pretty prosperous ranch going.

"How did you find us?" Luke asked as a broad grin split his face.

"It wasn't easy."

Rachel stared at the man she'd shared a meal with on her trip out to Montana, surprised to have run into him again in such a remote location. She took a step forward when his gaze landed on her.

"Cash, this is—"

"Miss Davenport, it's a pleasure to see you again." Cash removed his hat and made a slight bow.

Surprise crossed Rachel's face. "Hello, Mr. Coulter. It's good to see you."

Dax and Luke exchanged looks, wondering when and how the two knew each other.

"I see you've already met." Dax's eyes narrowed, his voice low and guarded.

Cash glanced at him. "We shared a train ride on our way out west. Miss Davenport left for Montana, while I rode to Denver." He looked back at Rachel. "I never thought we'd run into each other again."

"Neither did I, Mr. Coulter. My uncle's clinic, the one I mentioned to you, is located here. What brings you to Splendor?"

His face took on a grave expression as he turned toward Dax and Luke. "The Mayes brothers."

"So you believe Whitey and Duff rode all the way from Texas to hunt Luke and me down?" Dax asked.

"I'm certain of it. From what I heard, they have three other men with them. Might be their cousins, the Olin brothers, but I'm not sure. I haven't been able to find any wanted posters on those three."

"They're rumored to be the men helping the Mayes boys with their robberies. Could've been part of the group Luke, Pat, and I chased out of Red Gulch when Pat was killed." Dax folded his arms and leaned back in his chair.

"And you say they're camped south of town?" Gabe asked.

"I got close enough to see Duff and Whitey. I didn't recognize the third one. Sheriff Sterling said five rode out of Big Pine a few mornings ago, so there's no telling where the other two are."

"We hired two men, boss, but Olin isn't the last name they used." Hank stood at the sound of pounding on the front door, returning a moment later. "Bull wanted us to know King Tolbert and his daughter are riding in."

Dax looked at Luke. "I guess we'd better find out what they want."

King spotted the sheriff's horse as he dismounted. At least he wouldn't need to make the trip to town like he'd planned.

"Tolbert." Dax nodded at King and his daughter.

"We need to talk." Tolbert glanced at Gabe, who'd joined Dax and Luke on the front porch with a fourth man he didn't recognize.

"Come inside." Dax followed, asking Hank to take Abigail into the kitchen so she could visit with Bernice before he joined the other men in the study.

King hesitated when Cash took a seat next to Luke.

"Cash, this is King Tolbert. He owns the ranch on our eastern border," Dax said. "Tolbert, Cash Coulter. He's a longtime friend of ours. You already know Gabe and Hank."

The introduction seemed to put Tolbert at ease.

"What's on your mind?" Luke asked, puzzled as to what would bring Tolbert to them.

"I've gotten some disturbing news about one of my men. I need to know if it's accurate."

"Go on." Dax sat back, already knowing the man Tolbert wanted to discuss.

"Did you know my foreman, Parnell Drake, during the war?"

Cash's eyes locked on King's at the mention of the man suspected of killing his kin. He considered speaking up, then decided it would be best to see how the rest of the conversion played out.

Dax exchanged a look with Luke. "I did." His voice held a tightness which signaled his opinion of the man.

"Tell me about him."

"It's simple. He was a sergeant under my command. Had a history of being brutal in

304

combat, as well as with his men. He deserted the night before a big battle. I never laid eyes on him again until we arrived in Splendor."

"You never saw fit to inform me of his background?"

"Wasn't my business. I figured you'd already checked him out."

King paced to the window and shot a look at Gabe. "Is the man wanted?"

"Other than being a deserter? No, not that I've seen. I can check in Big Pine and elsewhere, see if I can find out anything more."

Cash continued to sit in silence. Although he believed Drake to be the man who'd murdered his uncle, aunt, and cousins on their Louisiana farm, he had no proof other than the word of a former slave who'd worked the farm with his uncle after the war. The cold truth was, no one would take the word of an ex-slave. Cash needed more proof, or the man to confess.

"What are you thinking?" Dax asked King.

"I believe the man wants to run you and your brother out, or kill you. Get rid of anyone who knows of his past."

"So you're saying he's the one behind the assaults on the ranch and our men?" As Dax considered it, it made sense Drake would be the man behind the attacks. More so than Tolbert instigating what amounted to a range war on his neighbors.

"I don't have proof but, yes, that's my guess."

"What do you plan do with him?" Hank asked.

King looked at Gabe. "The men who were with Drake the night of the stampede are back. I think it's a good time for you to speak with them."

"I agree. No better time than now." Gabe stood. "Cash, I'd like to meet with you tomorrow about the location of the Mayes' camp. You've got wanted posters on the two brothers. I want them behind bars before there's any trouble in Splendor."

"We're going with you," Luke said, including Dax in his comment.

Gabe eyed the two men. "I don't want this to turn into a slaughter. They're to be arrested and stand trial."

"We're still Texas Rangers. We don't need your permission to go after them." Dax folded his arms across his chest and leaned against the desk.

"True," Gabe relented. "But we do it together, my way."

Dax glanced at Luke. "Agreed. We'll meet you tomorrow morning at the jail."

"Who are you talking about?" King asked.

"I'll explain on the way to your place," Gabe answered.

The men turned as Rachel opened the study door. Dax pushed away from the desk, taking a couple of steps toward her.

"Excuse me, gentlemen." Her eyes met Dax's. "I'm leaving now. I'll be back in a couple of days to check on the men again."

"Wait up a minute. I'd like a word with you." Dax followed her outside with Gabe, Hank, and

Tolbert right behind them, leaving Luke and Cash alone.

Cash crooked a brow. "Is there something going on between Dax and Miss Davenport?"

Luke placed his hands on his hips and shook his head. "Darned if I know."

"Thank you for coming out." Dax stood beside Rachel and Old Pete, wishing they had time for coffee and conversation. "How about staying for supper? I'll ride back to town with you afterwards."

"I don't know, Dax. It seems it would be best to start back now."

"Best for whom?"

She gazed up at him, seeing the turbulence in his gray eyes. "For both of us." She pressed her lips together and wished she knew another answer. "I'm going to ask Uncle Charles to come out to check on Tat and Johnny. Perhaps being away from me will help you decide what you want." Rachel reached out to lay a hand on his arm. "I can't be around you and pretend I don't love you, Dax." She waited, praying he'd say something to give her hope they might have a future.

Dax pursed his lips, not able to say the words she wanted to hear. He loved her, but acknowledging it now would be the same as saying he'd stay and he wasn't ready to make that commitment—at least not yet.

307

"Rachel, I ..." His voice faded, a look of resigned acceptance clear on his face.

Rachel nodded in an attempt to hide the heart-breaking disappointment that gripped her. "Well, I'd better go." She pulled herself up onto the saddle, adjusted her split skirt and focused straight ahead, then turned Old Pete toward Splendor.

Dax kept his eyes trained on her until she disappeared. He knew something he cherished was about to slip away. He wanted to reach out, grab it, stop it from disappearing, but he didn't know quite how to do it—or if he should.

He no longer had to wonder how she felt. She loved him and he hadn't responded. Dax accepted if anything more were to happen between them, it would be up to him. She'd left the decision in his hands.

He took off his hat and wiped an arm across his brow, wishing he understood what drove him to want to ride hundreds of miles south to a place not truly his home, leaving behind a flourishing ranch, his brother, and a woman he loved. He feared the answer had nothing to do with Texas, but with his own need to be free of commitment. And he knew, to Rachel, it wasn't just a commitment.

Dax inhaled a deep breath, letting it out in a slow stream. He had to focus on the threats coming from Drake and the Mayes brothers. Once those were settled, he'd redirect his attention to his future, and a life with or without Rachel.

Chapter Nineteen

"Who else?" Gabe leaned back in the chair, frustrated at the lack of progress and evasive answers from the men who'd been with Drake the night of the stampede. Each swore they hadn't seen or heard anything out of the ordinary, and all were adamant that Drake hadn't ordered an attack on the Pelletier cattle.

"Just Swaggert and Pruett, who are close to Drake. My belief is they'll say whatever's needed to keep suspicion off of them," Tolbert said. "I'm not surprised none of the men we've spoken to were involved. I let most all the men Drake brought with him go. Other than Swaggert and Pruett, the men have been with me since before Drake."

"Were the two with him when you hired Drake?"

"They were. He said they'd been together for years."

"Well, let's hear what they have to say." Gabe stood, stretching his arms above his head while waiting for King to get the men. He walked over to the cabinet to pour a whiskey when King reappeared, his face red with anger.

"They're gone."

"Who?"

"Drake, Pruett, and Swaggert took off while we were talking with the others."

"Did they say anything before they left?" Gabe moved toward the entry door as he spoke.

"I didn't ask." King followed him outside and toward the bunkhouse. He stepped in front of Gabe and pushed the door open.

All activity stopped and the men turned toward their boss and the sheriff.

"Did Drake or the others say anything about where they were headed or why they were leaving?" Gabe asked, moving into the circle the men had formed in the center of the room.

A few shook their heads, others mumbled, "No."

"Their gear is gone, boss." One of the men pointed to a spot where they kept their belongings.

"I'd better go warn Dax and Luke." Gabe grabbed Blackheart and was on his way within minutes, leaving Tolbert to deal with the situation at his ranch.

Ellis, Bull, and the two new men who called themselves Ted and Bob, stood on the corral rails watching Joe take one more turn on the green horse. As with his other attempts, the horse bucked in a wild rhythm, surging from one end of the fenced area to the other. However, unlike the previous two rides, Joe managed to hang on until the horse became exhausted. He took his time, not rushing the animal, while letting it know he was the boss.

"Good ride." Bull slapped Joe on the back as he left the corral, brushing dirt and hay from his clothes.

"Anyone know who rode in with the sheriff today?" Jed Olin asked.

"Hank says he's a friend of the Pelletiers. Knew them back in Savannah before the war," Bull said. "I guess he's some kind of bounty hunter. Says there's some outlaws from Texas tracking them down for killing their brother."

"I wonder if that's when Pat got killed," Ellis said as they made their way into the barn.

"Don't know." Bull grabbed a frayed rope and sat down as the others occupied themselves with other chores. "Seems like a lot of trouble has been plaguing this ranch since Pat died."

Bill and Jed stayed a few minutes longer listening to Bull and Ellis, but heard nothing more.

"Ted and I are going to wash off in the creek," Bill said as the two started to leave.

"It isn't Saturday," Ellis joked as they left.

"What do you think of them?" Bull asked him, watching as the men walked away.

"Bob and Ted? They sure don't seem to know cattle like I thought they would. Guess they're better than nothing."

Bull grunted. "I'm not sure they're better than nothing." He turned back to his work, ignoring the men who'd walked out of sight.

"What do you want to do, Bill?" Jed's eyes darted around the area between the barn, bunkhouse, and main house. One of them had to warn the others.

"We can't both go. They'll get suspicious." Bill thought a minute. "We'll ride toward the creek. You'll take off from there to let the others know what's going on. I'll tell everyone you had a hankering to go by the Wild Rose. Just get yourself back here as soon as you can."

Dax, Luke, and Cash sat around the supper table with Hank and Bernice, laughing at the stories the three recalled from their childhood in Savannah. To the men who'd fought for the Confederacy and then returned to a home they no longer recognized, it seemed like a lifetime ago.

"What made you decide to turn to bounty hunting?" Hank asked Cash as Bernice handed him a plate filled with roast beef.

"I didn't make the decision. A friend of mine is a sheriff outside of Savannah. He needed help finding a man accused of murdering a neighbor. It took about a week to find and turn him in."

"That led to the next one?" Luke asked.

"In a way." Cash sat back in his chair, deciding this would be the best time to tell them of his search for Drake. "I'd ridden to Louisiana to visit my uncle, aunt, and cousins. They owned a farm near the Texas border and helped raise me before my parents moved to Savannah. A small place, a few head of cattle, pigs, and various crops. My uncle worked it with one other man—an ex-slave, Rawley, who'd been with them for years—and my two cousins. I arrived in the nearest town to learn they'd all been killed— murdered by persons unknown. I found Rawley still living at the farm, trying to take care of the place on his own. He swore he told the sheriff he knew who killed them."

"They never arrested anyone?" Dax asked.

"Didn't even search." His voice held a deceptive calm, hiding the anger he felt for those who ignored what Rawley had told them. "You may have forgotten how the word of a slave, or ex-slave, is ignored and counted as less than nothing. They didn't believe him. Some even wanted to hang *him* for the murders. Might have done it if the local preacher hadn't come to his aid and talked some sense into the others. He brought in some tracker who convinced the town it couldn't have been done by one man, not with the tracks of multiple horses and other evidence he turned up." Cash took a deep breath, trying to control the rage that still consumed him when he thought of the evil which destroyed his family.

"Did the man give you a name?" Dax asked, frustration burning in him at the sheer brutality.

"The leader introduced himself when the gang rode up asking for water and feed for the horses. Even though he was in the barn, Rawley said he heard it clear as day. Parnell Drake."

Bernice gasped at the mention of Tolbert's foreman, as Luke and Hank let out muttered curses.

Dax sat forward in his chair, leaning his arms on the table, his eyes locked on Cash. "You're certain?"

"No mistake. Problem is, there's no wanted poster or warrant for him since they didn't believe Rawley."

"That's when you decided to track him down yourself?"

"Yes, Drake and whoever rode with him."

"What did you plan to do once you found them?" Dax would do whatever he could to help his friend, short of gunning someone down without cause.

"I'll do what needs to be done." Cash pushed from his chair and stood, pacing away from the table at the same time loud pounding came from the entry door. He yanked it open to see Gabe, tired and windblown.

"I need to speak with Dax and Luke."

"We're here," Dax called. "Come on inside. We just finished supper." He noticed the look of deep concern on Gabe's face.

"Drake and his two partners, Pruett and Swaggert, have disappeared. Rode out of Tolbert's ranch while we were talking with the other men."

"Shit," Cash muttered and walked toward the hook where he'd hung his gun belt.

"Where do you think you're going?" Dax asked.

Cash finished strapping on his guns, then glanced over his shoulder as he grabbed his hat. "They need to be found and brought in before they disappear." He started out the door, but came to a halt when Gabe grasped his arm.

"Do you know something about them I don't?" Gabe asked, confused at Cash's sudden interest.

Cash glanced at Luke and Dax. "They'll explain." Once again, he turned to leave.

"Wait. You have no idea where they are, if they're holed up someplace or halfway across the Territory Range by now. If you want to help us, stay and we'll go with you to track Drake after we've brought in the Mayes gang." Dax stood next to his friend, his calm voice penetrating Cash's overwhelming need to take off after the men he suspected of gunning down his relatives.

Cash's hands moved to his waist as his head tilted up and he searched the dark sky. He knew Dax was right. He hated waiting, knowing the men he hunted were close. He let out a deep breath, pushing away the urge to do what he wanted. Putting the Mayes brothers behind bars had to come first. He stepped back inside and shot a look at the sheriff. "Grab some supper and coffee, then I'll explain what I know about Drake and his men."

"You're sure that's what you heard?" Duff asked Jed as his cousin finished explaining the new arrival at the Pelletier ranch.

"Certain. The man's been tracking us for weeks."

"Dammit, Duff. I told you we were being followed." Whitey's gut had warned him more than once they were being hunted, the same as they were hunting the Rangers.

"Quiet. I need to think." Duff paced away a few feet, pondering the possibilities for continuing their mission and still getting away alive. When the gang had started in Texas, the decision had been simple.

They'd learned the Rangers were in a small Montana town with no sheriff and no law nearby. Now they had a sheriff plus a bounty hunter to contend with, as well as losing the element of surprise. He turned back to Jed.

"Do they suspect you and Bill are with us?"

"Not from what I can tell." Jed chewed on a piece of hardtack, dipping it in his coffee every couple of bites.

"And you're certain the bounty hunter told them he knows where we're camped?"

"That's what the old man said."

"All right. First, we need to move our camp. Tonight."

"Where to?" Clark asked.

"Have you spotted any places to hide closer to their ranch?" Duff asked Jed.

"A couple of canyons leading into the Territory Ranch might work. The closest is at the base of Redemption Mountain, which butts up to the Pelletier place."

"We'll follow you there tonight, then you can ride back to join Bill. No sense pulling either of you out yet."

"Then what?" Whitey's voice still rippled with the anger he felt at his suspicions being ignored.

Duff faced his brother. "We get them alone and kill them."

Rachel watched the sunrise from the hill behind their house. She'd found peace on more than one morning by carrying a cup of coffee up to the top and watching the yellow ball peek above the trees, washing the area in early light. Even though the nights still required a shawl or coat, the days were warming. She loved this spot and fantasized about building a small home right here one day so she could see the sun rise each morning and the moon rise at night.

She thought of Dax. Had it been only yesterday she'd told him she loved him and he didn't respond? The ride back to town had been long and painful with the realization he didn't share her feelings. How wrong she'd been to think he felt the same. At least she could now accept the truth about his reasons for leaving. They had everything to do with following his dream in Texas and nothing to do with her. She had, in fact, been a stop along his journey. It seemed odd she held no embarrassment or resentment about announcing her feelings. In fact, she felt the opposite. She'd rather he knew than always wonder how he would have responded if he'd known.

Rachel and her uncle had talked at length when she returned, making the decision to start their visits to the outer ranches today. He wasn't expected to check on Tat and Johnny for a few days, which would give them plenty of time to visit the ranches on his list.

They'd take the wagon south out of town, toward the Murton ranch, then several miles further to the Weston ranch where he could check on their daughter, Janie, and possibly stay the night. Tomorrow, they'd travel to the Kuhn place, then make a last stop at the Frey ranch, staying the night before riding back to town the next day. Charles had seen only the Westons over the long winter and early spring, although he'd heard from Stan Peterman at the general store that all the families had made trips into Splendor a couple of times since Christmas. His concern wasn't so much for the adults as for the children.

"Rachel, I thought I'd find you up here." She looked up to see her uncle standing close by, watching the last bit of the sun coming up over the horizon. "We should get going if we hope to make it to the Weston ranch tonight."

"You're sure you're up for this?" She stood, tossing out the last of her coffee.

"The wagon is loaded and Old Pete is hitched up. I'm ready." He smiled down at her. She knew this type of medicine excited him—traveling to distant locations to meet with families who had little, if any, access to standard medical care. Even if they didn't need him right now, they would at some point and they'd already be comfortable with him.

"All right. Let's get started."

It didn't take Rachel long to throw a few items in a satchel, grab her coat, bonnet, and gloves, and meet Charles at the wagon. As she started to climb up, she stopped and ran back inside. Within minutes, she returned.

"I'm ready now." She cast him a smile. "Almost forgot my gun. Does anyone in town know we're going?" Rachel both looked forward to and dreaded the trip. She had little experience in the wild areas outside of town and knew of occasional reports of tragic endings to those who traveled alone.

"I spoke with Horace Clausen at the bank and Stan Peterman at the general store. They'll tell everyone else." He slapped the reins. "Peterman gave me directions along a portion of the river. He says it will take about four hours to get there, which will be a perfect time to stop and eat. It was smart of you to have Noah Brandt check on Old Pete when you got back yesterday. More than likely, he would have thrown at least one shoe halfway through the trip."

"He's a good man. We're lucky to have him."

Charles turned toward Rachel at her comment. She had yet to mention Dax since she'd returned from checking on Tat and Johnny, although she had asked him to continue their care while she stayed in Splendor. Both men were improving with each visit, enough so leaving town for three or four days wouldn't be a problem. He knew his niece had strong feelings for the oldest brother, and his instincts told him Dax felt the same. He didn't understand what stood in their way.

It took about an hour to reach the first ranch, and seconds for Tilly Murton to step outside to greet them. "What a wonderful surprise." She

319

waited for Rachel to climb down, then gave her new friend a quick hug. Tilly looked across the wagon. "Hello, Doctor Worthington. I'll go get Ty and Gil." She had made it halfway to the barn when her husband appeared, covered in dirt and hay.

Ty looked up to spot his wife and sweep her into a careful hug, letting her feet dangle inches from the ground.

"Ty, put me down." Her laughter rang through the air as she turned her head toward the wagon. "We have company."

He glanced up and set Tilly down, keeping his arm around her, and walked over to greet their guests. "Doc, Rachel, it's good to see you. What brings you out this way?" He shook Charles' hand and gave Rachel a brief hug.

"Nothing other than a sense it was time to visit some of my patients who don't get to town much. It would be good to check on Tilly while we're out this way." He glanced at her, seeing the blush washing her face. "How are you doing?"

"I feel wonderful." Tilly's hand absently moved up to splay across her stomach.

"Why don't we go inside and you can finish checking on Tilly while we rustle up some food?" Ty grasped her hand and started up the steps.

"We'll meet you at the restaurant," Luke called as Dax broke off from the group and walked toward the clinic. The brothers, plus Gabe and Cash, had spent a frustrating morning trying to locate Duff and Whitey Mayes. The camp where Cash first saw them had been abandoned, although the warm ashes from the fire told the men they'd missed their prey by hours. Even Cash's solid tracking skills lost their trail over rocky paths and flowing streams.

"Doc, Rachel." Dax pounded on the clinic door, getting no response. He looked up and down the boardwalk, then walked to the house in the back, thinking Rachel and the doctor might be taking their midday meal. Still no answer. He stalked back around to the front as Horace Clausen emerged from the bank.

"You looking for the doc?"

"I am. Have you seen him or Rachel today?"

"Spoke to him yesterday evening. He said they planned to visit some distant ranches and check on the families."

"Any idea where?"

"Let's see. As I recall, Charles mentioned stopping at the Murton place before heading toward the Weston, Kuhn, and Frey ranches. There's little chance they'll be back before day after tomorrow."

"And you're sure it was just the two of them?" Dax pulled off his hat and ran his fingers through his hair. He couldn't help the sense of foreboding at the knowledge they'd traveled alone into what amounted to wilderness country where the Mayes brothers and possibly Drake and his men might be hiding.

"As far as I know. Why?"

Dax spent a few minutes filling Clausen in on the outlaw gang, as well as Parnell Drake.

"Where's the sheriff now?"

"In the restaurant." Dax and Horace headed toward it at a fast pace.

"There he is. Looks like he's got Clausen with him," Luke said as he signaled Dax.

It didn't take the men long to formulate a plan to notify the citizens of the possible threat from both groups.

"My guess is Duff and Whitey Mayes want Dax and me, but they may not be above robbing the bank while they're in town. It might be best if you could close up for a couple of days." Luke folded his arms across his chest and leaned back in his chair.

"I can't close down until the robbers are found. It could take days or weeks." Clausen pulled a handkerchief from a pocket and wiped his face.

"What about posting guards?" Cash asked. "Perhaps a show of force would dissuade them from trying something in Splendor."

"It's a good thought, except who would we get?" Clausen asked. "Most of the townspeople have guns and know how to use them, but they're not guards."

"Let's not get ahead of ourselves. We know they're after us." Dax nodded toward his brother. "Seems doubtful they'd come after Luke and me, then try to stage a holdup at the bank."

"Dax is right. Their targets are the men who killed their brother, which means they must get to Dax and Luke first. We have to make sure they don't get what they want." Gabe signaled Suzanne for more coffee, then waited until she'd left to continue. "They don't want to catch them with a group of people as there's more chance of one of them getting shot."

"They'd have to follow us all of the time," Luke said.

"Or have someone on the inside who knows where you'll be each day." Cash sipped the hot coffee.

The table fell silent as the men contemplated Cash's words. It could mean someone they knew and trusted had been feeding information to the Mayes brothers.

"You believe someone tipped them off about you finding their camp?" Dax asked.

"I do." Cash set his cup down and glanced outside. "Have you hired any new men?"

"Two came on a few days ago. Quiet. They do what they're told but, from what Hank says, don't join in." Dax thought about his first introduction to the two men and the irritation he felt at Ted Jones for eyeing Rachel.

"What are their names?" Cash asked.

"Bob and Ted Jones."

"Could be they're part of the Mayes group. There isn't much out on the three Olin brothers, not like there is on Duff and Whitey. I'd keep an eye on them and anyone else you aren't sure about," Gabe said.

Dax nodded as he thought through the rest of the men and wondered who might be feeding information to the Mayes brothers, or even to Drake. He hoped the ex-sergeant had simply decided to leave Montana. At this point, Dax didn't care what happened to the man as long as he no longer posed a threat.

"Anything I can do?" Horace Clausen had remained silent during the exchange. Since moving out from back east, he'd had little experience with the type of men being discussed. The bank had never been threatened by robbers.

"Make sure the people who work for you are aware that known bank robbers have been spotted not far from Splendor, and tell them to be vigilant. If they make it into the bank, give them what they want and let them leave. We don't want anyone hurt." Gabe didn't like not having additional men to keep watch on the bank, but he had no choice. His focus had to be on the immediate risk—finding a way to protect Dax and Luke.

"Guess I'll be going now. Keep me informed."

Again silence enveloped the group as the banker walked away. Trouble seemed to be surrounding their small town and there weren't enough men to protect everyone.

"Did you speak with the doctor and Rachel?" Luke asked.

"She and the doc left early today, heading south of town to visit some families." The fact Rachel might be riding right into the path of the Mayes group or Drake gnawed at Dax, yet he'd convinced himself the men were after him and Luke, not the town doctor and his niece. In his mind, Dax felt certain there'd be no reason for the outlaws to go after innocents who had little connection to the Pelletiers—at least no connection anyone knew about.

"Do you think they're in danger?" Cash asked.

"I wouldn't think so. They're after Luke and me, not anyone else. The fact is, they might be safer outside of town right now." Dax hoped he was right. "Guess we'd better get back to the ranch and let the others know we haven't found anyone yet."

"I'll grab Noah and start spreading the word in town about what's going on, then I'll ride out to your place. I want to find out more about possible hiding places for those men. Hank, Bull, and some of others might have ideas. The gang has to be holed up someplace and I want to know where." Gabe stood. "As for Drake, maybe the man will show some brains and get out of the territory."

Chapter Twenty

"They took off early this morning. I heard they were headed to our old camp south of town." Bill had ridden away from the rest of the Pelletier cowhands toward the new camp in the hills west of the ranch. Not only had the group found a secluded canyon a couple of miles from where the cattle grazed, they'd also discovered caves covered by thick brush and trees.

"How many men are with the herd, and who's left back at their house?" Duff asked.

"As far as I know, it's the old man and his wife, plus the two injured men. Everyone else is with the herd." Bill scratched his stubbled chin. "There must be close to twenty men either with the herd or checking for strays. They leave a few men with the herd at night. The rest, which I'm guessing to be about twelve men, will go back to the bunkhouse. The Pelletiers almost always ride back to the ranch, so you're looking at maybe fourteen men."

"I'm looking for better odds than that."

"We can't keep waiting, Duff," Whitey protested. "We need to make our move soon. They know we're looking for them—"

"And that's why we wait. We need them to think we've left the area, given up on going after them. That's when we attack."

"We didn't sign up for this to take a year of our lives. We've got banks to rob and we're wasting time. I say we ride in tonight and take them while they sleep." Whitey stood inches from his brother, his features hard.

Duff pushed him back, causing Whitey to stumble and fall. "Get out of my face. I say we wait and that's what we'll do." He started to turn, then stopped when he heard the cocking of a gun. He looked over his shoulder to see Whitey, still on the ground, his gun drawn and pointed at Duff.

Before Whitey knew what happened, Duff spun and kicked the gun from his hand, landed another kick to his jaw, then planted a boot on his brother's chest while pulling his own gun, pointing it at Whitey's head.

"Don't ever threaten me again. Next time you do, I'll use this." Duff lowered the revolver a few inches closer to Whitey's face. "You understand me?"

Whitey wiped blood from his face and nodded. "Sure, Duff. I understand."

"Good." Duff stepped backward, keeping his gaze trained on Whitey, holstering his gun. He surprised himself with how quick he'd moved with his bad leg, but now it hurt like a son of a bitch.

Bill looked between the two brothers, believing it wouldn't be long before one of them did shoot the other over the reason for their trip.

"I've got to head back. Either Jed or I will let you know what's happening." Bill mounted his horse and started off toward the herd, glad to get away from the tension at their camp. He and Jed would need to find the opportunity soon, or someone besides the two Texas Rangers would end up dead.

"Seems to me everyone is doing fine here. Janie certainly recovered well." Charles closed up the satchel he'd carried into the Weston house. "You certain it's no problem for us to stay the night?"

"As long as you and your niece don't mind bedding down in the same room as our youngest." Lee Weston stood a few feet away, arms crossed over his lean chest.

"That's fine with us. We hope to get an early start in the morning. Ty Murton told me the Kuhn place is a couple of hours from here."

"Sounds about right. As long as the weather holds, you'll be fine." Lee bent down to pick up Janie.

"I suspect you don't get many visitors out this way." Charles had met Leander Weston two other times. Once when he'd brought his oldest son into the clinic, and the second when he and his wife had brought Janie into town a few weeks ago.

The first time, Weston had ridden most of the day, listening to his son's hacking cough and feeling his temperature rise. If he'd waited one more day, the chances were slim his son would've survived. It had taken two days to break the fever and another two to get enough food in the boy to make the return trip to their ranch. Lee had waited less time to bring Janie to town. A good indication the family valued his skills.

"Not many. A group of riders passed by last night, but didn't stop. Maybe four or five men. They stopped a few yards from the barn and I thought they might ask to stay the night. I'm glad they didn't." He bounced his daughter a few times before she squirmed to be set down. "Good thing. I don't much care for nighttime visitors. Usually means trouble of some sort."

"I know what you mean."

They turned as Rachel and Mrs. Weston walked in, a couple of kids at their heels.

"I'll finish up supper. Won't take long, then we can put the little ones to bed." Marci Weston's eyes sparkled when she looked up at her husband, her short, round frame in sharp contrast to his tall, lean body.

Two hours later, the last lantern had been extinguished and the house fell silent. Rachel lay next to Janie, staring at the ceiling and letting her mind wander to Dax. No matter how much she willed herself to think of other things, her thoughts had strayed little from him the last couple of days. She'd come to terms with his decision to leave and believed it to be the right choice for both of them.

Rachel now accepted how much she *did* want to marry and raise a family in Splendor. Even with the occasional danger, unpredictable weather, and unending work, there wasn't any other place she wanted to live. In a few short months, it had become her home and she felt grateful her uncle had encouraged her to give it a chance. Her mind sorted through the possibilities of the men already in Splendor. Except for Dax, no one held any appeal. Not even Gabe Evans. Although the man was quite handsome, educated, and easy to talk to, there simply was not the attraction she felt toward Dax. Besides, he had the same desire to roam the country without commitments.

She considered some of the cowhands, finally allowing a smile to break cross her face as she contemplated an unorthodox approach, at least for women. Perhaps she'd check into a mail order husband. She raised a hand to stifle a laugh. Why not? Men did it, why couldn't a woman? She closed her eyes and turned on her side, promising herself to at least consider the unconventional approach to starting a family.

"What now?" Lem Pruett set down his whiskey and glanced around the Big Pine saloon. For the last few days, he, Drake, and Archie Swaggert had been staying in the hotel, trying to figure out the best way to deal with the Pelletier brothers, and trying to stay out of the sheriff's sight.

Drake didn't know of any wanted posters out on them. They'd been able to commit their crimes and get out of the areas before anyone suspected them of the murders and thefts that had occurred.

"We stay out of sight for a few days, let them think we've left the area."

Lem and Archie glanced at each other, not liking the plan.

"I don't know. Seems it would be best to get out of here and not wait around. Why push our luck when we can go someplace where they won't find us?" Archie asked.

Drake thought this over. As much as he wanted to rid his life of the general and his brother, it made little sense to draw more attention to themselves. No one knew of their past and he didn't want to stir up suspicions now.

"Maybe that would be best. At least for now." Drake narrowed his eyes as the saloon door swung open and a group of cowboys sauntered toward an empty table. He relaxed and took another sip of whiskey.

"Where would we go?" Archie asked.

"From what I hear, Colorado's growing and ranchers are always looking for good men. We'll ride straight toward Denver."

"What happens if they still come after us?" Lem asked.

Drake looked between the two. He'd known them since before the war, yet he wouldn't hesitate to ride away if one of them took a bullet. He'd leave them behind without a thought.

"They won't."

The Pelletiers had no real proof the three had been involved in the shootings at the ranch. No one knew of their actions since the war ended, and they couldn't be tied to the murders committed on their way to Montana. Drake felt certain once they left Montana, nobody would care one way or another what happened to three ex-Confederate soldiers.

"The way I figure it, we'll come away with a sizable profit this year if we can keep close to the same head count. Calving is heavy right now. We find ourselves another good bull and we'll be set for next season." Luke spread out the paper and pointed to the numbers he'd worked on for several days. "We have plenty of good land and water. Enough to triple the herd, at least." He looked up at Dax, the glint of excitement in his eyes a welcome change from the trouble they faced.

"If we double the herd, how many additional men will we need?" Dax picked up one of the papers, studying the columns and noting the estimated expenses and profit.

"Best guess, not more than another ten or twelve men. Of course, it depends on how good they are. We will need more wranglers, unless we spend the money for horses already broke. Right now, Bull and Joe are the best we have. Once they're healed, Tat and Johnny are as good, maybe better, so that will give us four."

"You forgot yourself," Dax said, remembering how Luke had been the main person in Savannah to train their green horses.

Luke smiled, although he didn't take the bait. "I'm fine letting others handle the task." He pursed his lips as his brows furrowed. "Truth is,

I'd like to get Bull off breaking horses and let the three younger men take over."

"Bull's a natural leader and not afraid to take on new responsibilities."

"I believe he'll be key to the success of the ranch as we grow." Luke grabbed a map. "I've outlined the property boundaries. This is where we meet up with Tolbert's land." He pointed to a section east of their ranch house. "And down here is our common border with the Frey brothers, Frank and Hiram. After Tolbert and us, the Freys own the largest ranch in the area."

Luke pushed from his chair and walked around the desk to stand next to Dax. "I'm still hoping you'll stay, at least a year."

Dax glanced at his brother, noticing the lines around his eyes, a few premature streaks of silver in his auburn hair. He'd always seen Luke as young, carefree, and ready for any adventure. What he'd failed to notice was how the war, their duties as Texas Rangers, and the responsibilities of the ranch had mellowed and matured him beyond his years. He'd handled everything Dax had thrown at him since the war ended, never complaining and always performing well above what would be expected of other men.

In that instant, Dax knew he couldn't leave Luke to handle the task of building the ranch alone. No matter how conflicted he felt about staying in Splendor or returning to Texas, his brother needed him. He pulled his gaze away from Luke and trained it outside again, watching as Joe groomed his horse in the rays of the evening sun.

"I just might do that."

Luke's sharp eyes landed on his brother's face and could see Dax had made his decision. He couldn't speak through the relief coursing through him. Instead, he clasped Dax on the shoulder and squeezed, letting the gesture convey how much the decision meant to him.

"The Territory Range includes long narrow valleys, caves, and hundreds of deer trials. Truth is, a man, or group of men, could get lost in there for a long time if they have enough food and water." Hank scratched the stubble on his face and thought of places the Mayes gang could hide and still have easy access to the ranch.

Dax, Luke, Cash, Hank, Bull, and Ellis sat on the porch after supper, keeping watch and hoping trouble didn't come at them tonight. A shooter could hide a hundred yards out and still have a good chance of getting either of the brothers.

"If you ask me, I think you two should stay out of sight and let the rest of us look for them. No sense in making yourselves targets." Bull didn't like waiting around for someone to take pot shots at either of his bosses. He preferred action to sitting.

"You mean hide?" Luke shook his head, indicating his disgust at the suggestion.

Cash snorted at the incredulous look on his friend's face.

"Better than getting shot." Bull didn't back down. They'd be in a real fix if the outlaws got what they came after.

"There'll be no hiding." Dax's firm response left no further argument. "We need to figure out how they're getting information and follow them. Someone on this ranch knows where their camp is located."

"Agreed. But who?" Hank sat back in the rocker, considering which of the men might betray the rest of them. "We have five new men from Idaho, plus the two others who rode in earlier this week. We don't know much about any of them."

"It's not Tat or Johnny. They've been laid up and couldn't have warned the gang we had learned of their camp. That narrows it down to three from Idaho and the two newest hires." Dax raked a hand over his face and looked at Ellis. "Do you remember if any of the five were with the herd the night we learned of the Mayes camp?"

"Well, let's see." He looked toward the bunkhouse, trying to recall how the men had been placed. He looked at Bull. "You recall after Joe rode the new mustang we all went into the barn. Bob and Ted were with us, right?"

"They were."

"I believe everyone else had stayed with the herd. The only men at the ranch were me, Bull, Joe, Bob, Ted and, of course, Tat and Johnny." Ellis looked once more at Bull.

"Ted and Bob took off, saying something about going to the creek."

"Wildfire Creek?" Luke asked, knowing it meandered around the main ranch property.

"That's my guess," Bull answered. "The closest spot is half a mile away. I don't recall seeing Ted again, although Bob wandered in a couple hours later."

"I don't like it." The hairs on the back of Cash's neck bristled as he connected some missing pieces. "Ah, hell. I should've thought of this earlier. I sent a telegram to Austin, asking for the names of the cousins. The response said their names are Clark, Bill, and Jed Olin."

Dax's eyes widened. "You're thinking Bob and Ted are actually Bill and Jed Olin?"

"I do."

Bill crouched low, hidden behind a bush around the corner of the house and out of sight of the men talking in quiet tones on the porch. Even though they kept their voices low, he could make out most of what they said. The last sent a chill through him. They were out of time. Bill turned and moved in rapid steps into the darkness of the trees, skirting behind the foreman's house Hank and Bernice shared, quietly entering the bunkhouse.

He signaled to Jed—a quick nod, the one they'd prearranged if they were discovered. Jed grabbed his gun belt and, leaving his other belongings behind, followed Bill outside. They slipped into the barn from the back, grabbed their saddles and tack, and entered the corral.

"Did you hear that?" Cash asked as he stood and started down the porch steps.

Dax and Luke followed, while Bull and Ellis ran to the large corral on the opposite side of the barn. Someone or something was disturbing the horses. The sounds came again, this time louder.

Cash reached the corral as the gate burst open and two riders shot through the opening, staying low in their saddles. Jed and Bill pulled their guns and fired behind them, taking no time to aim. They rode in the opposite direction of the camp, toward where their brother and cousins waited.

Dax and the others ducked, drawing their guns and firing at the retreating riders. Several bullets buzzed past the Olin brothers, missing by inches.

Dax's bullet found its mark.

Jed heard Bill groan. He looked behind him to see his brother slump in his saddle before toppling to the ground. He didn't stop, just kicked his horse harder and prayed his brother would be all right.

"One's down." Dax kept his gun pointed straight ahead and ran toward the man he'd shot, who writhed on the ground. He knelt beside Bob, seeing the man's eyes begin to glaze over. He grabbed his shoulders and held him still. "Are you Bill Olin?"

Bill gritted his teeth and glared at Dax.

"Where is the camp?" Dax spoke louder and shook the man, trying to get anything he could from him before the opportunity was lost. Luke knelt next to them and glanced down at a wound no one could survive.

Bill's eyes moved from one Pelletier to the other, hate radiating as his rage bored into each of them. At that moment, each knew what they faced. A family who'd do anything to avenge the death of their own, without conscience or remorse, eliminating anyone who got in their way.

"How is he?" Cash continued to watch the second man until he rounded a bend and rode out of sight. It appeared he'd made a sharp turn, heading west, away from town and toward the mountains.

"Dead." Dax stood and stared down at the body of Bill Olin. "Now there are four." He turned toward the house, his back straight and mind focused. He'd wasted enough time, waited long enough to resume the role into which he'd been born.

Chapter Twenty-One

"Thank you for coming all this way, Doc. I can't tell you what it means to us." Becky Kuhn held his hand in both of hers and squeezed. "You sure you won't stay the night?"

"We're grateful for the invitation. Regrettably, we need to reach the Frey ranch before sunset. I understand it's about three hours north of here." Charles set his satchel in the back of the wagon as Rachel climbed onto the seat.

"Take that road and stay on it until you reach a fork." She pointed to a rutted wagon trail behind the house. "You can either go left, toward the west, or veer to the right. Take the right trail until you reach the creek and follow it to the Frey place."

"Is it anywhere near the Pelletier property?" Charles asked.

"Well, I don't believe I know the Pelletiers. The Frey property does share a common line with Pat Hanes' ranch, though."

"I guess you haven't heard. Pat Hanes died in Texas. The new owners are Dax and Luke Pelletier, two Rangers who rode with Mr. Hanes. I'm sorry you didn't know."

Becky placed a hand over her mouth and Charles could see her eyes water. "Pat was such a good man. Fair and hard working. We need more people like him in the territory." She brushed away a tear and stepped away from the wagon as Charles slapped the reins.

The morning had dawned clear and somewhat chilly for being so close to summer. It had taken two hours to reach the Kuhn ranch after staying the night with the Westons. Now, one more family and they'd be on their way back to Splendor.

Rachel kept glancing behind them, wondering if anything in Splendor had changed since they left. She reminded herself they'd only been gone two days. What could happen in such a short period of time?

They stopped after a couple of hours to stretch and let Old Pete rest. Rachel unhitched him and led him to the creek, while her uncle took a brief walk. They expected to arrive at the Frey ranch within another hour.

She stood next to her horse and watched the water bubble up as it carved a path through the trees. Mrs. Petermann told her the creeks and rivers would run high for a few months, then level off by the end of summer. Timmy offered to take her fishing with him, saying he'd show her all the best spots. Rachel had never held a fishing pole, and had only seen fish spread out at the Boston docks and at the neighborhood fish market. She still had so much to experience in this new land and felt excitement ripple through her as she thought of everything she had yet to see.

"Rachel, are you about ready?"

"Coming." She tugged on Old Pete's halter and, within minutes, had him hitched to the wagon.

An hour later, they spotted the roofline of the Frey barn and the ranch house came into view several yards away. Of all the ranches they'd visited, this one had to be the most spectacular. Located at the eastern base of the Territory Range, the main house sat in a green valley with a large creek and hundreds of pines forming a semi-circle around the various buildings. According to her uncle, the Frey brothers, Frank and Hiram, owned one of the larger spreads in the region.

Charles reined Old Pete to a stop as two men emerged from the cavernous barn and waved. "Hey, Doc. Sure didn't expect to see you out this way."

"Sometimes I have to get away for a spell." Charles climbed down and shook hands with both men.

"Frank, Hiram, this is my niece and nurse, Rachel Davenport. She traveled out from Boston a few months ago to help me at the clinic."

Frank reached up to help her down. "Pleased to meet you, Miss Davenport."

"How about something to drink?" Hiram asked and ushered them into the large, two-story house. "Pardon the mess, but it's just us bachelors in this big place and we aren't the best housekeepers."

"Didn't you have someone to help out?" Charles asked as they took seats in the dining room.

"We did, but she took off to be with her daughter's family at Christmas. Sent us a telegram saying she decided to stay. It's hard to get anyone to live this far out, especially with two cantankerous old men." Frank placed glasses of water in front of their guests before pouring whiskeys for the three men. "Can I get you something else, Miss Davenport?"

Rachel glanced at the whiskey, remembering the time she shared a drink with Dax and realized she hadn't thought of him all day. "No, water is fine, Mr. Frey."

"So what brings you out this way?" Frank sipped at his whiskey, then chased it down with some water.

"Checking on the outlying ranches. We've been to see Ty Murton's family, the Westons, the Kuhns, and now you two. How are you both doing?" Charles knew the answer before he asked the question. These two brothers were as tough as they came, both outlasting two wives.

"Fit as mules. A few of the men came down with some type of fever over the winter, but they all pulled through fine. Didn't touch Frank or me. How are the other ranchers doing?"

"Good. A couple of the children caught something, but they're doing fine now. Anybody else out this way I should stop and see?"

"Nope. We're it, unless you want to travel a bit more north and east to Pat Hanes' old place." Frank poured each of the men another drink. "He was a good man."

"I never had the opportunity to meet him. If you haven't met them, the new owners are good

342

people. You know they rode with Hanes as Texas Rangers?"

"We heard a couple brothers took over the place. Didn't know they were Rangers with Pat. Reverend Paige and his wife visited a couple of weeks ago and told us what happened. Guess we should ride over and pay our respects."

"How far is the Pelletier ranch from here?" Rachel asked, trying not to sound too interested.

"About two hours. The Westons and Kuhns live the farthest out. By the time you reach us, you're only about three hours from Splendor. Seems long because the road is such a mess." Frank set down his glass and stood. "Now, you two will have supper and stay with us tonight, right?"

"It'd be our pleasure." Charles drained his glass, glad they were almost home.

"You left Bill behind?" Clark fumed at his younger brother, Jed, who'd ridden into camp late the night before after everyone else had turned in. Clark had woken early to see Jed's horse, but not Bill's.

"They figured out who we were. We tried to get away and almost made it, until a bullet got Bill in the back. He fell from his horse. If I'd gone back, they would've gotten me, too. What did you expect me to do?" Jed ran a hand through his hair, distress and guilt still haunting him at having to leave his brother behind. "There's no chance he survived." He collapsed onto a tree stump and rested his elbows on his knees, hands grasping his head.

Clark stalked over and grasped Jed's shirt, yanking him up to within inches of his face. "You know what? You're going back to make sure he's not still alive. If he is, we get him out of there." He let go of Jed with a forceful shove and took a deep breath, his initial rage turning to despair.

Duff and Whitey watched, knowing how their cousins felt. They'd felt the same anger and grief when the Rangers killed Deke.

"Jed can't go back yet. We'll need him here," Duff said, trying to diffuse the tension.

Whitey walked toward Jed and offered him a hand up. His cousin had made the right decision to ride off without Bill. Even if he survived, Jed would've achieved nothing by surrendering.

Clark turned back to Jed. "Did they follow you?"

"No. I stopped a couple of times, but no one followed."

"They will. There's no chance the Rangers will let this one go." Duff picked up his rifle. "We need to be ready for them."

"What are you suggesting?" Whitey didn't want to give up. The need for vengeance burned even stronger within him.

"Is that bounty hunter still with them?" Duff asked Jed.

"Yeah. His name's Cash Coulter. From what I hear, he's an excellent tracker."

"Good. We'll use that to our advantage." He motioned for Whitey, Clark, and Jed to come close as he explained what he had in mind.

Dax, Luke, Cash, and Bull had waited at the ranch, while Joe rode into town to fetch Gabe. It hadn't taken the sheriff and Noah long to join the group preparing to ride after the outlaws. Joe, Ellis, and a few other men stayed at the ranch in case the gang decided to come back. Gabe thought the chance remote, believing they'd try to ambush the makeshift posse on the trail.

"The tracks are so clear you'd almost believe they were trying to lead us somewhere." Cash crouched down next to a group of horse tracks. They'd found the deserted camp an hour before and followed the trail south.

Dax crouched down next to Cash and studied the tracks. "Why do you say that?"

"What would you do if a group of men followed you? You'd do your best to hide your tracks by riding over rocks, or cutting in and out of the creek. Instead, there are four distinct sets of horse tracks heading in a clear direction." Cash stood and looked further up the trail.

"Which way?" Dax asked.

"South."

The trail meandered through low hills, continuing to head south, then west before connecting with the river, signaling the boarder of the neighbor's property. Not once did Cash lose the tracks. He could sense something wasn't right.

Luke rode to the front and reined Prince next to Cash and Dax. Gabe, Noah, and Bull stopped right behind him.

"This is the boundary between our land and the Frey brothers," Luke said, indicating the river.

"Do you know anything about them?" Gabe asked.

"Just what Clausen at the bank told me. They've been in the territory a long time and both are widowers. They run a large herd each year and are well respected in Splendor."

"Doesn't sound like they're the type of men to hide outlaws. Duff Mayes may be leading his men around the hills until he finds a spot to cross over the Territory Range. He must know we're after them. It would be a mistake on his part to stay in the area." Gabe rested his hands on the saddle horn and scanned the horizon.

"We're wasting time speculating. Let's move." Dax took off, anxious to find the men who were out to kill him and Luke. Gabe may have a point about them leaving the area—however, Dax's gut told him otherwise. He didn't believe they'd accept the death of their cousin without seeking vengeance. Their need for revenge would only increase because of the loss of another one of their own.

"I see three men near the barn talking." Whitey sat perched on a rock overlooking the Frey ranch house.

"No one else?" Duff asked.

"Not that I can see from here."

"Any guns?"

"One's wearing a gun belt. I don't see anything on the other two." Whitey lowered his field glasses and jumped to the ground.

"Let's spread out and get ready to ride. We'll grab the three and hold them in the house until the Rangers show up."

"What makes you think they'll care one way or another about us holding a couple of hostages?" Clark asked.

"They're still Rangers, aren't they? There's no chance they'll let us kill a couple of their neighbors without doing whatever they can to save them. They'll have no choice but to agree to do what we want."

"The odds are they'll have more men with them, like the sheriff and a couple of their ranch hands," Jed said.

"It doesn't matter. Once we have the Rangers, anyone they came with will have to let us ride out. If they balk, we'll do something to make them listen." Duff swung up on his horse. "Clark, I want you and Jed to ride around to the other side. Whitey and I will come in from here. Look for my signal."

It didn't take long for Clark and Jed to circle the ranch house. Duff and Whitey took a brush-covered path down a narrow slope and stopped as close as they could without being seen. The three men still stood by the barn. From his vantage point, Duff could see they were a little older than he'd first thought, but it didn't mean they posed no threat. He looked up and waved a red bandanna to signal the time had come.

The four rode in from opposite directions, shooting into the air, surprising Frank, Hiram, and Charles, who tried to duck into the barn. Bullets slamming into the wooden siding stopped them. Hiram turned, gun in hand, and fired, nicking Clark before Whitey put a bullet in Hiram's leg.

Frank dropped to the ground next to him, pulling a handkerchief out of his pocket to stop the flow of blood as Charles kept his hands in the air, taking a couple of steps toward his wagon.

"That man needs help. I'm a doctor. I need to get my medical bag out of the wagon."

Duff continued to point his gun toward the three while looking into the back of the wagon. One black satchel lay behind the seat.

"Go ahead, but understand there's four of us watching you." He glanced over at Clark and saw red seeping through his shirt. "I want the doc to look at your arm when he's done with the old man."

"It's nothing. Let's get them inside. I'm not comfortable sitting in the daylight with those men chasing us."

Charles looked up at the gunman's comment and wondered who hunted these men.

"I can stand." Hiram tried to sit, groaning when Charles pushed him down.

"Quiet. I'm trying to hear what they're saying," Frank hissed as he leaned close to the riders a few feet away.

"You." Duff pointed his gun at Frank. "Help get him up and into the house." Duff moved his horse closer. "You'll have to finish inside."

Charles got on one side of Hiram while Frank took the other, lifting him under his arms and starting toward the house.

Rachel stared out a slit in the front room curtains and leveled a rifle at the oldest of the outlaws. She'd almost run outside when the shots rang out, but the quick approach of the gunmen stopped her.

"Hurry them up, Duff. We need to get out of sight." Whitey dismounted, then waited for Clark to do the same before grabbing the reins of both horses and heading for the barn. "Jed, get Duff's horse."

Rachel set her gaze on the youngest of the gunmen. He looked familiar—his height, walk, and somewhat cocky stance triggered something, but she couldn't place his name or where'd she'd seen him. Her eyes shifted as Charles and Frank helped Hiram up the steps. She had to make a decision now or lose her chance to eliminate one of the outlaws. Rachel sighted the rifle and began to squeeze the trigger, then stopped, deciding the risk of the gunmen killing someone was too great. Instead, she lowered the rifle, grabbed her revolver from a nearby table, and dashed through the house, hoping to find a hiding place. She slipped up the back stairs, staying as quiet as possible, checking each room until she located a storage closet at the back of the second floor. The front door slammed open at the same time she pulled the closet door shut.

"Whitey, tie him up while the doctor finishes with the other one." Duff pointed to Frank, then turned his attention to Clark. "Get your arm taken care of, then check the rest of the house."

"Is there anyone else here?" Whitey asked Frank as he secured the rope around his hands and legs.

"No. It's just the three of us." Frank grimaced as the tight knots cut into his skin.

Whitey eyed him. Something in Frank's voice had him on edge. "You sure about that?"

"Of course I am. All the others are out with the cattle." Frank wondered where Rachel had found a place to hide and hoped she stayed there. "What do you want with us? We don't keep much money here."

"Of course you do, but money isn't what we want." Whitey finished securing the rope, then stood and looked down at the rancher. "We're after the men hunting us."

"And who is chasing you?"

"Whitey, what's taking so long?" Duff asked as he walked into the room. "Help Jed check out the rest of the house. The doctor is taking care of Clark's arm. We need to set up before they get here."

"They're here, Dax. I'm certain of it." Cash sat atop his horse and looked back toward the large, two-story house below. He'd circled the ranch area, finding what he felt sure were tracks from the outlaw's horses. "I don't understand why they'd stop here and not ride out of the territory."

"Dax, look down there." Luke pointed to the wagon with a horse they both recognized.

"Old Pete." Dax's heart began to pound when the thought of the doctor being inside the home with a group of killers. Could Rachel be with him?

"What is it?" Noah asked.

"That's Doc Worthington's wagon and horse. Old Pete is hard to miss." Luke slid off Prince and walked to the edge of the brush that concealed them. He took a quick glance around before disappearing down the slope and crouching behind a thick shrub. He shot a look over his shoulder when he heard someone follow.

"Someone needs to find out what's going on inside and determine if the Mayes and Olin brothers are here." Dax squatted next to his brother and tried to tap down the apprehension enveloping him.

"I'll go. Remember, this is what I did for much of the war—surveyed enemy territory prior to a battle." Luke started to stand before feeling Dax's hand on his arm.

"Go down from the back, and stay where we can see you. Do you remember our signal?" Dax asked.

"Of course." Luke whistled low, indicating he could still make the cricket sound the two had used since their youth to warn each other of trouble.

Dax didn't like Luke going down alone, even though he knew two would increase the odds someone would spot them. They stood, bending low while they made their way up the slope.

"What's going on?" Cash asked. Gabe, Noah, and Bull stood behind him as Dax and Luke approached them.

"Luke's going in from the back to see who's in the house."

"I'll go with him."

"Thanks, Cash, but it's best if I go alone." Luke checked his Remington and the knife he had concealed in a scabbard around his ankle. "I won't take chances. A quick check and I'll be back."

"Don't be a hero," Dax warned, concern evident in his eyes.

"Hey, you know me." Luke smiled and took off at a brisk pace along the trail, disappearing into the dense brush.

"Yeah, that's what concerns me," Dax muttered as Cash clasped his shoulder.

"He'll be fine. The kid's always had the damndest luck."

Dax thought of Cash's words and found he had to agree. Luke had always been able to sneak in and out of places without detection. The skill had pushed him up the ranks until he'd been promoted to major just months before the war's end.

"Now we wait." Gabe took a position so he could see the back of the house as well as movement from the front. "I hope the people who own the house aren't in there."

Chapter Twenty-Two

Rachel could hear boots on the stairs. By the sounds of it, more than one person intended to search the second floor. She huddled further back into the closet, trying to conceal herself behind old clothes while keeping the gun trained on the door. If they found her, at least she'd be able to get off one shot.

"You check the rooms in the back, while I look in these," Whitey said to Jed, indicating the three rooms near the front stairs. Compared to most ranch homes, this one boasted several upstairs bedrooms, enough for at least two families with children. The downstairs had a couple of bedrooms plus a study, as well as the kitchen with pantry, dining room, and front area. One set of stairs led up from the entry hall, while another accessed the second level near the pantry.

Whitey searched three bedrooms, checking under beds and inside wardrobes. He found no one.

Jed checked rooms closest to the back stairs until one door remained. He slowly pulled it open, then jerked it wide when he saw it held clothes and wooden crates. He glanced down the hall at Whitey. "Nothing here."

Jed lowered his revolver to his side before taking one more look inside. His eyes locked on the barrel of a gun pointed toward his chest. He began to raise his weapon and aim when a blast sounded and a searing pain ripped through his shoulder. His gun fell from his fingers as he gripped his injured arm.

Rachel could hear boots pounding toward her and aimed once more, getting another shot off as Whitey pushed Jed aside and aimed. The bullet grazed Whitey's leg, but he didn't stop. A strong hand reached in and pulled Rachel from the closet. She tried to use her gun to defend herself, but a hard slap to her face stopped her. The outlaw shoved her into a nearby wall, knocking her out. Rachel collapsed to the floor.

"What the hell?"

Whitey looked up to see Duff standing next to him, staring at the women on the floor.

"Jed needs help." He grabbed a shirt from the closet and wrapped it around his leg to stop the bleeding. "Mine's nothing." He levered himself up from the floor.

Duff scanned Jed's wound. "You're lucky, boy. Looks like it ripped clean through. Get downstairs and have the doc patch you up."

Jed nodded, gripping his injured shoulder as he walked past the woman on the floor. He stopped for a moment, his eyes locking on her face, and realized he knew her. The doc's nurse, the one he'd seen at the Pelletier ranch. The woman who Dax Pelletier indicated, with the slightest of gestures, belonged to him.

"Duff, I know this woman." Jed continued to stare at Rachel.

"You know a lot of women."

"You don't understand. She's a nurse and came by the ranch while Bill and I were there."

"Yeah?" Duff looked at Jed before switching his gaze to Rachel.

"She's Dax Pelletier's woman."

Luke had no trouble making his way unseen to the back of the house. He could see into the kitchen, but not much else. He crept low under the windows toward the side visible to Dax and the others, crouching down in an attempt to hear inside. Loud voices rang through the front area, but the words weren't clear. He took off his hat before rising to look inside.

From what Luke remembered, two widowed brothers. Frank and Hiram Frey, owned the ranch. Doc Worthington worked on someone spread out on the floor. He guessed the man with the wounded leg was one of them, and made a quick decision to go back around the house to see if he could locate the second one.

He signaled to Dax before moving at a determined pace around the house. A few minutes later, he looked into what appeared to be a study to see another man tied to a chair, a gag in his mouth. Behind him stood a man Luke didn't recognize, but assumed to be one of the cousins. He recognized the other man standing next to him from the wanted posters. Duff Mayes.

Luke turned to leave when a shot rang out, followed by a second one. He wasted no time

355

sprinting up the hill and following the path to where everyone waited. His mind already worked through various scenarios about what the shots meant, and the best way to rescue those inside and arrest the outlaws.

"I've got to get down there." Dax took a step down the hill before Cash and Gabe grabbed his arms.

"Not yet. Wait until Luke gets back." Cash tightened his grip on his friend, seeing the determination on his face.

"Let go of me." Dax's strained voice hissed out as he tried to shake the men off.

"We do this together or, I swear, we'll tie you to a tree." Gabe's hard-edged voice pulled Dax from the fear that gripped him at the sound of the gunshots. "She'll be all right. They won't harm her."

Dax looked at the sheriff, not yet comprehending.

"They need her to draw you out."

Dax didn't speak, but Gabe could see acceptance cross his face.

Luke came up and took in the scene before him as Gabe and Cash loosened their hold on his brother.

"What did you see?" Dax asked, his voice tense.

"It's the Mayes and Olin brothers. They have the doc and two other men, who I'm guessing are the Frey brothers." He looked at Dax and cleared his throat. "I didn't see Rachel, but they must have her."

Dax swore. He scrubbed a hand over his face and took a deep breath. "The shots?"

"I heard them, same as you." They both knew the odds favored one of the hostages being shot.

Dax worked to rein in the anxiety consuming him. He needed his control, the leadership he'd shown in battle, if they were to get Rachel and the others out alive.

God help the man who hurts her in any way, Dax thought, and turned toward the others. Three solemn faces stared back at him.

"What do you want us to do, boss?" Bull asked, ready to ride straight in and free the doc and Miss Davenport.

Dax turned back to Luke. "Tell us everything you saw."

Duff Mayes stood over Rachel, a savage smile on his face. "So you're Pelletier's woman." The triumph in his voice confirmed her fears. He meant to use her to lure Dax in, then kill him.

"Your man is wrong. Mr. Pelletier means no more to me than any other man my uncle and I help when someone's sick or injured." She glared at Duff, raising her chin in defiance and locking her eyes with his. They'd tied her to a chair with ropes securing her hands and legs.

"That's not what Jed says."

"Well, Jed is wrong. I have no idea why he thinks there is anything else between Mr. Pelletier and me because there isn't." She glanced at her uncle, hoping he understood her intent.

"She's lying, Duff. I saw the way he looked at her. There's definitely more between them than her being their nurse." Jed grimaced as Charles finished bandaging his shoulder.

"That's the best I can do. You're lucky the bullet went through your shoulder and missed your heart. My niece is generally a better shot than that."

Jed jumped to his feet and pushed Charles onto the divan. "Shut up, old man."

"Enough, Jed. Take him to the study and tie him up."

"What then?" Jed asked as he pulled Charles to his feet.

"We wait."

"Are there any questions?" Dax asked as the men considered the idea for freeing the prisoners.

"None from me." Cash pulled out his gun and checked it once more before shoving it back in its holster.

"Where do you want me once I let their horses loose?" Bull asked.

"Stay at the barn. Don't move forward until my signal. If any of the gang somehow get out the front door, shoot them."

Bull nodded, hoping at least one would make it out. Anyone who took Miss Davenport and the doc hostage deserved what they got.

Noah looked at Gabe, knowing he could take out at least two men in quick succession from a

358

hundred yards, if needed. He hadn't pulled the trigger of a gun in over two years, not since he'd left the fighting behind and ventured west with Gabe.

Dax noticed the exchange between the two men. "Do you have something to add, Noah?"

Noah swallowed hard before speaking. "Luke, you said there's a clear view into the study from the front of the house, correct?"

"It looked that way to me. The house has a series of windows along the front, facing the barn."

Noah turned his gaze to Dax, mentally preparing himself to do whatever they needed. "If any of the gang is in the study, I can get them both without harming any of the prisoners." His voice held a hint of resignation.

Dax suspected Noah possessed skills he'd never shared with anyone except Gabe. Skills he preferred not to use, but would if pushed.

"You're certain?"

"Yes, sir. No doubt in my mind."

Dax narrowed his gaze at him. "All right. You go in with Bull and take a position so you can see into the study. As soon as you're set, Bull will signal the rest of us. When we hear your first shot, we'll move in."

"Quick and clean," Gabe muttered, clasping Noah on the shoulder.

"Quick and clean," Noah responded as he pulled his Spencer repeating rifle from its scabbard.

"Where are they?" Duff asked no one in particular as time wore on with no sign of the Pelletiers.

"They'll come," Clark responded from his chair positioned at the window in the front.

Duff and Clark had taken positions in one room, while Whitey and Jed kept watch from the study. Hiram remained on the floor near Rachel, who squirmed in her chair, trying to loosen the tight ropes.

"Sit still, girl. You'll just make the knots tighter." Duff had been watching Rachel's efforts, admiring her spunk, hoping she'd be what they needed to draw in the Pelletiers.

She glared back, having no intention of sitting quietly while he lured Dax to his death. "You're wasting your time. Mr. Pelletier is too smart to fall for what you have planned."

"And what would that be?" Duff decided to go along. Perhaps she'd tell them something important about the man or his brother.

"It's obvious you believe he'll give himself over to you in exchange for me. He won't. The man doesn't like to be backed into a corner or forced to do something against his principles, which is your plan. He'll find another way to get to you and, by nightfall, all four of you will be dead." At least she prayed it would play out that way. She did not want Dax's death on her conscience.

Duff stood and walked over to glare down at her, noting the way her eyes sparked in anger. "I see you believe what you say, girl. Too bad it won't work out the way you want." He checked

360

her bonds before pacing to look out each window, noticing nothing unusual.

Rachel considered another tactic. "I need to use the privy," she said, looking toward Duff.

"Can't it wait?" he asked.

"No. I'm afraid not. I've put it off too long already."

Duff holstered his gun, removed the ropes around her ankles, and pulled her up to stand next to him. "Come on." He gripped her arm to lead her outside.

"A whiskey sure would taste good right now." Clark rubbed his arm where Hiram's bullet had grazed him. Charles had cleaned it up, yet the intense ache remained. Alcohol would do a lot to deaden the pain.

Duff stopped and shot a harsh look at this cousin. "Nothing until those Rangers are in their graves."

Duff's words sent chills down Rachel's back. She closed her eyes and prayed Dax and Luke were nowhere near the Frey ranch.

"Did you hear her?" Luke asked. He and Dax had taken positions under a window outside the room where Rachel had upbraided Duff Mayes. "She seems to think a lot of you."

Dax focused on the task, trying not to think of the women he loved being in danger because of him. If it weren't for his profession, the Mayes brothers wouldn't be after him and Luke, and would never have followed them to Splendor.

As if reading his mind, Luke spun the barrel of his revolver and spoke in a whisper. "You wouldn't have met Rachel if we hadn't brought Pat back for burial. None of this is your fault. The men in there are ruthless and out for revenge. None of us would be in this fix if they hadn't decided to become bank robbers and murderers." He scooted a foot to the corner of the house, confirming Bull and Noah were in place. "Now, let's get your woman and the others out of there."

Gabe and Cash had taken positions in the back, ready to move in at Dax's signal. Noah would give Bull a nod. He'd signal Luke, who would signal Gabe, then they'd wait for Noah's first shot.

"There it is," Luke said when Bull signaled Noah had the men in sight. Luke turned to Gabe and raised a hand. Everyone went on alert.

One shot rang out, followed by another not two seconds later.

"Damn," Bull muttered when he saw first one man fall, then another.

"What the hell?" Duff yanked Rachel in front of him as the door in the back burst open. He spun around, using her as a shield.

The sound of shattering glass preceded a wail from Clark, who fell from his chair by the front window, writhing in pain before cursing and falling silent.

Duff pulled Rachel with him as he backed up and looked into the study. Jed and Whitey lay on the floor, their eyes fixed open.

"Stop right there, Duff. You won't get out of here." Dax leveled his gun at the outlaw. He and

Luke had come through the front door as Cash and Gabe, guns centered on Duff, moved in from the kitchen.

"Give up and let the woman go. Everyone else is dead. You're the last one." Gabe took another step closer, ready to shoot if Duff did anything except lower his gun, which he now held to Rachel's head.

Dax's gaze settled on Rachel. He saw an iron clad resolve, but no fear.

"Let her go. She's done nothing. It's me you want. I'm the one who killed Deke." Luke moved into the room, distancing himself from Dax and the others in an attempt to draw Duff's attention.

"I'll kill you," Mayes roared and moved his gun toward Luke.

Dax shot a look at Rachel and mouthed one word..."*Duck!*"

In an instant, Rachel responded, wrenching herself from Duff's grip and spinning to the side. Bullets ripped through the air as five men emptied their guns into the outlaw. A grim smile crossed Luke's face as he looked to the door to see Bull, smoke rising from his revolver.

From her spot against the wall, Rachel stared at the outlaw's lifeless body. She felt herself begin to shake.

"Rachel?"

She pulled her gaze from the carnage to see Dax kneeling beside her, loosening the rope from her hands, and checking for any sign of injury. He lifted her into his arms and strode to the divan, setting her down and moving his hands over her, still not certain she hadn't been hurt.

363

With the worst over, a cold sweat broke out on Dax's face. He found it hard to take a breath or speak.

"I'm all right, Dax." Her soft voice drifted over him as he cupped her face with his hands and bent to place a kiss on her lips.

He could feel her shake and wrapped his arms around her, pulling her close, needing the contact to reassure himself she'd be all right.

"Rachel, I..." His voice cracked as Rachel placed a finger to his lips.

"It's over, Dax. You took care of the men hunting you, and everything will be fine." In her heart, Rachel knew this to be a lie. The danger had been eliminated and they'd all return to their regular lives. She'd continue to work with her uncle, and Dax would leave, taking her heart with him. Texas had become his dream and she'd do nothing to stand in his way.

Dax pulled her tight and closed his eyes. He couldn't pinpoint the exact moment when his desire to leave Montana vanished and his need to stay in Splendor with Rachel became as essential as breathing. For the first time in years, he prayed. He'd made so many mistakes. He loved and needed her, and now he had to find a way to make it right.

Chapter Twenty-Three

"All I'm saying is I've never seen anything like it. Noah aimed his Spencer, took a breath, and in a couple of seconds, the first two men were down, bullet holes dead-center in their foreheads. He got the third one a few seconds later. Most townspeople believed he'd come out west because he wouldn't fight. You know what Gabe said after all of them went down?" Bull secured the rope around the last of the dead outlaws they'd loaded into Doc Worthington's wagon.

"No. What?" Luke glanced over his shoulder as Dax helped Rachel into the wagon.

"He slapped Noah on the shoulder and said, 'Nice work, Major.' He'd been an officer. Who would've thought it?"

Luke's gaze rested on Noah and Gabe, who stood next to their horses, talking in low voices. He understood from some townspeople that Noah never spoke of his service in the Union Army, letting people assume whatever they wanted. In Luke's mind, Noah had been an unknown factor before today. Now everyone at the Frey ranch knew what he could do. Luke turned his attention toward heated voices a few feet away.

"There's no need for you and Luke to accompany us, Dax. I'm fine and so is Uncle Charles. Besides, the sheriff and Mr. Brandt will be riding back to Splendor with us." Rachel's voice held a ring of finality not many used with Dax.

"I don't like it." Dax planted his feet and crossed his arms, glaring up at her. "We still don't know where Drake and the others are. Those men are as dangerous as the ones lying in your wagon."

"They have no reason to attack us."

"That's what I thought about the Mayes and Olin brothers."

Both stopped as Charles climbed in next to Rachel and picked up the reins. "The sheriff and Noah are ready to go. I know it's inadequate, Dax, but thanks again for saving us."

"No need for thanks. We're glad it ended well for all of us." Dax shifted his gaze to Rachel and started to speak, but Charles slapped the reins and the wagon lurched forward. He hooked his thumbs in the waistband of his pants and watched until the wagon moved around a bend and out of sight, Gabe and Noah riding on either side. The opportunity to tell her how he felt, try to turn his prior actions around, had vanished. He stared at the empty dirt road, already contemplating how to convince Rachel he'd made his choice and it included her. An unwelcome fear squeezed his chest.

What if she'd given up on any chance with him and had moved on? He hadn't let the thought matter to him before. Contemplating Rachel with another man had been something he'd pushed to the back of his mind in an attempt to persuade himself he didn't care. He now knew it was a lie. Dax realized he'd do whatever he could, fight any battle necessary to win her back.

Charles shook his head and shot a look at his niece before focusing once again on the road ahead. He couldn't remember knowing two people whose feelings for each other had been so obvious. Their pathetic attempts to hide the attraction would have been funny if it wasn't causing Rachel so much pain. He kept telling himself it wasn't his business. Rachel's choices were hers alone, yet he couldn't ignore the way his self-confident niece had withdrawn into a world far removed from the one she'd seemed to be building during her first months in Splendor. His gut told him the change had everything to do with Dax Pelletier.

"Did you know I was in love once?" Charles didn't know what had caused him to speak of something few people knew.

Rachel shifted on the wooden seat and concentrated on her uncle, fascinated by his question. "No. I suppose I always believed your work to be your only love." How ridiculous her comment sounded. Why wouldn't her uncle have desired love, hoping to find a woman to build his life around? The fact she'd never given it a thought made her feel immature and selfish.

"It is now, but it wasn't always that way."

They rode in silence for a few minutes, Rachel hoping he'd continue, not sure if she should question him further. Finally, her curiosity could no longer be contained. "Will you tell me about her?"

She could see his hands tighten, then loosen on the reins. He leaned back in the seat and looked out on the trail before speaking, "Her name was Clare. She had the most beautiful soft, brown eyes. They were large and round and seemed to question everything. She always kept her hair tucked under her bonnet, but one day, the wind blew so hard the bonnet flew off, causing her bright red hair to fall out of its bun and cascade down her back. In that moment, I fell in love."

Rachel folded her hands in her lap and waited, her attention fully focused on her uncle.

"You know how prominent our family had been in Boston social circles. Our obligations were set out at birth—the type of person to marry, their background and education. Little room existed for love." He glanced away from Rachel, then back to the road. "Clare's father had been a dock worker his entire life. Her brother also worked the docks, as did most of her relatives. Honest, hardworking, and full of life, her family was not at all concerned with social status, although I knew Clare's father was acutely aware of our differences. Somehow, my father noticed the attention I paid Clare. He spoke with her father, offering him money and work in the Worthington family business if he made sure Clare no longer allowed me to court her." His head turned toward Rachel and she could see a wistfulness and longing never before present in her uncle's eyes. "I suppose the money and an opportunity to move away from the hard labor of the docks were too much temptation. He took the offer and I saw Clare just one more time."

"I'm so sorry. It must have been awful for you." Rachel reached over and placed a hand on his arm.

Charles continued as if she hadn't spoken.

"She snuck out one night to meet me. I asked her to wait until I could support us without the family money. We promised each other we'd wait. I started my medical studies, deciding to focus on something my father couldn't control, and looked forward to the day Clare and I would be together. A few months later, I received word she'd left Boston with a man her father had chosen for her. He'd learned of our promise and made certain she'd be unable to keep hers. It took a while before I accepted she'd never be mine." He let out a disgusted sigh and looked down at Rachel's hand on his arm before placing one of his hands on top. "My father's interference changed the future. It's why I chose to leave home and build a new life as far away from family as possible."

Rachel didn't know how to respond. She could almost feel the pain he must have felt all those years ago when he lost the one woman he loved.

"Looking back, I should have grabbed the opportunity and left Boston with Clare. To this day, I'm still haunted by my lack of courage to act on my feelings. Love isn't easy. It's hard won and harder to keep. If, at some point, you have a chance to build a life with the man you love, grab it and don't look back."

Over the miles it took to reach Splendor, her uncle's words replayed over and over in Rachel's mind. She'd given her heart to Dax and he'd made it clear he didn't share her feelings. Even if he stayed, nothing more would develop between them. There was no question in her mind he liked, cared about, and desired her. But love? She had to accept the fact that desire didn't equate to love, at least not for him.

Her future had certainly changed from the vision she had of it a few years before. Edging closer to her mid-twenties, Rachel began to doubt she'd ever find the type of mutual love her uncle spoke about. She knew her feelings for Dax were real. He'd always be the man of her heart.

Perhaps her idea of a few nights before, the one which had seemed so silly, might not be what she needed. She accepted her love for Dax, even if he didn't share her feelings. Perhaps she should consider a practical approach. As long as a man could be faithful, support a family, and be a good example to their children, why couldn't she advertise for a mail order husband? Certainly there must be a man out there who would find the prospect of a life with her acceptable.

By the time their wagon came to a halt behind the clinic, she'd made up her mind. She'd visit Bernie Griggs at the Western Union office in the morning. He might have an idea how to begin and, more important, how to send out an advertisement for a husband.

"What do you mean he's gone?" Dax's voice blasted through the dining room.

"Everything all right out here?" Hank asked as he emerged from the kitchen, Bernice right behind him. Luke and Dax acted as if they hadn't heard him.

"He left a note. Here." Luke held out the paper he'd found on the table next to Cash's bed.

Dax read the brief message before tossing it on the table. "How long do you think he's been gone?"

"I don't know. Hours, most likely." Luke looked as upset as Dax about Cash leaving to find Drake without waiting for them.

"Did he ever mention to you where he planned to start?"

"Not a word. I don't think Cash ever planned for us to go with him."

Dax walked to the window and looked out toward the barn. Several men were saddling horses, getting ready to ride toward the herd.

"I guess there's no sense going after him. We don't even know where to start."

The three had talked of leaving in two days, after Dax and Luke set up a rotating schedule for the herd and finished a few other chores. They'd decided to ride to Tolbert's ranch to let him know about the shootings at the Frey ranch. Afterwards, they were free to leave. Cash seemed fine with all of it last night as they'd sat on the front porch drinking coffee. Now he was gone.

"Not much we can do at this point. I sure hope he keeps us posted." Luke jammed his hat on his head before strapping his gun belt around his waist.

"So do I." Dax didn't like it. Their friend was on a hunt for vengeance, already declaring Drake and his two partners guilty. In his own mind, Dax felt the same. He just didn't like anyone taking the law into their own hands. "Nothing we can do now."

He'd change his plans and focus on the two most urgent issues in his life—the ranch and Rachel. He'd decided to give her a few days, then he'd do what he could to win her back.

"Is Rachel at home?" Dax stood outside, looking at Charles and rotating his hat brim.

"Not right now. Did she know you were coming by?" Charles scratched his chin, trying to remember where she'd said she needed to go.

"No. We haven't spoken since the incident at the Frey ranch."

"Well, come on in and wait with me. I could use the company and I doubt she'll be gone long. How about some coffee? Or perhaps a whiskey would be more to your liking?"

"Coffee would be fine."

Dax followed Charles to the kitchen, wondering where Rachel had gone. He also wondered what her reaction would be when she came home to find him there. He'd waited several days before riding into town to tell her of his decision to stay in Splendor. The angst he felt started a few miles from town. Before then, he'd been confident she'd welcome his decision. With luck, she'd also accept him into her life.

Charles handed Dax his coffee at the same moment the door burst open and Rachel walked in, holding what appeared to be a couple of telegrams. She came to a halt when she saw Dax.

"Dax. What are you doing here?" Her voice sounded cheerful but distant, as if she couldn't imagine why he'd stopped by.

"I came to invite you to supper."

Rachel removed her bonnet, setting it on a nearby chair, placing the telegrams alongside it. She already received two replies to the advertisement Bernie had sent out a few days before. There'd been no time to read them at the telegraph office—too many others were standing around and this was something requiring privacy. She wanted nothing more than to be alone to see what type of man might want to be a mail order husband.

"I'd planned to have supper with my uncle."

"I can fix my own meal. Go ahead and have supper with Dax." Charles left them standing in the front room as he headed toward the kitchen.

Rachel glanced over her shoulder at Charles, then back at Dax, feeling she had no choice.

"Supper would be lovely. Is this all right?" She indicated her dress and bonnet.

You'd look beautiful in anything, Dax thought. "What you're wearing is fine." He opened the door, allowing her to precede him outside, then held out his arm to her.

They walked the short distance to Suzanne's restaurant, took a table by the window, and ordered the night's special. Rachel had been aware of Dax studying her from the moment they left her house, as if he had something to say and couldn't quite find a way to get the words out. She hoped he wouldn't bring up the same, tired subject of his love for Texas and his intentions to leave. His intentions were all too clear to her.

"How have you been since the shooting?" His question shouldn't have come as a surprise as they hadn't seen each other since the day the four men were killed.

"I've been good, although it isn't something I ever want to experience again." Her eyes drifted toward the view of the mountains outside, her features not displaying how much the event did affect her. "There've been a few dreams— nightmares, really. I've been able to get back to sleep, though. I guess, under the circumstances, it's normal."

Suzanne set down their meals. "Anything else I can get you two?"

"This looks wonderful," Rachel said, glancing down at the steak and potato supper, her mouth watering at the aroma.

Suzanne smiled back. "Don't forget there's pie." She patted Rachel on the shoulder and left the couple alone.

Dax waited for Rachel to start before cutting his first slice of steak. He chewed slowly, contemplating what he wanted to say.

"I still get nightmares from the war. There doesn't seem to be much I can do about them, so I've learned to accept they're a part of my life."

"Is it the same dream each time?"

"Mostly. It's a battle with soldiers running around, not sure of their place. I step up to say something just before a cannonball explodes around us. The smoke clears and all I hear are the moans and screams of my men." He set down his fork and motioned for Suzanne.

"What can I get you?"

"Do you remember the offer of whiskey you made?"

Suzanne offered a slight smile. "I sure do. Let me get it for you."

Rachel's puzzled expression followed Suzanne as she disappeared into the kitchen. A moment later, she emerged with a bottle of whiskey and two glasses.

"Here you are." She filled each glass. "Let me know if you'd like more."

Dax picked his up, indicating to Rachel she should do the same. "Here's to the start of many suppers together, Rachel."

He noticed her slight hesitation before touching the edge of his glass with hers and taking a sip. She set down the glass as her brows furrowed, her stomach beginning to churn at his toast.

"I don't understand."

"I've made the decision to stay in Splendor and help Luke with the ranch." He waited, hoping she'd provide the response he'd imagined. Excitement over his announcement, or perhaps a declaration of how much his staying meant to her. He received neither.

Her face sobered, although she did smile. Not the bright, radiant smile he'd seen a few times. This one held a look of disbelief, her skepticism obvious.

"For how long?" She picked up her fork and knife to cut off another slice of meat. She put it in her mouth, letting the juice roll around while contemplating how his announcement might affect her.

Dax narrowed his eyes at what appeared to be complete indifference. Irritation thrummed through him at how she seemed not to care one way or another. "Permanent. I don't plan to return to Texas."

She set down her silverware and leaned forward, her face signaling nothing. "How nice, Dax. I believe you'll come to love the town as much as the rest of us."

Confusion at her lack of enthusiasm ripped through Dax. She'd told him she loved him. Had she changed her mind? Now she acted as if his decision to stay meant nothing to her.

He crossed his arms and settled his gaze on her. "You have nothing else to say about my staying?" His voice held an edge—part frustration, part anger.

"I'm not sure what else you expect me to say. You'll be needed at the ranch, and Luke is most likely pleased with your decision." She fiddled with the napkin in her lap, twisting it one way and then another, waiting to see if he'd offer anything further. Rachel longed for him to indicate his feelings for her. Staying in Splendor was a big step for Dax, but did it have anything to do with her? Or was it based solely on an obligation to his brother?

"Yes, he is pleased."

"Why are you staying? What changed your mind?" Tell me you're staying because of me, Rachel prayed.

He wanted to say the words, tell her he realized how much he loved her, but they lodged in his throat. "I finally accepted the ranch held too much potential to walk away. Luke's set on staying and, well...I couldn't turn my back on him."

"I see." She'd hoped for more, but accepted he couldn't say what he didn't feel. Love wasn't something you could force on another and it was her curse she felt it for Dax.

They lapsed into a tense, uncomfortable silence, neither knowing what else to say. She needed Dax to profess his feelings, if he held any for her.

"Are you two finished?" Suzanne walked up, shifting her gaze from one to the other. She could see something sparked between them and thought it best to keep quiet.

Dax handed Suzanne some bills before pulling out Rachel's chair. She could feel the friction build between them. He held out his arm and she wrapped a hand around it.

"Thank you, Dax. I had a nice time." Her voice sounded hollow, yet she meant every word.

"Did you? Or would supper with Gabe or Luke have been just as entertaining?"

She tore her hand from his arm and stepped back, fisting her hands and placing them on her hips, her eyes sparking with anger. "What do you mean?"

He didn't back down. His jaw worked at the same time his chest tightened. He needed to get himself under control, make sense of the fury which threatened to overtake him. He had no experience in this, didn't know what to say. He'd never been in love before and had no idea what she expected from him.

"I mean, you appear to enjoy your evenings with any man, except me, who escorts you to supper."

"If that's what you think—"

"It is."

She let her arms drop and searched for calm. Rachel had always been even tempered, rarely letting anything or anyone get to her. Even in the army hospital, with cannons thundering around them and guns blasting, rocking the tables where they worked, she'd been steady. Everything changed when Dax entered her life. She'd been on edge, fighting for control from almost the first time they'd met. Now he stood before her, making statements which made no sense.

"Fine. I see no reason for us to spend any more time together." She turned toward the clinic, lifting her skirt so as not to trip, and stomped down the boardwalk. She made it to her front door when an arm reached in front her, blocking the entrance to the house.

Dax stood next to her, his face impassive. "I apologize if I offended you. It was not my intention."

"What *was* your intention?" She turned toward him. He could see the confusion in her eyes. He felt the same—confused and conflicted. The evening had turned out nothing like he'd hoped.

"My intention was to spend an evening with you and share my news, hoping you'd be pleased with the decision."

"I am pleased." She took a step back, his nearness almost overwhelming. "You're a good man, honest and caring. Perhaps you'll find peace in Splendor."

"I hope so." His voice sounded hollow and distant. He bent down to place a kiss on her cheek. "Goodnight, Rachel."

"Goodnight, Dax."

Rachel sat on her bed, rereading both of the telegrams she'd received in response to her advertisement. Mr. Griggs at the telegraph office had sent her information to Denver, Independence, Kansas City, and Big Pine with a request to pass it along to the local newspaper. One had been sent by a widower in his thirties with a ranch near Denver. The other from a businessman in Kansas City. He didn't give his age or if he'd been married. Neither mentioned children. Both indicated they'd be sending a letter with more information.

379

She set them aside and crawled under the covers, wondering if she'd made a mistake in being so bold. She knew of no other woman who'd ever resorted to placing an advertisement for a husband. Men did it, searching for wives by placing ads in eastern newspapers. Although the number of women traveling west had increased, there still seemed to be a notable shortage of women available for marriage.

She thought it'd be easier to meet someone suitable who already lived out west and knew the challenges. After all, she did expect him to be the main supporter for a family.

She buried her face in her hands and felt a growing sense of unease. Mr. Griggs had assured her he'd keep the contents of her telegram and any responses private, yet she felt a tinge of doubt. For a moment, she wished she could go back in time and pull her scribbled note from Griggs' hand. How humiliated she'd be if someone knew what she'd done. She didn't need her uncle or anyone else in Splendor to discover her decision to identify a suitable man.

Although the days had warmed, the nights still felt chilly, and she pulled a blanket up under her chin. She thought again of the two responses and wondered if either of these men were anywhere near as handsome as Dax. It didn't matter. She wasn't doing this to find a replacement for the man she loved. She knew it wouldn't happen. Her reasons were quite sensible, not at all associated with seeking love. She couldn't have the man she wanted, so she'd find someone who could accept her for the woman she was—hardworking, honest, kind, and with a desire to have a family before she got too old. She'd get over Dax and never look back.

He could take his ranch and, well...jump down a deep, dark hole.

Chapter Twenty-Four

"Let me get this straight. You took Rachel to supper, told her the news, and she acted indifferent?" Luke had a hard time believing she hadn't launched herself into Dax's arms at the news.

"That's what I'm saying." Dax swung hay into the feeder outside the barn. The hard labor felt good, causing his muscles to burn while sweat dripped from his face in the early afternoon heat. He'd lain awake most of the night, replaying in his mind the conversation with Rachel, still not understanding her response. How could she declare her love for him a few weeks before, then act as if his decision to stay meant nothing to her?

Luke removed his hat, pumped water into his hands, and splashed it on his face and neck. Even with the heat, the temperature topped out nowhere near the scorching days of a Texas summer or the thick dampness of Savannah. The sky had turned a deep blue with patches of white clouds passing thousands of feet above. They'd been told to enjoy the clear skies while they could. Thunderstorms could break loose at any time, without warning, sometimes causing flash floods and making roads impassable for days.

Still, Luke felt fortunate. He woke up each day to an incredible sunrise and sweeping vistas. And Dax had decided to stay.

"You told her *why* you've decided to stay, right?"

"Of course I told her. It didn't seem to matter."

Luke scrubbed a hand over his face, still unable to comprehend Rachel's reaction, or lack thereof, to Dax's news. Well, all women were a mystery, no doubt about it. Maybe she'd given up after he told her his plans to leave. Perhaps in time, after it became obvious he had no plans to return to Texas, she'd come around and give them another chance.

"What are you going to do now?"

"Leave her alone, at least for a while. We need to concentrate on the ranch anyway. I plan to ride to Big Pine later this week for supplies I can't find in Splendor. Why don't you come with me?"

"I believe I will. It might be time for us to check the local saloon and see what kind of mischief we can get ourselves into." Luke smiled at the thought of having a couple of nights out without the prying eyes of the well-meaning citizens of Splendor. Life in a small town could be wonderful, but it could certainly cut into your social activities.

"Hello, Bernie. What brings you here?"

"Morning, Doc. Is Miss Rachel at home?"

"She's out back. Come inside and I'll get her for you. How about something to drink while you wait?"

"No, thanks. I have to get back to the office." Bernie stood inside, thinking it may have been best to send word to Rachel about the letters instead of coming here. It could be hard to pass them off to her without the doc seeing. He thought a moment, then shuffled the order of the letters.

"Bernie Griggs is here to see you." Charles watched as she hung the last of the wet clothes on the line and smiled to himself. He couldn't remember a time he'd ever seen her mother, his sister, do laundry.

Rachel glanced over her shoulder at her uncle, hoping Mr. Griggs hadn't said anything to him. "I'll be right in."

She wiped her hands on the apron she wore and followed Charles into the house. "Hello, Mr. Griggs. You wanted to see me?"

"That's right. A letter came for you. Looks like it might be from your mother." He held out three envelopes, hoping the doctor didn't pay too much attention.

Rachel grasped the letters and looked down at the first one. Sure enough, it had come from her mother. "Why, it *is* from my mother. Thanks so much for bringing it by." She flashed a grateful smile at Bernie.

"No problem at all, Miss Rachel. Hope it's good news. Well, I'd best be going."

She stuffed the other two envelopes into her apron pocket and tore open the one from her mother. Most of the time, her mother's letters were filled with news of Boston, who'd gotten married or had children. This one was different.

"Uncle Charles, listen to this." She walked to the kitchen and began to read.

I don't want you to worry, but your father has been ill for several weeks. His doctor believes he's working too much and needs rest. Of course, he's ignored the advice, at least up until a week ago. I had to take him to the hospital as he couldn't stop coughing. The doctor told him, in no uncertain terms, he needs a change, at least for a few months.

If it wouldn't be too much of a burden, I thought we'd travel to visit you and Charles. Is there room for us, or would we need to make other arrangements? Please let me know as soon as you discuss this with Charles. I hope to hear good news from you soon. Love, Mother.

She looked up at her uncle and saw a grin split his face. "You know, it may be what your mother needs to convince herself you're all right and not being held captive by the savages she's so certain surround us." He chuckled at the thought of his sister coming across the country by rail, then by stagecoach, and finally by wagon to Splendor. He wondered if she realized what the journey involved.

"We do have the third bedroom."

"It'll be good for them to share a room."

Rachel shot a look at her uncle, then started to laugh. She couldn't remember her mother and father ever sharing a bedroom. Of course, they would've had to share a bed at some point. She was proof of it.

"I suppose if it's too much for them, we can get Suzanne to put them up at her boardinghouse." She folded the letter and stuck in her apron with the others. "I guess I'll walk to the telegraph office and send a reply."

She dashed outside, then stepped between two buildings and pulled out the other two envelopes, one from Denver and the other from Kansas City. She looked around, making sure she was alone, and ripped the first one open.

Jeremy DeWitt owned a cattle ranch north of Denver. His wife had died a few years before while giving birth to a son, who was now three years old. Mr. DeWitt said their life was good, except his son needed a mother. Her heart tugged at the void she'd be able to fill, and perhaps there'd be the likelihood of other children. She'd mentioned it in her ad—she wanted a family. Rachel broke away from her thoughts and read the last line of his letter.

Would you be able to move to Colorado?

She shook her head, knowing a move to Colorado would be impossible. Her mail order husband would need to come to Splendor. She folded Jeremy's letter and stuffed it into her apron, then opened the second one.

The contents had the slight smell of roses as if the oil from petals had been used on the paper. The writing held a distinct flourish, more common of female writers. She unfolded the letter and began to read. Asa Smythe owned a number of establishments in Kansas City, as well as other towns. Managers handled the daily operations and he found himself living the life of someone with much free time. He had never been married. His unencumbered status made it easy for him to live wherever he wanted. Her eyes lit on the second to last sentence—Asa was fifty-three years old. Rachel nearly choked. He was thirty years her senior.

It ended with a question.

Would you be available to spend time with me if I traveled to Montana?

Two responses, neither suitable. She'd wait. Rachel folded the second letter and returned it to her apron, then walked the short distance to the telegraph office. She had to get a response back to her mother.

"Hello, Mr. Griggs."

"Hello, Rachel. I was going to go back by your house after work, but now there's no need." He pulled a letter from behind the counter and held it out. "I must've dropped this in my hurry to get to your place earlier."

Rachel took the letter, noticing it had been sent from Independence. "Thank you."

Bernie lowered his voice. "Any good news from the others?"

She shook her head. "Both are interesting, but neither are right."

"Perhaps that one will be perfect." He glanced at the letter in her hand, then looked up as someone entered the office. "Hello, Horace. I'll be right with you."

"No hurry, Bernie. Good afternoon, Miss Davenport," the banker said.

"Hello, Mr. Clausen."

"What can I do for you, Rachel?" Bernie asked.

"I need to send a response to my mother's letter, but it needs to get to her right away. I assume a telegram would be best."

"Yes. She might even have it by this evening. Tell me what you'd like to say."

Dearest Mother, Please come right away. We are excited to see you. Let us know your arrival date. Love, Rachel.

"I'll get this right out."

"Thank you, Mr. Griggs. I'd better get to back to the clinic. Good afternoon, Mr. Clausen."

Once more, she ducked between buildings, glanced around, and opened the newest letter. The name at the top read Orin Coker. He had sold his ranch near Independence and wanted to start over in either Montana or Colorado. His parents had passed years before, he'd never married, had a good bit of money set aside, and was twenty-seven years old. If she needed someone who talked a lot, he might not be the best choice as people told him he was pretty shy. Other than that, he said he was pretty normal.

A soft chuckle escaped her lips at his choice of words. Orin said he stood five foot ten and, to the best of his knowledge, he weighed around a hundred and ninety pounds. He ended the letter by saying he was free to travel to Splendor to meet with her.

Rachel read the letter through twice more before tucking it away. She'd send a response in a day or so, once she had time to think about Mr. Coker. So far, his seemed the most promising reply yet. Perhaps it hadn't been such a bad idea after all.

"What do you have there, Dax?" Luke joined his brother, who sat on a chair outside their hotel in Big Pine. He sat on the porch rail and rested his hands on either side for support.

They'd enjoyed a good couple of days in Big Pine and would leave for Splendor the following morning. Both had eaten at the fanciest restaurant twice, played cards, and learned a great deal about the Territorial Capital. It was information which could prove handy as they expanded the ranch. Luke had spent some time with one of the saloon girls, a pretty one named Dolly. He hadn't pushed Dax. His brother needed space and time to relax away from the ranch.

"It's the town paper. Came out his morning." Dax picked up the cup of coffee he'd brought outside, took a sip, and continued to scan the paper. "I didn't realize Big Pine had grown so much. You should see the number of ads."

"What's being sold?"

"Land, of course, and horses, plus tack. There's a windmill for sale, several wagons, and ..." His voice slowed and Luke noticed he pulled the paper closer to his face. "What the hell?"

Luke shot him a glance. "Something you don't like?"

"If it's what it appears, then damn straight I don't like it. Here." He shoved the paper at Luke and pointed to the ad.

Luke's eyes widened as he read.

Wanted—husband. A kind, considerate, hardworking man who's willing to marry a nurse in a small town a day's journey north of Big Pine, Montana. Must be able to provide an income and want a family. Reply to Mr. Griggs in Splendor, Montana.

"Do you think Rachel wrote this?" Luke asked, already accepting she'd placed the advertisement, but not believing it.

Dax stood, hands on his hips, and glared down at this brother. "Damn right I do. I'm not waiting until tomorrow. You want to ride along, I'll be leaving within an hour."

Luke read the posting once more before responding, "That's not the way to do it, Dax. There's got to be a reason Rachel did this because anyone who's seen the two of you together knows how she feels." He stood and locked eyes with Dax. "You did tell her you love her, right?"

Dax's eyes darted away from Luke's and didn't return. It was all the confirmation Luke needed.

"You didn't tell her?" The incredulous tone in Luke's voice was clear.

Dax shifted his feet and crossed his arms. "No."

"Ah, hell." Luke took a breath. Even he understood a woman needed to hear the words, no matter how obvious it seemed to a man. "No wonder she acted like she did and placed this ridiculous ad. All right, there has to be something you can do besides confront her straight on." He stood and walked a few feet away, then spun around. "I've got it."

"You have another reply." Bernie Griggs held out a telegram. "It came through from Big Pine. Maybe this will be the one."

She took the message, glanced around, and unfolded it.

"Why don't you have a seat while I step into the back?" Bernie pointed to a nearby chair and left the room.

Rachel took a seat and started to read. It was from a Montana rancher who lived a good distance from Big Pine. He gave his name as Cole Brockman, never married, with no prospects as few women lived in his part of the territory. He wanted a wife and children, worked hard, and would be willing to expand his holdings near Splendor. He stood over six feet tall. The last sentence gave her pause.

Arriving in Splendor in two days and would like to call on you for supper. Respectfully, Cole Brockman.

Rachel took a deep breath as she placed a hand on her chest. He certainly seemed determined. She started to fold the telegram and place it in her reticule, then opened it and once more read the contents. He'd be in town

Saturday. She stood, her knees shaking a little as the reality hit her she'd be meeting a man who knew she actively sought a husband. Too late to turn back now, she thought.

When Mr. Griggs returned, she gave him a brief response to send to Cole Brockman. She signed it *Miss Rachel Davenport*.

"Well, don't you look good?" Luke put his hands on his hips and walked around Dax, checking the outfit he'd chosen to impress Rachel—black slacks and shirt with a steel gray brocade vest. He'd purchased a shiny black string tie in Big Pine before they'd returned to their ranch. Luke noticed two embellishments. Dax wore a silver and gold belt buckle, and a gold pocket watch. "She'll have to be a strong woman to not be swayed by a handsome gent like you."

Dax glared at his brother, already feeling his body tense at the thought of trying to impress Rachel. In the past, he'd always been himself, dressed the way he always did, and didn't go to any extremes to garner her attention. How everything had changed. The woman he loved had placed an advertisement for a mail order husband in Big Pine, and possibly in other cities, as well.

He swallowed a lump in his throat, wishing for the hundredth time he'd told her straight out he loved her. What had he been thinking? She'd been open with him about her love. Why hadn't he been able to do the same? Well, now he was paying for it.

"Do you need me to get Hannibal ready?" Luke's playful attitude had sobered. Until now, it hadn't occurred to him Rachel could've moved on, dismissed Dax, and made up her mind he wasn't the man for her. He could see the tension build in his brother. Luke had never been in love, and if this was what he had to look forward to, perhaps it would be best if he simply stayed as far away from it as possible.

Dax looked in the mirror once more, then turned toward Luke. "Thanks, but Hannibal's ready." He grabbed coins and bills from his dresser, settled his hat, and started for the stairs. "Guess it's time to get going."

Luke followed him downstairs and outside, watching as he mounted his horse.

"I'll be at the saloon with Bull and some others if you have a mind to stop by later." Luke held a hand out to Dax. "Good luck, brother."

Dax shook his hand, touched a finger to the edge of his hat, and rode off, preparing himself to face whatever Rachel decided.

"Let me understand this. You've never met the man, yet he's riding from some ranch hours away to take you to supper?" Charles watched Rachel pace back and forth across their front room, wringing an embroidered handkerchief between her hands, occasionally peeking out the curtain.

393

"Yes, that's correct." She knew her uncle deserved an explanation, but now wasn't the time.

"You do know his name, right?"

"Of course. It's Cole Brockman."

"Anyone in Splendor ever hear of him?" Charles didn't like the situation. His only comfort was knowing there was just one place Brockman could take his niece for supper—Suzanne Briar's restaurant.

"I didn't ask." She glanced at her uncle, then back at her hands, which twisted the poor fabric until it formed a knot. She'd selected her most beautiful gown, the one everyone in Boston complimented when she wore it in the past. Who knew what he'd think of it, though. At least it set off her auburn hair and green eyes. No one in Splendor wore anything as fancy and she began to doubt her selection. Should she run back into her room and change into her blue day dress?

"Rachel, I believe I hear someone walking toward the house." Her uncle tried to remain calm. This wasn't what he'd anticipated when Rachel had told him a gentleman would be calling on her tonight.

She froze in place, took a deep breath, and waited.

Dax stood outside, ready to knock, but his arm stopped in midair. What if she refused to go to supper once she realized who'd answered the ad? Luke's idea seemed good at the time. Now all

Dax could feel was doubt. He'd led hundreds of men into battle over and over again, but somehow, he was having trouble mustering the courage to face one woman. The thought galled him. The confidence he'd carried his entire life seemed to have deserted him and he didn't like it. Not one damn bit.

He checked his pocket watch once more, removed his hat, and took a breath. He raised his hand and rapped three times, then stepped back.

Rachel's courage left her at the sound. What had she been thinking, advertising for a husband? She must have been mad.

"Do you want me to get it?" Charles began to push from his chair.

"No. I'll get it." She swallowed the huge lump in her throat. Her heart thumped so fast, she had to place a hand over it to try and calm the pace.

Six steps. That's all it took to reach the door and place her hand on the knob.

The rapping sound occurred again and she jumped. She glanced over her shoulder at her uncle, whose expression had turned from concern to amusement, and rallied herself. This behavior couldn't continue. She stepped right back up to the door, grabbed the handle, pulled, and let out a shriek at who stood in front of her.

Rachel realized she'd placed a hand over her mouth to stifle her startled reaction. She dropped her hand and glared at Dax. "What are you doing here? You can't be here, not now. I have a gentleman caller arriving any minute." Her agitated words poured out, and all he did was continue to stare, the broadest smile she'd ever seen from him flashing back at her.

Dax let her flounder a few seconds before his expression sobered and he stepped forward. "I'm Cole Brockman. I've come to take Miss Rachel Davenport to supper." He watched as her eyes grew wide and her jaw dropped. She tried to respond, without success. He'd never seen her so discomfited.

"Cole Brockman?" she stammered as she took in the sight of him. My God, he truly was the finest looking man she'd ever seen. And those lips. She could almost feel them on hers and shivered at the thought.

"Yes, ma'am. We communicated by telegram. You are Miss Davenport, right?" He found he enjoyed the role he'd assumed and Rachel's utter shock at him standing there.

Finding her composure, she squared her shoulders and pulled herself erect, settling her gaze on his. "You know who I am Dax, and I know perfectly well you are *not* Cole Brockman."

"I most certainly am Cole Brockman, and I answered your advertisement for a mail order husband."

Rachel could hear her uncle clear his throat and cough from across the room.

"This is the posting you placed in Big Pine, correct?" Dax slid a hand into a pocket and pulled out a folded piece of newsprint.

She broke her gaze long enough to see the advertisement in his hand. She reached out to snatch it from him, but he was too quick. "Oh, no. I'm hanging onto this." He slid it back into his pocket. "Did you also place it in other cities?"

"That's none of your business." She felt her face heat. "Who is the real Cole Brockman and where is he?" She had her hands fisted at her sides, sparks coming from her eyes as she tried to look around him.

"Well, the fact is, my full name is Dax Cole Brockman Pelletier. A southern tradition, I'm afraid. Brockman was my mother's maiden name. So, you see, you got exactly what was promised." He took in the look of utter astonishment on her face and worked to control the amusement he felt. Somehow, he knew she hadn't begun to accept the humor in their situation.

He could see the instant she began to put all the pieces together.

"You were in Big Pine and saw the post?" Her voice still held an edge, even though the tone had softened.

"Yes, ma'am."

Embarrassment and humiliation washed over her. She buried her face in her hands and started to stumble backwards before a strong hand grasped her arm.

"It's going to be all right, Rachel. Have supper with me. Please." His gentle, deep voice washed over her and she began to relax.

She let her hands drop from her face and slowly lifted her gaze to his. Rachel could see no mockery or humor, only a plea to spend time with him. She nodded, unable to get her voice to work over the emotions surging through her.

Dax looked past her to Charles and nodded. Her uncle winked in return and offered a broad smile.

They strolled at a slow pace to Suzanne's, Rachel's hand tucked firm under Dax's right arm, his left hand resting on top. Neither spoke as they made the short walk.

All eyes turned their way as Suzanne showed them to a table. It had been set up in a back corner, candles and wildflowers adorning the tablecloth. Rachel knew Dax had been the one behind the request. He pulled out her chair and, instead of taking a seat across from her, he took the one to her left, giving them more privacy from the other diners. Still, neither spoke.

Suzanne poured glasses of wine and set the bottle on the table before serving their suppers.

"Everything looks wonderful." Rachel stared down at her plate, still avoiding eye contact with Dax. The embarrassment at his knowledge of the advertisement had subsided somewhat, although she still felt her face warm knowing he'd discovered her intentions.

"Have I mentioned how beautiful you are?" Dax hadn't taken his eyes from her since the moment they'd started toward the restaurant.

"Why, no, I don't believe you have." Her eyes sparkled as the corners of her mouth tilted up.

"I should tell you every day because it's true." He dragged his gaze away long enough to eat a few bites of his supper. He set down his silverware and sat back in his chair, making a decision to say something before he lost his nerve. "You told me once you loved me. Do you still feel the same?"

Rachel stopped with her fork midway to her mouth. She hadn't expected him to come right out and ask. "Yes, I still love you." She set her fork down and folded her hands in her lap, clasping her fingers tight and wondering where the conversation was going.

"Then why place the advertisement after I told you I'd decided to stay?"

She took a breath, exhaling slowly. "There seemed to be something missing from your announcement." Her voice wasn't much above a whisper.

"Such as I'm in love with you?" His voice thrummed through her as he placed a hand on top of hers. "I do love you, Rachel. I've know it for a long time."

She couldn't speak, certain that if she did, she'd make a complete fool of herself.

"Come on. Let's take a walk. I'll ask Suzanne to hold our dessert for another night."

The summer night air felt warmer than usual, yet Dax settled his arm around her and pulled her close. They walked away from the restaurant and past the school across from the livery.

Dax bent down to place a kiss below her ear. "No more advertisements, right?" he whispered as he pulled her around to face him and his mouth claimed hers.

She could smell the unique scent of him— soap and leather and a muskiness which excited her. She clung to his shoulders as his mouth trailed kisses down her neck, then up to the sensitive spot behind her ear. His lips traveled a slow, sure path along her jaw before claiming her mouth again in a kiss that sent waves of heat scorching through her. She moaned when his hands splayed across her back, drawing her tight against him.

He moved a hand from her back to the swell of her hip, letting his other hand rest at the back of her head, holding her in place. He couldn't get enough of her. She was in his blood, had become a part of him.

He ended the kiss and pulled back. She opened her eyes and he looked into her dilated pupils. He noticed the blush to her cheeks, how her lips had swollen from his kisses. He knew he'd never grow tired of looking at this woman.

"We have to stop or I'll end up dragging you behind the bushes." He smiled down at her with a slow easy grin, exciting her further. She willed herself to relax. "I'd better take you home."

They covered the short distance in a few minutes, Rachel opening the door to see a note on the table next to the chair where her uncle usually sat. She picked it up, walked a few feet away and read it, then looked at Dax.

"Uncle Charles is at the Wild Rose, playing cards. He says not to wait up for him as he'll be late." She scrunched her nose slightly. "He never plays cards."

Dax watched her, knowing he should leave, but not wanting to walk out the door.

Reality dawned on Rachel. She looked up into his eyes as the corners of her mouth lifted, and she raised her eyebrows.

"Ah, hell." Dax muttered, walking toward her in long, purposeful strides, his eyes smoldering, his face set. As he drew near, he tore the hat from his head and threw it on a chair. In one fluid movement, he wrapped an arm around her waist and pulled her tight against him, gripping the back of her head with his free hand.

"I can't fight it. I want you too much." The words came out in a low growl a split second before his mouth descended on hers. He lifted Rachel into his arms and carried her to her room, not losing contact of his mouth on hers.

They made love, Dax taking it slow. He discovered he was her first, and knew he'd be her last. They spoke of marriage, children, the clinic, and living on the ranch, until neither could resist the other any longer.

The clock on her wall chimed midnight as he left her bed and dressed.

"I'll be back to speak with your uncle tomorrow." He bent and placed a soft kiss on her mouth before shutting the bedroom door behind him.

He'd just grabbed his hat when the front door opened and Charles walked in.

The doctor glanced at Dax, looked behind him at Rachel's closed door, then let his gaze settle on the man before him. "I suppose we need to talk. First, I need some whiskey. Same for you?"

"Yes, sir."

Dax rotated his hat in his hands, feeling his stomach tighten.

Charles handed Dax a glass, tilted his in a salute, and threw back the amber liquid. Dax did the same.

"Appears you'll be marrying her."

"Yes, sir. With your permission."

"You've got it. Now, get the hell out of here and let this old man get some sleep."

Epilogue

Dax hadn't set foot in a church for longer than he could remember. But if Rachel wanted a church wedding, that's what she would have. He stood at the front near the altar, Luke next to him and Reverend Paige behind them. It had been two months since he'd proposed and he felt more than ready to make Rachel his.

He looked out into a church overflowing with people. Neither Rachel nor he had lived in Splendor long, yet the entire community had come out for their wedding. A surge of warmth passed through him. He'd never felt this sense of connection, not even in Savannah where he'd grown up. He sensed Luke's eyes on him.

"What?"

"You sure you're ready for this?"

Dax could see the way his brother's eyes crinkled at the corner and his mouth quirked up. Without Luke's help, Dax might have lost Rachel. He owed his brother a lot.

"More than ready."

Luke laughed and clasped his brother on the back as the piano began to play.

Dax's eyes lit on the most stunning sight he'd ever seen. Rachel, in her white wedding dress, offering a brilliant smile meant just for him. She stopped beside him and he could see her lips move. *I love you.* His heart flipped. Dax didn't remember much more of the ceremony.

Suzanne, with the help of the church women, put out a big spread. Music played, punch flowed, and men tried to hide the fact they'd given their drinks a little extra boost.

King Tolbert stood next to his daughter, Abigail, and surveyed the gathering. Although he'd been attracted to Rachel, he was happy for her and Dax. He now needed to begin his search for an appropriate suitor for Abby.

Few in Splendor fit his precise requirements for a son-in-law. Luke Pelletier might be the only one, and he'd seen no spark between them. Certainly not Gabe Evans. The man was a hardened solider and gunman, not at all suitable for his daughter. The one other bachelor close enough to Abby's age to make him a possible suitor was Noah Brandt. He chuckled at the thought of his daughter being attracted to the shy, taciturn blacksmith. He'd seen them on several occasions talking, always about horses or some such topic. No, his daughter would never be drawn to a man like Brandt. However, King did want to speak to Brandt on an important topic.

"Abigail, I need to speak with someone a moment. Will you be all right on your own?"

"Of course, Father." She'd been hoping her father would find a reason to leave her alone. Abby had been watching Noah throughout the ceremony and celebration, but there'd been no opportunity to speak with him. Now could be her chance. She watched her father move from one group to another, shaking hands and making small talk, before deciding the time had come for her to move through the crowd toward Noah. No sooner had she made the decision when her father walked right up to him, shook his hand, and began what appeared to be an in depth conversation of some kind.

Abby watched for a few minutes, disappointed at the lost opportunity. Once her father finished, she felt certain he'd be ready to leave for their ranch.

"Would you care to dance, Miss Tolbert?"

Abby glanced at the handsome cowboy standing next to her. Gil Murton, the same person who'd had a crush on her since they were young.

"Hello, Gil. It's so good to see you again. I'd love to dance with you." She took his hand and felt immediately drawn into the laughter and music of the people on the dance floor. He whirled her around the floor to the lively song. When it ended, he asked for one more dance, which she accepted, never once noticing two men glaring at her from the sidelines. Her father and Noah, both for their own reasons.

When the second song finished, Gil escorted her off the dance floor. She looked behind him to see her father approach. "Father, you remember Gil Murton."

King glanced at her, then Gil, giving the boy a hard stare. "Of course. I understand your brother married recently. A saloon girl, I believe."

Abby glared at her father and his blatant attempt to belittle Gil's family.

To his credit, Gil didn't take the bait. "Yes. Ty married a wonderful woman. They're expecting their first child any day now."

"I see. Well, we must be going, Abby." King grasped her elbow.

"Good to see you, Gil," Abby said as her father guided her away.

Without a backward glance at the young man, Tolbert escorted her to their buggy.

Dax and Rachel watched the exchange, wondering about what had been said. Abby's look of rage had been hard to miss, yet it wasn't something either cared to figure out on their wedding day.

"I'm glad your parents were here for the wedding." Dax nodded toward Mr. and Mrs. Davenport, who stood across the room in deep conversation with Horace Clausen.

"So am I, although it was a bit touchy when I introduced you and they heard your southern accent, General."

Dax wrapped an arm around her waist and pulled her close. "Now they're enamored with my extreme charm." He placed a kiss on her neck, eliciting a laugh.

Rachel's gaze wandered to the magnificent Pinto tied to the back of their buggy—her wedding gift from her husband. "He is beautiful, Dax. Thank you so much."

"What will you call him?"

"I've been thinking about it and believe I'll call him Dancer."

Dax looked at the three-year-old mare he'd gotten on his last trip to Big Pine. The lively animal would be a good match for his wife.

He turned Rachel in his arms, placing a kiss on her cheek. The celebration had gone on for over two hours and Dax could think of another place he'd rather be.

"Do you think anyone would notice if we disappeared?"

She smiled at him. "Should we chance it?"

"Okay, you two. Don't be making any plans to run off just yet." Luke walked up and handed both a whiskey. "I understand this is your drink of choice, Mrs. Pelletier."

"It certainly is."

The three toasted as they watched the crowd.

"It's a good town. I'm glad you made the decision to stay." Luke took another sip of whiskey, then faced Dax.

"I've been thinking. Everyone still calls our ranch the old Hanes place or, sometimes, the Pelletier ranch. I believe we need a real name for it."

"What do you have in mind?" Dax began to imagine all the options Luke might say.

"Redemption's Edge."

Dax looked at Luke, then shifted his gaze to Rachel. They let the name roll around their heads before each smiled.

He clasped Luke on the shoulder as they all raised their glasses before Dax made one more toast. "To Redemption's Edge."

"And its great success," Luke added.

They finished their drinks as Luke's eyes locked on someone near the food table. "Excuse me a minute." He winked at them both, then walked away.

Rachel watched Luke stopped in front of a lovely young woman with golden brown hair. "Who's he talking to?"

Dax shifted his eyes from his wife to Luke. "That's Ginny. She works for Amos Henderson."

"At the saloon?" Rachel's asked, her surprise obvious.

He chuckled. "Yes. Amos has a little different arrangement with her than the other girls. She serves drinks, nothing more. Ginny and her sister came into town with the settlers a few months back. She told Amos they had no real reason to travel on to Oregon with the others, so they stayed."

"And Luke's fascinated by her." Rachel took another sip of her whiskey.

"From what Al at the Rose said, he couldn't take his eyes off Ginny the first time they met." Dax nuzzled her neck. "Not much different from the way I felt about you." He glanced around, then grabbed Rachel's hand. "Come on."

Dax whistled for Hannibal and waited while the large animal obeyed the command. He lifted Rachel onto the saddle, then swung up behind her, wrapping an arm around her waist before placing a soft kiss on her neck.

"Are you ready?" Dax asked, anxious to get her to the ranch.

Before she could respond, they both looked up to see what appeared to be a lone rider, slumped in his saddle, coming toward them. It wasn't until he was within a few yards that they saw the arrow protruding from his back.

"My, God, Dax. He's hurt. I need to help him."

Dax shook his head, frustrated by the delay, yet knowing he had no choice. He dismounted before helping her down and grabbing the reins of the stranger's horse. Dax wrapped his arms around the wounded man and pulled him from the saddle, laying him on the ground as a group of wedding guests formed a circle around them.

"Does anyone know him?" Dax asked, looking up at those peering down.

The responses confirmed no one recognized the injured man.

"Get him to the clinic." Doc Worthington ordered.

"I'll get the wagon," Noah said.

Dax, Luke, and Bull placed their arms under him as Noah pulled alongside.

"Attacked us..." The words were strained, raspy, and barely audible.

"Who attacked you?" Dax asked.

The man's eyes opened to mere slits. "They're coming..."

"Who's coming?" Dax question became more urgent.

"Indians."

Thank you for taking the time to read Redemption's Edge. If you enjoyed it, please consider telling your friends or posting a short review. Word of mouth is an author's best friend and much appreciated.

Please join my reader's group and sign up to be notified of my New Releases at http://www.shirleendavies.com/contact-me.html

About the Author

Shirleen Davies writes romance—historical, contemporary, and romantic suspense. She grew up in Southern California, attended Oregon State University, and has degrees from San Diego State University and the University of Maryland. During the day she provides consulting services to small and mid-sized businesses. But her real passion is writing emotionally charged stories of flawed people who find redemption through love and acceptance. She now lives with her husband in a beautiful town in northern Arizona.

Shirleen loves to hear from her readers.

Write to her at: shirleen@shirleendavies.com
Visit her website:
http://www.shirleendavies.com
Sign up to be notified of New Releases:
http://www.shirleendavies.com/contact-me.html
Comment on her blog:
http://www.shirleendavies.com/blog.html
Facebook Fan Page:
https://www.facebook.com/ShirleenDaviesAuthor
Twitter: http://twitter.com/shirleendavies
Google+:
http://www.gplusid.com/shirleendavies

LinkedIn:
http://www.linkedin.com/in/shirleendaviesauthor
Pinterest:
http://www.pinterest.com/shirleendavies

Other Books by Shirleen Davies

Tougher than the Rest – Book One
MacLarens of Fire Mountain Historical Western Romance Series

"A passionate, fast-paced story set in the untamed western frontier by an exciting new voice in historical romance."

Niall MacLaren is the oldest of four brothers, and the undisputed leader of the family. A widower, and single father, his focus is on building the MacLaren ranch into the largest and most successful in northern Arizona. He is serious about two things—his responsibility to the family and his future marriage to the wealthy, well-connected widow who will secure his place in the territory's destiny.

Katherine is determined to live the life she's dreamed about. With a job waiting for her in the growing town of Los Angeles, California, the young teacher from Philadelphia begins a journey across the United States with only a couple of trunks and her spinster companion. Life is perfect for this adventurous, beautiful young woman, until an accident throws her into the arms of the one man who can destroy it all.

Fighting his growing attraction and strong desire for the beautiful stranger, Niall is more determined than ever to push emotions aside to focus on his goals of wealth and political gain. But looking into the clear, blue eyes of the woman who could ruin everything, Niall discovers he will have to harden his heart and be tougher than he's ever been in his life...Tougher than the Rest.

Faster than the Rest – Book Two
MacLarens of Fire Mountain Historical Western Romance Series

"Headstrong, brash, confident, and complex, the MacLarens of Fire Mountain will captivate you with strong characters set in the wild and rugged western frontier."

Handsome, ruthless, young U.S. Marshal Jamie MacLaren had lost everything—his parents, his family connections, and his childhood sweetheart—but now he's back in Fire Mountain and ready for another chance. Just as he successfully reconnects with his family and starts to rebuild his life, he gets the unexpected and unwanted assignment of rescuing the woman who broke his heart.

Beautiful, wealthy Victoria Wicklin chose money and power over love, but is now fighting for her life—or is she? Who has she become in the seven years since she left Fire Mountain to take up her life in San Francisco? Is she really as innocent as she says?

Marshal MacLaren struggles to learn the truth and do his job, but the past and present lead him in different directions as his heart and brain wage battle. Is Victoria a victim or a villain? Is life offering him another chance, or just another heartbreak?

As Jamie and Victoria struggle to uncover past secrets and come to grips with their shared passion, another danger arises. A life-altering danger that is out of their control and threatens to destroy any chance for a shared future.

Harder than the Rest – Book Three
MacLarens of Fire Mountain Historical Western Romance Series

"They are men you want on your side. Hard, confident, and loyal, the MacLarens of Fire Mountain will seize your attention from the first page."

Will MacLaren is a hardened, plain-speaking bounty hunter. His life centers on finding men guilty of horrendous crimes and making sure justice is done. There is no place in his world for the carefree attitude he carried years before when a tragic event destroyed his dreams.

Amanda is the daughter of a successful Colorado rancher. Determined and proud, she works hard to prove she is as capable as any man and worthy to be her father's heir. When a stranger arrives, her independent nature collides with the strong pull toward the handsome ranch hand. But is he what he seems and could his secrets endanger her as well as her family?

The last thing Will needs is to feel passion for another woman. But Amanda elicits feelings he thought were long buried. Can Will's desire for her change him? Or will the vengeance he seeks against the one man he wants to destroy—a dangerous opponent without a conscious—continue to control his life?

Stronger than the Rest – Book Four
MacLarens of Fire Mountain Historical Western Romance Series

"Smart, tough, and capable, the MacLarens protect their own no matter the odds. Set against America's rugged frontier, the stories of the men from Fire Mountain are complex, fast-paced, and a must read for anyone who enjoys non-stop action and romance."

Drew MacLaren is focused and strong. He has achieved all of his goals except one—to return to the MacLaren ranch and build the best horse breeding program in the west. His successful career as an attorney is about to give way to his ranching roots when a bullet changes everything.

Tess Taylor is the quiet, serious daughter of a Colorado ranch family with dreams of her own. Her shy nature keeps her from developing friendships outside of her close-knit family until Drew enters her life. Their relationship grows. Then a bullet, meant for another, leaves him paralyzed and determined to distance himself from the one woman he's come to love.

Convinced he is no longer the man Tess needs, Drew focuses on regaining the use of his legs and recapturing a life he thought lost. But danger of another kind threatens those he cares about—including Tess—forcing him to rethink his future.

Can Drew overcome the barriers that stand between him, the safety of his friends and family, and a life with the woman he loves? To do it all, he has to be strong. Stronger than the Rest.

Deadlier than the Rest – Book Five
MacLarens of Fire Mountain Historical Western Romance Series

"A passionate, heartwarming story of the iconic MacLarens of Fire Mountain. This captivating historical western romance grabs your attention from the start with an engrossing story encompassing two romances set against the rugged backdrop of the burgeoning western frontier."

Connor MacLaren's search has already stolen eight years of his life. Now he is close to finding what he seeks—Meggie, his missing sister. His quest leads him to the growing city of Salt Lake and an encounter with the most captivating woman he has ever met.

Grace is the third wife of a Mormon farmer, forced into a life far different from what she'd have chosen. Her independent spirit longs for choices governed only by her own heart and mind. To achieve her dreams, she must hide behind secrets and half-truths, even as her heart pulls her towards the ruggedly handsome Connor.

Known as cool and uncompromising, Connor MacLaren lives by a few, firm rules that have served him well and kept him alive. However, danger stalks Connor, even to the front range of the beautiful Wasatch Mountains, threatening those he cares about and impacting his ability to find his sister.

Can Connor protect himself from those who seek his death? Will his eight-year search lead him to his sister while unlocking the secrets he knows are held tight within Grace, the woman who has captured his heart?

Read this heartening story of duty, honor, passion, and love in book five of the MacLarens of Fire Mountain series.

Wilder than the Rest – Book Six

MacLarens of Fire Mountain Historical Western Romance Series

"A captivating historical western romance set in the burgeoning and treacherous city of San Francisco. Go along for the ride in this gripping story that seizes your attention from the very first page."

"If you're a reader who wants to discover an entire family of characters you can fall in love with, this is the series for you." – Authors to Watch

Pierce is a rough man, but happy in his new life as a Special Agent. Tasked with defending the rights of the federal government, Pierce is a cunning gunslinger always ready to tackle the next job. That is, until he finds out that his new job involves Mollie Jamison.

Mollie can be a lot to handle. Headstrong and independent, Mollie has chosen a life of danger and intrigue guaranteed to prove her liquor-loving father wrong. She will make something of herself, and no one, not even arrogant Pierce MacLaren, will stand in her way.

A secret mission brings them together, but will their attraction to each other prove deadly in their hunt for justice? The payoff for success is high, much higher than any assignment either has taken before. But will the damage to their hearts and souls be too much to bear? Can Pierce and Mollie find a way to overcome their misgivings and work together as one?

Second Summer – Book One
MacLarens of Fire Mountain
Contemporary Romance Series

"In this passionate Contemporary Romance, author Shirleen Davies introduces her readers to the modern day MacLarens starting with Heath MacLaren, the head of the family."

The Chairman of both the MacLaren Cattle Co. and MacLaren Land Development, Heath MacLaren is a success professionally—his personal life is another matter.

Following a divorce after a long, loveless marriage, Heath spends his time with women who are beautiful and passionate, yet unable to provide what he longs for . . .

Heath has never experienced love even though he witnesses it every day between his younger brother, Jace, and wife, Caroline. He wants what they have, yet spends his time with women too young to understand what drives him and too focused on themselves to be true companions.

It's been two years since Annie's husband died, leaving her to build a new life. He was her soul mate and confidante. She has no desire to find a replacement, yet longs for male friendship.

Annie's closest friend in Fire Mountain, Caroline MacLaren, is determined to see Annie come out of her shell after almost two years of mourning. A chance meeting with Heath turns into an offer to be a part of the MacLaren Foundation Board and an opportunity for a life outside her home sanctuary which has also become her prison. The platonic friendship that builds between Annie and Heath points to a future where each may rely on the other without the bonds a romance would entail.

However, without consciously seeking it, each yearns for more . . .

The MacLaren Development Company is booming with Heath at the helm. His meetings at a partner company with the young, beautiful marketing director, who makes no secret of her desire for him, are a temptation. But is she the type of woman he truly wants?

Annie's acceptance of the deep, yet passionless, friendship with Heath sustains her, lulling her to believe it is all she needs. At least until Heath drops a bombshell, forcing Annie to realize that what she took for friendship is actually a deep, lasting love. One she doesn't want to lose.

Each must decide to settle—or fight for it all.

Hard Landing – Book Two
MacLarens of Fire Mountain
Contemporary Romance Series

Trey MacLaren is a confident, poised Navy pilot. He's focused, loyal, ethical, and a natural leader. He is also on his way to what he hopes will be a lasting relationship and marriage with fellow pilot, Jesse Evans.

Jesse has always been driven. Her graduation from the Naval Academy and acceptance into the pilot training program are all she thought she wanted—until she discovered love with Trey MacLaren

Trey and Jesse's lives are filled with fast flying, friends, and the demands of their military careers. Lives each has settled into with a passion. At least until the day Trey receives a letter that could change his and Jesse's lives forever.

It's been over two years since Trey has seen the woman in Pensacola. Her unexpected letter stuns him and pushes Jesse into a tailspin from which she might not pull back.

Each must make a choice. Will the choice Trey makes cause him to lose Jesse forever? Will she follow her heart or her head as she fights for a chance to save the love she's found? Will their independent decisions collide, forcing them to give up on a life together?

One More Day – Book Three
MacLarens of Fire Mountain
Contemporary Romance Series

Cameron "Cam" Sinclair is smart, driven, and dedicated, with an easygoing temperament that belies his strong will and the personal ambitions he holds close. Besides his family, his job as head of IT at the MacLaren Cattle Company and his position as a Search and Rescue volunteer are all he needs to make him happy. At least that's what he thinks until he meets, and is instantly drawn to, fellow SAR volunteer, Lainey Devlin.

Lainey is compassionate, independent, and ready to break away from her manipulative and controlling fiancé. Just as her decision is made, she's called into a major search and rescue effort, where once again, her path crosses with the intriguing, and much too handsome, Cam Sinclair. But Lainey's plans are set. An opportunity to buy a flourishing preschool in northern Arizona is her chance to make a fresh start, and nothing, not even her fierce attraction to Cam Sinclair, will impede her plans.

As Lainey begins to settle into her new life, an unexpected danger arises —threats from an unknown assailant—someone who doesn't believe she belongs in Fire Mountain. The more Lainey begins to love her new home, the greater the danger becomes. Can she accept the help and protection Cam offers while ignoring her consuming desire for him?

Even if Lainey accepts her attraction to Cam, will he ever be able to come to terms with his own driving ambition and allow himself to consider a different life than the one he's always pictured? A life with the one woman who offers more than he'd ever hoped to find?

Redemption's Edge – Book One
Redemption Mountain – Historical Western Romance Series

"A heartwarming, passionate story of loss, forgiveness, and redemption set in the untamed frontier during the tumultuous years following the Civil War. Ms. Davies' engaging and complex characters draw you in from the start, creating an exciting introduction to this new historical western romance series."

"Redemption's Edge is a strong and engaging introduction to her new historical western romance series."

Dax Pelletier is ready for a new life, far away from the one he left behind in Savannah following the South's devastating defeat in the Civil War. The ex-Confederate general wants nothing more to do with commanding men and confronting the tough truths of leadership.

Rachel Davenport possesses skills unlike those of her Boston socialite peers—skills honed as a nurse in field hospitals during the Civil War. Eschewing her northeastern suitors and changed by the carnage she's seen, Rachel decides to accept her uncle's invitation to assist him at his clinic in the dangerous and wild frontier of Montana.

Now a Texas Ranger, a promise to a friend takes Dax and his brother, Luke, to the untamed territory of Montana. He'll fulfill his oath and return to Austin, at least that's what he believes.

The small town of Splendor is what Rachel needs after life in a large city. In a few short months, she's grown to love the people as well as the majestic beauty of the untamed frontier. She's settled into a life unlike any she has ever thought possible.

Thinking his battle days are over, he now faces dangers of a different kind—one by those from his past who seek vengeance, and another from Rachel, the woman who's captured his heart.

Made in the USA
San Bernardino, CA
11 December 2017